BREAKERS

Also by William McCloskey

Fiction:
Warriors
Raiders
Highliners
The Mallore Affair

Nonfiction:
Their Fathers' Work: Casting Nets with the World's Fishermen
Fish Decks: Seafarers of the North Atlantic

BREAKERS

A NOVEL

William B. McCloskey Jr.

Skyhorse Publishing

Skyhorse Publishing books may be purchased in bulk at special discounts for sales promotion, corporate gifts, fund-raising, or educational purposes. Special editions can also be created to specifications. For details, contact the Special Sales Department, Skyhorse Publishing, 307 West 36th Street, 11th Floor, New York, NY 10018 or info@skyhorsepublishing.com.

Skyhorse® and Skyhorse Publishing® are registered trademarks of Skyhorse Publishing, Inc.®, a Delaware corporation.

Visit our website at www.skyhorsepublishing.com.

10 9 8 7 6 5 4 3 2 1

Library of Congress Cataloging-in-Publication Data is available on file.
ISBN: 978-1-62636-002-0

Printed in the United States of America

TO ANN

MY WIFE AND BEST FRIEND

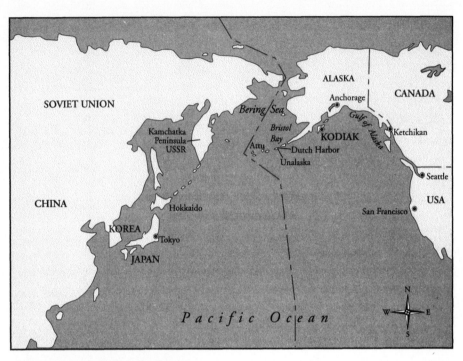

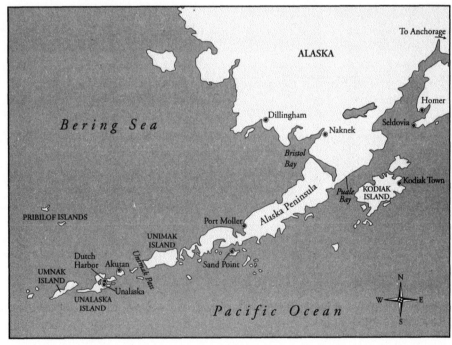

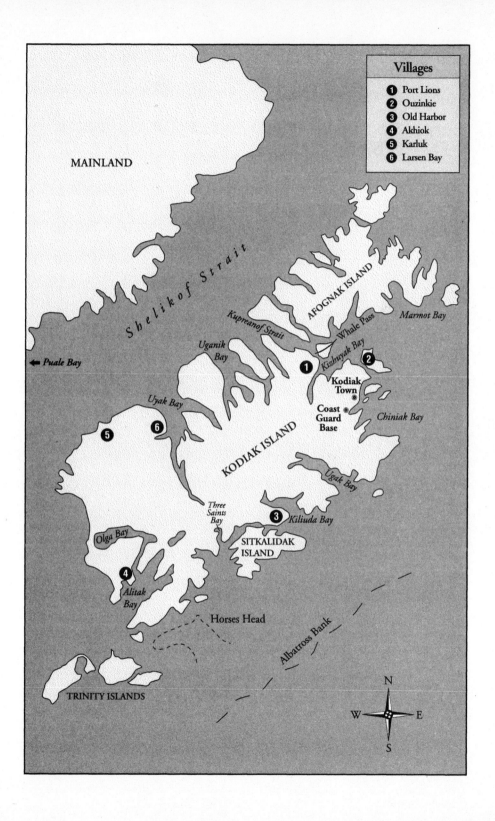

MAINLAND

Shelikof Strait

AFOGNAK ISLAND

Marmot Bay

Kupreanof Strait

Whale Pass

Kizhuyak Bay

Uganik Bay

← *Puale Bay*

1

2

Kodiak Town

Coast Guard Base

Chiniak Bay

Uyak Bay

6

5

KODIAK ISLAND

Ugak Bay

Three Saints Bay

3 *Kiliuda Bay*

Olga Bay

SITKALIDAK ISLAND

4

Alitak Bay

Horses Head

Albatross Bank

TRINITY ISLANDS

N
W — E
S

ACKNOWLEDGMENTS

One of an author's final pleasures, after finishing a book and nursing it through rewrites and copy edits, is to remember the experiences besides actual writing that fed into the finished work, and then to thank those whose help and forbearance made the experiences possible.

Among fishing skippers who hired me I want to thank Thorvold Olsen (king crab and salmon out of Kodiak), Magne Nes (salmon, Bristol Bay), and Monte Riley (salmon, Kodiak). Also among hospitable skippers Leiv Loklingholm (king crab, Bering Sea), John Crivello (salmon, Bristol Bay), and Guy Piercy (salmon, Bristol Bay).

For experts' insight I am indebted (without holding them responsible for how I've used their information) to Dave Milholland, Bristol Bay fishing veteran; Dr. Karin McCloskey, my emergency transport pediatrician daughter; Jay Hastings, lawyer and advisor to the Japanese; Peter Schmidt, founder and CEO of Marco Marine; David Smith, Marco senior naval architect, and two of the already-legendary cannery bosses of Bristol Bay, now retired: Harold Brindle of Red Salmon/Columbia Ward and Ivan Fox of the former New England Fish Company.

At Lyons Press, Nick Lyons for his faith going back to the acceptance of *Highliners* for republication, and to Tony Lyons of the new generation for continuing support. And to my editor Enrica Gadler for insightful suggestions and velvet-gloved prods based on her remarkable ability to identify with the characters of my imagination.

Others who fit less easily into categories but who were generous with varieties of advice, time, and logistical support: Tom Casey, fisheries professional whose enthusiasm for the ways of Hank Crawford has remained strong for two decades; Alan MacNow, who opened the door to Japan;

Pat Kern, insightful Baltimore neighbor who eased me into the computer age; Chuck Bundrant, founder and driving force of Trident Seafoods; and Bart Eaton of Trident and past crabbing skipper in the Bering Sea.

Then there is my family, the precious glue that holds together the great matters of importance: my parents Bill and Evelyn now of memory, daughter Karin and grandson Will, son Wynn, and wife Ann to whom this book is dedicated with gratitude and love.

CONTENTS

xi

PROLOGUE
THE CALDRON

Sea life boils throughout the water column off Alaska. On the seafloor crawl thick king crabs with sluggish claws, and spidery tanner crabs, both in search of baby halibut, cod, and other bottomfish. Meanwhile, mature bottomfish search for baby crabs. Deeper yet, in trenches below the seafloor, mill fat black sablefish. In the center of the water column swarm cloudy masses of minute plankton—simple-celled animals and vegetables the size of pinheads—which are gobbled by pollack, herring, capelin, and all manner of other fish and crustaceans. Not all creatures commit to a single plane. Big squids and little shrimp stay deep during the day but storm to the surface at night. Halibut lie half buried in mud with only watchful eyes exposed, then flash upward at the sight of prey. Cod also hover near the bottom, but scoot anywhere to follow opportunities higher in the water.

Swimming near the surface are schools of plankton-feeding salmon and other anadromous fish that hatch in fresh water, migrate to salt water, then return to fresh water to spawn. Marine mammals, ranging in size from clam-crunching otters to majestic whales, roam the Alaskan waters from floor to surface feeding as they please. Above them, seabirds dive and peck at such surface-cruising fish as their beaks can handle.

Plankton to whales, all follow their predatory rhythms. Big eats little all the way up the line, and life flourishes throughout the caldron.

Sea creatures reproduce most abundantly in the cold waters of the world that are underlaid by continental shelves. Few seas are as cold, and few shelves are as vast, as those in the Gulf of Alaska and the Bering Sea.

Winds that blow over the relative shallows of continental shelves cause the waters to circulate from seafloor to surface, unlike in deepest ocean where currents drive the water only horizontally. The wind-driven circulation upwells seafloor nutrients from the lightless depths. Traveling upwards with the nutrients and feeding on them are the plankton. When the plankton approach the surface they absorb the light available there—which they need as much as food in order to grow—and they multiply by the billions. In tropical water the warmth matures them so rapidly that they zip through life and die within hours, but in cold water plankton stay roiling through the column alive and fresh. They anchor the aquatic food chain.

Into this rhythm enters man, the universal predator of land, air, and sea, whom nature has programmed as relentlessly as the plankton to eat or die. With hook, spear, net, and cage this two-legged intruder has devised ways to inject himself among the sea's occupants and take his nourishment as efficiently as the cod. He enters the oceans with cunning and skill.

The twin caldrons of the Bering Sea and the Gulf of Alaska thus teem with both fish and fishermen. The fish and marine mammals have no choice but to be there. Seabirds cannot roam too far from water. The fishermen who choose to enter the system may have other options on land, but on water they must accept some of the most primal forces of God's universe. They live with sunrises, storms, and tides, self-reliant and alive, absorbed for the time into nature's ocean cycle.

PART I
1978
ALASKA

1

STORM FIELDS

SHELIKOF STRAIT APPROACHING KODIAK, 3 JULY 1978

Minute by minute the northeaster gained momentum as it tunneled its force between the dim, snowy mountains on either side of the strait. A swell bigger than the rest rolled toward them, built into a foaming monster, and tried to engulf the bow. Instead, the boat rolled up steeply and gracefully before the sea could break in force, and globs of water that drummed on the wheelhouse roof dissipated into thick ripples down the windows. I don't feel like bucking this today, Hank Crawford thought without heat.

The others whooped, enjoying the ride, their feet in sandals braced apart on the pitching, carpeted deck of the wheelhouse. Good boat. And he knew how to handle her, that's why they could laugh. Another wave came, then another. He steered smoothly to meet them. Where better could he be, after all, than here aboard his own boat, in control, heading home, the hold plugged with salmon? It barely mattered, much, that he was tendering other guys' reds from Chignik instead of catching them with Jones and the rest off Igvak. That was the price for owning too big a boat to limit-seine between crab seasons. What the hell, this is my time, he decided, feeling mellow about it, and this is my place.

"Shitty weather, eh Hank ol' boss?" yawned Seth, swaying with the motion.

"Never seen worse, man the lifeboats."

"Man, remember two winters ago in the Bering, way north around Misty Moon and Pribilofs in the Bering? Man, gusting a hundred, ice all over the crab pots? Had to crawl ass-level just to chip ice? That's the day, man, I thought we was . . ." When Seth trailed off, Hank knew worse memories had returned.

John and Mo, the other crewmen, remained quiet when the two old-timers started reminiscing. Their history aboard the *Jody S* covered months instead of years. "Hey, you apes," said Hank to draw them in. "Signing up to box tomorrow?"

"Not me," John declared. His big eyes seemed always serious and disapproving. "Going as far from town as you can get. My girlfriend and a book."

"Sure, Boss, hell yes," said Mo in a voice as sturdy as his arms. "Do it for the boat, okay?"

"I didn't mean you had to."

"Only one Fourth of July a year—I want to. How about you, Boss, you going to take on somebody?"

Hank steered them through a drumming wave, and called over the noise: "No chance. There's Jody if I want a fight." They all laughed.

One of the waves rose out of all proportion, its rhythm broken by a cross swell, and the bow suddenly thudded into a wall of sea rather than riding over it. Catapults of water shot toward them. "Duck!" cried Hank, crouching. The force moved through as if no reinforced glass intervened, crashing the windows to engulf them in kicking, pulling water. It covered Hank with frightening coldness. Spitting bitter salt, eyes nearly blinded from the sting, he struggled upright into a blast of wind, his hand still clasped on the steering lever. The boat veered to port with a jolt like a kick. Without control they'd broach! He gunned the engine and steered to starboard. This took the boat on a sickening roll that slammed water and debris around his legs. The next wave broke and covered them with new water that surged through the door to the bunks and galley below.

He kept his voice calm. "Seth, check engine door, start bilge pumps. Mo, John, open survival suits, don't panic." Seth's burly figure stumbled away dripping, faster than the others could merely gain their feet. With one hand steering Hank grabbed both sideband and VHF microphones: "All-ships, *Adele H* and allships, this is *Jody S, Jody S*, just north of Miners

Point Shelikof Strait, stand by, *Jody S* two miles off Miners Point just north—" He held off declaring Mayday, but kept his grip on the mike. Who'd be around? Most boats fishing Igvak would have headed home to Kodiak for the holiday. To his men, shouting to make sure Seth heard: "Turning hard to starboard, hold tight, *Seth hold tight*."

He maneuvered the boat onto the crest of a lesser wave, then throttled full ahead and turned the rudder hard. She dipped, rolled, and rose, to slamming wood and metal, as water swept his feet. "Oh Jesus!" wailed John. Seth and Mo bellowed obscenities. There was a moment of disoriented chaos, then blessed stability. Thank God for power, the boat had pivoted before the next trough caught it, and they rode on an exact opposite course with seas astern. He adjusted to quarter the seas for retreat into Uganik Bay. The violent pitch became a bouncing roll.

"Seth! You okay?"

"Yeah, but wet as a fucker. Bilge pumping good, both engine room and hold. But fuckin' water everywhere in the bunks and galley. Need help down here."

"*Jody S*, *Jody S*, you read me? Over," from the sideband. It was Jones Henry's voice, from the *Adele H*, wiry and calm but urgent.

Hank motioned the other two below. John stood wide-eyed and trembling, barely able to hold himself upright, his wet hair slapped to his head like seaweed, a mess of debris plastered around his legs. He might have been twenty-two, but he looked as helpless as a kid of ten. Mo, younger in years, had already managed to extract three of the survival suits from their thick bags despite a bleeding gash in his arm. He quickly laid the heavy foam rubber garments on the chart table and started to go. Pausing halfway he returned, punched John on the shoulder, and led him along.

"*Jody S*, *Jody S*, you read me? Over."

"Stand by, Jones," snapped Hank, and let the microphone dangle. He watched each roll anxiously. She bounced back from port, but paused sluggishly to starboard before returning. The unevenness meant more than mere water sloshing below. Some weight had shifted permanently, leaving a steady list extreme enough for another trick sea to capsize them. Everything in the engine room was bolted, the big objects on deck secured. That left the hold; fish must have shifted when they turned. Could he risk guys on deck? Leaning far out the lee side, he watched the stern where water slapped over the rail and gurgled across the main hatch. Ahead he could see surf breaking below the high bluff of Miners Point, they were that close to shelter, but if another rogue wave caught them, running unstable . . . He bit his lip, trying to decide as he shouted for Seth and the others.

"*Jody S*—"

"*Adele H*, *Adele H*, this is *Jody S*. Howdy Jones. Strong nor'easter out here, warning all boats." He considered, decided it would be no secret. "Big sea stove in our windows. Got a starboard list but soon under control, headed for Uganik. No emergency but you might stand by. Out for now."

Seth had cuts on his face and grease everywhere on the light clothing he wore. Even his eyebrows dripped grease. Laugh about it later. Hank said that their salmon might have shifted, and Seth required no further explanation. The sideband began to sputter with voices led urgently by Jones, asking if he needed help, demanding a confirmed position. Hank studied the restless water, ignoring the calls but relieved to be monitored. Decide quickly. "Seth take over here. We'll slow to minimize the waves and find you the easiest course to steer while I go down—"

Seth grabbed his survival suit from the pile and began pushing his feet into the booted legs. "I'm deck boss here, not you. You steer. Tie a line around my waist, and this rubber thing'll float me if I get washed over. Just promise to fuckin' turn around for me."

It made sense. "We'll throw John over to save you instead," Hank said to lighten it.

"No way . . . ," murmured John uneasily.

"Hey, that'll do it," Seth hooted.

Hank watched tensely through the limited view around the housing as Seth, belayed to a line and suited in the clumsy orange rubber coverall that enclosed everything but his face, helped Mo lift the heavy hatch cover, then jumped through the opening into the fish. Despite his own care, water kept breaking over the rail to unbalance them. Where the hell was John, he should be helping! Oh. Mo had a similar line tied around his waist, presumably tended by John out of sight since it stayed taut with jerking exactitude.

Seth wriggled into the mass of salmon slanted high to starboard, and began pedaling his legs to start them moving. Sluggishly the load began to shift. As the boat slowly regained balance, several high gusts blew and a wave lapped into the hold. "Mo! Tell him to get out, we're okay now."

Mo conveyed the message and called: "Says the boards on the starboard bins, they're broken loose, he's going to put them back, that's why the fish shifted, says won't take long."

The gray water kept rolling. No lee for at least another mile and a half. The orange figure slipped from view. Boards thumped as Seth worked them back into their tracks, then silence. "What's he doing? Tell him that's good enough."

Mo leaned into the hold just as a wave poured over his back. He cursed automatically and grinned up: "Pitching fish into the port-side bin. Says too bad we have so fuckin' many. Want me to go help?"

"No, no, mind his line, tell him hurry."

Suddenly a wave swept broadside, inundated the hatch opening, and drove Mo across the deck. Water filled the hold so high that fish floated out. Hank started down, crying, "Pull his line, pull, *Pull!*" then backtracked at the thought of losing the boat without control. He switched the steering to autopilot, and raced down the ladder to deck through the galley, shoving John aside in the doorway. Mo tugged at Seth's line, but it hung on some hidden snag. Hank submerged his head in the hold to grip the line better, yanked it in different directions until the snag freed, and pulled desperately until a blessed piece of orange appeared. The survival suit kept Seth afloat but he was limp. They grunted him out by the arms as waves hit the boat freely. Lost heading, throttle must have slipped to neutral, Hank thought. What should he do? What choice? They rested Seth head down, bent at the midriff over the rim of the hatch, to grip his legs and pull him out the rest of the way. On an impulse Hank pounded Seth's back, bringing a gush of water from his mouth, followed by gagging and coughing. Thank God, thank God. He pounded again, then rushed back toward the wheelhouse.

John stood mesmerized, blocking the doorway with one leg braced inside, his hands knuckled white around Mo's belay line. Hank shoved him aside roughly. "Go help, dammit!" John stumbled to obey. "Carry Seth up to the wheelhouse!"

At the controls Hank pushed the throttle and regained way to gun as hard as he dared toward the mouth of Uganik Bay. Even though the wind blew off their stern quarter it penetrated the glassless windows to chill his wet clothing—nothing but shirt and jeans since he'd been riding in the impregnable comfort of a heated wheelhouse. With the hold awash, dribbling out fish, they now rode more stable but lower. The deck dipped at the waterline. A wave could now flood through the galley from astern and pour down to the engine room. Like running in mud, how could he be in all places? Mo backed up the ladder with shoulders bent, his arms locked around Seth's chest as he dragged him. Hank rushed to take over: "Quick, go back and dog the galley door, quick!"

"Done, Boss. It's okay, I got him, he's puked a lot and talked a little." Hank slapped Mo on the shoulder and returned to the controls.

John trailed behind, holding Seth's legs as he muttered: "Oh Jesus, never seen anything like this, and heavy . . ."

When we're safe, Hank decided, this boy goes. They propped Seth against the chart cabinet on the soggy carpet, kicking broken glass aside. Hank knelt and shook him. "Hey, open your eyes, say something that makes sense so we know you're not as gassed as you look."

"Next time, I'll fuh . . . fuckin' steer."

Mo started to peel down Seth's survival suit but, "Leave it on, keeps him warm," said Hank hastily, not adding that the boat might still capsize. They raised Seth's legs and drained water trapped in the suit as John grumbled that no wonder those legs had been so heavy. Water gushed out at Seth's neck and he complained obscenely that they were drowning him a second time. Hank could have shouted and hugged him in relief, but said, "Reminds me of killing Rasputin, they had to try five or six different ways. Keep trying, Mo."

"What's Rasputin, Boss?"

"*Jody S, Jody S*, you read me?" from the sideband. Hank grabbed the mike and reassured Jones Henry. "I'm steaming back toward you through Kupreanof," Jones continued. "You need me?"

"Thanks, thanks, no, turn back and go on, but thanks, don't lose your tide. See you tomorrow in town."

Jones's tone relaxed. "Stove in your wheelhouse windows you say. That ain't *my* twenty percent of the *Jody S*, is it?"

"Sorry, partner, what else would it be?"

By the time they reached Uganik Bay and easy water, Seth had wriggled himself free of the clumsy survival suit, and he and the others were making heavy jokes as they salvaged and picked through the mess. The pump in the fish hold gradually lowered the water and then drained it, so that they rode with freeboard again. Probably only a hundred of their few thousand fish had floated away. Mo found boards to shore up the lower half of the windows. Water had swept through the galley and among the bunks where sleeping bags and clothes had tumbled to the wet deck. They now wore an assortment of woolens, mostly wet, covered by oilskins that helped block the cold air.

Hank stayed at the wheel. He ducked occasionally into his adjacent skipper's cabin to separate wet books, papers, and clothes, then returned to watch for setnets and other obstructions. Fingers of snow remained on top of the mountains around the bay, innocent-looking pockets deep enough to bury a hiker. Rich green covered the lower slopes. The growth resembled grass from a distance, but he knew it for a wiry jungle two or three feet high. A bear pawed salmon from one of the stream mouths, glanced up at the sound of their engine, retreated a pace, then returned to dinner. Overhead, eagles soared on powerful wings, gliding around each other in easy patterns. A sea otter, afloat with all four paws in the air and a half-eaten clam on its belly, plopped from sight when the boat approached. Hank usually enjoyed the sights of nature's process, but today he thought of rocks not far beneath the surface waiting to rip a boat's hull. It was a world that made way for man but gave him no quarter.

The boat passed through a series of sheltered inlets that allowed a passage skirting the rest of Shelikof Strait. The inland route took longer, and with time already lost they'd have to wait for the next slack at Whale Pass, not reaching Kodiak until morning. He remained tense enough that when John brought a bologna sandwich he waved it aside.

It was nearly ten in the evening. The sun, still an hour from setting, shone through the ceiling of gray-clouded sky to slice bands of orange across the green slopes and glow pink on the snowy higher peaks in the center of Kodiak Island. The place had a spooky quiet, a deceptive peace only yards from the tumultuous whitecaps beyond the entrance. Should never have risked Seth in the hold. (But Seth may have saved them from capsizing.) If he himself had entered the hold as he intended, would the others—no help from John—have been able to pull him free while keeping the boat stable, or would he now be discovering the secrets of the hereafter? How often would his luck hold? The image of Seth, unconscious, made him want to cover his head. My God, each of his choices bore death's shadow. Some day he'd decide wrong.

Down below, Seth yelled something jovial about cruddy socks that wouldn't need washing now. Mo took up the noise with yells about cruddy shorts, and, judging from the guffaws and splats of wet cloth they had launched a battle. He needed an explosion too, his body ached for it. Instead, he leaned out a window and wrung water from his sleeping bag.

Seth and Mo grab-assed until they generated the energy to finish cleaning. John did everything they told him, willingly. He must have sensed the thread by which he hung. By midnight they had reached Viekoda Bay. The sky was nearly dark, and Hank decided to drop anchor rather than risk standing watches. If the others were as drained as he, they all needed sleep. Mo, with a noisy groan of relief, fell onto his wet bunk without bothering to remove oilskins or boots, and in a minute he was snoring. John undressed, and huddled under a salt-clammy blanket. Seth wandered aft, ostensibly to check damage, but he remained to kick at the hatch absently and look out over the water.

Bone-weary, his stomach still knotted, Hank hesitated by the damp bunk in his cabin, then climbed to the bridge on top of the wheelhouse to stare at the black mountains and black water. The smell of vegetation wafted in, with a strength increased by their days of nothing but sea odors. He was sick of wondering what he should have done better, but putting it from mind gave no peace since it remained as malaise. Could have killed Seth! If he went back to crewing on somebody else's boat—Jones would have him gleefully—he'd still make enough, yet be done with the decisions. And when the time came to horseplay he'd let off steam, gobble a fistful of food, crash into his bunk, and be snoring in a minute.

Seth appeared and settled quietly on the storage chest beside him. They said nothing for a long time. Hank counted the years they'd been together—eight from the time as greenhorn deck slaves on that old Norwegian's dragger, shoveling shrimp until they ached; four from the time they nearly died together on the life raft with Jones, Ivan, and Steve. No one had ever shared more of his life's grit. He broke the silence to keep from getting maudlin. "Can't sleep?"

"Guess I like smelling the air. You all right?" Hank said that he was. "No sense your feeling bad over anything happened today. You done the right thing each step of the way as far as I could see. As any of us could see."

"I thank you for saying it. I'm not that sure myself."

Seth rolled some pot from his leather pouch, took a drag, and passed it over. "Paper's half soggy but she'll draw." Hank refused. He had tried to discourage Seth from smoking the stuff, with the mitigating knowledge that he and Jody had stopped only since the kids came. "You need it, come on, everything has a time and place, in the words of Henry Crawford."

Hank laughed. "Is that the kind of shit I feed you guys?" He took the joint, lit, and drew, holding the smoke in his lungs until a cough forced it out. The lightest finger of repose passed through him. He lit again to fortify it. "Well, you know, Jody would give me hell if I lost a deck boss, so I got a little shaken."

"*You* got shaken? Those damn survival suits might keep the water out, but they just as like to keep it in. Hot inside? Like flushing a toilet the way I pumped sweat, man. There I was down in the gurry kickin' fish, and after a minute the sweat started bangin' into my eyes, and the hands in that thing? Try wiping your face some time with big stiff flippers! I didn't mind a bit that little cold shower." He rolled another joint and took a long, slow draw before handing it across. "Thought for a minute you wouldn't get me in time. My arm got tangled, one of those boards, it must have jammed against me. That was last I remembered. Then next thing I woke up, I thought Fuck, I got to puke, guess he got to me after all."

"I didn't want to lose a good survival suit." The smoke was mellowing him enough to require no more than a slight further push to make him emotional. "Too bad you weren't quick enough, before you stopped being useful, to grab those fish that floated away."

"I appreciate it anyhow, you bearded fuck," Seth said quietly.

Hank steadied his voice. "Any time, buddy."

The darkness deepened so that the water finally merged with the mountains, and the outline of the mountains against the sky became a blur. Brush crackled a few hundred feet away as some nocturnal animal moved about, and a plop of water signaled a salmon jumper who might in daylight have betrayed his entire school to the nets, but the brief night around them remained essentially silent.

"John goes," Hank declared.

"Come on, he works hard on deck and he tries. I was dead-ass like that myself once, I don't know about you."

"Come on yourself, Seth. Some guys don't have the right reflexes. You want to protect every wimp, ever since the life raft and what you think happened. Sorry I mentioned it."

"I gave up and disgraced myself, you can say it. And I don't want to see nobody go through what I did after that, not for something I can help. Remember how we dodged the rats, bunked in that warehouse waiting for any skipper to take us? Well John, he hitchhiked all the way from Kansas, then pounded docks and worked the slimer lines just like we did for months and months before Jimmy broke his arm and you took him on."

"My mistake, he looked strong. A kid who'd given up college after a couple of years like you, like I might have. I thought he'd make good company. Hundreds of kids pound the docks, Seth. The only thing you might owe them is a free chow in the galley now and then."

"Anyhow, I've spent good hours training this guy. Give him another chance."

Hank rose and stretched. "One more trip. Out of pity for a deck boss whose brain sprang a leak today. If John can handle the gear, it's only because you taught him by rote. He doesn't understand how it works. You'll teach him emergencies the same way? A thousand different emergencies?"

"He'll click in soon."

"Let's get some sleep."

2

Punchbag Blues

Next morning as they approached Kodiak harbor drumbeats thumped across the water. Parades had already begun. As they passed the boat harbor en route to the canneries they could see bobbing gold tassels on banners that the Coast Guard marchers carried past the reviewing stand, then the swirling high school pompoms. They'd missed the morning ceremony for those lost at sea during the year. Hank had planned to ring the bell himself for Joe Larson, lost crabbing off the Aleutians in December, then to spend a minute holding Steve and Ivan in his mind's eye to keep alive their memory.

Jody and Jones Henry waited with the cannery crew to catch their lines. She wore slacks under a plaid shirt beginning to bulge. The ponytail of her auburn hair caught the light even under a gray sky, as she followed the course of the boat with eyes narrowed at sight of the boarded windows. Hank at the wheel attempted a grin and waved, but she only nodded.

Jones, head tilted beneath a visor cap, wore his usual denim fleece-lined jacket over oilskin pants. A brailerload of dripping sockeyes rose from the *Adele H* moored nearby. He took in the damage with a few glances, then returned to work.

When Jody came aboard she stopped at each of the men in turn. "Mo, that bandage on your arm . . . John? You look all right, I'm glad. Seth, your face is cut, did you put anything on it?" When she reached Hank in the wheelhouse she said nothing, just hugged his waist as he encircled her with his arms and held her. He breathed the clean smell of her hair, and savored the warmth of her body. The bulge was a precious part of it. The others busied themselves on deck. Mo and John pitched fish from the hold, including Seth's share, while Seth did Hank's job steadying the brailer and recording weights.

"Well," she said at length, releasing him, "this place is a mess."

"Should have seen it twelve hours ago."

"Are you hiding wounds under those clothes, or is it just what I see?" He shrugged, enjoying the attention, and found her a bruise to kiss. "Poor baby." Then, seriously: "You're tired. Was it bad?" He told her it wasn't anymore, and she became cheerfully businesslike. "When Jones said your windows were smashed, I ordered new ones cut right away, and called the Seattle insurance people. Any other damage?"

"Don't think so. Later." He put his arm around her again, and brushed his beard gently against her forehead in the way she liked. "I missed you, that's the bad part." They swayed together like teenagers at a prom, reluctant to release each other. "Kids good, I guess?" She nodded against his chest. "How's the friend inside?"

"I'd kick him back if I could."

A cannery hand came to say that Swede needed to see them. "Well," said Hank as they climbed the open metal stairs in the noisy, echoing cannery, after passing a line of kids and Filipinos gutting belt-loads of salmon, "drink's what I need." At the bend, out of sight, he hugged her shoulder and touched her ear with his tongue. "I know what I need most. Let's not stay long."

She put her hand to his mouth. "Darling, I'm goddamned spotting. Don't ask the details, you'd just get sick. Dr. Bob says we ought to leave it alone for a few weeks to play safe."

"You're in some kind of danger?"

"Calm down. It's part of the whole stupid business."

Maybe he shouldn't have been so persistent about their having a third. What if it injured her? He went limp and drooped his head to make a joke of it but the day, which had begun to seem agreeable despite fatigue and the repairs ahead, had lost its promise.

Swede Scorden, his lean jaw set as if he were still biting one of the cigars his doctor had made him relinquish, held a phone and blanketed the reports and papers on his desk with notes scribbled in a heavy pen. He motioned them to chairs, opened a desk drawer and produced a bottle, pushed it toward them, and set out glasses one by one, without lifting his gaze.

"Want me to get you a chaser?" Hank whispered. Jody shook her head, but stopped him pouring at the one-finger mark. He gave himself a full tumbler, and drank half at one gulp. She frowned. He winked back as the Scotch burned smoothly down his throat.

At a break in his conversation Swede snapped: "Any damage besides the windows?"

"Shaft might be twisted but I don't think so. Get Slim, we'll start on it clockaround tomorrow. How long will new windows take? Why'd you call us to Kodiak anyway, instead of delivering ashore in Chignik? Cash buyers are all over the place there, taking your fish."

"I needed product here to keep my goons busy."

"You don't even let your poor goons off to watch the parade," laughed Jody.

"And they come back drunk? Hold on." Swede told somebody on the phone to check figures again and get them straight this time. "LSD confirmed? Then fire 'em. Whole crew. Leave *Orion* tied to the pier, I'll send replacement. Next opening's when, six tomorrow night? High tide's at four? Meet the first morning plane. No, they don't work ashore for me either after drugs. Boot 'em from the compound. I'll pay fare back to Seattle to get rid of 'em, but they camp at the airport until they fly." He slammed down the phone, and spoke pleasantly. "Bristol Bay. Ever been there? Not to be missed."

Hank turned to Jody. "You heard. He's still the prick of the fleet, still the cannery boss from the Middle Ages."

"So. Cash buyers in Chignik you say?"

Hank took another swallow. "Paying a twelve cents premium. Watch out. Crews get restless when they see the numbers on those buyers' signs. Your deals with skippers don't reach the crews."

"Any boats contracted to me, caught delivering to cash buyers, go off my list." Swede reached to find his cigar and snorted to remember he had none. "Unless my tender lets them down."

"Guys don't need your company store anymore."

"Oh? When a boat busts its windows they're still ready to kiss any part of me that sticks out. You know cash buyers who stock parts and keep a skilled boatwright on the payroll? Jody, how did such a mushhead land you? Go on, drink up, pour another, pass it over."

"You machos," said Jody drily. "Hank's had enough. And Swede, you dealer . . ." Her eyes narrowed. "Who's the *Darcy B* cash-buying for in Chignik? I hear it's for Swede Scorden."

"That's crazy!" declared Hank.

Swede half smiled. "Who told you that?"

Jody smiled back. "Deny it."

"Hank, cage your wife. No, get rid of *him*, Jody. Come back alone any time, you're the brain. Don't look so shocked, sonny. Everybody in this game hedges his bets. Look at him, all virtue. Join the world, Crawford. All's fair." He poured, then shoved the bottle back across the table.

"No more for us," Jody declared.

Hank, scowling, purposefully drained and refilled his glass. He'd begun to feel it and didn't care. Cagey prick. Competing against his own men but holding them to the rules! And Jody, she knew and didn't tell him. Hell with staying sober. Nothing he could do with her today required temperance. He rose to the window and glanced over masts, gray choppy water, and the low spruces of Near Island. Couldn't the sun ever shine in Kodiak? And the smashed *Jody S* moored below. Ought to be down there on deck where he belonged. A brailerload of dripping salmon swung from the hold and rose to the pier, where a kid in oversized yellow cannery oilskins emptied it onto a conveyor belt. The fish thumped out stiffly, oozing blood and gurry, reds that had sparkled silver in the nets a day or two ago. Sorry stuff. And the boards across *Jody S*'s windows looked sorry, battered, irresponsible. Jones Henry, still in oilskins from his own boat's delivery, emerged from the *Jody S* wheelhouse checking damage. As a partner, Jones had the right, even at only twenty percent remaining, but he, Hank, should be there in control. He took one more swallow as he headed toward the door and his boat.

"Hold it, Crawford, I'm not through," barked Swede sharply enough to stop him. "Jody, make him sit. Listen, Hank. All hell's loose in Bristol Bay. Reds are plugging the nets. I just fired my tender crew up there on the *Orion*, and you're beached till we fix your boat. Now you take a rest tonight, let Jody be nice to you. Then, nine-thirty flight tomorrow, you and your boys fly to Naknek and take over the *Orion*."

Hank laughed roughly, annoyed. "My boat needs fixing. I'll be here to see it's done right."

"Jody can supervise your repairs here, you know that." Swede's voice smoothed. "You worked to kick the Japs off our fish. Don't you want to see its success? We've backed them off the Aleutians, they've stopped intercepting our reds headed to the Bering, and the reds are plugging our nets in Bristol Bay. It makes hauling reds in Chignik look like dollhouse."

Jody deftly appropriated the glass, then held his arm. "I'll take this one home. Seth can bring the boat around."

Hank pulled away. She should understand! Tendering was shit, hauling other boats' dead catches like a mule, never hands on fish that still thrashed. Not what a fisherman did. "We're not for hire anymore."

"Tell him what he knows, Jody. You need money for your big Marco one-oh-eight. Whether you *need* a new monster boat or not. The thing is, Crawford, I can trust you and your boys because you're too dumb to cheat me."

"Swede you old fucker, hear this. Bristol Bay is not my turf. Little gillnetters? I'd as soon pick potatoes. I've never fished there, I don't plan to."

"Fish, Hank, fish! Big reds, sockeyes. Money! All you do is collect and take 'em in to the cannery."

"No."

"Then listen. Three thousand, cash, under the table. Then two-fifty a day for you, a hundred and sixty for each of your men. End of season adjustment for a good captain." Hank guided Jody through the door too firmly for her to pull away. "Jody, I need the idiot."

"I think we have to take a walk," said Jody quietly. "We'll let you know."

"Four thousand," Swede snapped, "My donation to the new boat and we settle it right now."

Jody looked at Hank and her eyes narrowed. "We'll take a walk, Swede, and let you know." They descended the metal stairs to a forklift area by the gutting lines. Hank started toward the quay and his boat. Jody guided him firmly the opposite way to the managers' parking lot. They stopped by their station wagon and she squared in front of him. "Unless that storm really threw you, Hank . . ."

"I'm fine!" He wanted time with her, and his injured boat needed him, and he knew that he was going to be persuaded.

"Every thousand we put toward the new boat is one less to pay the bank at interest." The Scotch had spread its warm fingers. He shrugged. Back at the office they shook hands with Swede, but Hank bargained to leave on a later plane that would still let him catch the tide, and that any later adjustment would include his men.

With the decision made, his anger subsided. But he insisted on going to his boat. Jones Henry had left, and they could see his *Adele H* nearing the harbor breakwater a mile away. Seth virtually strutted when told to take the *Jody S* around after they unloaded and hosed.

"I need to stretch. Leave the car here. Let's see some Fourth of July before you nail me in." They walked hand in hand along the potholed road that connected the canneries and town. It was as deserted as a Sunday off-season except for parked vehicles leading to town past the docks, net loft, and hardware store. A band still played. They could feel the thump of drums and brass before they distinguished a tune. "The kids need to see this. Where are they?"

"They're in town. Adele gave me the day off to comfort the ship-wrecked fisherman."

The words made Hank lighthearted. The right wife, okay kids whom he'd soon see, friends, a sound boat soon ready to fish again. He slid around to face and hold her, and stomp-danced in time to the band. She laughed in the throaty way he never tired of hearing, and followed his lead.

People clogged the roads around the square, many of them strangers. Not many years past, before the town started growing, such a percentage of unfamiliar faces would have been remarkable. The parade had just finished, and the tag end of a marching band, trailed by horsemen in cowboy hats, dispersed by the ferry pier where a Japanese research ship lay moored. Nearby, the Coast Guard cutter *Confidence* was open for holiday inspection. The local politicians, ministers, and Coast Guard brass who had formed the reviewing party stood handshaking each other. The crowd drifted toward the cutter and the boxing ring in front of the American Legion Hall.

Hank had no desire to discuss his accident, but it had become the day's news in the fishing community. People stopped to ask questions, commiserate, offer advice, reminisce about their own close calls. He listened and answered, trying to be polite while he kicked one foot against the other. When Jones Henry—up from his boat and changed into shore clothes—joked wryly about the damage he changed the subject. The massive dose of Swede's Scotch had left him logy. He needed to run, play thumping basketball, anything but talk.

"Daddy, Daddy!" Henny raced to claim him, bouncing on sturdy fat legs. Hank swept him up, twirled him with mock growling sounds as the child squealed, then hugged him tight. Dawn, barely toddling, called and he grabbed her in his other arm. The minute he smooched her wonderfully soft cheek she demanded release and squirmed back to the ground, independent as a cat. Henny pummeled him and called for another swing overhead. "Hey, kumquat, go easy," shouted Hank, increasing the roughhouse. He loved the easy power with which he could handle his boy, and the feel of the kicking little body.

"I hope that poor child survives to reach adulthood," said Adele Henry. She wore the expensive fur-trimmed brown suede coat Jones had bought her in Paris, over a sweater and puffy slacks. Women her age should stick to dresses, Hank thought mildly.

"Come on, Mother," growled Jones beside her. "You'd put him in lace pants if you had the chance. He'll be pulling nets with us in five, six years, he'd better learn to bounce."

"Oh yes, pull nets. That's what you thought with your own boys, daddy, and with that talk you drove one straight into being a computer salesman, and poor Russ never settled to anything. Jody, don't you think Hank's being too rough?"

"I think he knows when to stop." Jody said it with cheerful offhandedness, but with an edge that made Hank glance over. The wide mouth was smiling, but the eyes narrowed just enough to send a signal. He gave Henny a final bear hug and set him down. The boy began to cry—no whimper, Hank noted, but a good, lusty yowl. "I told you so," said Adele, and bent to pick him up. Henny pushed her away, his face red and woebegone, and wrapped his arm around Hank's leg. Hank tried to keep his grin in check as he lifted the boy high, with enough gentleness to keep Jody appeased, then draped him over his shoulder like a sack and patted his bottom.

"Me too," said Dawn. He cradled her up to his other shoulder, then maneuvered her back down as she started to squirm, stealing a peck on the cheek in the process.

Hank finally told Jones the details of the Shelikof Strait accident, and listened politely to his former skipper's advice on what he should have done. Jones might still own twenty percent of the boat, but it made Hank restless to be instructed. Traffic drifted around them. Hank held back until Adele complained that the line to visit the Coast Guard ship was getting longer and longer, and they'd already had to wait as long as it took to get into the Louvre in Paris, France. "He wants to make sure Seth brings his boat over safely," said Jody. He liked the way she understood without needing diagrams. Adele was a grand person, but she had never tuned so to Jones. He kept Henny draped over his shoulder as the women left to save them places.

"You're lucky," said Jones. "That Jody."

"You're lucky too, don't groan at me. How many dames would have put up with you all these years?"

"I never hear the end of them two weeks in Europe."

"Best investment you ever made."

"I saw enough of Frenchies during the war. This time they fed us snails. Figure the rest for yourself."

They watched critically as the *Jody S* left the cannery pier and glided through the breakwater to its mooring at the floats. Seth stood on the bridge, erect and grave, with Mo and John behind him practically at attention. Hank frowned. They actually enjoyed his absence! Shouldn't have jumped into Swede's Scotch that way, and then let Jody bully him, should have brought in his own boat. The mooring accomplished, Seth sauntered among the other boats with John and Mo still a pace to the rear. His stocky body had an easy, powerhouse sway that might have amused Hank at another time. Was that why Seth wanted to keep John, to have a sycophant who followed behind and kissed his ass?

As Seth ascended the gangway from the floats and saw Hank watching, he drew a breath that pulled his shirt against the buttons. "All delivered," he announced expansively, without bothering to append the word "Boss" that Hank often denied to Jody he desired of his men. (At least, Hank told himself, I'm honest enough to recognize the contradiction. After all, though Seth was younger, he and Seth had once crewed together as equals, so why shouldn't the guy avoid that word?) Hank shifted his boy to a piggyback position, using the activity to cover any reservations that his face might have shown, and complimented Seth.

It helped none that John declared in a studiously serious voice: "That was the smoothest docking I've ever seen."

"Glad you've got enough reflexes left to tell," said Hank curtly, and felt petty at once as John averted his eyes and fell behind. He felt more foolish still as Seth observed to Jones that there was nobody like "ol' Boss" for bringing any boat alongside in any kind of shitty weather.

What did he have against John, after all? The kid was a little bit refined, not comfortably rough. He shaved and combed, and even now wore a clean yellow stay-press shirt instead of plaid flannel with sawed sleeves like the others. The campus still clung to him. The boats had removed all traces of Seth's single year at Berkeley. He himself, a Johns Hopkins bachelor and former Navy JG, could turn his background off or on to suit the circumstance. The hands that held his son's legs were thick, strong fisherman's hands. A kid from Kansas like John should have big hands and hail from the wheat fields if he wanted to make it on a fishing boat, not from some accounting school. Was that all he had against the guy?

John might have been subdued, but he kept rubbing his sideburns as he glanced about restlessly. His black hair, plastered like a mold when wet, blew soft and long in the breeze, and he kept adjusting his cap over it. Hank felt compelled to make amends. "That Cindy you keep mentioning, she's somewhere around the corner? Take off and find her, man."

"I guess she got tired of waiting. I told her we'd be in yesterday like every other boat, or at least by early this morning."

"Earlier might have found you dead," Hank snapped. Henny on his shoulders began to aim playful slaps on his forehead. "Stop that!" he said too loudly, then took the child's hands and swung them lightly to soften it. He told his crewmen, didn't ask them, "By the way, get your fun now. We're going to fly tomorrow to Bristol Bay at eleven-thirty, to take over one of Swede's tenders." Seth said he'd always heard about those Naknek sockeyes, so, great! If Seth thought that, so did Mo. John pulled a long face. "We can do without you," said Hank.

John considered. He probably guessed the threat to his berth on the *Jody S* if he stayed behind. "I'll come."

"Well," Mo declared, "I better go over and sign for the boxing. Two or three of us from the other boats, we plan to mix it up together, make it like—see whose boat's best, you know? Ham Davis from the *Star Wars*,

Smeltzer from the *Lynn D*, Butch from the *Joe and Edna*. Ham especially, eh Boss? With you and his skipper's always giving each other a hard time?"

"Hell yes," said Hank. "I'll put fifty bucks on that one, and I'll flush out Tolly besides."

"You mean you'll fight Tolly Smith, skipper to skipper, after Ham and me's had it out?"

"No, no, we'll drink and cheer."

Jones looked around. "I've got another fifty says you'll take Ham, but don't tell the old lady. Mebbe you won't mind knocking down the *Star Wars* candidate for both *Jody S* and *Adele H* together, since my boys ain't so young?"

Mo swelled visibly. "Honored, skipper, honored." He slapped Seth on the shoulder. "You taking on anybody?"

"Only apes punch it out," said Seth cheerfully.

"I used to box a little," said John. The others glanced at him, then continued with their plans.

First Hank and Jones were obliged to join the women for a tour of the cutter *Confidence*. When the route took them past the Japanese research ship Jones halted, as Hank feared he might. "What are those cursed buggers doing here on an American Holiday?"

"Just good will." Hank kept it light. "Gals are waiting. Come on."

"Never trust a Jap alive. Treacherous from Pearl Harbor to the end, to this very minute. On the Canal they'd surrender with a hand grenade in their shirt, blow us up with them.

"Guadalcanal, you've told me. Terrible. I know. But the gals are waiting."

"Believe it!"

The queue at the gangway moved aboard at last. The Coast Guard ship was enough a piece of the seafaring scene that the two had visited her on business and knew some of the men. Jones grumbled: "We never had to shuffle through some line just to bump against a crowd of old hens and land-lubbers who don't know the difference between a winch and a fiddly." ("Be quiet, daddy," snapped Adele. "You've never taken this old hen to the Coast Guard before, so be a gentleman about it. And I'm sure Jody knows a fiddly when she sees one.") On the other hand Henny, who still rode Hank's shoulder, struck such a romance with the 20mm guns mounted on the bow—he ack-acked exuberantly while his feet thumped a tattoo—that Hank relaxed and laughed as he cushioned his chest against the hard little heels.

Swede's whiskey still kept him dizzy but had no effect on his ability to cradle Dawn and let her down again whenever he chose, while steadying Henny. He joked with the gunner's mate on duty by the 20mm. The kid, scrubbed for the occasion, kept trying to explain his charge in more detail than anyone around wanted to hear. Hank let the words pass over him, interjecting a knowledgeable question now and then, as Henny took his fill of the guns. Ever since his first ride with the Coast Guard years before, a kid himself from Jones Henry's boat searching for bodies after the old Whale Pass disaster, the cleanliness and order of military ships had both attracted and repelled him. Navy service had made him part of the community, but duty in its fleet still seemed sterile—at least impersonal—compared to fishing boats. The men aboard were seafarers of a different sort, regulated not by the feeding habits of fish but by commands over a speaker. Could this gun-struck kid tie even a bowline?

He remembered well: That wardroom coffee so long on the burner its acrid odor scorched the room; wet heat from the marshy Vietnam jungles that no amount of air conditioning dispelled; orders given and orders taken. He glanced up at the long array of windows on the *Connie*'s bridge, located higher than any mere ten-foot sea could reach. On watch aboard one Navy ship of his duty he'd borne responsibility for nearly a hundred men. He'd handled a ship that could have swallowed a fishing boat in its hold without listing. It *had* been exhilarating. The kid who fretted his hours over a 20mm gun probably got to fire it now and then, to taste the smoke and feel the force he had unleashed. What a small, grubby command he himself had settled for, after all—to shepherd boatfuls of fish into a cannery dock, when he might by now be maneuvering a great gray warship into Hong Kong or Naples or Rio to the accompaniment of jets spouting from harbor tugs. He squeezed Henny's legs, firm and smooth and vulnerable, to reassure himself.

An officer in dress blues and braided cap strode over. His face, still young, had creases at the mouth as he smiled. "Tommy!" growled Jones warmly. He and Hank were greeted in turn by name. "Now here's a man," Jones continued, placing a hand on the officer's shoulder. "We're going to lose him to Washington, D.C., and I expect he'll set them politicians straight. Commander Tom Hill, he's captain aboard here and he's one man the foreign buggers watch out for."

"I've heard," said Adele, impressed. "And you know Jones?"

"We need support from men like Jones and Hank, Mrs. Henry. And they give it. Hi Jody."

"Tell her," said Jones. "Tell her how you caught a Jap just last winter in the dead of night, sneaked up on him fishing our fish in our water. Hank sent us the article. If it wasn't for fellows like this, the foreign buggers would keep raping our fish even worse than they do. Now you tell me, Tommy. Our boys Ted Stevens and Don Young in D.C., they worked all those years for the two-hundred-mile law they passed last year, but the foreigners still fish right under our noses."

"Some of you big fishermen didn't read the fine print," said Jody pleasantly. "Hank's tried to tell you. The foreigners can bargain with the State Department for any quota that Americans can't catch."

"You hear that, Daddy? Jody keeps informed even if you don't." Jones frowned at his wife but said nothing. As they left the ship, Adele took his arm. "But I must say Daddy knows everybody, even though we spend winters now in San Pedro. Not the president of France, of course, when we went to France last year. But just since we've been back this summer, when Governor Hammond came through campaigning for his re-election, and then Mr. Hickel against him, it was 'Hi Jay' and 'Hello Wally,' and you should have heard the 'Hi Jones' right back."

"You got to know the big fellows to get anything done," said Jones, mollified.

Hank stayed apart, still daydream-skippering a warship into Rio or Hong Kong. Or skippering a cutter like Tommy's. A few months earlier he had ridden the *Confidence* as a guest to observe the extent of the foreign fleet still off Alaska: longliners and draggers by the sickening hundreds, still allowed to fish American waters and get away with what they could. Some obeyed the rules, others evaded them cleverly. Tommy, a true hunter, cruised silent in the winter dark, when the foreigners, used to being watched only in daylight, relaxed. Nighttime boardings, the ship's boat over quickly with a large party rather than the usual one or two. As some of Tommy's men fanned out to inspect both holds and crevices, others occupied the captain and mates with paperwork. Meanwhile, the boat zoomed astern to search for illegal catch hurriedly dumped. His operation had the excitement of the chase, with the occasional big one as reward. Commander Hank could have stalked these superfish.

"Don't you think so?" asked Jody.

"What, dear?"

"*Sleep*, Hank. You don't listen. A while back we were coming to town for just a minute and then going home, because you were so tired—"

They stopped. "*You* said I was tired, honey, I didn't." Abruptly he lifted Henny to the ground and swung Dawn into his place, a gesture against favoritism. "I'm just fine. We've got to go cheer Mo when he boxes."

Her mouth tightened. He knew she found the boxing stupid since crewmen needed their hands, but why should she be angry? She'd said herself they couldn't have sex. Dawn began to squirm. He raised her up and down several times, both to divert her and to use a few muscles, but soon Henny had regained the shoulders. Tired? Hell, he now had energy that needed steaming off. Sleep was the last thing he needed. They headed toward the Legion Hall in a drizzle too light to disperse anyone. Firecrackers popped from a rooftop, and others answered from the harbor. Beer cans crunched underfoot as they drew closer to the ring. The town was in full swing. People clapped his shoulder and offered drinks.

Mike Stimson, Jody's old skipper, hailed them. A gold chain bounced against his open shirt and a gold watch gleamed on the thick arm that held out a bottle of the best. Jody laughed and took the first nip. (Should she be drinking when pregnant? And like that in front of the kids? It was all right for men . . .) Mike declared loudly—not for the first time—that fishing had no more piss and zing since losing his cook and head net-puller eight years ago. The praise brought the wide smile to Jody's face, and when she invited Mike to make her an offer the direct, sassy eyes flashed as they had routinely a half dozen years before. Hank took it in secure good humor. He declared how peaceful and free life would be again if Jody found somebody else's head to bang with a frying pan, but his hand eased around her shoulder.

The boxing ring stood on a raised platform. The bouts had already begun. Hank knew the two crewmen who dodged each other's gloves as a referee trailed them. By the steps below stood Tim from the Legion—he'd evidently closed his filling station for the day—coordinating the matches with microphone and clipboard. Beside him waited two kids in white T-shirts, joking nervously, their Coast Guard jumpers draped on a nearby rail. Just behind them pranced Mo, and Ham from the *Star Wars*, performing elaborate bends and stretches. Seth stood alongside, drinking from one beer can and holding two others.

"I got him scared already, Boss," called Mo, beating his chest. His beefy shoulders hid the muscles beneath like plaster on a wall. Glad I'm not going into the ring with him, Hank thought appreciatively. Ham, a big homely boy who grinned more than he talked, had the build to match Mo's. Even match. Walt, the deck boss aboard *Star Wars*, started slapping oil onto Ham's arms. Seth countered, rubbing beer over Mo.

"Where's your skipper hiding?" said Hank. In answer, Tolly Smith bear-hugged him from behind, then tickled Henny until the child kicked so hard that Hank had to swing him to the ground. Tolly grabbed him back up for a noisy roughhouse, then held still as Henny touched the gold ring in his ear. The two had reached an agreement that Henny could play with it if he didn't pull. Henny usually remembered since a further privilege, playing with the big gold nugget around Uncle Tolly's neck, hinged on his honoring the pact.

"Okay, man, this is it," Tolly declared. "I'm tired of your corking me on the grounds. I'd never cork *him*, Jody, that's all lies. Our two deck apes'll have it out, and justice will prevail when your boy hits the canvas. You dumb enough to bet on it?"

Hank tried to sound casual as he caught Tolly's eye. "No need for that. Come on, Jones, let's buy him a drink."

"Hell with that," said Jody. "If you place bets it'll be in front of the budget directors."

"Daddy's certainly not making any bets," said Adele. "Are you, Daddy?"

"Be quiet, woman. You don't know anything."

"Ho ho ho!" Tolly stuck out his chest and looked around grandly. "I used to know these people when they roamed free as buffalos, the way *I* still do. Jody, you'd make your own bets back then. And as for this shaggy corker"—he tousled Hank's hair—"remember when you was a greenhorn college kid at Swede's old cannery? Closest to a beard he had back then was when he forgot his safety razor. I taught him all he knew, that summer."

"You still dump cologne like mouthwash and stink like a whore's kitchen," said Hank easily, finger-combing his hair back into place. "Some of us change for the better."

The announcer called the next fight as the two in the ring, one with a reddened cheek turning purple, tapped gloves and retired to scattered applause. Below, the Coast Guard kids mounted the steps to begin. Seth and Walt started massaging their charges in earnest, and Mo had removed the bandage from his arm. Beside them stood John, typically both in and out of it, holding everybody's beer cans.

"Hundred bucks," said Tolly. "That's starters, that says my *Star Wars* is top boat in the ring."

"No sweat there," said Hank, hoping Jody would not embarrass him. She merely shrugged. "*Jody S* gladly covers that to make a little party money." He had planned to reach a hundred after opening with fifty, but now he'd be forced higher. Jones, glaring at his wife, made good his promise to stake fifty on the honor of the *Adele H*, and Tolly accepted with an inevitable jibe at the age and infirmity of Jones's crew. Adele's raised eyebrow promised later discussion, but she held her peace.

The boxing caught Henny's attention and he grappled his way back to Hank's shoulders. "My daddy do that!" he declared, and started imitating the punches with such vigor that Hank had to steady him.

The Coasties slugged earnestly, although by the end of the two-minute round their initiatives became less and less frequent. Soon Mo and Ham were strutting up the steps as the announcer gave their names and boats, and declared that by their request this would be best two out of three rounds. They're so young and full of themselves! Hank thought. He himself was hardly old at thirty-three—Jones pushing sixty was still a hard man to outfish—but when was the last time he'd strutted? Down the mud-ice ruts of Dutch Harbor, maybe, after delivering a deck load of king crab. Or passing out cigars throughout Kodiak when Henny was born, after missing the actual birth by two days as he tried to dovetail a Bering crab run with Jody's bio clock. (She'd said herself that meeting boat payments was all the more important if they were going to have a family.) When Dawn was born they both agreed he'd stay with the crabs. Hell with that, this time. Other men helped deliver their kids and this would be his final chance.

Mo and Ham spent little time circling and testing their footwork before one and then the other leapt in with a jab. Their usual friendly faces wore fight scowls. Mo sent a right that thumped against Ham's chest without budging him. Then Ham grabbed the opening to land a hard blow to Mo's jaw. The two broke, danced for a moment, and headed straight into each other again. This time Mo's swift hook found its way to Ham's cheek. Ham delivered one to Mo's solar plexus that budged him only a foot, and the two ended in a clinch that the referee broke.

Hank, Jody, Jones, and Tolly cheered and grimaced with their men. Only Adele, holding tight to Dawn's hand, took it coolly. Henny, on top of Hank's shoulders, became a crowing extension of his father. At the two-minute bell the fighters streamed sweat, but they still pranced like race-horses. The referee called the round a tie. Jody pushed through to the corner where Seth was sponging Mo to shout her encouragement.

"Two young men who need their hands for fishing," said Adele. "It's foolish, but they *are* beautiful, aren't they?"

Tolly returned from his man, grinning. "Double you both."

"Covered for *Jody S*," Hank declared.

Jones hesitated. "Cover him, Daddy, cover him," snapped Adele. "Don't let your man down now."

John, the detached crewman, joined them. He declared to no one in particular that Mo lacked strategy, that anybody could see the opening Ham left when he put too much body in his jab. And Ham for his part was dumb if he didn't see that Mo's left jaw hurt and he'd left himself open on the right by protecting it. And Mo's arm after all had that fresh cut on it that you could work over, since all's fair above the waist.

Hank turned on John furiously as Tolly laughed, "Sonofabitch, thanks," and hurried back to his man just as the bell rang to start round two. "Lean on his left jaw, Ham," he shouted up. Back with Hank he said, "Nice boy you have there, goes for a fellow's cut arm."

"Well, they were just my observations," said John. "I'd offered Mo advice and he wasn't interested, so I figured nobody cared."

Ham heeded his skipper's call and worked Mo's jaw, but Mo took self-protection lightly enough that he managed a punishing blow for each opening Ham left in the process. But high stakes or not, Ham avoided Mo's wounded arm. By the end of the round, their bounce diminished, the two walked solemnly to their corners to cheers from the audience as the announcer declared that this was a fight, finally, ladies and gentlemen. Their seconds watered them with vigorous concern.

The referee called the round for Ham. Hank put down Henny, ignoring his objections, and grabbed John's arm more roughly than intended. "If you've got any goddamned advice this time, advise your shipmate."

"Don't shove me like that, please, Skipper."

Mo in his corner was breathing hard. He listened to John when Hank told him to, but the instructions were so detailed (they'd been clear enough when John was mouthing off in front of Tolly!) that Hank knew Mo was not assimilating them.

"Yeah, Boss, my jaw hurts, but don't worry, I got him on the run. You watch, this round."

Back with the others, Tolly suggested they triple their original bets. Hank and Jones agreed, tensely.

Despite Ham's advantage, Mo managed in the third round to knock him down for a count of four after storming in with an offensive at the starting bell. Both men slammed each other equally, and Hank groaned for his crewman's jaw. When the final bell separated them they stood panting and slumped, eyeing each other with their scowls still in place. The knockdown earned Mo the round. The referee declared the entire bout a tie, and asked if they wanted to go another round for sudden death. The audience yelled its approval.

"Sure, I guess," said Mo slowly. "Hell yes."

"Hell, sure, yeah," said Ham with equal slowness.

Hank turned to Tolly. "We need those guys to fish. A tie suit you?"

"Tie's fine. Let's stop it."

The two skippers shouted up praise and ordered their men down. Mo and Ham drew simultaneous breaths of relief—they resembled each other closely—grinned, hugged, and left the ring together as another pair of crewmen took their place. On the ground, Seth and Walt happily poured beer over their charges. Somebody's bottle, passed mouth to mouth, was quickly emptied by the group slapping their fighters' backs.

"My daddy do that?" asked Henny excitedly, pointing to the ring. Hank tickled him to divert his attention, but the child said through his yelps and giggles, "Do that, Daddy, do that!" What would it be like to spar with old Tolly? Something for Henny to remember about his dad. They'd be almost an even match—Tolly a hair shorter but maybe more solid. Hadn't put on gloves for about five years, be fun . . . As he took his snort from a bottle he warned himself it was probably the booze that had him so full of balls, but this insight left as soon as the bottle passed on to Jones. "Think you could last a round up there with me?" he asked Tolly casually, in private.

"Not me, buddy. I set nets and make bets." Well, thought Hank comfortably, I tried.

Somebody had to go into the Legion Hall to bring out drinks, since the children were with them. The skippers began to argue without heat over who should buy. It was more a ceremony, making little difference. Each would buy eventually.

"I never saw such a bunch of old men for making up their minds," said John with half a smile. "Let this one be on me. What's everybody drinking?"

Nothing this asshole said was right! "You mean you're tired of advising the enemy and want to take on the rest of us?" Hank's voice rose to the kind of roar he usually reserved for the deck with the engine gunning. "Instead of advice, why aren't you up in that ring if you know so much? That too close to the real thing?" The group suddenly became a center of silence in the noisy square.

"I'm not afraid, if that's what you mean," said John slowly. His face had a bland expression that could have masked deep feelings, but the apparent detachment made Hank even angrier. "And while we're at it—Boss—stop riding me. And I don't like anybody shoving me. I try to do my work —"

"Feeble try!"

John considered for a moment. Then, in a husky voice that had at last lost its cool: "Want to go up there in the ring with me yourself?"

"You're fuckin' A!"

Jody came between and pushed them apart. "Stop this bullshit."

Her tone usually gave Hank pause, but he brushed past them all and strode to the steps of the ring. "Sign on a match here, Tim." he said calmly. The ring was empty, waiting. The others protested, Seth with vehement concern, Jody so coldly he knew he'd hear of it later. He permitted himself a few perfunctory stretches, but within minutes of their exchange he and John were stripped to the waist, gloved, and facing each other on the raised platform.

Hank fought with spirit. But John was a dozen years his junior and, it turned out, a college varsity boxer. By the end of the two-minute round

Hank had been forced to pick himself from the floor twice, and although John's nose bled the decision was clearly his.

The party continued for a while. But it hardly amounted to much since Jody, after watching the fight to its conclusion, took a taxi home with the kids before Hank descended from the ring. Tolly produced a box of multiple-string firecrackers. They banged with enough noise that Seth and Mo said they were just the thing. But halfway through the box Tolly stopped, because nobody was really paying attention.

3

BEHAVING

Next morning at breakfast Jody remained cool, although she served his favorite pancakes and sausage. Henny chattered around, still talking about his daddy in the boxing ring. Now and then he'd hit himself in the face, cry "bop bop," and fall to the floor. The fact that Hank had been the loser didn't bother him. Outside the window, fog obscured all but pale shapes of houses and the harbor masts. Good. The plane to Bristol Bay wouldn't fly.

Hank regarded the greasy sausage glumly, and picked at the pancakes without his usual lay-on of butter and syrup. Doughy inside. Not the time to complain about it as he would on the boat and growl for a fresh batch. Was he getting old to have a hangover hold him down? And he ached! Just two minutes in the ring, and his legs, back, and arms felt like they'd been pounded for days, never mind the sore chin. Hadn't looked in the mirror. Face bruises? Have to laugh them off. Thirty-three wasn't old compared to Jones Henry. Not old when he did indeed own the *Jody S* all paid, at least eighty percent of it, and was about to graduate to a 108-foot crabber that could fish any sea. But old enough compared to that damned John. Now if he fired the kid he'd look like a prick skipper who couldn't take his knocks. Might have remembered from Navy days. Fraternize with the enlisted, no matter how much they're guys like yourself, and somewhere it gets screwed. He pushed at the sausage. Didn't want new adventure. Not before some home life. Bristol Bay was all unknown, new waters. Didn't have the energy. Should be with his *Jody S* to see her repaired properly before deserting her for the new crabber.

Dawn, released from her high chair, toddled to him and draped over his leg. But when he leaned to pick her up she squirmed away with a giggle. "Bop bop," said Henny, and pummeled his other leg. It hit a sore spot but Hank controlled his wince. He suddenly thought of an opener to start Jody talking. "B-I-R-T-H-D-A-Y," he spelled out and nodded toward Henny. "Soon, right?"

"Last week," said Jody drily. "Adele brought a cake. You gave him that toy truck over there."

"Hey, four-year-old!"

"That'll be next year, big daddy."

"Oh, sure, three. I meant three." No way around it. He faced her. "I had a few drinks, like the old days. I'm sorry."

"In the old days we were free kids and you were just another fisherman. Now you're a respected highliner and your children imitate you. It's a question of behavior."

He felt a sudden emptiness. "You've changed."

"I've gone the next step in our lives. You'd better catch up."

"It was bad out there. Then it kept going wrong ashore. All I did—"

"Well, I wouldn't mind a few drinks every day myself." She stood holding a spatula, the new baby bulging beneath her apron. Her hair was tied with loose neatness. Everything she wore looked good. He glanced at the new candles in the wedding-gift silver holders and the good plates stacked unused at the end of the table. She'd prepared a special meal last night, as always when he returned from the sea, and he'd blown it. And all his boat clothes, soggy and ripe when they came to harbor, now lay clean and folded.

Gently he disengaged Dawn who held his knee again, and Henny on the other side who had begun to crawl to his lap. He rose and put his arms around her. The baby bulge pressed his stomach. Rather than barrier it made him love her all the more. "I'm a slob. I'm sorry."

"Well, even a slob had better eat his breakfast."

"Not hungry. Hangover."

"*Too* bad." Her voice had lightened. It would be all right. "Nourishment clears the system, buster, shovel it in, then finish packing. There's work to do." He kissed her, and controlled the wince when his jaw touched her face. Didn't control it enough. She laughed, and imitated Henny. "Bop bop. Big fishermen take a long time to learn." He laughed gladly.

"Look, we'll tell Swede to stuff it on Bristol Bay, it's not too late. I want to hang around home a while before I go to Westward. While they fix the *Jody S*, maybe I'll stack seine a trip or two with Jones. . . ."

She spread their accounts over the table. Insurance should cover the *Jody S*'s smashed windows so shrug that off. But money! Last season's king crab might have generated enough cash to think of a bigger boat, the shrimp had pushed in a nice winter bonus, and tendering the *Jody S* for Swede in Chignik had brought another chunk. But, Jody pointed out: "That's only a hundred five thousand less to borrow from the bank for a boat that costs one million six hundred thousand before pots and gear. We'll sell *Jody S* for at least six hundred thousand of that after Jones's twenty percent. Thank this new Capital Construction that keeps it from disappearing in taxes, the government did *that* one right for a change." She added Swede's new seven-thousand-dollar bribe. "And you know you can expect another ten thousand in Bristol Bay, at least. Since you've got to have your new crabber so you can bounce with the big guys . . ."

"Hold on, we're in this together."

"Your ego, Hank. I could live with ninety-foot *Jody S*."

"But you *approved*."

"I didn't interfere. Let's not argue this, you're getting your boat and I support it. Just forget this talk of freedom to lay around the house when Swede offers money. We'll relax some other year."

"We didn't have any time together last winter either."

She tapped her belly. "I think this happened on a warm January night in Hawaii."

"Okay, two weeks. Nice two weeks."

By early afternoon the fog had dispersed enough for the eleven-thirty flight to leave, resulting only in the kind of delay that Kodiak travelers took for granted. Jody gathered them in the station wagon—Seth and Mo from the boat with boots tied to their knapsacks, and John, who bunked ashore, in front of the laundromat with a bag of clean-smelling clothes that he folded and packed as they rode.

Henny climbed around Hank's lap as might have been expected. For some annoying reason, Dawn, the wiggleworm, settled on John's lap. Hank watched from the corner of his eye, hoping that John would betray his nature by pushing her away, but instead the asshole talked to her gently, gave one of his seldom smiles, and worked his packing around her.

Hank had tried in front of a mirror, but could do nothing to disguise the cut cheek and a chin discoloration where John's fists had landed most effectively. John's face bore no reciprical satisfaction. At the airport they avoided each other and addressed only the others. Mo also said nothing, but from a sense of blissful peace. He'd upheld the honor of his shipmates, and a mapwork of purpling bruises on his face bore evidence.

Seth carried the conversation as they waited. "I had a buddy fished Bristol Bay once. He said anything goes out there, you name it."

Hank knew the reputation. The place had its legends from generations now too old to fish, as had Chignik Lagoon, Karluk, and the Copper River Flats. He might have graduated to fishing for species not considered by the old-timers, in bigger boats than they knew, but salmon remained the great basic. Now that he'd committed he felt anticipation. But he kept a glum face in front of Jody, and gave her repeated unnecessary instructions on supervising the *Jody S*'s repaired windows. Jody, in turn, offered no tart reply as she might have in private, respecting his position in front of the crew.

As they started to board, a truck drove up and Swede strode out trailed by a cannery kid with his bags. His signature red tractor cap, worn at an aggressive tilt in the old days, was now planted squarely like a businessman's fedora. "Can't see the last of you!" said Hank in good humor.

"Time I got up there to run things." To Jody he confided: "It's my summer vacation. You needn't tell Mary that. The old rules apply in Bristol Bay, that's what I like. Kodiak's gotten to be a goddamn teacup city." Inside the twelve-passenger plane both Swede and Hank headed for the cockpit seat by the pilot. "Well, you take it, Crawford. I'm being nice today."

"Swede's going soft," said the pilot. "You must have something he wants, Hank."

The ride took them first over the interior mountains of Kodiak Island, snowed on the peaks even in July. Hank could see the island's bays laid out as if on a map. The plane passed over fingered Uganik Bay. The roofs and pier of the cannery complex where he had once worked as a greenhorn passed below, a cluster of toy squares surrounded by forest wilderness. Seiners at anchor hugged the inlets awaiting the next opening. At a word from Fish and Game skiffs would roar, corks would encircle stray finners, dripping nets would creak up through power blocks to spread aloft like sails. Hustle of lines and rings, salmon thrashing aboard around your legs. Jones Henry would be steaming there even now. Hank closed his eyes. Bright had been every touch and smell. So grand, fishing on the little deck of the *Rondelay* with Jones, cuffed into eager shape by Steve and Ivan.

If he hadn't pushed himself to be such a balls-driving skipper, Steve and Ivan might still be alive. When he looked out again he saw the She-likof Strait that had smashed out his windows two days before. The water now sparkled calmly. What? said the water. Me, attack you? Impossible. Your dream.

They left the innocent water behind and began crossing the main-land's range of snowy volcanic cones. Mountains at least retained their sin-ister beauty without changing the way water did. Hank's malaise in the face of nature's cold immensity ran its course. He pulled at his beard and called merry answers to the pilot's shouts. At length the peaks and cones gave way to flat brown marshland pocked with dark pools. The pools reflected blue from the sky as they passed over them one by one: they mir-rored even the clouds.

The pilot swooped low to buzz a bear and send it lumbering, then scattered a handful of caribou. The acrobatics sparked whoops from Seth and Mo. Hank grinned back at them. Swede slept, a man who had seen it all. John soberly watched through his window as did the four other passen-gers. Seth and Mo, twin bears themselves in jeans and shaggy checked shirts, bounced across the narrow aisle from window to window to watch the animals below. "Seatbelts, guys, sorry!" yelled the pilot. When they obeyed he strafed the caribou again on their side of the plane.

The little airport at King Salmon was as busy as a freight depot. A flight from Anchorage had just landed and others had preceded it. People shouted and called. There were swarthy, taciturn Aleuts—the men wiry and the women round—and driven bearded whites of all ages with red scarred hands. All walked with purpose. Outside, the sun beat hot and dust swirled. Tractors pulled loads of baggage straight from the plane's bays to a bare lot. Truck drivers jockeyed to back against piles of crates, boxes, machine parts, and rolled nets. Others with clipboards checked over the piles. A dusty knot of young people in clean denims stood apart, gripping knapsacks unscuffed by use. They seemed collectively unsure.

Swede's eyes darted. He snapped his fingers and a man hurried over to take his bags. "I parked outside this mess, Swede, follow me," said the man. He gestured toward the knot of youngsters: "That wet-looking bunch is bodies for the slime line. I have the van. We can take them, or they can bounce on top the parts shipment in Joe's pickup if he has room, or I'll come back if you want privacy."

"They're no good to me out here. Pile 'em in, but leave legroom for my four men."

The dusty knot, male and female, crowded in back of the van with their bags, some forced to sit or even lie on each other's laps, but the driver firmly kept the ordered legroom for Hank's crew. Swede sat in front, with Hank between him and the driver. The kids in back joked uncertainly, a cross between swagger and vulnerability that Hank recognized with amused nostalgia: students come for an Alaskan adventure to work in a cannery. Seth and Mo, enjoying their status, kept aloof silence, but John began questioning them. He was soon comparing colleges and advising them about mosquito repellant and clean socks.

"Got your *Orion* all stocked and waiting, Swede," said the driver. "Those crew we fired, they camped the night at the airport since you didn't want them around, and I booked them out first flight to Anchorage this morning. They're gone." Swede did not bother to reply.

The road traversed flat scrubland, dreary without the mountains that framed the Alaska Hank knew best. A half hour later, without passing a single house, they turned onto an unmarked dirt road that led through wiry brush. "You kids listen up," called out the driver. "Don't you wander outside the compound, especially at night. There's bears. Understand?" Several voices assured him soberly.

The compound consisted of weathered but painted frame buildings interconnected by boardwalks. It was a larger version of the remote canneries on Kodiak Island: a village here compared to a settlement. Long structures with sheltered porches had roughly painted signs that labeled them "Henhouse" and "Stud Barn." Other signs identified "Laundry," "Raingear," "Bathhouse," "Galley Keep Out," and "Store." Down a hill, where sheds the size of warehouses puffed steam, corrugated roofs blocked a full view of the water. Beyond flowed a quarter-mile width of river empty of traffic. Gulls circled around islands of tide-bared mud.

The van stopped in front of a house on the highest rise labeled "Office." Its porch faced a wide causeway leading down directly to the wharf a city block away. People and forklift trucks crowded the wharf and lower causeway. Swede, without comment or instruction to the others, jumped out and pulled Hank with him to a red golf cart that waited by the office steps. He motioned Hank to stand beside him in the cart, turned the key left in the ignition, and headed downhill toward the wharf so quickly that Hank grabbed for balance. Swede drove in a straight line. Everyone opened a path for him. The causeway led past buildings labeled "Flash Freeze," "Blacksmith," "Machine Shop," "Net Loft," and others.

The wharf, which stretched out of sight around all the sheds, was noisy and crowded. They looked down on dozens of boats more than twenty feet below. In rows they resembled toy models, all made nearly alike with a small cabin forward, an open deck aft, and a roller at the stern. "The basic Bay gillnetter," said Swede.

"Bathtubs with stovepipes for masts," joked Hank.

"No longer than 32 feet by law, but able work machines." The boats rested on bare mud, supporting each other rail to rail. Beneath their exposed keels fanned a lacework of dry gulleys. Water lapped at only the outermost boat. Men stood on the wharf lowering boxes of groceries. Far below on the small decks others received them.

"Tides here like no other," said Swede. "Give it an hour, and you'll see all those little gillnetters bouncing against each other." He led Hank along the wharf to a long clumsy vessel. Three metal tanks higher than a man's head, connected by pipes and valves, filled most of the deck. The monstrosity intruded among the graceful small boats like an ox among calves. "There's your tender, *Orion*."

Any pleasure Hank had anticipated vanished. "That's a fuckin' scow, not a boat."

"You know it. Floating box, chilled seawater worth its weight and don't forget. She holds four hundred thousand pounds if you distribute right, that's seventy to eighty thousand Bristol Bay sockeye reds a haul. All you have to do is horse her back and forth with the tides from the grounds to the cannery. Easy money."

Hank thought of his own *Jody S* with its trim bow that sliced through water with the bounce of the men who rode her. He should be back supervising her repair rather than pissing like this for money to replace her. All Henny's and Dawn's eager daddy-touches, all the press of Jody and her mystic burden, lay wasted back in Kodiak and inexorably running their course without him. "Shit, Swede . . ."

A bald man whose stomach pushed against greasy coveralls saun- tered onto deck from the *Orion*'s housing, picking his teeth. "That's your engineer," said Swede. "Doke Stutz. Don't underestimate. He knows the river and he knows the bay. Done it season after season. He'll keep you clued."

"I thought it was just me and my crew."

"Wrong thought, Crawford. You and your apes don't know fuck-all about an old power plant like *Orion*'s. And you're not to crash my barge trying to learn Bay currents." He called down and Doke looked up.

"Where's my new meat?" Doke demanded. "We got to go on the ebb in two hours." Swede introduced them. "Well, get down here then, skipper. Where's your boys? They got scrubbing to do."

Hank remained silent.

Swede turned uncharacteristically smooth. "It's no different than ten- dering for me at Chignik except for the tides, Hank. All right, you had your own boat there, I know you fishermen want to make love to your own little tubs. My sympathies. Don't smash your windows next time. Just after high slack here you'll ride out the ebb. The next opening's at six, and by mid- night you can expect deliveries, so let your apes sleep once you anchor. Plan always to do the river at high slack." Swede swept his arm toward the water broken by sandbars and the flat terrain beyond. "You're looking at the Naknek River. Around the bend's the village of Naknek, you can see it all in three minutes some time. A runt tide here's twenty feet, it increases from there, so ebb or flood current can peak at over two knots and sand bars rise while you watch. Pay attention to the tables. One flood tide each day is about four feet higher than the other. That's the best to ride. Head out from the river mouth to where Doke shows you among the other ten- ders. Drop your hook. Fly the company flag where my boats can see from all sides. Expect to leave on one slack flood and return loaded on another. Like candy from a baby, Crawford."

"Scorden, when I get my new crabber paid for, you'll never shaft me like this again."

Swede laughed, more harshly than necessary. "You break my heart. I've been rich and gone bust twice, and now I sometimes lick ass like you young pissheads never think you will. Jap ass this time. Say never as much as you like, Hank. Just don't let the reality break you." He walked toward his golf cart. "You'll enjoy it out there."

Hank dug hands into his pockets, and looked away from the scow to avoid any exchange with the fat engineer (who had, in fact, continued forward without paying him further attention). Men in boots and deck shoes leapt with purpose from deck to deck of the small gillnetters, shouting, pitched for action. He knew that excitement. Fish waited out there. Nets alive. They were going fishing while he'd merely collect their harvest after it had died and turned to slime.

The van pulled alongside, now empty of cannery kids, and his crewmen unloaded their bags. "Yours here, Boss," said Mo, keeping it shouldered along with his own. "Where we headed?" Hank pointed to the *Orion*. "That thing?" said Seth, and whistled ruefully.

"It looks stable for once," said John. "I guess we won't have to worry about breaking windows and capsizing."

Hank chose to ignore it. At his direction Mo scampered down a slippery metal ladder, received their bags lowered by rope to the scow's deck, and stowed them in the wheelhouse. A steam whistle blew from somewhere that echoed against the corrugated building fronts like a train in fog. "Mug-up time, fellows," called the van driver. Men from the boats were climbing up other ladders to form a line by a closed door at one of the sheds. Other people in hairnets and paper caps, men and women both, streamed from every opening of the long buildings and headed along the boardwalks toward another destination. They wore stiff landlubber boots which gave them a lumpy walk unlike the foot-to-deck roll of the men from the boats.

The van driver told them to pile in. "Swede said take the skipper to the office for signups, but first to ride you all to the exec hall and mug you down."

"Is that where the fishermen are headed?" asked Hank.

"No, they get their own place with a few doughnuts over there by that line. You don't want to bother with that when Swede throws you the red carpet and real food."

"We'll mug-up with the fishermen," Hank declared. Seth and Mo agreed at once.

"You guys crazy?" asked John, quickly combing his thick black hair. "When we can meet the people who run this place, look around, and get a decent chow besides?"

"I think it would be good if you went there," said Hank stiffly. Maybe the asshole would get lost and miss the tide.

John half-entered the van, looked back for them to follow, hesitated as Hank, trailed by Seth and Mo, sauntered toward the line of fishermen. "Don't you guys ever look beyond your noses?" When they made no reply he shrugged, seated himself, and rolled shut the door.

Hank and the others joined the line of fishermen, but they stood isolated. The closest group, men thick and middle-aged, spoke a language he couldn't recognize, maybe Slavic. Others who grouped behind them spoke half in English and half in a rough Italian. A small knot of men had the brown, faintly Oriental faces of Aleuts.

When the door opened, they climbed a narrow stair to a large, bright room with long tables. The line led past doughnuts, heavy pastries, bread, and slabs of bologna, finally to urns of coffee. "Good sinkers," said Mo with a full mouth as he slathered margarine on the bread and made a thick bologna sandwich. "John don't know what he's missing."

They sat on benches at a long table beside the thick men speaking Slavic, who turned friendly when Hank asked knowledgeable fishing questions. They were Croats who lived in Anacortes, second generation, came up every year. "Everybody fishes in their own groups," one declared. "So do the Squareheads, and the Wops, and the Aloots and Eskimos if anybody but theirselves knows the difference."

The van driver appeared beside Hank, annoyed and anxious, to say that he'd thought the jerk he'd driven to the dining room was the skipper the way he acted, and Swede would ream his ass if he didn't get the real skipper up to the office. Seth and Mo found the idea of mistaking the Boss so hilarious that they had to stop eating to laugh it out.

At the office, Swede's manager went over invoice procedure, radio codes, and lists of the boats committed to delivering, all of it familiar to Hank from tendering with the *Jody S*. But it turned out that duties were expected beyond those of collecting and delivering: sales of basic groceries, laundry and shower privileges, even emergency engine parts and spot welding. Once this fleet left the docks the openings might continue without a break, and the tender was their supply line. It made him little more than a storekeeper. But having now committed he paid attention gravely.

Two hours later they had stowed their gear on the scow and explored their new quarters. Hank aired the wheelhouse, which smelled of stale beer and smoke but had a new leather padded captain's chair that both reclined and swiveled. The controls, radios, loran, and radar all looked workable without extra studying, although the actual feel of her in the water could only be learned underway. His own cabin, adjacent to the wheelhouse, was even larger than his cabin aboard the projected new crabber. Almost like shoreside living. Maybe bring up Jody and the kids if he stuck with it. (Sudden ugly vision. Lifejackets and tethered harness, no exceptions, for Henny and Dawn.)

The galley and mess deck were spacious. Other spaces had washing machines, dryers, showers, and toilets. The previous crew, in their quick enforced departure, had left a mess of butts, paperbacks, beer cans, and sour linens. Mo brewed coffee, and collected everything from the galley table to wash it. John, who returned brusquely and said nothing when kidded about being mistaken for the Boss, turned-to to scrub even the toilets under Seth's direction. Hank, seated at the galley table studying his new documents, noted that at least John worked hard without complaint.

The door to the engine room flew open to a rush of machinery noise, then slammed shut as Doke, the inherited engineer, lumbered in wiping his hands. He stopped by Hank as he stuffed the rag into his coveralls. "That's my seat."

Hank waved at the scattered papers. "I'm pretty well spread here."

"That's where I always sit. That's my seat."

Hank considered and decided to be agreeable. He slid his papers and mug to the other end of the table curved against banked seats. Doke squeezed in—his gut made it an effort—hunched glumly, and lit a cigarette. The man's thick hands, black under the creases and nails, trembled. "Your engines ready for underway?" Hank asked pleasantly.

"You never need to ask that, skipper. Fuel and water tanks topped, everything." He pointed to Mo who had his hands in suds at the sink. "Tell your boys not to waste water."

"You've seen a few seasons up here, Swede says."

"You could say that."

"Been aboard here long?"

"Long enough to see a dozen crews come and go. Most last a season. Your boy going to bring back an ashtray or do you want me to throw my butts to the deck?"

Mo dried an ashtray and brought it along with two mugs of coffee. Doke pushed his away. "I only drink tea. Coffee scrapes my ulcers." He pointed to an airtight can. "That's my special tea bags. Mine. I count 'em, so don't try anything. And scald my cup first, with water you see bubbling, not just lukewarm. You steep it for a minute and a quarter, no more no less, that's seventy-five seconds if you need a diagram, and you won't have no trouble with me sending it back." Mo frowned with concentration as he listened, then turned to comply.

"That's a job you'd better do for yourself," said Hank. "Then it'll never be wrong."

"I'm the engineer, not the cook."

"My guys'll be glad to serve you coffee like the rest of us, or tea as it comes."

Doke rose heavily. "I'll talk to Swede about this."

The tide had risen enough that only six or seven feet separated the deck from the pier, but Doke's belly made him slow and clumsy on the slippery ladder. Hank stayed at the table on purpose, but watched through the hatchway.

"You told him," muttered Seth.

Without answering Hank went back to the wheelhouse and studied sandbars and depths on the chart. He'd have to be independent of this pisser. Be polite, even kind if possible noting ulcers and shaky hands, but no dependence. The chart table vibrated from the engine on standby. The pisser probably knew his business. Outside the window the mudflats had disappeared under rising water. Craft moved everywhere, pushing against streaks of incoming tide. The little gillnetters tied around him—now seaborne and light as the surrounding gulls—rose and fell on swells. White exhaust puffed from sterns as boats passed under the mooring lines of other boats and escaped the pack to reach open water. Men at the lines now wore their oilskins, ready for spray and action. Some of the younger ones whooped. He felt the excitement building. Even his flat-bottomed scow came slowly alive with water beneath her.

On the wharf, Swede drove up in his red golf cart as the fat engineer gripped it from behind, and jumped down the ladder to deck. Hank readied himself. A moment later, while the engineer was still positioning himself to descend from wharf to deck, Swede entered the wheelhouse and stopped to catch his breath. He now wore his tractor cap at the same fierce angle that had defined his authority when Hank stood before him as an awed green-horn at another remote cannery fifteen years ago. The jaw was now less fixed, but the face had wiry lines grown permanent from the eternal scowl.

"My guys hop to it, Swede, but they don't take shit."

"Doke was here before you were born. Back in hard times when they fished under sail. He'll never let you down. Give him slack."

"I already have. This teabag shit pushed it too far."

"Teabag? What's that? The man says you took his seat and told your crew not to bring him things. That's not galley procedure with a senior man."

Hank laughed. "He's more an old baby than I thought."

"He helped convert *Orion* from a military dry barge twenty years ago. It's more his home than wherever he lives the rest of the year. Knows every kink in those tanks' refrigeration. Knows how to keep thousands of fish at quality 31 degrees. Master welder besides. I assume you and your boys can weld in a pinch, but watch Doke and you'll all learn something. And by the way. Stop calling my *Orion* a scow." Swede lightened his tone. "Scows around here are those big tubs open to the sun that can't keep salmon fresh for more than a few hours, need to cover 'em with burlap at that. You've got a queen-of-the-fleet power barge that can hold your cargo fresh for days. Just close your eyes and forget the tanks on deck. Those klunks refrigerate and old Doke keeps them working. You're passing through, Crawford. He knows Bristol Bay better than you'll ever, so roll with him. Don't make me keep saying it. I need you both."

"Nobody'll take his seat, tell him. I never meant to. And he can expect his food brought to table if he can't get it himself, but no chef's specials. Tell him to behave like an adult and we'll get along."

"I don't have time to be a chaplain. There's a Seattle shipment waiting to enter on this tide, eight hundred thousand flattened cans for one-pound talls, overdue a month, plus butter, dishrags, machine parts, all overdue, and you're hogging my wharf space. Get to sea, Hank, and don't give me any more grief. We've stopped the Japs from intercepting Bristol Bay salmon

with our new two-hundred-mile law. You should appreciate that. Now sockeyes are pouring in for the history books. Ours! So move it!"

Hank watched Swede on deck, cajoling the old baby who waved his
arms indignantly but then subsided to listen with sullen mouth. By now
most of the boats around him had cast off. Time to go. In good spirits he
called down: "Swede! Get your ass off my ship so we can move. Mr.
Doke, sir, I don't need to ask if your engines are ready because I know
they are. Right?" He pulled a signal cord that should have sounded a
whistle, and it did: a good hooting blast. Seth and Mo were on deck in an
instant, and John soon trailed behind. "Get up there and be useful, Swede.
Cast us off!"

Hank eased the throttle forward and felt it take hold, then tooted as
the lines slacked. On the wharf, Swede lifted the aft hawser from the bol-
lard and sent it slapping to deck at Mo's feet, then held the bow line long
enough for Seth to pull it in dry. Hank swung on the spring line, testing the
current, then signaled and off it came too. Swede gave a rare grin and a
thumbs up. The *Orion* was pushing water. She responded like the work-ox
she was. Hank nosed her cautiously into the current, which gave him a
long clumsy sidle into the channel rather than the quick possession that
was his style on the *Jody S*, but care controlled unwelcome surprises.

Having stowed the lines, his men gathered in the wheelhouse and
sought out perches for the ride ahead. This was going to be new for them
all.

4

MONTEREY BABE

Day and motion never ended in Bristol Bay. Hank watched a dark vermilion sunset streak the midnight sky and ripple on the water even as an orange dawn began to glow a few degrees away. Ships' lights enough for a town lined the horizon. Smaller lights dipped and rose on swells that merely splashed against the stolid hull of the anchored *Orion*.

The crew was sleeping until the next boat came to deliver. Old Doke had withdrawn into his bolted cabin which he kept padlocked during the day. The company's flag, illuminated, flapped overhead in a steady breeze. Other tenders, like the *Orion* anchored just outside Fish and Game's fishing boundary, kept enough space between them to pivot with the tide. Lights on the freighters at distant anchor etched masts and glowed dimly on superstructures. There were also red and green lights in motion that focused less easily, dimly outlining the little gillnetters.

Hank, on the bridge, scanned through binoculars. He watched a bag of fish swing aboard the nearest tender from a boat alongside. On a nearby gillnetter that hugged the fishing boundary, two men worked under deck lights that glinted on their oilskins as they pulled their nets over the roller. The net came in slowly, burdened with lumps of entangled fish. Hank's hands and shoulders itched with the desire to grip web and feel the flap of those big, angry salmon. Net so heavy with fish that the men had no time to pick it. Fish and web piled around their legs. So much fish, such weight, that a third man, probably the skipper, ran on deck and helped to pull. Without the *Orion*'s steady thrum of generators he could probably have heard their shouts. Did hear.

47

He had slept poorly during the few days so far aboard *Orion* although the quarters were comfortable enough. Two deliveries back to the cannery proved he could handle the Naknek River's tides and currents. He was earning his keep with the volume of fish the little boats delivered. But as a spectator. *Scow*! The abundance equalled any plug of crab or salmon he'd ever fished, and it kept pulsing in. On cloudy days he could look into the water and watch the dark bullet shapes swimming past in drill, crowded nearly thick enough to be scooped aboard. Down against the hull he could sense the brush of salmon despite their instinctive veer from objects in their path. Mystical, driven creatures. Their soul was all instinct when Nature told them to return to birth water. Their drive to death heightened the unquiet night. Nothing slept except the sidetracked men of the *Orion*.

Doke's heavy breathing heralded his climb to the wheelhouse. "What you want, skipper, want to get your boys off their asses. Here comes a delivery."

For all his dreaming over expanses, he'd missed a gillnetter just drawing alongside to port. The *Monterey Babe*, regular customer. Feeling foolish, he jerked the alarm and bounded down ladders to deck. He received lines with a nod from the breezy son while the jowly dad, his head poked out of the window, maneuvered the boat's wooden hull alongside so lightly that it barely touched the fenders.

John appeared first on *Orion*'s deck, brisk and businesslike, oilskin coat buttoned, clipboard under his arm. Seth and Mo trailed sleepily, snapping the suspenders of their oilskin pants. Mo climbed up and opened the tank's hatch. John pivoted his upraised hand and nodded up at Doke, who had taken his place at the boom controls below the wheelhouse. Doke nodded back and pulled a lever. To a grind of gears the heavy scale lowered from the boom. John controlled it with a guy line and swung it to the gillnetter. Father and son on the gillnetter's deck hooked a bag of fish to the scale, and at John's signal Doke levered it up. Seth and Mo pulled the dripping bag across the two rails and steadied it, suspended. John recorded the weight. The younger fisherman peered also at the scale face and scribbled the reading. At John's nod, the bag rose. Seth yanked the draw cord and the fish tumbled into the tank.

It all went like clockwork. Hank stood apart, not needed. The bags of fish were nothing that Seth and Mo couldn't handle by themselves. Doke let no one handle his controls. He now responded to John's slightest nod, while still routinely pausing at any signal or instruction from Hank as if it might be incompetent. John had aptitude for the ledgers and for ordering supplies. Why waste it? First time the fellow had been useful.

Yet John had become subtly the man in charge on deck despite Seth's seniority—the man who controlled the clipboard in work dominated by tabulation. (Storekeeping, not fishing!) John still pitched in to help move a hatch, and dressed for messy work he seldom needed to do, but look at the way he wore full oilskins against an occasional splash of gurry when Seth and Mo, who handled the stuff directly, seldom bothered with their coats.

One day as Hank killed time with a magazine at his wheelhouse perch, noise of an argument rose from deck. He walked to the bridge and looked down. The *Orion*'s boom, controlled by Doke, was raising a canvas bag full of salmon from the gillnetter *Esther N* tied alongside. John signaled and the load stopped, suspended under the scale. He and a lean crewman named Jack from the *Esther*, both holding clipboards, watched the dial on the scale that weighed the bag.

"Like before, it's *now* you read it," exclaimed Jack, and scribbled a figure.

John waited calmly. Seth and Mo stood alongside. "Come on, man," muttered Seth. "This is chicken shit."

"Wait. Wait," said Gains coolly. An entire minute passed while gurry and blood dripped from the bag. At last he entered a figure on his own sheet. "Thousand twenty-one."

"Bull," Jack exclaimed. "Thousand twenty-*three*!"

"You can hardly expect us to pay you for two pounds of slime."

"What the fuck kind of prick are you?"

"I answer to the company." Gains signaled Doke, the bag rose, Seth yanked the cord, and the fish were disgorged into the hold. The boom carried the collapsed canvas back to the *Esther* where Jack's partner detached it and hooked in another.

Hank called John to the wheelhouse. "No need to be that tight. Just give the scale a couple of seconds to settle."

John studied him, then shook his head. "I just don't understand you. We're not a charity."

"But I'm in charge." Hank watched him return to deck, and lingered to make sure he complied. Storekeeper. Company man. Jack, partner on the *Esther N*, had called it right—company prick. No fisherman there.

But no fishing boat this, either. By the time the salmon had reached delivery stage they were X-ed with bloody net marks, and a metallic stench rose from their bodies. No amount of washing and sliming would restore their brightness as it did for seine-caught and line-caught salmon. And the land, on days when blowing rain didn't obscure the shore, was flat, brown, swampy. None of Kodiak's still-snowy mountains and luscious July green. Time and place had left Hank Crawford behind, here.

He'd studied the chart until he knew the names: official ones like Peterson Point, Deadman Sands, Johnston Hill, and Halfmoon Bay, and others penciled in by previous skippers: Dogleg, Fishhook, Banana Tree, Gravel Pit, Honey Hole. He could see from depth marks how the fish funneled past or through them. But he wasn't dropping nets, merely collecting other men's harvest. A ring of fat from idleness tugged against his belt.

Another day, when the *Orion* had just anchored for business after delivery to the cannery, the *Monterey Babe* again drew alongside. Hank stood with hands in pockets, watching the father and son briskly open hatches and adjust the thick hook to bags of fish. Their little boat, freshly painted probably a month before, had already gained the scuffed look of heavy fishing that left no time for niceties, from the rail bared to the wood where bags of fish swung, to torn oilskins strapped against the housing, worn tires for fenders, and the chipped A in the name MONTEREY BABE on the stern. "Busy out there, eh?"

The father only grunted, but the son said brightly, "Smokin', man, smokin'. If we had time to go ashore I'd find me an extra hand." The crane raised a dripping bag from the *Babe*'s hold. "Stand aside, sir." Hank complied. The bag bulged triple the thickness of the son's waist. Two fish flopped from the top. Hank's hands wanted to grab even these stiff, net-bloodied sockeyes. The bag passed two feet from his face. Brassy smell of harvest.

When the loading finished, the son leapt over the rails to *Orion*'s deck and finished the paperwork with John. He called back: "Take a shit, Dad?"

"Who needs fancy toilets out here? Come fish!"

"Well *I* do. Only take a minute." The son winked at Hank, and sprinted around the housing to the facility. The father began hosing their deck and holds.

Hank scratched his increased waist. Even handling a pressure hose would feel good. On clear days light never left the sky, but now in drizzly rain both sky and water beyond the boats had turned black. Millions of sockeyes waited and milled in that black. Behind him his crew had hosed the trail of gurry and wandered back inside until the next delivery. They'd be anchored, collecting like this, through at least another full day.

"So it's smoking out there?" he ventured to the father, a thick man of about fifty with a leathery face that sagged in pouches.

"Best in my thirty years here."

"Come from where? Monterey?"

"Monterey, California, sir."

"Guess you have radio VHS?"

"Ain't we talked to you on it?"

"Enough out there to keep three men busy, eh?"

"Better believe it."

"So you'll expect to plug your boat every few hours and be delivering back here?"

"That's how it's going, sir."

By the time the son returned, Hank had convinced himself. The tender was anchored safely, the crew self-sufficient without him. Radio contact in case of emergency. Wasn't it to Swede's advantage if he, Hank, understood more of Bristol Bay fishing than just the delivery? He tried to sound casual, not like the eager juvenile he felt inside, as he proposed crewing for a trip.

"You ever fished before?" demanded the father, with no thought now of adding "sir." Like any job applicant, Hank outlined his qualifications.

The son picked up on the offer at once. He turned to his father who said something in what Hank assumed to be Italian. Rather than embarrassed, Hank felt lighthearted even as they discussed him. The son declared heartily in English: "We can always dump his ass back aboard here if he don't work out. Come on, Dad. We don't need that extra bunk. All the crap we got stored there? Push it in the forepeak."

"The man ain't coming to sleep. He'll slow us down, Chris. Might of fished, but I don't hear he's picked gillnets. *E non parla Italiano, lui. È straniero.*"

"*Va ben', Papa. Possiamo parlare, e non capisce niente, eh?*" The father pivoted up his palms, shrugged, and went inside. "My old man," said Chris, "He takes a minute for any new idea. Hurry get your gear."

On the mess deck Hank hastily justified his temporary departure. "I'm riding out for a trip to learn more about the fishery. Seth, you're relief skipper." Doke, in his corner slot on the mess deck, maneuvered a toothpick and scowled.

Seth shook his head. "Here I was thinkin' of asking Chris myself to do a trip. Those guys are *fishing*. Sets my ass crazy just taking their dead fish, Mo and me doing half a man's work between us."

"Me too, Boss," echoed Mo. "Lucky you. Go ahead, we can handle stuff here."

John looked up from logging neatly clipped invoices. "Ride that tub when you have this? You can smell that younger Speccio fellow above his fish every time they deliver. I'll never understand you people."

"No, you won't," said Hank.

Doke began to clean his nails with a toothpick. "Swede ain't going to like this. He put you here to buy fish. I helped design this boat, I been here that long. And you never seen me on one of them little gillnetters."

"That's why I feel good about going for a few hours," said Hank smoothly. "Look at all the experience I leave behind at your table there."

The *Monterey Babe*'s whistle tooted impatiently. Hank bounded up the ladder to his cabin, stuffed an armful of sweats and socks into a bag, and on the way to the main deck grabbed boots and oilskins. Another boat was just coming alongside to deliver. "Delivery ahoy!" he called gaily into the mess deck. "Shake it!" He tossed his gear to Chris in the boat, released the painter, and leapt over the rails to the deck of the *Babe*. Seconds later he watched the *Orion* from the distance of water as Doke climbed ponderously to his place in the control bay and the others came from the housing.

The *Babe*'s deck beneath him bounced alive as the hull played in and out of sea chop. From the *Orion*'s deck Seth shouted, "Plug her, Hank, plug the fucker." Hank contained the whoop he felt like returning. The air, the very woodwork, smelled of fish. He could have been the green excited kid of sixteen years ago just berthed on Jones Henry's *Rondelay* for his first trip as a fisherman. A shower of spray slapped him. Salty taste. Cold. The water that looked nearly flat from the *Orion*'s stolid platform had swells and ripples, perhaps unseen currents, a literature of vitalities that only a small boat could elicit.

"Hey, man," said Chris. "Get inside. The old man likes to bang through the water. This'll be Niagara Falls in a minute." Another shower caught Hank's back as he bent in the low doorway to enter the cabin. Chris behind him, wetter than he, cursed cheerfully and shoved to hurry him.

The boat's pleasant wave-bounce from deck in fresh air became enclosed motion in the cramped, dark wheelhouse. Hank gasped at the stew of fish odors that combined with ripe clothes and diesel, all intensified by heat at least thirty degrees higher than outside. It triggered a bubble of nausea. His own boat was so much larger and cleaner that he'd forgotten. Don't get seasick, he told himself. He breathed deeply. Each breath seemed less toxic until, like a diver accustoming himself to pressure, he reached an equilibrium. Good smells. Part of the game.

The father stood on a platform behind the wheel, leaning into the window to peer through spray that peppered the glass. Wet-rippled lights from other boats spun past in the dark. "Yeah, I don' know," he said into a microphone cupped between his neck and shoulder. "You fishing right on the line? You doin' okay there?"

"I don' know, I don' know," said a voice roughened by transmission over the speaker. "If you can call it okay a Mimi-Rodolfo. Anyways, I guess we'll set here through the flood. I don' know. Goin' back to the net now, I guess. Over and out."

"Fuckin' Mimi-Rodolfo, he says," announced the father after replacing the microphone. "Don' *know*, he says!" He laughed and pushed the throttle. The boat leapt high in the water and thudded back, then steadied at an increased speed.

"My dad's name is Vito," said Chris. "He'll talk enough after we've set, but don't disturb him now. For your info, a Mimi-Rodolfo among our guys means plugged nets. It's our radio band but any slob can listen. We change codes about every two weeks. Right now only a Tosca's better, sometimes they call it a Scarpia, get it? A so-so run, we're calling it a Fanciulla. But if somebody says it's a Madam Butterfly forget it, just anchor and go to sleep. Later we'll switch to Rossini, confuse these squareheads and oley Joes and bohunks that don't know Barber of Seville from the Green Bay Packers." He led Hank to an inner cabin where the heat and odors deepened. A dim light sheltered with red plastic showed a tier of three bunks against one bulkhead and a narrow table against the other, with a two-burner stove between. Utensils and plates clicked in racks that held them tightly, but smudged clothing hung and swayed everywhere. "Here, this top bunk's yours, help me clear it. Just stuff the junk I hand you up forward there."

They needed to sway and balance as the boat pitched. Chris handed him a greasy box from the bunk, then another. Hank's nausea returned. He clamped his mouth, started to breathe deeply, then dared not. At last he rushed back through the wheelhouse to open deck, grabbed the lee rail, and vomited. Cold water drenched him. The boat slowed with a surge.

"Want to go back?" said Chris quietly. "I made him slow down. I can make him turn back."

"Shit no! Thanks. Tell him pick up speed again."

"What's that, Dad?" said Chris into the cabin. The boat suddenly turned with a roll and reversed course. "Hank, Dad says he's taking you back."

"No! No!" Hank wiped his mouth with a wet sleeve and staggered inside. "Hey Captain! Vito! Turn around, man. I'm a fisherman like you. Just getting sea legs. I'm okay."

Vito continued to peer ahead. "You see, buddy," he said soberly, without changing course, "I got a living to make, no salary like you on that big tender. Got no time to break in a greenhorn when the fish is smoking. This is a little boat, just papa and son. Other boats, we all fish together like family, everybody's friends back in Monterey. You're a big captain, don' know about these things."

"I do. I respect that. I respect it." The lights of the *Orion* were nearing. Its silhouette in the gray dawn loomed above two bouncing gillnetters tied alongside, delivering. Through the water-streaked window Hank could see the figure of John coolly standing with his clipboard. "Turn back. Don't do this to me. Please! Look, no crew share for me this trip. I don't care, I'll even pay you."

"Dad," said Chris firmly. "*Voltarla.*"

"*Non mi piace quest'.*"

"*Voltarla*, Papa!"

"*Eh, va ben', va ben'.*" Vito shrugged, slowed the boat, and turned. The boat bucked a swell, then leveled into it. "Losing time, all this!" He pushed the throttle and they sped back in their original direction.

Hank felt himself breathing heavily. "Thanks, Chris," he said, trying to keep what dignity remained him.

"Got puke on your whiskers, buddy. Here's a rag. Take your time."

How low will this week take me? Hank wondered as he wiped his beard on deck, taking spray indifferently. A refreshing salty wind swept ripples over the water. By now the dim early light showed black outlines of gillnetter housings when they popped above the swells. They looked lonesome, vulnerable, gay, inviting. He shivered, wet. To start the week, his own boat three times the size of these took a sea that nearly drowned his crew. Then his lowest crewman boxed his ass to the mat. Jody got pissed. Swede bullied him into minding a scow. Now this, down to puking and begging all in a week, when he'd thought he owned the world. He returned to the cabin to help Chris clear the bunk. His wet clothes soon dried on him in the heat. Lie down? Chris suggested. Hank refused and followed to the wheelhouse. The two leaned against the bulkhead by a window. Chris took a light from his father's cigarette.

The number of boats increased. Vito veered the boat around a cluster while they all peered at nets coming up astern. The collective glow of deck lights showed that some nets had entrapped a fish every foot or two. Hank exclaimed. But their own boat kept going. "Those are all bohunks from Anacortes," said Chris. "Yugoslavia, whatever the hell. You don't want to fish with them, they got different ways, don't deliver to our cannery anyhow. And up ahead's a bunch of squarehead boats from Ballard near Seattle, not even American some of them, cousins and uncles come straight from Norway then go back, forget it. You like spaghetti? We don't bother with much else out here so you'd better. My wife, she puts her sauce in jars for us, my mom puts *hers* in jars for us, we alternate and don't take sides, you know? 'Sure,' I say, 'yours is best, honey,' when I get home. 'You don't tell Mama.' Then whisper to Mama, 'Sure, yours is best. Don't tell Angela.' Hell, you got to keep 'em happy. Eh Papa?"

"Get me the *Tide*."

Chris pulled a copy of *Tide Tables* from the rack, its paper cover torn and thumbed limp. He held a flashlight in his mouth and started to run his finger down a marked page.

Hank glanced at the clock. "You've got one hour and twenty-three minutes before ebb starts."

Father and son exchanged a glance. "You carry that shit in your head?" asked Vito.

"I checked the *Tables* before we left."

"The man's on the *nail*, Papa," Chris chuckled from the book. "Where you headed, Dogleg or Banana Tree?"

"Banana," said Vito after a pause. Chris noted to Hank without heat that the old man liked to keep his secrets.

An hour later they slowed into a small enclave of wooden gillnetters like their own. A light drizzle turned boat lights into beads and halos through the window. Vito eased alongside the scuffed rail of an anchored boat named *Miss Rosa*, turned the wheel over to Chris, and stomped to deck. A man his own age came from the other cabin simultaneously. The two talked in Italian, with gestures.

"That's my Uncle Tony," said Chris. "They're brothers. Always talk strategy strategy before a set. Far as I ever saw it don't make a difference to the fish. But it makes *them* feel good, you know? Old-timers? They've been there. They fished the open double-enders under sail until 1952."

"Under sail with these tides? You mean at least with an engine kicker."

"No, man, fuckin' under sail all the way. Two other of the old man's brothers, they drownded back then when a rip tide broached them against Deadman Sands near Honey Hole and no way they could back off. Never mind, you'll hear. When the old man and Uncle Tony loosen up to you— you're new ears so they will, don't worry—you'll wish for some escape road back to your tender." A pair of younger men with black mustaches came out and stood with thumbs hitched at the top of their oil pants. "My cousins. Joey there, he's married to my sister. Here, take the wheel a minute, just keep her steady while I tie us alongside and bum some eggs since we got a new man aboard."

When Vito returned he frowned at the sight of Hank at his wheel, even though they were now tied alongside the *Rosa* and he'd come to shut off the engine. Without ceremony he and Chris removed boots and coveralls though nothing else, and crawled into their tight-layered bunks. "Couple hours' shut-eye," Chris explained. Their snores began at once. Hank followed suit, although it took a long time for him to fall asleep. Four hours later he woke to the starting engine and, like a good crewman, dressed quickly and appeared on deck. Chris had just untied them from the *Rosa* and water was widening between the two boats.

Hank helped Chris open two small hatches and adjust canvas receiving bags in each. Then they peered from the rails for signs of fish. So did the cousins on the *Rosa*. The net, its meshes made of wiry green monofilament, lay fluffed in layers around a thick drum astern. Far away, near a low rise of gray sand, a glinting silver shape wriggled halfway into the air and splashed back. "Jumper way off portside," muttered Hank, not pointing, unsure of their protocol with other boats nearby. Chris called to his father and waved the news to his cousins.

"Yeah Vito, we seen that jumper," said Tony over the radio. "Joey here, he wants to go closer into the bar, way shallow, you know Joey. Me, I don' know, looks good out here."

"We share," said Chris. "And Joey and me, sometimes they listen to us, sometimes they don't. In there's the fuckin' fish, not way out here." Vito tooted a whistle. Chris shrugged and threw over a buoy attached to the net. The net paid out slowly astern over the big roller. The water's friction helped pull it as the boat advanced. The net disappeared, then surfaced to become a line of white corks regular as beads.

Vito communicated with whistle toots and Chris called back one-word shouts, all of it code to Hank. During a pause, Chris gestured toward a section of net still on deck where ends had been joined. "That's a shackle, what's left. Fifty fathoms of web. Three hundred feet. The law says nine hundred feet only, that's three shackles for us. Some guys put together more shackles with less web on each. Nine hundred feet's enough, man, when they come smokin'. Whoa!" He pointed, and shouted to his dad. A beaded cork a hundred yards astern dipped from sight. "Maybe we're lucky today anyhow." Vito tooted. Chris undogged the roller and the boat zoomed ahead, laying the rest without further signals. The *Rosa* cruised leeward along the *Babe*'s corks as Uncle Tony peered from the wheelhouse window. Then the *Rosa* roared quickly away and the cousins started laying their own net in the water.

The two boats towed with a comfortable distance between them, but close enough for shouts back and forth. After a few calls, Chris stretched, then lay back on the hatch. The water was gray and calm. It lapped against the hull. Hank settled beside Chris, looking up at peaceful gray-and-white patterns of sky while a light drizzle picked at his face.

Chris chuckled. "My cousins got the same problem with their dads—my uncles you know—all the old-time guys. We learned from them, we respect them. But now they're gettin' older they play everything cautious. They just like to ride the net, like now. Papa never wants to fish in around the sandbars, especially to slip in, go dry, wait for the flood. Don't tell me they never did it before in those famous old days. But now Papa says, like: 'I seen too much of those wood double-enders lose centerboard, get blown, swamp, guys drown.' And I says 'Sure, back in sail days you got no engine. Now it's different. Sneak in shallow on Gravel Spit, say, and you got *fish*.' And Papa or Uncle Tony ends it with, like: 'You're young is what's wrong. Got no sense.' But my cousins and me? Fish outside like this all the time? Come on. That ain't the action. What do *you* think?"

"I think I'll be smart and stay out of it."

"Ahhh . . ." Chris slapped Hank's shoulder in good humor. "Well, it don't matter. But my cousins and me? We're not even sure we need this union anymore, you know? But for Papa and Uncle Tony you say 'Association', you might as well be saying Holy Mother Church. So my cousins and me we lay off that one. But . . . we get restless, sometimes throw our weight. I think since you're here I'll take us in close next tide."

Eventually Chris made spaghetti and they ate. After the net had soaked about two hours Vito yawned. "See what we got." Chris and Hank pulled into wet-gear as Vito tooted to tell his brother they were hauling. On deck Chris waited for the engine to go into neutral, hit the power takeoff button, and started the roller drum that held the net. Vito bustled from the wheelhouse buttoning his oilskin jacket. He stepped beside Chris, grabbed a hand hook from beneath the rail, and eased Hank aside.

"Hank can do it, Dad."

"Man's inexperienced."

"For horsing in web? Come on."

"Let him watch."

Chris laughed. "You don't need to be a Wop to haul web."

"I've tol' you don't use that word. Used to mean things."

"Hank, see that spare hook under the rail? No, not the wood handle, that's mine. You good at picking fish?"

"Finest," muttered Hank, both amused and insulted. Now he'd have to be good, while in truth he'd never picked fish from a gillnet.

The first meshes slipped over the roller empty and dripping. Vito and

Chris pulled the incoming net forward on deck and continued guiding it in. "Whoa," said Chris automatically as the first two salmon came aboard trapped in mesh. One hung only by its jaw. Chris flicked it free, and the five-pound flapping creature thumped by their boots. Web encased the other sockeye. A deft twist of Vito's hook dislodged it.

Three fish came next, tangled about a foot apart. Hank stepped in, held one firmly, and tried to loop it free. The body slipped against his glove and stayed trapped—indeed, became more enmeshed. Without comment Vito snatched the fish, hooked out a wad of strands under its gills, and sent the creature flying to deck.

At the coupling between the second and third shackles Vito stopped the roller. Automatically he and Chris began tossing loose fish forward into the canvas bags, then shaking free those lightly tangled. Hank followed. They cleared the boards of about thirty fish, then pulled in the rest of the net and heaped it on deck, fish and all.

"Good enough," said Vito. He hosed himself, and from the wheelhouse radioed, "Fuckin' Fanciulla, I don' know, guess we'll drop the hook a while, wait for flood." He gunned the boat free of others around them. Chris at his dad's toot released the anchor.

Hank kneeled determinedly into the netted fish. He freed a few easily, but to his chagrin Chris glanced over just as he struggled with a carcass, now dead and bloody, that entangled further with each yank of the hook. Chris tapped his shoulder, and in a few seconds had slipped head and gills through one web and the stiffening body through another. "Easy does it, man. You'll learn. Right now hose down. We ain't squareheads that don't eat till it's over. You like your eggs fried or boiled?"

In the cabin Vito asked Hank if he'd ever seen anything like this kind of fishing and received the appreciative reply he wanted. It turned him expansive. He began to tell how soft all this was compared to the old days under sail with no hydraulic roller to help with the pulling. "You think there wasn't hernias?" By the time they had finished spaghetti and eggs washed down with Chianti, the *Rosa* and another cousin's boat had tied alongside. The two other crews came over for coffee, crowding against bunks and seats. The air filled with smoke. Everyone treated Hank courteously—they all had delivered to the *Orion* and knew he was the fellow replacing the dopeheads—but ignored him.

Their talk rambled through engines and nets and bilge pumps, then settled into baseball. Chris's Little League team back home for Sacred Heart, he'd better tighten up his third base and outfield the minute he got home. Blessed Ascension always had that advantage, its coach not going to Bristol Bay and all, and you never saw worse cutthroats.

"Dodgers and Orioles," said Vito. "They'll do World Series. Take my word."

"L.A., maybe, you got Tommy Lasorda, he's manager, o.k? But Boston, Boston for the American. Don't forget the Red Sox got Lynn and Rice."

"Naah, Yankees, Yankees for the American," said one of the cousins. "You think Joey DiMagg's old team is gonna let us down?"

Vito reached under his mattress for a wallet and slapped down a hundred-dollar bill. "This says L.A.-Baltimore."

"You got it," declared his brother. "Mark the books. Who's dumb enough to cover me? I got a hundred says L.A.-Boston."

"Covered!"

Chris took a ledger from the rack beside the *Tide Tables* and registered the bets. One of the cousins fetched a similar book from the *Rosa* and wrote in it. Vito replaced the bill in his wallet. They began to wonder what the canneries would pay by the end of the season. "Hundred bucks says it breaks one-fifty," declared Vito.

"Naah, you crazy? Hundred bucks says under one-ten, raise you fifty."

Suddenly they fell silent and looked at Hank. He laughed. "I'm not management. You really think the price will go that high? From fifty-eight cents last year?"

After a while they all went back out to pick the remaining fish from the nets while they talked across the rails, continuing the points of baseball. Chris leaned to Hank over the fish and muttered: "You want the whole treatment, ought to hear 'em in the Club back home, those old men, betting the nags."

Hank picked and listened comfortably. The little grove of stunted evergreens they called Banana Tree, the single growth on a brown hill that fixed the location, faded and disappeared in foggy drizzle along with the hill itself. Occasionally another boat cruised by from the Italian fleet and stopped to banter, and other engines could be heard just out of sight, but the three boats stayed a pocket to themselves. More bets entered the books. Hank made one himself, and Chris banged him on the back as the others called their approval.

"Now," Chris announced as they wound the clean-hosed net back on the roller. "This next set, flood soon, we're going close in to the bars."

"*Non mi piace*," said Vito firmly. "What if it starts to blow, blows up swells, what if that engine breaks down? Where are you? Back in sail days is where."

"Just the same, Papa, we're goin' in." Chris's cousin on the *Rosa* declared that they were going in too. Vito and his brother grumbled further but acquiesced.

The two boats eased toward humps of sand where gulls strutted, but separated to allow distance between them. Both crews paid out their nets. The *Monterey Babe* grounded with a soft scrape and the water's gentle rock stopped. As the tide lowered further, exposed sand rose around them. The nets became kite-tails that floated until they too snaked dry. Soon land surrounded them on all sides.

"Shut the engine, Papa. I got a belt I oughta change."

"Do it on the water."

"*Papa*. Nothin's going to happen here."

Vito turned off the engine. In the sudden quiet, rivulets of water gurgled and the gulls squawked like petulant children. Hank watched two gulls attack a salmon stranded in a puddle. They went for the eyes. When Hank realized what was happening he searched for things to throw. After a while the fish stopped flapping. Two other sockeyes emerged as a puddle drained and a collective noise rose from the gulls. Hank jumped over the rail, gripped tight until he knew the sand held him, then ran over and rescued the fish.

"Hey!" declared Chris heartily. "Our new man here, he can't stop fishing."

Hank grinned, feeling self-conscious. "Let 'em die in dignity at least." He threw the two fish by their tails up to deck, then retrieved another.

"Get back aboard," fretted Vito. "You never know what'll happen, gone dry on the sands."

Aboard the *Rosa*, beached a few hundred feet away, Joey and his brother stood on the stern and shot gulls. "Naaa," said Chris mildly. "I kill

enough what I hafta." He changed the belt, then the oil. Vito started the
engine again at once. Chris shrugged, and heated more coffee.

The steady withdrawal of water stopped, then virtually on the minute
started to rise again around the far edge of sand. It bubbled progressively
up the tail of net, covering it an inch at a time. The white corks floated one
by one, rigid until the web they supported cleared bottom, then undulating
with the flow of current. Chris watched through binoculars, muttering,
"Come on, baby, don' let me down." A splash against the submerged net.
"Whoa. Comin' in." Splashes consumed a cork, then another. Suddenly
spray whitened the water along the length of the corks, and fishtails
thrashed above the surface. Chris whooped, and even Vito grunted.

The thrashes progressed in a line toward them as water reclaimed the
sand. "Smokin' man, smokin'," declared Chris reverently. "Didn't I say?
In ten years it's never been like this year since we stopped the Japs' intercept."

Within a minute, half the exposed corks had disappeared. Others
became centers of frenzy as big silver fish tangled in meshes near the surface. Shouts from the *Rosa* proved that their net was filling too. They
drank in the sight as they waited for rising water to refloat the boats. Hank
restrained a dance and shout. It could have been again his first time at the
net. His hands itched to grip the twisting fish. Like seeing the Lord's table
laid open in all its bounty.

At last they floated. The current at once pulled them into its line,
almost violently. The net weighted with fish steadied them as firmly as any
anchor, but the pressure made the net so taut against the drum that they
could roll it in only by backing engine cautiously to create slack. "Dangerous, I don' know," muttered Vito at the remote controls astern. He continued to worry as he throttled and neutraled expertly to keep web from the
propeller.

Netted fish rose in lumps over the roller. The drum slipped without
moving them as the soft bodies squeaked beneath. Hank grabbed web with
Chris to ease them. Like pulling rocks! The concentration continued. Soon
it turned grunt work just to drag the laden net over the drum and heft it
astern. Except for the occasional snagged fish loosened with a shake, the
tangled sockeyes became a hill around them on deck, then a mountain.
First Hank's feet slipped on fish, then became so engulfed in the soup of

web and fish that he needed to grip his boot tops to suck free. He laughed and pulled dizzily as the creatures thrashed against his legs, panting to echo Chris's excited "Whoa!"

The *Rosa* nearby also hauled in. Hank glanced through sweat to see their net in profile against the stern. It rose taut between water and roller with fish hung from the web like grapes on a vine.

It took two hours to bring aboard the nine hundred feet of web. As soon as the last of the net trailed safely free of the propeller, Vito hurried them to deeper water. They moved sluggishly compared to their usual bounce since the weight of fish had lowered their freeboard. Water rippled only inches below the rail.

"We oughta throw some fish back. What if a storm?"

"*Papa*!"

When they dropped anchor the increasing flood current snapped them quickly bow-on against the flow and pulled the anchor line taut. "Fuckin' Tosca," radioed Vito, keeping his face as long as his voice. "I don' know, maybe better next tide, guess we'll drop the hook a while, hope for better."

The *Rosa* came alongside, riding similarly low. For safety each boat used its own anchor rather than tying together. The men on the *Rosa* faced a similar mountain of harvest. Both crews started picking around darkfall. Each cleared a space to sit, with web and fish over legs and lap, and called back and forth. Bets, recorded by messy hands on streaked paper for later transfer, centered on fish count both in each hold and throughout the Bay. Hank now had his own page in the bets ledger.

They picked throughout the dark and into a grudging dawn while rain dumped from above and the sea splashed from below. Deck lights glistened on wet metal, oilskins, slime-covered deck and canvas, salmon with red crisscross net marks, everything. The chilly dead fish as they aged emitted increasing coppery odors. Occasionally someone stretched and made coffee. The bets and jokes lagged for a while, but then another of the Monterey boats anchored nearby with plugged nets and it all started fresh. Hank bantered contentedly with the rest.

About three a.m. in dim light, with only the first of the shackles cleared and rewound on the drum, all hands hosed and went inside. Chris fried fresh salmon with spaghetti for all three crews. Nobody hurried, even though the radio crackled with news of the continued run they might have pushed to tap again.

Work resumed. The dead sockeyes had lost all sheen and turned soapy. Hank was now facile with the pick, although some tangles stayed so thick that he'd mangle a fish to renewed kidding. It bothered nobody. Cutting a leg of web to widen the hole through which to draw the fish would have made sense but he saw none of the others doing it, and it was their gear. Cold sank through his oilskins to his thermals. His fingers burned from yanking the thin monofilament webbing that cut like wire, his legs started to cramp, and pains stabbed down his wrists.

Not that he was unhappy in good boat company, but any euphoria over live salmon abundance had long passed. All fishing had monotony, but extracting these net-bloodied creatures was more like sorting garbage. He'd wallowed enough in dead salmon delivered from seiners, crawling into holds up to his waist in fish to pitch them into a brailer. But the fish had first poured free from the net, thumping into the hold in flashes of silver. Well, that distinction represented the sensibilities of Henry Crawford—it made no difference to the salmon. Both seines and gillnets interrupted the salmon's drive home so that they died with a five-minute gasp, cheated of their duty-spawn for the next generation and a bedraggled fadeout. Did salmon care? he wondered pleasantly without caring himself, and called over an embellishment to one of the cousins' jokes.

When they broke again to eat, this time on the *Rosa*, one entire shackle remained to be picked. The canvas bags now bulged in six holds, and the remaining fish swilled in a red gurry that only regular hosing thinned.

Hank watched the clock. Still a while before the high slack on which *Orion* should return to the cannery, assuming it had a load, but the scow needed to start ahead of the tide to reach the river mouth. Ought to radio them. But on radio he'd risk a pointed question from John that the fleet could misinterpret, or gee-whizzing from Seth that might be worse. He was out learning the fishery, of course, but . . . (Would Jody call it that? Once she'd have understood.) He explained his concern to Chris who conveyed it to everyone else. Nobody seemed unhappy. Within minutes black smoke spouted from the three boats' stacks as engines turned and anchors rose.

A chilly hour and a half later—all but the skippers at the wheel remained on deck picking fish and taking spray—the misted lights of the tender fleet approached like a wall. Beneath the *Orion*'s high rail Hank grinned up, dripping, surrounded by his hill of fish. Seth and Mo cheered. Camera flash as John silently recorded the event. The *Babe* and the others tied in a line behind the *Orion* while they picked the last of their fish. Vito turned jovial. By the time Hank climbed back aboard his own command to receive the salmon he had helped catch, Vito was joking to everybody about the high-class crewman he'd trained to pick fish.

In raining dark the *Orion* started for the cannery. The fat engineer settled in the galley at his place, drinking tea he had brewed himself. He'd not spoken since Hank came back aboard. "I see you enjoyed yourself," said John, who, his duties finished, then showered and went to bed. Seth and Mo trooped to the wheelhouse to hear about the fishing. Hank at the controls drank black coffee to keep alert—he'd worked nearly clockaround for two days—as he steered through an increased maze of lights approaching the Naknek River mouth. It became difficult to match his men's high spirits, and harder yet to keep from yawning.

Lights ahead seemed to float, and passing tufts of fog made them blink. "Seth . . ." He kept it casual. "Think that's a red flasher ahead or a running light?"

"Hell, that's somebody's port side. Gillnetter maybe, probably you saw it dip in a wave."

He had studied the river mouth over and over. Their radar position was slightly off, but within the leeway he could allow. Uneasily, however, he slowed.

The *Orion* thudded to a halt that threw them to deck. Dishes shattered in the galley below. They had grounded.

5

RECKONINGS

Bristol Bay groundings are common enough. The bottom is sand or mud. It took Hank a tense half hour to reverse engines and move free on the still-rising tide. A falling tide might have left him dry a dozen hours for all to see. His luck held, and he knew it.

When they docked at 2 A.M., Swede stood in the rain while his men received their lines. He motioned Hank into his cart, gunned up the hill, and ushered him to a room in one of the barracks, all without speaking. Finally: "Sleep it off. I'll send your things in the morning."

"What do you mean by that?"

"When I hire a skipper I hire him full-time. Your boys can stay or not."

Hank wondered angrily how Swede knew, and whether it would have made a difference without the grounding. He started a defensive reply, then suddenly felt ashamed. "It won't happen again."

"I know it won't. See 'em at the office for a flight back to Kodiak." He tossed Hank a key. "Turn this in when you go."

Hank followed down the hallway, unbelieving. "You don't have anybody to take over."

"You underestimate Doke Stutz."

Swede had already reached the porch and started down the steps. Hank kept his voice low by the windows of nearby rooms. "Come back out of the rain where we can talk." Swede only turned where he stood. "Look. I don't like to be fired. Who made me come up here? What did that Doke fart tell you? I went on a trip with fishermen to get a feel for the place, then hit sand in shitty weather, that's all. Now I appreciate things in Bristol Bay

I didn't before." Swede hesitated. "Get back here, man. We've got a long way to go in this business together."

"I remember firing you once."

Hank relaxed. "You demoted me from shrimp foreman to a shovel, once. Back when I was a green kid. I didn't let you fire me. Don't worry. You still piss battery acid."

"Follow." Swede's cramped office had skeltered ledgers on shelves and mud tracks on the floor. Radio voices droned from the speaker. He unlocked a drawer and produced a bottle.

Whiskey gave neither man pleasure, nor any of the old bonding. The glasses remained nearly full. Swede coldly stated his terms. Hank acquiesced. (The fishing lark by itself would have made boat jokes, but to be fired for grounding . . .) Doke's petty mess deck privileges were to be honored, and never a foot of Hank's was to leave his own deck at sea. Hank had enough honesty to know his relief and to accept in good grace.

Swede on his part told Hank to keep the key and use the room when the *Orion* docked between tides, and authorized his men to eat in the mess hall without charge. "But tell your apes to keep it to themselves. I don't run a Salvation Army. The Speccio types all have their same rooms year after year—they've been here so long they're scenery, I respect them—but they pay for chow ashore. Frankly, those old-time Dagos would never leave the dock if I made it too comfortable."

Hank put down the key and rose to go. "Guess I'll sleep aboard where I belong. I'll want to phone Jody in the morning, then we'll ship with the tide."

Swede pushed over his telephone. "Call the lady now. You ever see that line by the phone I keep outside for the apes? The town's got a half dozen circuits, that's all, and you'll wait hours after people wake up." He poured their untasted whiskey back into the bottle, locked it away, and rose to leave. "Close the door behind you. By the way, that new crabber you're building. I assume it has the horsepower to pull a groundfish trawl?"

"That's not how I'll use it."

"Groundfish may be your future."

"What? Cent-a-pound trash the Japs make into fish paste? With good crab and shrimp out there?"

"You trust good times like the stock hotshots of 1928."

"Come on, Swede, there's no future for groundfish except on factory ships, strictly foreign ones." Hank drew a breath and settled in. He had argued this before, and voicing it kept him reassured. "You ever caught a pollack? It's half mush before it's dead. No American plant would buy the stuff. It rots before it gets to shore, so rule that out. Now. The alternative. Can you see Americans three months at sea on a shitty factory trawler gutting those things into paste?"

Swede waved him aside. "I'm only telling you that the stuff's out there for somebody to catch, and it might as well be you. Do you live in a vacuum? Ever heard of JV's—joint ventures? Washington just approved a JV for Koreans to bring in two factory ships—not to fish, just to process—and buy pollack from American boats, since Koreans don't have quota anymore to catch enough for themselves. Don't think the Russians and Japs are far behind."

"I might sound like Jones Henry on this, but JV's are the State Department's way to ass-kiss foreign governments into trade deals. It lets foreigners keep cluttering our two hundred miles. We'll start depending on them after all we did to kick them off."

"So do you waste the stuff? The State Department won't do that. It'll give it back to the foreigners."

"Then let somebody else catch it. Come on. Joint ventures are for guys without the balls to handle my big crab pots. They say you just float the trawl bag over to the factory without it ever coming aboard your own boat. Not for me. Delivering bags of mush to Koreans, kissing Jap ass? Asian peril. Forget it."

"Your vision's smaller than I thought."

Hank spread his arms. "Swede, I love my work. It's because I catch critters big enough to wrestle with. Real food, not mush. Factory fishing's the wet and cold without the buzz. Your ass is so tied up in business you've forgotten what that's like, if you ever knew. And I hate deals. This tendering shit with you is bad enough."

"Pay attention, Hank, don't fall behind. Big fish eat the runts. If you think small like that, why are you hocking yourself for nearly two million dollars of boat? The more you invest, the more deals you'll need."

Hank thought it over, and laughed uneasily. "Better pray for me, Mr. Scorden."

A door opened and a light switched on in the deserted outer office. "Mr. Soren? You are there?" A short Japanese man entered. His starched brown coveralls bore a round chest insignia in Japanese. "Mr. Soren, salmon egg line has young girls who talk and do not concentrate. You must make them pay attention to business."

Swede's voice lost its heat. "It's three in the morning, Mr. Togamashi. American kids work better if they talk. Especially on graveyard shifts."

"But they are paid to work and they are not serious. They set bad example. It will be necesary for me to make report."

Swede avoided Hank's amazed grin. "Okay, Mr. Togamashi, let's see what we can do. Hank, pick up the phone and wait for a connection. It may take a few minutes. Love to Jody." He started out, paused, then closed the door. The lines in his face still held the trademark scowl except for a smile like a grimace. "The rules I learned came from a different time. Thank God people still put salmon in cans. I do that very well. But Japanese—" he lowered his voice—"*Jap* money's paying so much for frozen reds this year I'm not sure we can compete the price and still make canned reds pay. In which case the Japs over my head might convert the canneries and everybody in them. Jap money's bought control where you stand, don't think otherwise. When I warned that big fish eat the runts, I didn't mean just you. Tell your buddy Jones Henry or don't, it might give him apoplexy. But up here we didn't win World War Two."

Hank found no words to reply. After Swede left, it took a half hour of garbled phone signals before he reached a sleepy Jody. Her voice started a rush in him of loneliness and desire. She understood the reason for his call at such an hour but her voice remained matter-of-fact. Boat repair would take another two weeks. Dawn had a cold. He began to tell about the scow with room for her and the kids, but she talked over him in a way he knew when he'd come from a long trip. Once started she needed to talk.

She'd registered Henny for nursery school in the fall, she said, and the kid talked of nothing else. They were invited to a farewell party at the Coast Guard base for Commander Hill after his final cruise on the *Confidence*. Everybody expected a good pink salmon run, but hardly any pinks had shown up yet. The Koreans said they'd pay six cents a pound for JV groundfish, but no Kodiak boats were signing up. ("Good!" said Hank.) Some Danish delegation was in town looking at sites for a groundfish plant, and Chris Blackburn reported in the *Mirror* that they would pay twenty cents. Al Burch was taking the Danes around.

Jody continued. Hank listened hungrily to her voice. Oral Burch said he'd delivered his best month of shrimp ever, a million pounds, and the shrimpers had it out at Fishermen's Hall with the Fish and Game biologists who wanted to close down Kiliuda Bay for stock sampling. Oral quizzed them on how they set their trawl, and told them they'd better take a fisherman with them to do it right if they planned to spout off about closures.

Hank stretched and yawned easily. "I knew that was bunk about the shrimp disappearing. I hate to sound like Jones, but you've got to watch them biologists."

"Maybe Jones says what's on our minds whether we admit it or not. Here's one for you. I went with Adele and Jones to an open house on the Japanese research ship. Just before he left to fish pinks. Adele dragged him along for some reason. You can imagine how we heard about Japs on the Canal all the way there, and Adele telling him to act like a gentleman. Well, I didn't mind going. You should have seen the spread of crab legs and raw fish, and those prawns ten times as big as the ones we catch around here. But trust our Jones. He marched to the buffet table, and, sharp as rusty nails, I mean loud, he announced that we'd better eat all we could since it had been stolen from right under American noses. Poor Adele."

Hank laughed disproportionately, and Jody joined with her own husky laugh. He yearned to hold her. Lucky Jones, to be out on a little seiner where a fisherman belonged, and home every few days at that.

"That's about the news. I see through the window we're fogged in. Again."

"How's the little guy in the oven?"

"He waits to kick until I start to doze. I assume it's a he. No girl's that ornery."

"Your mother told me you'd kicked her black and blue."

"With the bridge tournaments and martinis? How would she remember? Oh. Your mom wrote a nice letter. She's so tactful, I don't know where she went wrong with you. Should she come to help during my confinement or is my own mother coming? It's Adele she'll fight to hold the newborn, not Mother Sedwick. Anyhow, I've booked them late August at the Inn."

"What's wrong with our house?"

"Nothing a new, bigger one wouldn't cure. God, you men, do you ever look around you? They'd be underfoot here and your mom knows it. Adele said they ought to stay with her. Your folks like Paris but I don't think they want to hear about it day and night."

"You've sure gotten catty."

"I've gotten bored. My company is children and wives. I hope you're making money."

"I miss you."

"Yes yes, I know. And we all miss *you*. Who's paying for this call?"

"Listen! This barge I'm running has space if nothing else." Before he could talk about her coming up with the kids static drowned his words. The phone went dead. He clicked and clicked, cursing, then scribbled a letter for her and left it with a note asking Swede to mail it.

Back at the *Orion* under bright wharf lights, Hank found Seth, Mo, and John assembled in oilskins, down on an adjacent scow. They were pushing paddles like shuffleboard players to corral fish against a revolving ladder of big scoops that raised them to a hopper on the wharf. "What the hell!" he exploded, and shouted down to them. The thump of heavy rock drowned his voice. All three—even John—worked at a competitive pitch, starting at a far end of the deck to push so hard that the fish bunched in hills and flopped over the paddles.

"Where's the dock foreman?" he demanded of somebody passing. Gone for a piss was the reply. Hank stormed into the plant. Inside he glowered over lines of workers who stood by conveyor belts of fish, gutting and sliming. Off in a section separated by thick flaps stood a glum Swede with the unhappy Japanese foreman, among girls in plastic aprons and caps surrounded by crates and tables full of red, glistening roe. He started for Swede himself when the dock foreman sauntered by. "Why the hell are my guys pushing fish?"

"I was shorthanded this early, and old Doke said he was in charge. Told those guys to hop to it."

"Well I'm in charge of the *Orion*. You fuckin' get your own men down there if you want to unload."

"Easy, easy. They didn't seem to mind."

"They fuckin' do now!" His anger increased as he strode dockside and yelled down to his men to drop their goddamn paddles and get to bed.

In the galley, Doke looked up from his tea mug. "Come to pack your gear, have you?" The man's beady eyes mirrored the mouth's satisfied twitch.

Hank stood over him. "I'm captain here, old man. You stay in your fucking engine room. Never again order my guys around. They'll fix your fucking tea for you, and see you get fed in your corner there. And when we leave at the end of the season you can take back your fucking scow. But get this straight, old fucker. Never again order my guys around."

Doke pulled back against the padded bench and his mouth quivered. "Swede didn't sack you?" His eyes darted. "You better not hit me."

"Got it straight?" The man nodded.

Seth and Mo came in merrily. They'd enjoyed working up a sweat. "Boss, you okay? Doke here said you was fired, and we was going to quit too, soon as we'd got our fill of fish."

"We sail out again at noon. Haven't you been up all night? Go sleep. Where's John?" Taking a shower. "All right, I'll tell him separately. Get this straight. You never again do the fucking dock gang's work. Doke does not give you orders."

"*Sure*, Boss. Fuckin' A."

John came in soberly, brushing his dark hair. Despite recent labor he now wore crisp clean denims. He shot a glance, aware that he'd missed something. Hank repeated his instruction. "Well, I'm glad to see you assert yourself, captain. Maybe now you *are* in charge." Hank realized that the man no longer addressed him either as Boss or by name.

The July sockeye season wore on. Doke kept his place, sullenly. He and John, despite their different concepts of the fastidious, worked as a team on deck and bonded after a fashion. Both had inflexible standards, and both stood apart. John alone respected Doke's claim to specially brewed tea. After Mo had with good will flubbed the job a few times to Doke's sour (but now cautious) reprimand, John took the job and did it always correctly. Doke for his part urged John to share his special tea, while still guarding that no one else—uninterested coffee drinkers all—raided his closed can.

Hank forced himself into detachment as sockeyes arrived in volleys from the little gillnetters. He stood at the rail to banter with the Italians when they delivered, but found cheerful excuses neither to join them fishing

again nor even to come aboard for mug-up. He assumed a barge captain's
rightful jobs at anchor—coordinating deliveries by radio, ordering supplies
and selling them to boats, logging the fish tickets, deciding levels of credit—while aware that John could have done it all better while he himself
would have preferred working on deck.

Jody indeed flew up with the children and spent nine days aboard the
Orion. Hank relaxed. The barge, neither his in spirit nor hers in fact,
became an oasis where neither ruled. They enjoyed each other, both in
companionship and physically, as they had in the old fishing days before
children grounded her ashore—and changed her nature, as Hank saw it.
Yet, in contradiction, he still hoped to name the new boat *Jody C* and have
her accept being Mrs. Crawford. The *S* for Sedwick bothered him whenever he thought of it. A man didn't fish under his wife's maiden name no matter how independent she wanted to see herself.

Jody's visit was a bright time for everyone despite increasing hours
on deck as salmon poured aboard. Under her civilizing influence Hank
actually spoke to Doke again beyond curt business, to find the old man
marginally pleasant once his defenses relaxed. By now, Hank respected
Doke's skill with tools and welding torch. Henny, tied in a life jacket and
harnessed to a steel eye on deck at a safe distance from dangerous brailer-
loads of fish, watched with endless fascination and chattered to men on the
boats until they looked forward to it and he became part of the scene. He
continued delightful scampers over his daddy. Dawn, to Hank's annoy-
ance, took to John who quietly enjoyed the child's attention. She sat beside
him at table and he cut her food.

Jody, freed of clinging children and not required to cook—Mo had
learned to cook basic food well enough—soon volunteered special dishes
and presided brightly at table. Doke began appearing for meals in a shirt
that was clean although ragged at the collar and sleeves. She returned to
Kodiak before season's end only because a zoning fight at the city council
needed wives to speak up against the merchants, with their fishermen at
sea.

By season's end, Hank had banked several thousand toward the new
boat. He and Doke shook hands in parting, and Hank even asked kindly
how the old man spent his winter. "Not much, skipper. After here I stay
with my *Orion* when she follows the fish to Kenai and maybe Ketchi Kan,

then go back to my boardinghouse in Seattle. Up here again in May. I catch a lot of TV, winters, in my room. Nobody there to bother me like here."

When a new skipper recruited by Swede came to relieve him in early August, Hank handed John his plane ticket. John handed it back. "You can be free of me," he said quietly. "One of the foremen took me on to help shut down the plant. Canneries interest me, you know."

Hank gladly mellowed even to John. "I'm not sure why the fish business attracts you, but I think your talents are for the shoreside part of it."

"Yes. But I needed some seagoing perspective. I've certainly seen my fill of that now."

Even the asshole's good-bye carried barbs! But they shook hands, and Hank wished him luck. It was time to face selling the *Jody S*, and making sure the new crabber in Seattle had everything he wanted.

6

WINNER-LOSER

And here he was, separated again from Jody. But he enjoyed the ship-yard's organized chaos of grinders and welding torches and booming hollow metal. From under the ways he admired his boat's gleaming propellers and pondered the transformation of blueprints into the reality of a hull rising above him like Everest. When no one was watching in the unionized yard, a sympathetic welder let him do two of the welds himself. He tasted the ozone and metal dust as well as breathed it—ate it—and bonded to the new boat in the process. It was at night that he missed Jody and fretted to be with her in the final month of pregnancy.

The loan had been negotiated before the shipyard began construction. The bank smoothly paid each step of completion. Startling, but exhilarating, how easy it was to obtain a million and a half dollars in credit, how little he'd needed to shop. A man with proven performance, he simply guaranteed his assets.

Tolly Smith, his old buddy from early salmon days and now rival skipper on the grounds, also roamed town babying a new boat in time for the September crabs. Perpetual strutting bachelor Tolly, who had never removed the gold ring from his ear, crowed over such easy new boat loans. "They'll get their money back easy, the banks. You know it man, or they wouldn't do it, the way crabs is everywhere and Japs pay top dollar. We're riding into the future, man, you and me, gravy gravy gravy. And look at back where we started."

The two shared information over beers, but obliquely. Rival yards were building their boats. Both yards provided the usual radar, loran, and

depth sounder, as well as king crabbing gear considered basic—pot han-
dler, pot launcher, line coiler—that Hank and Tolly each knew from well-
studied catalogues. On the other hand, added horsepower and the latest in
electronic color-display trackers could give each boat an edge that neither
man cared to share. Grins and jokes answered pointed questions.

Tolly's crewman Ham Davis strutted in with a self-assurance of
mission. He solemnly shook Hank's hand before reporting to his boss and
remained standing. Hank greeted him warmly. He'd known Ham a long
time as part of the general scene, but now liked him especially for his
gentleman's boxing match a few weeks earlier when he avoided Mo's
injured arm.

"Skipper Tolly. That big captain's chair you had made special? It just
came. Boatyard says it won't fit in the wheelhouse without they put up a
thicker stanchion to hold it, and then they've got to move the radar and other
stuff. Said to tell you it adds four hundred fifty bucks extra to installation."

Tolly leaned back and fingered the gold nugget and chain around his
neck. "Fuckin' robbers," he declared without heat. "Looks good that chair,
don't it?"

Ham ticked his head and grinned. "Beaut! Guy could be in his own
living room with TV. And a place for cups and all."

"Then we gotta have her. And don't forget she's got a vibrator."

"Nobody said!"

"So you tell the boatyard for me. Just add it to the bill, no sweat."

"Yes sir, you got it!" Ham glanced toward a dark corner by a wall
phone and became less confident. "Uh, Skipper? Okay if I take tomorrow
off?"

Tolly turned businesslike. "You just went home ten days to Idaho.
I'm pushing to make the Bering on time."

"It's these two girls Mo and me met last night at a dance hall? They
work days except Wednesdays tomorrow. Want to take us on a boat and
picnic to Lake Union and all."

"You getting in?"

The natural rosiness of Ham's cheeks deepened. "Maybe tonight, if
they think we'll go tomorrow."

"Better go then. Wet your dick while you can. Up in the Bering
you'll get only seawater wets it."

"Yessir! Thanks!"

"Hold it there," said Hank. He made his voice stern and annoyed although he was amused. "You're planning to handle both girls yourself? Mo works for me. Not a boo to me about his taking off, and he's got a shit-load of jobs tomorrow."

"Well . . . Captain Crawford . . ." Ham's face now matched the red on the "No Credit" sign over the bar. He glanced anxiously toward the dark corner. There stood Mo. Hank gestured him over.

Both skippers knew their men needed slack before the hard crabbing drive, but Hank with grave reluctance enjoyed bargaining a messy bilge task for Mo's freedom next day. He regarded the two big young crewmen impersonally. They were both escaped farm boys, twin tractors strong and steady, alert enough around heavy gear, sunny by nature, good to have aboard so long as others made the decisions. When they sauntered off, Hank watched half-wistful for his own old freedom.

Ham hurried back. "I forgot. The boatyard guy says he needs it in writing if you want that extra stuff."

Tolly flourished his hand and Ham scurried to the bartender for pen and paper. Tolly bent over the paper, suddenly all frowns as he scrawled letters one by one into words. "*Hsst*, man," he muttered to Hank. "Does 'hereby' have an *e* after the *r* or not?" Hank told him so discreetly that Ham and Mo joking quietly about their imminent conquest didn't notice. "And 'dessinate,' that got one *s* or two?" Hank spelled it, adding the *g*.

When Ham and Mo had left, Hank observed: "I don't know what kind of whore's chair you're putting in your wheelhouse, old boy. But don't make it so comfortable that you or your man on watch falls asleep."

Tolly winked and nodded wisely. "Ahh buddy, that's where the fuckin' vibrator comes in. You can set it to buzz every couple minutes for wakeup. I have come a *long* way."

"There's talk around," Hank ventured. "A future in pollack and groundfish for boats with enough extra horsepower to—besides pulling up crab pots—to drag a trawl."

Tolly held out his gold nugget. "See this, man? That's where your extra bucks should go. And a Maui condo. And on your boat best captain's chair money can buy, and don't forget the Jap hot tub for you and your guys after freeze-ass on deck."

Hank shifted, suddenly restless. Tolly fished hard and knew his stuff. Maybe he himself was steering wrong.

"You're only young once," Tolly continued. "Even if *you've* maybe dropped the ol' anchor with Jody. But megabucks to catch shitty little pollack that gets you three cents a pound, versus crabs that bring, what, sometime two *bucks* a pound? Jody must hit you over the head. Pollack's Jap-style Russia-style fish, let 'em have it." He leaned back and worked a gold tooth-pick drawn from his shirt pocket. "My boatyard tried to sell me on that goods. Raise your horses from eight hundred fifty to one thousand one hundred fuckin' fifty just for pollack? Man . . . Not that I wouldn't mind to run past everything else on the water. But sometimes you have to get smart enough to invest in what'll do you good. Make some boatyard richer by four hundred thousand bucks? No wonder they tried. But even a bank wouldn't be that stupid."

"Sure wouldn't," said Hank, and dropped the subject. He ordered another round, and gave the waiter a fifty-dollar bill with: "Round for those three guys over there too, and keep the change." It was the crew of a rival crabber on the Bering Sea grounds. They gave him a whoop and a wave, and he waved back with appropriate insults.

But advice from Swede was never idle. Big fish did eat the runts. Whatever he'd said to Swede's face, what good was owning two hundred miles of ocean if you still let foreigners sweep it dry? Besides greater horsepower, the naval architect at his own boatyard had sketched and priced for him the other parts of a trawl conversion: stern ramp covered by deck plates until needed, heavy net reel, special davits to support the weight of doors and full net.

"I'll just crab harder and take one more year to pay it off," he'd told Jody over the phone.

"Oh God, Hank. Can't you ever be satisfied?" Long silence except for Dawn and Henny squabbling in the background, then: "Anyhow, no bank would lend you that much more."

"Talked to them today. They think it's the idea of the future."

"Hank, stop spending! We had a good living with the *Jody S*, and barely payments compared to what you're doing."

It was a thought he avoided even in his mind. "Just think about it. I'll be calling again tomorrow."

"We even spend too much on these damned long distance calls."

"Come on, honey. Not with the money I'm making on the crabs. This is our time!" The bold Jody of fishing boat days, who'd called hundred-dollar rounds in Dutch Harbor as casually as the men, had certainly changed. But eventually he'd persuaded her.

So, while Tolly rattled on about gold and condos and the high cost of keeping his latest squeeze Jennifer happy, Hank smiled to himself. The davits and reel were to be shipped to Dutch Harbor, stored there, and assembled aboard when needed using a crane. Don't tell. Then someday at sea, throttle full speed (first make it a bet!), and take old buddy by surprise. When they left a half hour later he tucked another twenty for tip beside Tolly's twenty under the ashtray.

Hank monitored as his wife sold the *Jody S* without his presence and at a better price than he'd hoped for, coolly negotiating the paperwork herself. It pained him to relinquish any boat. They were both glad that the new owner, free of old-timer superstition, changed the boat's name (although *Plunderbird* sounded a wrong note). Jody also settled the new boat's name without fuss when he approached her cautiously. "Your family has two women, hasn't it?" He painted JODY DAWN on the bow and stern himself, so full of the occasion that he needed to flick water from his cheeks before anyone noticed.

Time began to squeeze. Jody would come due around Labor Day, and the Bering Sea king crab season opened September 10. Bad way to start paying the bank, to miss a single day on the grounds. The new boat stood in virtual completion. He watched restlessly the final touches of painters and electricians, hoping against delay. The workmen might have seemed unconcerned, but two days ahead of schedule the *Jody Dawn* splashed into water. Seth and Mo joined him after visiting their folks respectively in California and Iowa. (Seth announced expansively that he was maybe engaged, maybe.) With near-reverence they sailed their new home to Fishermen's Terminal to take aboard new crab pots and lines.

It remained to bring the boat north with a four-man crew half green. Hank had already hired two new crewmen in Kodiak, cold-bloodedly rejecting any applicant over twenty-two so that he could drive them to the furthest limit of young endurance, but a car accident beached one in a cast only days before he was to fly south. The Terminal docks teemed with healthy young guys seeking a site. Word got around. The supposed widow of Odysseus had fewer suitors. Hank had Seth mug-up the hopefuls while he looked them over. He prodded each verbally; never again would he hire a fastidious John. On deck the hopefuls vied to help stow the seven-hundred-pound pots lowered from the wharf. Would insurance cover a non-crew injury? Hank trusted to luck as he speeded up the crane to test them.

In the end he hired Terry Bricks, a kid not true to type in size but self-assured on deck and merry at the table. Inches shorter than Seth or Mo, Terry still dove like an ape at each pot swinging down and mastered it into position with thick shoulders, showing no fatigue. Hank shooed off the others. He wished them luck kindly, recognizing in some the greenhorn's longing to be part of a fishing crew he'd once felt himself. He now had the godlike capacity among men to choose and reject. During quiet moments he reflected on it and wondered how far in this direction his life would go.

Oddmund "Odds" Anderson, the crewman hired in Kodiak, was a quiet, careful man of half-Norwegian, half-Aleut descent, older-seeming than his actual age. He had worked five years full-time aboard his father's boat in town, and summers before that from age thirteen. His wife gutted salmon and picked crab in season in Swede's cannery. At twenty-one he already had two children, reason enough to work hard. Odds knew boats, albeit smaller ones than the *Jody Dawn*, and wanted to expand his horizon. Hank sympathized and also felt an obligation to include the local-born community in his own rising fortunes.

Hank now phoned Jody every night despite her concern at the cost. She insisted he not fly home. "Then you'll hold it back, won't you, till I get there? I don't want to be away like I was for Henny and Dawn." Her curt answer puzzled him.

The trip north with the sparkling new *Jody Dawn* took nearly a week. They made it in company with Tolly Smith's new *Star Wars Two* with CB banter between wheelhouses. After a pleasant run through Puget Sound, Hank first judged his new lady's responses in the unsheltered swells of Queen Charlotte Sound. Her wide hull took motion solidly. The departed *Jody S* had livelier action—not a desired feature for winter crabbing. It bothered him to have abandoned a boat once of his heart, and at that after smashing her windows on their last run together. But, when the rest were at chow, he roamed the wide new deck patting gear and savoring the fresh-minted smells. A glance astern over the water showed that Tolly was doing the same. With a grin he gunned the new engine within the limits of break-in speed. But for this restraint on both their engines, he and Tolly would have raced all the way to Kodiak.

Through Hecate Strait the low hills of spruce wafted the best of land odors. At Dixon Entrance, Tolly wanted to continue north through the Inside Passage for a midtrip party in Ketchikan or Sitka. "Count me out," said Hank; Jody was waiting. Tolly followed into the rough open Gulf of Alaska with appropriate remarks about the apron-string bonds of a once free corker. They hit a storm, not unusual in the Gulf, and for a day thudded into waves. The tightly lashed hill of pots on deck held, the squared steel frames grinding and clacking. Despite their unbalancing height the boat recentered briskly after each roll.

The Gulf seas were subsiding when a blip appeared on the radar, followed by a dark hull on the horizon. During the Seattle stay Hank had visited the National Marine Fisheries office to map, and thus avoid, the areas where foreigners could still fish. He examined charts as they approached the ship, while his crew peered through binoculars. The ship's bay at main deck level opened to the sea. They drew closer and made out a line hung with large fish that moved steadily into the bay. "They're longlining," Hank told Tolly. "Jap, Korean, or Taiwan. Oriental letters on the stern." Loran coordinates put the vessel outside any permitted foreign zone.

Seth pounded Mo's back. "Caught us an Oriental fucker!"

Their sideband radio reached the Coast Guard in Juneau. Headquarters dispatched a cutter with a Fisheries agent aboard, on patrol miles away in the legal foreign area. An officer on the cutter radioed Hank and Tolly to approach the ship close enough to observe its fishing but: "Don't scare him off before we get there. They're longlining? That would be for sablefish—black cod you call them. Stuff the rest of the Koreans and Japanese are fishing legally."

"Yahoo," said Tolly, "My girlfriend just gave me a camera. Let's get evidence." They had the advantage of seas high enough to partly conceal their boats as they approached. Tolly edged closer and closer. "But this camera viewfinder, it makes the ship no bigger than a shithouse in a cornfield."

"Don't spook him," Hank warned. Suddenly the fish-hung line dropped from the bay into the water, followed by a large object. Hank swore. "You've scared them. Looks like they've cut their longline and sunk it with a weight. And you never got close enough for a good photo, did you?" Tolly swore even harder. As they watched, the ship started to move away.

Hank gunned the *Jody Dawn* to close on the ship. He put Seth at the helm and tabulated underway hours to figure the speed he could safely push the new engine. He radioed the cutter and with loran coordinates confirmed their position. "She's headed north, course about three-four-five or seven, doing I judge twelve knots. We still can't read her name, but it doesn't seem to have Maru at the end so it's not Jap I guess."

"Read you. That course heads for the main Korean fleet. They'll try to get lost in it. I won't give you our position on open frequency, but you'd be interested. Stick with her."

"Look, Boss," cried Mo, "she's dumping fish overboard."

Hank told Mo and the two newcomers to get into survival suits, tie themselves to the rail, and retrieve some of the fish. "One of you lean over with the dip net, the other two hold his legs. Remember we're going fast, the water could tear it out of your hands. Let it go, Chrissake don't go with it."

"Right, Boss. Sure! Fuckin' evidence, right?"

Hank watched tensely with his own hand now on the control—nothing was worth a man overboard. An umbrella of spray cascaded over them from the bow. He slowed just as they passed some of the fish. Mo netted two black cod, about four pounds each. "That's enough," he shouted down. "Good work!"

"Plenty more, Boss," called Mo expansively.

"*No!*"

Back dry in the wheelhouse, Mo and the new man Terry whooped like children as spray arched from the bow at each thud into a wave. Hank controlled his own excitement, and noticed that Seth, a whooper in the past, also remained tensely cool. The man was growing up. (Engaged? Was that it?) The Korean gained distance, but barely. At 7 P.M. at least three hours of light remained. Tolly's boat fell farther astern. (First use of my extra power, thought Hank, and no time to bet Tolly first. But "Hey man, hey, what am I seeing!" from Tolly rewarded him.) Every quarter hour he radioed the Coast Guard their position.

Late sun turned horizon clouds golden and gilded the continuous beads of spray. A dot appeared on the radar and grew as they approached. "White hull, Boss," exclaimed Mo from his binoculars. "It's the Coast

Guard! The gooks have been running straight towards them!" The white cutter sped like cavalry to the rescue. The foreign ship slowed while *Jody Dawn* continued to close the gap. "We've boxed him in," laughed Hank.

Suddenly the ship reversed course toward the *Jody Dawn*. Water shot from both sides of its bow. Seth cried out hoarsely. Hank, in sudden horror, pictured the ship that once bore down on the life raft where he, Seth, Jones, Steve, and Ivan lay close to death looking up, when they'd thought rescue had come and found too late they'd not been seen. (A Jap, rushing mindlessly between grounds without a proper watch. Always Asians.) "You son of a bitch fucker!" he yelled. "Seth! Rifle by my bunk!" Then he remembered that the hunting guns lay at home in Kodiak, taken from the old *Jody S.* The ship bore steadily. Hank veered from course in time. The high rusty hull, its home port Seoul now clear on the bow, continued straight. Asian faces stared down. Seth, now on deck, shook his fist and screamed vituperations. He continued even after the ship had passed.

Hank reduced to mere headway speed. "Mo, take the wheel. Steady as she goes." He hurried down to deck. Seth continued to scream. Hank took his arm and led him inside. "Easy man, easy. It's okay, okay."

Seth clutched him and sobbed. "Man, it's like I seen it again just now, old Steve jump at the anchor to stave us off, then into the water and gone. Just like happening again. Them bastards never stop for you. And I was there like potatoes, given up. Only for you, saving me, I'd be down there now with Steve and Ivan."

"It's okay, okay." Hank hugged him, then tousled his hair. "We came out okay together, both of us. With old Jones mean as ever. Steve and Ivan's time had come. Nothing you could have done. Or me . . ." He wanted to sob himself, because it wasn't so. Not the time now for guilt. A minute later he led Seth into joking about it roughly.

"Boss, you better get up here," called Mo.

A rubber-sided skiff headed toward them. The Korean ship had stopped not far from the *Jody Dawn*, and the cutter lay-to close by. Mo reported, amazed with admiration, that the Coast Guard had fired a flare and then a shot. "And that gook boat, when it shut down, it made a backwash that threw three more of their fish on our deck. Boss, you should have been here. Seth sure told 'em. He okay?"

"Finest. Terry and Odds, go catch that Zodiac's line."

The Coast Guard officer in the Zodiac jumped aboard to examine the jettisoned black cod. The fish had clear hook marks in their mouths, and one had a torn side. The exposed meat was bright red, a dramatic contrast to the shining black skin. "Pretty fish," said the officer. "Bad eating except smoked they say. Asians eat anything." The officer invited Hank to witness the boarding and give his statement to Fisheries firsthand.

"Don't let 'em poison you, Boss," called Seth lustily, now back to himself, as Hank rode away in the Zodiac. "Don't let them gooks feed you black fish."

Hank sat in the rubber-sided skiff, but stood when he saw that the coxswain, crewman, and officer all remained upright facing slaps of cold spray. It *was* more fun. Water beaded on the fabric of their orange water-proof coveralls and cascaded down his oilskins. He licked salt from his lips. Cleansing, to ride over water and bring an enemy to justice.

The high Korean hull, deadly minutes before, loomed as a wall of layered brown and yellow rust. The coxswain dodged a bolus of sludge that popped from a scupper. Hank looked up sternly into flat anxious faces at the rail. Sweat it, boys, he thought with satisfaction. Water surged at the Jacob's ladder. He waited until the Zodiac rode a crest, jumped to the rungs, and scampered up before the next surge crested. Even the ladder was slimy. A Korean at the rail leaned down to help him with a pull under the arm. Hank shook it off and easily finished the climb. The Korean, in a hard hat, bowed and attempted a smile. Hank nodded curtly.

Orange Coast Guard figures moved over the deck and above on the bridge. Hank followed the officer through mottled green passageways that smelled sourly of cabbage, garlic, and old fish. His wool cap brushed the overhead and he ducked to go through a doorway. The fish stink deepened two decks below in a wide, dark space with a ceiling so low he needed to bend. Chilly wind and laps of spray blew through an open bay, probably the bay he'd seen drawing in the longline laden with fish. A half dozen Koreans near a bin of line and hooks bobbed with tentative smiles. Fish chunks clung to their thick rubber clothing.

"Caught them dumping a tub of bait through the scuppers," said a young American with a sandy mustache, whom the officer introduced as a Fisheries inspector. "Look at the fresh scraps on those hooks. We got 'em redhanded and they know it." It was the metallic crumminess of the place that impressed Hank. He kicked pieces of fish with his boot. Expect rust, but didn't they ever scrub and hose? The inspector lowered the flaps of his fur cap, pulled on thick gloves, and squeezed through a hatch onto a frosty ladder. The sound of thumps came from below him. Hank peered down at orange figures throwing stiff frozen fish like cordwood from a stack. The inspector grinned. "I'm here for hours. Not just black cod. Halibut, the poor stupes. Fishing a closed zone for stuff otherwise legal, but packing illegal fish besides. Got their ass this time."

Hank followed the officer up decks through a dim galley (Koreans at tables glanced anxiously—sour cabbage smell especially here), to the wheelhouse. Stifling wheelhouse heat: at least forty degrees hotter than the passageways. The Americans had shed their float coveralls. An older inspector in civvies leaned over the chart table copying data from log-books. An officer in khaki with lieutenant's bars on his collar stood questioning the captain, a round Korean of middle age with a large purple birthmark on his face. Both were polite. The Korean smiled often, once even giggled. He answered in English so slurred and broken, in such a low voice, that the lieutenant needed to ask often for repeats.

Hank wrote his report, glancing occasionally through the window at his new crabber and Tolly's equally fine boat rolling alongside. Seas rose as it grew dark. Time to return to their own business. The black cod these people poached were handsome fish, a kind satisfying to catch. Had anybody tried to eat them fresh before declaring them too oily for Americans? He'd seen and eaten stranger stuff in Vietnam, some of it laughable in the later telling, but some not bad. Maybe there was no need to give these quotas to foreigners.

Suddenly the Korean captain thumped to his knees. He bowed his head, clutched the lieutenant's legs, and began to cry. "Prease, no report, no arrest. In home Pusan I will prison." He struck his fist against his kidneys and then toward his teeth. "Will beating. Prease prease."

The lieutenant, a man in his late twenties, backed away. "It's done, fellow. Pull it together."

"Prease prease!" The purple birthmark, a swatch from temple to check, turned almost black.

The lieutenant's face flushed. He turned to Hank and the inspector. "I can't do anything. Somebody tell this guy."

As quickly as he had kneeled, the Korean rose and continued the interview, but with eerie calm. Hank watched, stunned. When the lieutenant thanked him for reporting the poacher he avoided the Korean's eyes, and quickly accepted a ride back to the *Jody Dawn*. Cold salt washed his face on the way, but he shivered not from the chill. Beaten for stealing fish that should be God's bounty? The man had known his risk of course. He shrugged off Seth's glee, and parried Tolly's queries on the CB except to say: "They were fishing all right." He remembered wary peasant eyes peering from corners of thatch when his Mekong River patrol beached at a Vietnamese village for questions. He was the intruder with his men—a scared but cool young ensign in power and sharpened for ambush. Obeying the rules of war, knowing he endangered such villagers if the Viet Cong took control, but under duty. Hapless people who might still be paying for their hospitality to the Americans who frightened them. He welcomed rough weather as they beat toward Kodiak. It kept him focused on the immediate.

7

CRAB HEAVEN

Sun shone on the green of Pillar Mountain as they steamed into Kodiak harbor. It was a rare blue-sky morning in early September. Steam poured from the fish plants along the Narrows where once, fourteen years before, he and Jones had survived the earthquake and tidal wave that had swept them like toys. He and Tolly tooted gaily when they entered the breakwater. Hank had reached Peggy Dyson, the Kodiak fisherman's wife committed to daily weather broadcasts, during her evening roundup the night before to tell Jody of their arrival. He searched the small group at the slip through binoculars, anticipation rising. His own dad and mother held the children's hands; nice, they'd made it! Jones but no Adele. Jennifer, Tolly's squeeze. They looked grave. Where was Jody? He nearly banged the pier in mooring, called for Seth to shut the engine, and leaped down. "Jody?" Henny climbed over him and Dawn clutched his leg. His mother in tears hugged him, "Go with Mr. Henry," she said, and collected the children. His father trailed up the ramp, patting Hank's shoulder.

Jody had started labor. Adele was with her. The men had no further details. "Nice boat," said Jones. "Too big for me."

"Is she having trouble?"

"Count on women to pull long faces."

His father started telling him about their long flight from Baltimore. Hank barely listened. As the car climbed the hill at Rezanof he blankly watched the blue-domed Russian church and the canneries and water below. Dust swirled. What could life be without her?

89

He ran from the car to the hospital door, and interrupted a Native couple at the desk to demand: "Mrs. Crawford, where?"

"You're behaving like Mr. Crawford," said the nurse calmly. "You've got papers to sign."

He grabbed them, fearing to see the word Death. All he saw was Maternity. "How is she? Where?"

"You fishermen daddies are so alike. Never there on time, then so agitated." She smiled. "It's a boy, Mr. Crawford. Congratulations. Now wait your turn."

"IS MY WIFE OKAY?"

"Tired, I should think."

At last he stood by her bed and choked as he bent to hug her. She lay with lidded eyes, her hair sweat-tangled on the pillow. Adele bustled beside him, crying also.

"For Christ's sake, you two," muttered Jody. "I did all the work." She laughed weakly. It sounded hoarse. "Now Dawn and I have to put up with another penis in the house."

A girl would have pleased him too, but a son was so good! He hugged the warm, fretting bundle, carefully brushed a cheek against the precious small head to avoid scratching with his beard, and fingered fists that had the sturdy delicacy of paper clips. He and Jody had discussed names for boy or girl: now they'd escaped the diplomatic tangle over hints to name a girl after his mother or Adele. "Does Peter still sound good to you, honey? After your dad?"

"As long as that's Peter the Final." She fell asleep.

Hank danced with his bundle. "Hey Pete, Petey fella, Mr. Pete, Mr. Pete, Mr. Pete." He hid tears as best he could from Adele at the window and the men peeking by the door.

"I'll have that back," said a nurse. "Now all of you clear out." Hank relinquished his son after a hug, then kissed Jody gently.

Two days later when Jody came home and he could act unchallenged by nurses, he unwrapped the bundle, enjoying its soft skin, and tucked the infant inside his shirt against his bare chest. The warm creature snuggled, animal to animal.

"Hank dear, what on earth are you doing to that child?" said his mother, amused.

"Little critters like warmth. He's my little critter."

"Don't you let him slide," warned Adele.

A droobling sound. Hank grimaced, but kept the baby in place long enough to show it didn't matter. Adele noticed, and whispered the news to his mother and to Jody in bed. The women watched while talking with pointed nonchalance. "Well," said Hank after five minutes, "That's enough for now, Pete." He bent over the crib. "Down you go, Mr. Honey."

Jody laughed her throaty laugh. "Not so fast, Big Daddy. It happened on your watch. Change your critter." Caught, he did. The three women enjoyed the sight, and joined together in making unflattering comments on his diaper technique around kicking little legs.

Tolly and Seth had winked, waving bottles, but the presence of his parents kept Hank from going on a fisherman's bash for new son and boat. At home he shared cigars and bourbon with his dad while his mother took her fill of the children. (Henny and Dawn found her a novelty easier to manipulate than even Adele.) The senior Henry Crawford soon shed his tweed jacket and silk tie for a red-and-black checked wool shirt, but he remained a studied East Coast version of roughing it. The effort endeared him to Hank, as did the rural scarf with which his mom garnished her tailored suit, all protected by a bright flowered apron when she pitched in to nurse or clean. Better than emulating Adele's lime green slacks, Hank thought.

But *Jody Dawn* did have to be christened. With Tolly's *Star Wars Two* tied alongside they made it a double affair. Tolly had groused since arriving over the need to hurry westward and stake out grounds, but with his girlfriend's attentions, and the glory of the captured Korean longliner brought to the Coast Guard base drawing reporters even from the *Wall Street Journal*, he lingered. Jody recovered with amazing speed. Three days after leaving the hospital she sat on the *Jody Dawn*'s main deck, sipping only a diluted Scotch since she was nursing, while the party whirled around her. Hank had brought a padded chair from Jones's house in the pickup truck, then with Mo cross-hand carried her aboard to general cheers. Adele and Mother Crawford both stayed home, so she had no need to worry about her children until time to nurse again.

Many toasts hailed the capture of the Korean longliner. Jones declared over and over, his arms around Hank and Tolly, that it took good

American fishermen to track down the foreign buggers. Tolly expounded on the capture to anyone who asked. Jennifer, snuggled against his side, enjoyed the focus as much as he. Mo, and Tolly's crewman Ham, now buddies ashore after their July 4th boxing match, formed another chest-puffing center of attention, surrounded by more females than their own girlfriends of the moment. Hank avoided the subject and gave only curt answers. Reporters in town had found him equally taciturn.

On deck, the senior Crawford insisted that water would be fine with his bourbon, but gladly used the soda that Hank, when he thought of it, dispatched Terry to buy. Hank was pleased that his dad, while losing no poise, conversed with fishermen as if he cared about and enjoyed them. They in turn relaxed with him. Jones—after silently inspecting the boat's every compartment (as did Tolly)—challenged Crawford senior on the deficiencies of President Carter, assuming that anybody from the East endorsed the fellow and his wishy-wash. But the two agreed, the one with salty denunciation and the other in resigned humor. The fact that Alaskan decks and East Coast offices were worlds apart had never bothered Hank; their common ground surprised him. He might be more of a piece than he'd imagined. On an impulse he strode to his dad and hugged him. The older man lightly hugged him back, not comfortable, but with eyes warmly affectionate.

No one at the party except the new crewman Odds turned aggressively drunk in the old way of Ivan. Hank watched quietly. Was it the half-Aleut blood, proof that Natives couldn't hold liquor? Ivan, rest his dogged noble soul, also shared that mix, but Steve had been there to intercept. Maybe, while avoiding another asshole deckhand like John, he'd made a different mistake.

By seven, Jody's eyes had lost vitality. She declared fatigue but insisted he stay. Seth and Mo, solemn in their mission, carried her over the gangway to the truck. Hank's father frowned at him for staying (but then there had been parental disapproval all around for bringing her down), and followed to drive while the crewmen rode in back. Tolly and his men noisily returned to their boat, shooed off remaining revelers, and a half hour later left their slip with whistles and shouts, bound for the Bering Sea.

Hank told Odds to get home to his wife and refused him more drink. Odds, normally quiet and obedient, picked up a hammer scowling. Before he could advance, Terry darted to snatch it. Odds turned on him fiercely, then grunted and lumbered off the boat. It quashed the party. Soon even Jones had left with his crew.

Hank leaned against the stack of crab pots, not drunk but not sober. Should he sack Odds and hire someone less known so close to departure? Terry brought coffee, and quipped happily that it had been some party. He shrugged off the incident with Odds. "He works good and hard. Don't worry. I'll look out for him." Hank studied the short, husky youth and nodded. That strength and cheer might do it.

Late light streaked the sky and burned orange on masts and hillside houses. No vessel of the *Jody Dawn*'s size remained in the harbor: all gone westward where he should be, to waters rough and lonely a hundred miles from land. One of the old wooden halibut schooners, then another, glided into harbor past the breakwater. End of a halibut opening. Young men stood on the schooner decks in seasoned oilskins, bearded but not seasoned in face like the gloomy old Norwegians of his own apprenticeship who grew scarcer with the passage of time. All of that history. He'd participated in its course. Now he charted history of his own. The thought made him weary.

Across on the next pier Jones and his men, now in coveralls, thumped around their limit seiner. Machinery whined on other boats of the salmon fleet, and men called out as they removed power blocks and installed pot haulers for king crab season. Soon they'd all steam a mere few hours down the island to grounds within sight of the mountains and a quick run into lovely, sheltered bays. Home every week or so. Why hadn't he stayed like that? Now he'd invested too heavily to remain small. And was leaving Jody behind.

"Can't wait to get back out there," said Terry. "Put those big pots to work, you know? Slingin' them big ol' keepers."

"Finest." A pause. "You never speak of your wife, Terry."

"Oh. Well, we're like separated. You know what it is when you go fishing. Sometimes a woman—not yours, you lucky—they don't understand. When you fish you never think of them all the time. You just *can't* 'cause you're not there, you got to worry about the boat. They don't understand."

"Yes, well, you're right, Jody does understand. She fished herself before the kids came along."

"You see? Now my old lady, my ex I guess, you'd think in Tillamook where she grew up—both of us grew up there right on the coast of Oregon —you'd think like with the boats and all the men fishing, she'd know."

At home that night Hank was markedly affectionate. With kids asleep and parents gone to the inn, he lay holding her in bed. They kissed and snuggled. No toughness or banter. "I'm so glad you're my wife."

"I'm glad too."

Don't ever leave me, he thought, but dared not put it into words. What had he done, to commit to a monster boat that would keep them apart even more than before?

His dad echoed that thought next day in private as Hank packed his sea bag. "This doesn't seem a good time for you to go fishing, son." Hank explained that when the king crab season opened on September 10 it was grabs during only the limit of the opening. This was the money to pay off *Jody Dawn*, money at a level unmatched during the year, the money on which the banks predicated their big boat loans. Not just to him. All would be there fighting. A day missed could cost thousands. The harder you fished, the more boat you owned when the season closed. That simple. "I see," said his father, and he did.

His mother wondered more openly as she burped little Pete and the two children competed for Hank's legs and attention. "Really, Hank, your duty's with your family right now. It was bad enough to have you gone when Jody delivered. You might have planned that better although it's not for me to say." She walked over and patted his arm. Her hands were developing big brown discolorations. "Time with your family's so precious. It goes so fast. Take your boat out some other time, dear." Both Jody and Adele laughed, and explained, but she shook her head. Hank listened gloomily, grateful for Jody's support. He left the room as soon as he could.

Time grew short. They had a picnic. Next morning the *Jody Dawn* prepared to leave its slip. Hank's parents were smiling and so was Jody. Henny and Dawn, in puffy orange life jackets, capered up and down the float under the eye of Adele. Seth and Mo, as senior crew, kept businesslike expressions while they checked yet again the lashings on the pots, but when Jody summoned them for a good luck kiss they broke into grins. Odds glumly nodded to his wife, jumped aboard with the bow line, and coiled it without looking up. Terry twirled the stern line overhead like a cowboy and yahooed to nobody in particular.

Off they went. Jones blasted the horn from his boat in the opposite slip and his boys threw firecrackers. They would head soon for crabs at Horse's Head just down the coast, but by the time Hank returned, Adele would have dragged Jones south to San Pedro and his welding shop for the winter with pressure for another foray to France before the salmon next spring. They had worked it out, however much they scratched at each other. Hank sighed as he saw the last of his beloveds, and pulled the whistle gaily to cover it.

The first day saw them down the east coast of Kodiak Island, past foggy rock sentinels and then, as the sky cleared, past friendly bay mouths backed by mountains streaked with perpetual snow. It all had memory, from the rocks near Chiniak where he'd lured a bullying Russian trawler in days before two-hundred-mile, to sheltering Uyak and Kiliuda Bays where salmon and shrimp had teemed for his nets in season. At dusk, by the shelter of Sitkalidak Island, boats the size of Jones Henry's had already begun to assemble for the king crab opening still days away. Their lights twinkled in the distant funnel of Three Saints Bay.

"Old Harbor around the point, that's where I was born," said Odds, now perched on a wheelhouse bench with the others, his drunken belligerence forgotten. His voice was soft, the *r*'s deliberate. "Place all rebuilt after the earthquake. I've got plenty of aunts and uncles there if we ever want to go in." Hank acknowledged to encourage him. Odds pointed at the boat lights. "Three Saints, that's where the Russians first set up to fur trade, two hundred years ago. There's all kinds of history. But we came there first, my people."

Hank had always been unsure how openly he could speak to Natives about themselves without offending. "Do you, uh, your people, keep any Aleut customs?"

Odds seemed to have no reticence. "Go to Russian Church if that's what you mean. Big family dinner afterwards at Grandma's: Pop and Mom, aunts, sisters, cousins, everybody's kids. But Ivan, my uncle in your crew that died a few years ago in that wreck, he never came to family."

Hank and Seth exchanged glances. "Ivan's your uncle? I didn't know."

"A little crazy, but very serious about church. Guess he's pretty well forgotten."

"No! Not forgotten. A good, good man. A friend."

"Well, we always thought he was a little crazy. Never came to family. Pop said he never done anything right. Figured he finally died from doing something crazy."

"Don't *never* say that," snapped Seth, his voice near to cracking. "Ivan, he saved our lives. And when Ivan fished, he hung tough more than anybody here." Seth left the wheelhouse.

Hank drew a breath. "We work together, so I guess you should know." He told the story quietly. How the late *Adele III* caught fire and they abandoned her in a life raft that inflated upside down and had to be righted all wet with gear lost. How all of them—Jones Henry, Seth, Steve, Ivan, himself—drifted five days getting weaker, at last barely moving as wind rattled their torn canopy and cold sea splashed through. How a Japanese trawler they thought was heading to rescue them blindly ran them down instead and how Steve, fending off the high hull, drowned. How Ivan mourned the shipmate who had buffered him from the world—"*Steve* was Ivan's family, Odds"—but kept rubbing their feet and sheltering their bodies when they lay comatose. How when a Coast Guard helicopter found them at dusk, Ivan lifted them one by one into the rescue basket to be drawn aloft while seas rose and night darkened, then dropped into the water to be with Steve.

He said nothing of Seth's giving up first, Seth's eternal shame; or of his own guilt: how he, as skipper, had probably led them to the situation. Nor could he have told, without choking up, how when only the two of them remained in the newly unstable raft under the helicopter's prop wash, and he as captain decided to go last despite fear, Ivan had hugged him, then put him firmly in the basket.

Odds listened, grave and frowning. Mo and Terry knew when to keep quiet.

By next morning the last of Kodiak had been passed, and *Jody Dawn* rolled through the North Pacific. Waves turned alternately blue or gray depending on the sky. Everyone had settled into routine underway—sleeping, eating, standing watch. They picked at food and felt sluggish. The boat took seas with the rhythm of breathing. When water tumbled across the wide afterdeck, the high lashed pots shifted not an inch. Without heavy work it became a limbo time, when leisure made even washing dishes a chore. Thoughts of land and home intensified, but they also blurred as did again the memory of Ivan. Hank played with the new electronics in his new wheelhouse, watched his new crewmen, yearned for the warmth of his new son against his chest, all with desultory effort. Even newness became mere abstraction.

"I had a dog once . . . ," Terry would begin, but lose interest in the story himself.

Storm, fog, and whitecaps had gathered by the time they entered Unimak Pass so that only radar showed the blocks of land that heralded the Aleutian Islands. Hank bypassed Dutch Harbor—the new boat's large tanks had enough fuel and water, and he mistrusted Odds with the bars. He headed north toward the Pribilofs and his own tried grounds for early season. They passed other boats, stark on crests, then hidden in troughs twenty feet deep and more. With relief he found the water uninhabited over Hank's Hole, the spot where big males had collected in previous years, his private discovery from years of prospecting, exact position known only to himself and Jody, marked on a chart he kept even from Seth. Tolly began calling on the VHF. Hank stayed brief. People had things now like radio direction finders that could home in on a signal and spot you. He'd fish with friends later when the crabs migrated along known tracks.

Time to fish. Suddenly they all felt it. Before starting to set pots for next day's opening, Mo heaped out a breakfast of steak, spaghetti, and canned corn. Nothing remained on the platter but grease. Terry's quips became hilarious. Soon the heavy, square pots were being craned, swinging from the top of the stack. The men armed them with chopped bait and launched them over the side. Hank, at the wheelhouse controls, started his four men slowly. He watched the newcomers. With everyone keyed up they quickly reached the shotgun pace he favored. Both Terry and Odds had Mo's young bounce. They teamed but competed. Good sign, although the whole tale would await fatigue. Only Seth paced himself, a strong man but nearly thirty. The new boat had quick response despite its wide beam. A string of red plastic balls bearing the new *Jody Dawn* "JD" logo stretched farther and farther astern. All good.

Next day, with a radio signal from Fish and Game, it began. The first pot came up empty and stayed on deck. The second had three crabs, all males. Seth brought one to Hank, who gripped its claws to spread the legs the breadth of his reach, then kissed the big red-purple carapace while the others cheered. Terry and Odds had never heard of the ceremony. Terry chuckled and kissed the creature. Odds refused, but with a self-deprecating grin that didn't offend. "Bring your buddies!" called Hank and lobbed it into a wave.

Each successive pot contained more. Only a few were females to throw back. After a dozen pots the steel-framed cages—seven feet square and three feet high—contained enough crabs to block the sight of white-caps through the mesh. The crabs increased the seven-hundred-pound base weight by a thousand pounds and more.

Seth and Mo were proven. The new men kept pace. Terry on deck was a buzz bomb, everywhere, doing it right. Only Odds had never han-dled such pots before, but he had innate sea-sense from years on smaller boats. No one needed to coach him to wait for the deck to roll in the right direction before launching a pot or moving it. He measured keepers care-lessly, however, ignoring calipers the others used when in doubt even on the run. Hank alerted Seth, who caught Odds twice about to throw a crab with too small a carapace into the hold. "So close it makes no difference," argued Odds quietly. "Fucking big difference," Seth roared, "if an inspec-tor sees undersized and fines your ass." Odds shrugged, complained of damn regulations, but culled more carefully.

And the crabs were there: sluggish from the cold depths, their spiny shells the size of dinner plates, claws slowly groping for something to crush—food and money both. Under Seth the men alternated jobs to keep fresh. Only Odds, learning a new skill, snarled line when coiling it at top speed while the hydraulic roller wheeled up pots from sixty fathoms. Hank could afford no weak link. He allowed a slower pace with Odds at the rail, and saw the man improve.

Hank also broke rhythm each day to trade jobs with Seth and train him at the new helm, glad for an excuse to stretch on deck. Each time after two or three hours he returned panting, though stimulated, to the wheel-house, troubled by his fatigue. It was one thing to declare he'd hire only apes under twenty-two on his crab deck, but another at only thirty-three to wear down himself. And he noticed that Seth, five years his junior, seemed relieved for the break. Too soon. Steve and Ivan, the twin ghosts of his past, had been in nearly their late forties when the water claimed them, but still bulldogs on deck who needed no rest however long the fishing.

Each pot raised to the surface brought more big, purple crabs than could be culled on the instant. They cluttered the deck. Seas over the rail washed them from side to side until the men threw or boot-nudged them into the open tank of circulating water. Were other boats doing so well? As the abundance continued Hank began to speculate. *Jody Dawn* could be the first boat of the season to deliver, even to come in plugged. Throw down the gauntlet to be highliner! Seth and Mo agreed lustily, Terry with a cheerful "sure," Odds with sober acceptance. Hank pushed them as close to clockaround as he dared, allowing five hours' sleep, taking less himself. No one slacked. At last, crabs stopped sinking from sight in the holding tanks and bunched near the surface. Time to deliver. The creatures would die in tanks plugged any fuller, would smash against each other in heavy seas, suffocate. They left baited pots to soak and steamed to Dutch Harbor a hundred thirty miles south. All hands crashed into dead sleep except the watch.

They entered Dutch to a frosty dawn. Blue shadows coated snow on top of the sere mountains. Odds sucked in his breath at sight of the dark twin onion domes on the boxy Russian Orthodox church and declared he'd never seen anything so pretty. Their delivery plant lay near the church in Unalaska, the village across a narrow waterway from actual Dutch Harbor and the Navy's decaying World War II facilities that had been closed in 1947.

The plant manager welcomed them noisily. They had indeed brought the season's first delivery, reason for Hank to treat the attention cautiously lest other boats track him back to his Hole. A familiar knot of young men were already hunched by the gangway, hoping some change in fortune had made a crew berth available. Soon workers stood in the drained hold waist-deep in crabs, and brailers lifted the creatures to a chute that tumbled them into the building. Steam rose from inside. Sea-astringent odors overlaid with ammonia wafted out, the smell of crabs in cookers. Mo and Terry drooped no longer. They strutted from their cabins in clean, tight denims, ready to see what lay along the boardwalks and gravel road. Odds, buttoned carefully, prepared to visit the church. "Father Rostinoff back home,

he'll be glad. I guess you don't know it, how important Russian church is
to Aleut people." Hank gave him money to light a candle for Ivan, then
became again the Navy officer briefing his men before granting shore
leave. "No talk about where we're fishing. Back here in two hours."

"Aww, Boss . . . The bars won't even be open yet."

Exactly, thought Hank, avoiding a glance at Odds. "The minute the
hold's clean we go across to the Dutch side, load a hundred pots I stacked
there last year, then back to sea."

He went to the plant office to sign off on his delivery. A head of dark
hair and sideburns looked up from a desk outside the manager's office and
the man said evenly, "Well, I assumed you'd be along some time. Pushing
as usual I suppose, since you got here first." It was John, his former asshole
crewman. Neither offered to shake hands.

"So you're making out in the cannery business."

"*Freezer* business. Yes. Of course I'm glad for that look from down
under first, for background. But management's the place for action these
days, not slogging in oilskins."

"As long as somebody else slogs for you. Swede took you on, then?"

"Mr. Scorden?" John handed over a receipt, and pointed at the line to
be signed. "Not Mr. Scorden, no. A few of those cannery bosses still have
their place. But this part of the company's the future. You should understand that, with your new crabber and its capacity for groundfish. You see,
I do follow your fortunes. You're on our high-potential list."

Hank wanted to hit him. "There wouldn't be a fish business up here
without men like Swede who took gut chances. Men who went broke trying new processes, picked themselves up, figured things out."

"Oh, nobody denies the man his place in history. But the new fortune's in groundfish, and he's not with it. They don't invite me yet to the
managers' meetings, but I'm far enough along to hear what goes on. Last
week in Seattle Scorden was the only one who spoke against going ahead
with a trial surimi plant. If you're his friend you might want to caution
him. That's the way down."

A short Japanese in suit and tie bustled past. John stood quickly. "Mr.
Hitai. This is Henry Crawford, one of our better performers. He's just delivered a full hold, in his new boat with groundfish capability." The Japanese
regarded Hank from head to foot, inclined his head slightly, offered a limp

handshake, said that good performers were always welcome in the office, and hurried on. John sat again at once. He smiled. "Fact is, I'm going with Mr. Hitai to Tokyo next December. They want to look me over, I think, since I've already shown a pretty good knack for the business."

Hank signed the fish ticket and left. The glow had lessened from delivering first, although he knew his sudden malaise to be just anger. The asshole hadn't changed, and now he'd be around. And the fellow was wrong. Nobody would dump Swede after he'd produced year after year.

As they left harbor the sea quickly took them in motion. Hank calmed in the sharp salty air that was free of crab-factory stench ashore. They passed other boats just coming to deliver. Hank, feeling himself again, pumped his whistle at Tolly's *Star Wars Two* and wished his envious buddy better fishing ahead of the crowd next time.

Having tasted highlining they all wanted more, for honor and money both. With a hundred additional pots to work, and crabs pouring in, Hank quickened the pace. He reduced haul-and-reset time from ten minutes to eight, then seven. The new hydraulic machinery sped pots up from sixty fathoms as fast as the line could be coiled, and even Odds's deliberate hands now flicked line correctly on automatic. Wetness became part of life, whether from sweat or sea. Painful to start after stopping, better not to stop. When Hank cruised between strings of pots, the others flopped to deck in the heated corridor without removing boots and oilskins. They toughened to four hours' sleep. Crabs filled their every sight and crawled through truncated dreams. The creatures stopped being food, were money alone. The *Jody Dawn* became a crab-catching machine, its rhythm the hard rock that blared from the deck speaker.

When delivery time and blessed rest halted the crabbing machine temporarily, aches moved in like a tempest. In port however, their aches ignored, Seth and Mo headed at once to the Elbow Room for beers and then to a pizza shack. Seth might have announced a month before, after visiting his folks in California, that he was maybe engaged, and might have talked about it since, but he showed no further sign of commitment after meeting a girl who bossed one of the crab lines. She also found friends for Mo and Terry. Terry held back to make sure Odds didn't follow before joining them, but the Russian Church kept Odds from the bars. Although the small, old building opened only for services, a parishioner gave Odds a key, and he spent most hours in port—even in rainy dark—replacing weathered boards outside at his own expense.

At the plant, Hank endured John's presence as he waited for phone connections to Jody. Sometimes it never clicked. Alcohol had little savor. After each approximate week at sea the half dozen hours in port were too long without Jody, who once had sauntered the road here alongside him.

As autumn stormed in, night increased, seas towered higher in the dark, and hail slashed across lights. Water bubbled over deck as often as not. Hank needed to maneuver every minute to avoid seas that would sweep them. He drank ever more coffee and chewed countless antacids to keep down the coffee. Money, money, each hour another little chunk toward the million dollars still owed on *Jody Dawn*. Sometimes on deck, with everyone moving like zombies, rotten sea things came from the bottom and, led by Seth, they slammed them at each other, or broke into wild dances to the music. It restored adrenalin.

Life outside the boat existed less and less. The different warmths of Jody and the kids, the special new warmth of infant Pete, lay in limbo, comforts too distant to be real. Also other thoughts: John Gains slithering up the corporate ladder; Swede maybe threatened. Ivan and Steve became sputtering candles back safe in memory again. Occasionally he brooded on the arrested Korean captain, perhaps now being beaten? Another's reality, not his. He felt passing sad for it all. Then, suddenly, sun breaking through a cloud would pierce gold into the whitecaps, or sea birds in the dark would flash under deck lights, or a tumble of crabs would explode into shape and color. I'm in charge, it's happening because of me, he'd exult. This is my time, and this is my place!

He narrowed the gap between pots to six and a half minutes, then to six, taking turns on deck himself except in roughest weather when his helm had priority. In conscience once, after halting work when waves had snapped three lines in a row to pots now lost on the seafloor, and the deck slanted so that everything loose tumbled from side to side, he asked them around the galley table: "Want to slow down, guys?"

"But Boss," said Mo, "we're highlining."

Terry told a joke. They all laughed and then, except for Seth, who had the wheel, fell asleep where they sat.

PART II

1980–1981
BERING SEA,
ALASKA

8

Hank's Hole

"But it's an hour from town," said Jody. "And you just saw the road for yourself."

"Hour's run straight to heaven. Look at that view. After months at sea, that's how I want to see my water." The building site sloped down through great pine trees. He kicked at snow to clear a mat of fragrant needles. Trees and brush framed the bay. They blocked the shoreline and valanced the sky to confine the water like scenery in a picture. Kodiak town jutted like a peninsula miles away. Dock lights from the canneries sparkled under the gray March sky. "Smell that pine. And see those red berries? Get us a couple of big woofy dogs and never have to pen them. The kids'll love it."

"No electric line this far from town. And no water line."

Why doesn't she understand? he wondered. "We'll dig a well. Purest kind of water, good for the kids, no chemicals. And one thing the pioneers never had was a generator. We'll have enough electricity to party at midnight."

"And how will the kids get to school in the winter?"

"Four-wheel drive." His arm went around her shoulder. "Twenty acres, all to ourselves. Twenty acres! Just feel this solitude. Of course if you like, we can rent a room or two in town to stay over on bad nights. I guess we can afford that too, the way I'm scooping money from the crabs."

"Stay over, and leave the woofy dogs to eat berries?"

He laughed, glad she was joking. "Picture windows everywhere. Water view from the living room, fireplace in back. Bedrooms looking out

105

into the woods. Except maybe the master bedroom, put that upstairs looking over the water. Maybe a tower with windows in all directions. You'd
certainly go for that. Your own wheelhouse without getting wet."

"Steering where?"

"Shh." The real estate agent approached from the car, where she had
gone to fetch the plat. "Don't let on how turned on we are."

Two weeks later Hank flew back again from Dutch Harbor, having
left Seth to skipper for the last of the season's tanner crabs. He and Jody
signed the contract. To Hank's satisfaction he'd offered fifteen hundred
less and bargained a thousand reduction. He sketched plans for the house,
asking Jody what *she* wanted every step of the way. They included space in
the wet room for a washer and dryer, anticipating the time when a generator could power them. Windows were his special preoccupation—space
everywhere to look out and enjoy the surrounding beauty. A separate building would house the generator and workshop, and an open shed he'd build
himself would shelter off-season boat gear. An outhouse would have to do
for the time being of course (water view from the seat, through graceful
pine trunks), although he sketched in a proper bathroom and then, at Jody's
frown, a second one.

As soon as they signed the papers he rented a dozer, bumped it slowly two and a half hours from Kodiak over the potholed road, singing to
himself all the way, and cleared the house site of trees and scrub. Later he
rented a backhoe to scoop out enough foundation for drainage and even a
root cellar. Amazing, the skills he'd learned since coming to Alaska seventeen years ago as a greenhorn kid!

After bringing the *Jody Dawn* back from Dutch at the end of tanner
season—Seth could have done it, probably, but Hank could not admit this
to himself—he declared construction parties to lay foundation blocks, dig
privy holes, build sheds and such. Seth, Mo, and Terry all took it in sport,
gladly pitching in for endless beer and barbecue. Odds declined, always
with the self-deprecating smile that made it acceptable. He had his own
house and family in town to tend.

Henny and Dawn liked the place without question. The boy, nearly
five, stomped boots through slush and meltwater trailing his dad. Dawn, a
year younger, brought up the rear jealously, fussing at "Henry" (ignored)
to walk around puddles and behave. Tomboy like her mom, people said.

Pete, a toddler at one and a half, stayed close to his mother, unsure of the new surroundings. Jody tucked him under her arm like baggage as she moved from site to site. His little red boots kicked from behind and sometimes slipped off—they were Dawn's castoffs, still a size too large. Jody retrieved them from the mud and slipped them back on, often with more patience than she showed to the others.

At Jody's insistence they hired an architect to design the house despite Hank's confidence that he could do it himself. When construction began, he might have stayed to assist the contractor and save money, but it made sense to go for bigger money on the Bering Sea. By the time the *Jody Dawn* left harbor in August bound for Dutch, the new home had the definition of struts and rafters. He hated to leave. His hands wanted to saw boards and hammer nails. And could Jody supervise it, with her unnecessary new job career-counseling at the high school along with newly elected duties on town council? She had kids to raise! His wife didn't need to earn money. Almost half went to taxes on top of what he earned. Not quite half, with the state's amazing vote in April to cover all state income taxes with oil pipeline revenues. But still!

He watched harbor shapes recede until spruce-topped islands blocked all but white plumes rising from the fish plants. What a fool, to be leaving the crow of little Pete at every new sight, the chatter of Henny and Dawn splashing in his tracks, and Jody's warm smell and murmur in his tired arms at night.

At least the sun shone. The mountains of central Kodiak Island passed to starboard, vivid in the sweet-clear air. Little seiners worked the mouths and capes of the bays, Jones Henry's *Adele H* among them. Nets rose like sails on power blocks. He called Jones on the CB. "Partner! Catching any?"

"Seven brails last set," came Jones's wiry voice. "Five the one before. We ain't had time even to eat. Got to go, about to purse again. You keep count if you see Japs out there taking our fish."

Through binoculars Hank watched crews strain bulging moneybags of fish to the rail, could sense the flap of frenzied salmon around his legs. Why wasn't he there where he wanted to be! Yes, and back home. Tolly, buddy-riding to port aboard his *Star Wars Two*, radioed buoyantly, "Man, remember when we was stuck on those shitty little tubs, ass-deep in gurry every night pitching fish? And look at us now, riding free to the big money!"

Hank watched for logs washed to sea from a recent storm. Some bobbed treacherously just at the surface, hidden by any chop or swell. He remained alert but dreamed along. In a few more years Henny would be old enough to fish with his old man. Even now the kid's eyes caressed his daddy's boat. Once Hank had watched him—it made the world sing at the time—rub his cheek against the hull the way some children caress a kitten. But did he want to expose his beautiful boy to such danger? Well, by then they'd be so rich from crab that the old man could afford to seine peacefully, chasing the salmon from May to October, just scratching along if necessary, pulling into coves when rough weather hit, taking no chances whatever others might catch. And Dawn, sparky like her mom—couldn't leave her behind. A few years more, then Pete. Jody would cook. All-Crawford crew. By then he'd have cut Seth's umbilical, restored the dear guy's confidence that was still vulnerable to the lifeboat memory.

When they approached Three Saints Bay toward evening: "Time to party, man," radioed Tolly. "Have us a hunt and cookout, now the hens and storekeepers is left behind."

"Not for us. Long way to go."

If Hank had wanted to nurse his thoughts and avoid the guilt of pleasure away from his loved ones, he should have refused in an empty wheelhouse.

"That's a special place for my people, where the Russians first came," declared Odds, his swarthy face turning long. "Used to be a nice little Native village there called Nunamiut and a cannery. Be nice, to go in there."

"Hank," said Seth quietly, "It was all sort of a party, I guess, helping with your new house, but . . . you know?"

Hank glanced at their faces, all watching him gravely. Mean work awaited them. He turned his boat and radioed Tolly: "Race you in." The mood in the wheelhouse lightened at once. Hank did not need full power to arrive first at the shoals off Cape Liakik.

It was a comfortable bash. They made their beach fire on a sandspit, far enough in for safe harbor, but also far enough from stream mouths to avoid bears pawing the salmon that crowded to spawn. Seth and some of

Tolly's crew made a stab at hunting since they had rifles that needed exercise. It was off-season, but that was a rule made for tourists, and who was to see, or care with such abundance of the wilds? Insects discouraged them more than the law. The black flies bit like piranhas, while gnats fine as powder, when breathed in, set them coughing. Seth and the others soon returned with a shrug after firing a few rounds, and added wetted branches to the fire "to smoke them nippin' fuckers."

Above them, almost against their noses, towered the high jagged peaks that from sea provided a coastal landmark. "Ghosts up there watching us," said Odds. "Maybe they're called the Saints, but more up there watches than just saints." No one offered him a beer, and Hank noted gladly that he passed the cooler without a glance. Odds and Jeff, a fellow-Aleut crewman from Tolly's boat, took off through brush near the beach, barking like dogs to warn off bears and oblivious to the insects.

"Now how's a bear go?" whispered Terry. "Row-row-row, something like that? And a ghost? Maybe whoo-whoo-whoo. I'm just goin' to sneak around the other way and—"

"Sit down." Hank made it a command. "They'd likely shoot first and then look. Leave 'em alone."

"You want to make a joke of everything," groused Seth. "You ever get serious?" Terry grinned, and shrugged.

Mo and his friend Ham from the *Star Wars Two*, boxing and drinking buddies ashore—their present live-in girlfriends even looked alike—tossed a football between them. Soon they were aiming the ball like a bullet to see who could zero hardest at the other.

Seth, and Tolly's counterpart deck boss, Walt, waded in to their hips and snagged a few chum salmon still fresh enough from open sea to have firm flesh. From a spit over the fire delicious smells of searing fish skin blew along the beach.

The two skippers set an example and drank sparingly. Hank lay back, slapping flies usually before they bit, and gazed at blue sky and raw, striated rock. The sun in early afternoon had already disappeared from the narrow valley. It was all going right—boat, family, house—yet he felt clouded. Tolly chatted beside him on the relative virtues of Jennifer and some new girl he'd met in a bar. "I mean, take Jenny, we party fine in every way. But the woman has a temper. What if we married and she turned all temper? I've seen enough of that, man. Not that I'm ready to tie any knots. There's crabs to catch, you know? But Linda now, she's sweet all the time. And she laughs a lot. Smells bad down around her snatch if you know what I mean, but . . . What do *you* think?" Hank grunted noncommittal wisdom.

Terry waded in to snag more fish. He watched the spawners swim thick against his legs, suddenly threw his rod ashore and announced: "I'm goin' to catch one of these fellers with my bare hands. Who bets? Twenty bucks anybody!"

"Twenty, you got it," said Mo and Ham, each without a break in their tossing stride. "Twenty, you got it," called Hank, and Tolly echoed it. Seth shook his head, finally muttered, "Sure, twenty, don't drown."

The struggle made even the football tossers stop to watch. Terry disappeared twice under water, jumped up spitting and cursing. "Oh shit it's cold," he announced merrily. "I got to do it soon or my balls'll disappear in my gut." The third immersion took so long that Hank rose, and Seth started toward the water. Slowly Terry's head and shoulders emerged, his wet face a study of sly pleasure. Step by step he waded to shore. His arms locked a big chum salmon against his chest. "Shhh, don't wiggle, shoo baby, shooo. I got bucks ridin' on yoooou."

"He'll slip you yet," said Mo. "Thumb him in the gills."

"Naah, she's my *friend*, name's Alice, ain't goin' to hurt my Alice. Back she goes after I collect my bucks." Suddenly the fish thrashed its strong tail and slithered up past Terry's cheek like a popped cork, over his shoulder. Terry grabbed and lost his footing. Seth hurried in, offered a hand, and pulled him back up.

They had trouble through their laughs settling whether the bet had been won or lost. But Terry could not stop shivering. Hank rowed him back to the boat, made him peel down and wrap in blankets, and brewed hot tea.

Odds and Jeff returned triumphantly. Odds held a rotten sliver of board with a trace of gold paint that he declared must have been part of an icon in an old Orthodox church. "Father Rostinoff back home, he'll bless it I know and he'll probably put it on the altar. The couple times I come over here from Old Harbor with my cousins in their motorboat, I never found this. It means good luck today, good luck for the whole trip I bet."

They stayed through a full day, and might have lingered longer—

Tolly's boat had enough beer to keep it going, and once Hank gave in he relaxed—if a heavy wind hadn't scooped down from the mountains. Williwaws might follow to trap them.

Back at sea, the sparkling blue water of their Kodiak departure turned to roiling gray. A half mile out, the Three Saints peaks disappeared in wet haze. During the next day the rest of Kodiak Island and then the Shumagins passed only as traces on the radar. Everyone turned sluggish and slept except the watch. The urge to sleep extended day and night as the boat left the islands and plunged through busy water off the mountainous spine of the mainland. Once the sky cleared briefly to reveal the snowy cones of Pavlov and other dormant volcanoes. Wisps of smoke trailed from one. The smoke soon blended with clouds and the cones slipped back into hiding.

The volcanoes pulled Hank from his ease. Brief window onto violence. It waits on land and water around me, he realized. Remember the hours it took Terry to stop shivering after (as they all finally conceded) he'd caught his fish. He clocked emergency steps in his mind. Then, with a grunt, he short-blasted the deck siren and timed his men. Seth appeared in the wheelhouse first, pulling on one boot, squinting to hide the panic that Hank knew lurked ever since the lifeboat. None took more than a minute to appear despite coming from full sleep.

"Fire in the galley. What? Quick!"

Terry yawned. "Come on, Boss, I was just there. You know if it was real we could —"

"I said fire!" His tone made it frightening. They scrambled for hoses and extinguishers. Then he put them through man overboard and abandon ship, timing each. He watched critically—Terry small and quick, Odds and Mo large and deliberate, Seth driven, but all engaged as a team—and felt reassured. But: "Bunch of ass-draggers!" He blasted the siren. "It's fire again, this time lazarette. Move!" The second time around they quickened each response, and the third time cut further seconds. The drills energized them, and for a few hours the wheelhouse turned bright with Terry's joking.

Next day they reached Unimak Pass and entered the Bering Sea, appropriately with a sudden blow that scudded foam across gray waves. Hank began plotting his crab chase. Jody and the kids became a wraparound for sleep alone, thinned from the everyday.

In Dutch Harbor he loaded pots from his storage site alongside Tolly's. The two boats worked at the same wharf, it seemed at the same pace, but Hank gave Seth a nod. Quietly, so as not to draw attention, they drove to cut seconds off the load-time for each big square cage. Then, when Tolly's crew quit to sleep at 2 A.M. in the dark, Hank, with only a three-quarter load, slipped mooring and headed to sea.

"Done it again, Boss," crowed Mo. "On to Hank's Hole, right?"

"Shhh," Hank laughed, both proud and ashamed of himself.

Odds shook his head. "Your best buddy, our buddy boat. That ain't right."

"Tolly's guys worked on me about your famous Hole, back at Three Saints," said Terry. "I gave 'em loran coordinates."

"You *what*?"

"How do you know my coordinates?" demanded Hank. Now he'd have to fire the guy, automatic rule of the docks, and he'd trained Terry, liked him.

"I don't. It's your secret, you lock us out of the wheelhouse at Hank's Hole times. But it ain't way up to the Misty Moon Banks, is it? That's the only coordinates I know to give somebody, from a time with the halibut."

Hank laughed with relief.

"That ain't right either," said Odds. "Trick our buddies."

Seth ground knuckles into Terry's thick hair. "You are *some* fucker, you!" Terry ducked and laughed.

Mo, a head taller than Terry, lifted him and danced around the wheel-house. "And this fish-hugger just cost me twenty bucks besides. What'll I do with him, Boss?"

"Put me down."

"Boss? He wiggles like a fish. What'll I do with him?"

Before Hank could think of a funny answer Terry punched straight up into Mo's face. Mo cried out and dropped him, then stood bewildered, mopping blood.

Terry's voice was calm and even. "I'm sure sorry if I hurt you, Mo. My body ain't a playground. I'll fight you later, ashore, if you're mad, but I don't want to."

Hank quickly grabbed paper towels and handed them to Mo. "Go down and put ice on it."

"I'll get him ice." Terry slipped away.

"Be damned," said Seth. "Terry's always fun, like a kid. You all right, Mo?"

"Sure. I just done wrong, forget it. Terry's okay."

"Good," said Hank, relieved again. Crew fighting was a quick way down, and he liked each too much to get rid of either.

Terry hurried back with the ice wrapped in a towel. He gave it to Mo with one hand and lightly punched his arm with the other.

"It's okay, man," said Mo. "Thanks." He alone faced aft. Suddenly "Hey! *Star Wars'* deck lights just clicked off. He's unmoored, Boss, he's after us."

They crowded by the after window. Indeed, Tolly was in pursuit. As soon as Hank left the cannery zone he increased speed. They whooped as the boat thudded into heading waves. Water fanned from the bow to crash against the front windows. Mo tentatively patted Terry's shoulder. "Oh man, don't you call this the life?" Terry pounded Mo's back.

The *Star Wars Two*'s running lights began to swoop as Tolly also left harbor and gunned ahead. After a few miles, on the VHF: "Pretty sly, baby. But Tolly's on to you." Hank bit his lip, and despite his men's expectant looks did not reply. Within an hour Tolly's boat had grown smaller. *Star Wars Two was* underpowered. Hank at last picked up his microphone. "See you in a few days, babe. By the way, don't bother with any coordinates your spies might have picked up around the campfire." Tolly answered with cheerful obscenities.

By morning twilight Tolly was a speck on the horizon. When at last they had opened the distance beyond even radar range Hank adjusted course approximately toward Hank's Hole, and went below for Mo's traditional pre-crabbing steak dinner.

Sixty miles out, radar blips announced vessels ahead. By the time lights began to blink and enlarge against the overcast horizon, the head wind's clean briny odors bore the taint of fish under steam. "Only gook factory ships stink like that," observed Seth. "You mean we haven't kicked them all back home yet?"

"Guess not," said Hank. He scanned through binoculars as they closed. Several boats had the same cut as their own, with running lights that rose and disappeared in the swells. Only one cluster of lights, higher

and more numerous than the others, blinked steadily from the large outline
of a ship. "I think it's one of those things they're calling joint ventures.
Americans catch the fish and sell to the foreigners who can't catch them
anymore themselves."

"Americans, catch those crappy whatchamacallits? Pollack?" Seth
pulled off his cap—it advertised a local marine supplier—scratched his
tumble of straw-blond hair, and replaced it. A bald spot had begun to open
on the back of his head. "Two, three cents a pound for mushy little slime-
fish, not even big ones, when crabs bring a buck and more, things you
know you've got fuckin' food in your hand when you catch 'em? Don't
make sense. People say you gotta grow with the times, but some kind of
growing that is. Glad nobody's hoodwinked *us* on that one."

"Well . . . more like nine cents these days," said Hank. "High volume,
all those little fish, there could be money in it."

"Drag through the mud when you got nice big crabs," laughed Mo.
"Count us out, eh Boss?"

Pause. "Yup."

Jimmy Seegar, on the *Sea Challenger* out of Kodiak, raised him on
the CB. "You joining our JV, Hank?"

"Not a chance. How're you doing?"

"Worst decision I ever made. It's all scratch. Who said there was
goddamn pollack here for the taking? Bureaucrats, that's who. They lied.
We can barely keep this hungry Korean sonofabitch fed, this factory, and
they're gettin' restless. I'd of switched to pots gear three weeks ago and be
goin' for crab, but we signed a contract."

"That's rough," said Hank, but thought: *I'd* find fish. You need the
guts to search.

"Ever targeted pollack before, Hank?"

"Never. Never groundfish. I take it you're scanning through the
whole water column, not just the bottom?"

An accented voice interrupted. "American fisher-boat? New fisher-
boat? You have fish for us?" Hank answered in the negative. "How about
girlie-magazine? You have new girlie-magazine?"

"Oh, Mr. Sun, your boys are in luck," said Jimmy. His voice was not
friendly, although he made it seem so. "This new boat, no fish, but three
big, big whore-girlie from Kodiak want to come on board and play kissie-
kissie. You put down ladder?"

"Ohhh." The Asian voice caressed the sound from high in the throat. Then, barked orders over the speaker.

"Oh shit," laughed Jimmy. "First fun I've had in a month." A Jacob's ladder clattered down the rusty side of the ship, and faces in hardhats peered from above. "One of your apes wouldn't have a dress to put on, Hank?"

Hank throttled to speed. His opinion would only make an enemy on the Kodiak docks. "Got to go, Jimmy. Making a rendezvous. Good luck."

"New boat wish to come port-side instead starboard-side?" said the Asian voice anxiously. "No problem, you come."

"Pull out of it, Mr. Sun," said Jimmy, annoyed. "No fish, no girlie-girlie. Just my friend. Hang up. Good-bye."

"Hell," said Seth as they left the fleet astern. "I bet we'd have got Terry to go along if we'd had a dress. Anything to trick a gook, eh?"

Hank remained silent.

Throughout the day, and the night that followed, he called the crew occasionally to set prospector pots, and marked their location on the chart. At ten the following morning he folded the chart, and declared to the four lounging in the wheelhouse: "It's time, guys. Scoot." Mo, Terry, and Odds tumbled below obediently. Only Seth lingered, and frowned back. "Maybe I'll tell you next year," Hank soothed as he closed the wheelhouse door behind them and locked it. He brought out the specially marked chart from his padlocked bunk drawer, and adjusted course toward his Hole.

They all knew the routine. Mo left lunch on a tray at the door. Without prompting they readied the deck, emptied frozen herring into the tub, and began to fill bait cans. The loran coordinates closed. The depth sounder showed his Hole just where it had always been, some ten fathoms deeper than the rest of the seafloor around it, no more than a hundred fifty feet wide. On deck under Seth's careful direction, they lowered nine of the heavy pots slowly, one by one—easing them down attached to the hauler block rather than heaving them over the side as usual. Hank sang under his breath. Wind and chop did their best to drive him off course, but the *Jody Dawn* answered each twitch of his throttle like a mistress. He hovered her where he chose.

After filling the Hole he cruised the area setting prospector pots in other locations and marked them on the secret chart. One of the prospects, checked after soaking only an hour, came up with twelve keeper males. On the strength of it he set the rest of his deck load, some hundred pots, into a string. He'd milk the Hole and graze besides.

He could picture his prey a mile of fathoms below, in murk that barely brightened under rare full sun. Piles of sluggish giants awakened. They sidled toward the scent of food, claws quivering in expectation. They crawled through the funneled entrance, barely squeezed through the opening at the end perhaps trampling others in their greed. But when they reached the perforated bait can, ah—betrayal. It oozed savory oils but held the food tight. (Hell, even condemned prisoners got a last meal.) Only the luckiest crab figured its way back out through the tunnel. Greed had changed the destiny of Big John Crab—no, be fair, nature's drive to eat and survive—from predator of the deep, snatching his pleasure with deadly claws, to lumps in a salad. "If you eat-a me then I'll eat-a you," Hank sang. All creatures lived off each other. His luck to be top of the food chain, head species. Even if he turned holy and vegetarian, Nature wouldn't change.

Three hours later they raised pots from the Hole. King crabs packed each of the big cages so tight that soon some might have suffocated. Claws protruded from the mesh, sluggishly gripping at space. Each load tumbled to deck, all males, their spiny purple carapaces grand as alarm clocks. No cull necessary.

"Done it again, Boss," called Terry. "We are *hot*!"

Back down went the pots. Like picking apples from a tree so full it needed only a shake. A half dozen more such hauls from the Hole, along with any luck from the string he'd set, would fill their hold, send them to Dutch with the debutante load of the new season, first price, while other boats were still days from delivering. Two seasons of this would pay the rest of the *Jody Dawn*, a third and he'd own the new house with mortgage kissed into smoke. Wouldn't hurt to buy a condo in Hawaii instead of renting on their winter break.

"Boss! Look to port."

Silhouettes lined the horizon, vessels bigger than the *Jody Dawn*. They were spaced evenly, moving in his direction from the area of his prospect string—eleven radar blips, one larger than the others. His song stopped. He gunned the boat toward them, not sure what he planned to do. Binoculars picked out Asian characters on one rusty housing. The ships advanced on him like an army. By shortwave he raised Coast Guard operations in Kodiak. "There's a whole fleet of Orientals, Jap or Korean, trawlers I guess, dragging the hell where I've laid my crab pots. In *American* waters—I'm not outside two hundred miles." Reluctantly he gave his position.

"They probably have a GIFA," said the duty lieutenant. "Wait one I'll check."

"Giffa? Giffa? What the hell?"

"Governing International Fishery Agreement, sir. Wait one. Yeah, here. *Kashima Maru*, that's the name of the mothership. Japanese. You're a registered crabber, right? You should be receiving directives from the Commerce Department that show where Japan can fish its GIFAs. Looks like you're not in one of the regular crabbing zones that's protected."

"I'm in the waters of my own fucking country! And what was the fight to get the foreigners off our fish if they're still here?" He knew the answer, bitterly. State Department was trading fish for Sonys, as Jones Henry and others called it. He riffled through a packet of government announcements still in their envelopes. Jody had scribbled "Read this" across one of them. A Japanese factory fleet, goddamnit, fishing his very grounds with permission!

The announcement included the mothership's radio frequency. He called it. "*Kashima Maru, Kashima Maru*. This is *Jody Dawn*, American crab boat. You are fishing in an area where I have laid my gear, my crab pots. Orange buoys, orange buoys. Do you hear?" Only static in reply, and the faint sound of voices speaking what sounded to Hank like Japanese on their boat-to-boat frequency. The ships advanced in formation like an army of reapers, fishing grids with Japanese efficiency. Their nets would be spread across the bottom, dragging every inch of the seafloor along the total swath of their line.

The *Jody Dawn* reached one of the prospector pots just as a high rusty bow brushed it aside and then traveled over it. The ships had already overrun part of the string. Hank blew his siren, shouted over the deck speaker and the radio simultaneously "Stop! You're riding my gear, orange buoys, stop!"

The closest ship blasted its whistle. A man on the bridge waved him away urgently. Others appeared on the bow, shouting and gesturing. Hank nosed his boat away from the advancing hull. His men on deck shouted up curses and waved their fists. Mo grabbed a rotten sea object from the scupper, and threw it skillfully to arc over the high bow. At this, the Japanese began throwing dead fish. One turned a pressure hose on them.

"Do something to 'em, Boss!" cried Mo.

Seth turned wild. He disappeared into the cabin and came out with his rifle. Before the others could obey Hank's cry to stop him, he fired up at the Japanese who screamed and scattered. Hank's only course was to throttle ahead and run Seth out of range.

He went to the last of his string. "Bring them aboard," he shouted, his voice now hoarse. "Stack, don't take time to empty, save what we can." In rough sea with water foaming across deck, they needed to lash each pot to the rail. It took precious time. The heavy steel cages, weighing now some two thousand pounds each with crab inside, suddenly shifted. Seth cried out, his hand mashed. A Japanese voice barked over the radio, "American pirate, American pirate, murder-man, I report you to State Department, go home!" They managed thirteen pots before the trawlers bore down too close.

Hank raced ahead to his Hole. Seth, his hand dripping blood, stayed with the work even though Hank told him to go inside. They pulled up six of their pots, already half full, but needed to abandon the other three. Seth was crying from pain and frustration. Hank set course away from the ships and hove to only when miles separated them.

When the fleet had become distant silhouettes—although the stench of rendered fish blew back obscenely—Hank returned to his Hole. It had disappeared, filled by the trawls plowed over it. Hundreds of creatures lay caged and buried. Would others uncaught struggle their way up through silt to open seafloor, or die coffined like their mates?

All in all they lost over a hundred crab pots, each worth about three-hundred dollars, let alone the harvest gone. Saved were two pots whose straps and buoys had survived the trawlers' drag over the string. By the time they were raised, the pots contained some fifty large males each. Discovered and lost in a day were grounds of wondrous productivity. All the lost pots now lay dead on the seafloor with lines snapped and no way to recover them, traps to hold crabs prisoner until they starved.

Hank called the Coast Guard in Kodiak. "We've had an incident."

"So we've been informed." The speaker was now the base commander, and his tone was stiff.

"They destroyed our gear. One of our men's injured. Did the Jap . . . the Japanese . . . claim any . . . ?"

"Urge give no details over open frequency. Return to Dutch Harbor. Give your ETA. People from Washington are leaving tonight to meet you there."

Hank became equally formal in the style of his Navy days. "Read you. Twenty hours ETA depending on weather." He glanced at Seth who was in the wheelhouse with the others. Seth's hand was wrapped in ice, yet he was oiling his shotgun. "Got a man here with hand crushed. Request medical help meet us at the pier."

"I'll so relay."

When the messages had ended, Seth looked up and said evenly: "I didn't mean but to scare them. But those fuckers had it coming if I hit one."

"I hope they see it that way."

It was only after Hank had set return course, with seas thrashing the hull and night wrapped around them, that he realized he was trembling.

9

THE GREAT GAME

S eth's scattershot had nicked the arm of the man with the deck hose, and had driven a leak into the hose itself. Since both vessels were pitching, he could not have placed the bullets deliberately. But then, with different luck a man might be dead.

"You think you're a cowboy?" the lawyer sent by the State Department coldly demanded. "We're charging attempted murder." A delegate from the Japanese Embassy, who had accompanied him from Washington, nodded vigorously, his eyes aflame like a warrior in a samurai movie. There was no way to keep John Gains, the Asshole, out of it. He gravely attached himself to the Japanese, and offered translations.

The conference of officials, behind closed doors, took four hours. It scared the waiting Seth sufficiently that he wrote an apology with oriental flourishes added by the lawyer and Gains. After their urgent private coaching (with a muttered "do it!" from Hank), Seth even exchanged bows with the Japanese delegate, offered to pay for the hose and any medical bills, and requested that his apologies be conveyed to the man he'd shot. His bruised hand had one finger broken, now splinted.

The Japanese Embassy man turned cordial at once. The *Kashima Maru* deeply regretted the unintentional destruction of American gear, he announced, and its company wished to compensate the captain fully for the loss. More bows.

Hank did not escape that easily. Before it was over, State forced him to go to Anchorage to settle the matter, and saw to a fifteen-thousand-dollar fine. And while months later a bank draft in yen reached Kodiak for the

121

cost of the lost gear, it helped not at all in Dutch Harbor during the frenzy
of a September opening. He had indeed delivered a partial holdful of king
crabs before any other boat, and received a good price for it—thank heav-
en Swede Scorden now ran the front office and quickly produced a bottle
from his desk drawer. But Swede put it straight: "Ask me for any advance
or loan. But there's no damn pots for love or sale."

The *Jody Dawn* was impounded until settlement—Seth might have
skippered it for a run—so that the hearing and red tape cost him an entire
precious nine days off the grounds in a season that lasted little more than a
month. His ace, Hank's Hole, had been destroyed, and he now faced fishing common grounds with fewer pots than any other boat.

"Well, chalk it up to being as secretive and greedy as the foreigners,"
snapped Jody over the phone. He had expected her to be indignant for him.
Surely the old Jody on deck would have plotted secret grounds and yelled
insults at foreigners with the rest. But then she turned soothing, told him
they'd manage, and made him promise to stay cool.

His desire to hold her was overwhelming. "I'm catching tomorrow's
flight home for a couple of days."

"The hell you are. We can't afford it. Go catch some crabs." But as
the Anchorage stay became protracted, she left the children with Adele and
flew up for the weekend. They watched expenses carefully—he'd rented
the cheapest room despite its shabbiness—but she had not been so tender
and reassuring since the birth of Pete.

In Dutch Harbor the authorities permitted the crew to load what pots
they had still stored. Seth then moored the *Jody Dawn* out of the way at a
far end of the cannery pier. He stayed on board, refusing invitations to
drink at the Elbow Room. After the enforced apology he paced the empty
wheelhouse muttering to himself.

With no work required of him, Odds quietly disappeared into the
Native community. Ever since his volunteer work on the little Orthodox
church, doors in the village had opened to him and he had become, in fact,
an unofficial courier between this congregation and the one in Kodiak.

Mo and Terry had energy to squander. Now closer friends since the
punching incident, they took work together on the crab butchering line.
They competed during the entire twelve-hour shift to see who was faster at
pulling apart the big crustaceans. They needed to press the carapaces

between a rigid apron each wore and a chest-high iron wedge, then grip the legs (avoiding the slow but vicelike claws) and snap out hands in opposite directions. The execution was messy but quick. Crab offal covered their faces, more than the other workers who knew that the job paid the same hourly wage whatever their speed. (The workers in any case lacked the stamina and spirit of men who enjoyed hefting heavy gear on a pitching deck.) The foreman soon realized he had a bargain. He assigned them their own bin when the others complained of the flying mess. But: "Hose your faces now and then," he warned. "That shit can give you rash."

As soon as the morning plane from Anchorage returned Hank from his costly stay, he headed for the cannery office with papers to release his boat. The route led past the butchering bins. Waving aside a bright "Yo!" from Mo and Terry, with a frown at purple-red rashes that covered their faces and arms, he told them to get the others wherever they were and prepare to sail. They called after him to watch something but he waved it aside and hurried on. The route took him between the steaming cookers that emitted odors of hot crab and ammonia, then through the shaker lines where rock music dinned around setfaced men and women who banged crab legs to extract the meat. He averted his eyes. The sight of his harvest creatures dismembered gave him no pleasure.

At the office while waiting for the marshal he burst through Swede's door to vent himself. Swede must have seen him coming, and held out a shot of whiskey. Hank remained standing, started to gulp it, pushed it aside. "Did you hear what they did to me? That State Department bastard prolonged it up there on purpose."

"The 6 A.M. flight cleared your head I see."

"And that asshole John, sucking along with them. You might have pulled rank and told him to get lost."

"Sit, Crawford. I mean it. Your boat can wait another ten minutes." Swede walked over and locked his door. He had grown heavier over the years, no longer lean and darting. "Start with this and stick it in your craw. Your former deck ape John Gains is now my boss. The Japs take him regularly to Tokyo and they gave him corporate standing over there. He knows the game as if he'd invented it. Took courses in the language, all that, so in the top office they jabber along in Jap and leave me behind. Continue with this. He saved your Seth's ass from jail." Back at his desk he drank his own shotful, then Hank's besides, and returned the bottle to the drawer. "The man's not my friend. But he cashed in credits on this one. We had management around the table with State's lawyer and the Jap embassy man, and our own Jap brass. Everybody who counted—I didn't—wanted a crucifixion but Gains. You don't shoot at Jap fishermen these days. Should have done it to Koreans, nobody jumps for them. You say Gains sucked? Damn hard he did, Jap ass, federal ass, to save your boy. The man's a politician. Knows how to kiss. This time he did it for you."

Hank slowly took a seat.

"You think our peanut farmer in the White House wants an international showdown over a few fish? Two months to election, with hostages in Teheran and Russians in Afghanistan to explain? Happy Japs, happy trade, that's the State Department's mission here, not some Alaskan yokel's crab pots in the Bering Sea. You bet they slapped you. They meant to make your *Jody Dawn* the example to the fleet in case anybody else tried to be a hero. They'd planned double that fine, your boat impounded for the entire season, and jail for Seth, before your asshole John got sucking."

Hank fingered his beard, sorry he'd given up the shot. "I'm stupider than I'd realized."

"That's news. You're cannon fodder, Crawford. You're nothing but Rosenkrantz and Guildenstern, to put it your educated way." Swede produced the bottle again, and held it out with a raised eyebrow. He looked tired. Hank accepted. "If you haven't been reading *National Fisherman* or listening to Jones—who's prejudiced but has it clear—shall I tell you what's happening?"

"Yeah. See if you can make me love it, to lose gear to Jap factory machines. To watch American boats scrape bags of shitfish to sell to Koreans."

"Our famous two-hundred-mile law three years ago? It gave Americans all the fish and crab they could catch within the limits of sustaining healthy stocks."

"Save your kindergarten. Don't forget I went to Washington and helped lobby for that. I know all of it. And I know too fucking well how we gave in to State Department garks so they could give away the leftovers that we can't catch. But to dodge foreigners on my own grounds the way I had to before the law? And now with no recourse! We've lost half of what we fought for."

"Well, you do pay attention. You just don't understand. King crab? Americans like you already controlled it, and you've siphoned more and more tanner crab each year to reduce the surplus there that foreigners might take. But the pollack! Those mighty schools of pollack out there we call groundfish, that crab-spoiled Americans like you think you're too good to catch? They're now the big poker chips. Diplomats trade 'em for favors. Have you been so busy with new boat and babies and crabs that you find that news?"

"Just say your piece, Swede."

"Well now, the ones who get front choice for the surplus groundfish are the ones who once made the biggest investment to rape us in the first place, since they also happen to be the most strategic. Russia in some waters, but around here especially Japan, as Jones Henry who fought at Guadalcanal will tell you five times a day. Korea and Taiwan are nothing but little brothers, we just throw them leftovers. That's why Koreans play this joint venture business. They don't have enough pollack quota themselves to keep their rusty factory ships pumping. They have to buy from American boats. There's where joint ventures are good and you should be out there. You can make your mistakes in a new fishery at their expense."

"The JV Americans I've talked to out there scrape dirt. They're the ones losing, not the Koreans."

"But the product's there and it won't always be loss. You seem ignorant of the stakes. They're high. Fish by the million-ton. It's true, pioneers up here sometimes make the first moves and lose out. Twenty years ago I did that as you know, but going broke didn't kill me." Swede poured two more shots, drank his, poured another, then put away the bottle. "The best pioneers with balls survive to run the new show." He gulped the second shot, and added sourly: "Or the ones with luck. You have luck."

Hank gripped his shot without drinking it, and looked toward the door. The place smelled of ammonia from the crab vats below. Time to be on the water. Did Swede routinely drink this much before noon? There had been talk of his wife leaving him or at least living a separate life in Seattle. The lines in Swede's face, once leathery and sharp, had begun to puff. But his voice was focused as ever.

"JVs are the writing on the wall for foreigners. I'll repeat. They're the way for Americans to gear up and learn to handle groundfish without waiting for a domestic market that doesn't exist. Pollack in factory quantities makes fish paste, not an American product." Swede tapped his glass on the desk. "But it's money, Crawford, money in Asia. Start watching our Japanese brothers. They play a busy game. I'd say they're winning. To start, they have enough fish quota from Jimmy's State Department to fill their motherships, so they have nothing to do with joint ventures. Why help Americans learn to catch more of the fish they think they own, when they have the quota from us to catch it themselves? The more Americans find ways to catch, the more the Japs lose. Is that news to you?"

"I've been putting it together a different way."

"There's a game in progress. Russia's invested in JVs, but since they invaded Afghanistan, Carter's trying to freeze any fish quotas they've counted on from us. It's easy politics. Very popular. Forget that, from what I hear, the Russians have dealt honorably with American boats delivering to them off Oregon and Washington. The Koreans up here don't have the same good reputation. Some say they're trying to make their JVs fail, after which they might capture more quota. Bet on it, they and our Jap brothers are licking their lips at the prospect of that quota that Russia might lose, because somebody else will get it and they're the likely somebody.

"And the game continues. Our own company, the Jap-owned company I work for that used to be American, which indirectly you can thank for that drink you're holding, wallows in yen and plots to set up a groundfish plant here in Dutch Harbor in case Americans like you finally decide to gear for groundfish and push them off the grounds. You see how they've already bought into the king crabs they no longer catch here because Americans can take them all? They buy them from you and make the larger profit on the processing. We Japs—I'm one of 'em now—we're smart enough to cover ourselves however it blows. You going to drink that shot or not? Here, I'll take it."

Hank gulped the whiskey to avoid handing it over, and rose.

"To be fair, pollack die of old age like everything else. They might as well be caught for somebody's food. It's up to Americans to cash in. Some are interested. There's money from places besides Asia, like Christiana Bank in Oslo, to encourage building so-called American factory ships. The great international game here is no longer crab. Remember I warned you to get ready for groundfish?"

"Okay, okay, I took your advice and put extra power on *Jody Dawn*. But my guys hate the idea."

Swede held up his hand. "Since when does your crew jerk you around? Spare me excuses. Go. Get out. It's crab time. Boats are coming in plugged. Go catch your share."

Walking in a chilly dream, Hank took time to buy a bottle of the best Scotch ($115 at Dutch Harbor prices) and called on John Gains. The man now lodged in an office guarded by a secretary, reached through a private entrance and removed from the processing noise and smells. The secretary announced him, then pointed to a chair. Fifteen minutes later, biting back resentment, Hank had begun to write a note when John came from his office with an impersonal "Yes, uh, Hank?" Everything about him was in place from shined shoes to narrow tie knotted close to the neck.

"I understand Seth and I have reason to thank you."

Faintest of smiles. "Call it shipmates." He refused the bottle. "Thanks, but that's unnecessary. Excuse me, a meeting's in progress. Wish I could talk. Try another time. An appointment's best. Hope your luck improves." At the door he turned. "Incidentally, the *Kashima Maru* has moved its fleet to another area. They don't want gear conflicts any more than you do."

Hank left, unsatisfied and tense. He passed back through the plant. Mo and Terry still worked the butchering line. "Didn't I tell you we're going?" he exploded.

"Easy Boss," said Terry. "We sent the word to Odds and Seth. But we got to wait for the nurse back from lunch to give us enough salve for a week out there. This crab shit's bad for the skin."

"And now, Boss," declared Mo, "we want you to just watch for a minute. It's a bet we got riding. Which of us you think tears apart a crab cleanest? Just watch."

"That's no business of mine!" Hank shouted as he strode away. "Get to the boat if you want to crew for me."

"Ahh Boss, we'll be there," called Terry. "Little surprise waiting for you."

When Hank reached the *Jody Dawn*, indeed, his load of pots filled the deck three tiers high, more than he thought they still owned.

Seth, alone on the *Jody Dawn*, had heard a thump on deck a week before. He looked out to see a crewman from the *Midnight Sun* securing his boat alongside. As Seth watched, the *Sun*'s crane began to swing crab pots over, and its crew quietly lashed them to those on the *Jody Dawn*'s deck.

Arnie Larsen worked the controls from his bridge. "Hey," called Seth, "you think we're a barge or something?"

"Get your ass on deck and give a hand. Then maybe we take you for target practice so you get one or two in the head next time instead of a fuckin' arm and hose, eh?" A Norwegian "har-har" followed. The *Midnight Sun* donated seventeen pots.

Tolly's boat followed. "Give me the fuckin' slip, would you?" he called gaily. "Well, we didn't know you was going to a Jap shootout or we'd have followed harder. You are *some* fucker, man. We love you." He donated fifteen pots, and announced: "We got a secret receiver in one of 'em. Gives us your position wherever you go. You figure out which. But first we got to six-pack you, man."

Seth shook his head. It turned out, in fact, that Seth had become the hero of the fleet. Others came down to urge him ashore for toasts. He refused them all.

Four other boats had donated an approximate dozen pots each. The *Jody Dawn* needed only to change markings on the buoys. Seth had spent his time doing it.

Meanwhile, at the Elbow Room, the landmark drinking hole ("too near the church, really bad," observed Odds, who looked away whenever he passed the busy door), a box appeared on the bar labeled "Jody Dawn." It did not collect quarters like most donation boxes, but fifty- and hundred-dollar bills. By the time Hank put to sea again, a fifth of his fine had been collected.

10

NIGHTRIDE

Hank had barely found the crab again before Terry's gurry rash crept into his eyes and Mo's rash began to suppurate over his face. It was necessary to take them back to Dutch Harbor—sheepish and apologetic but frightened—for medevac to Anchorage.

Hank hired replacements from a dozen hopefuls living in tents and shacks who, once radio word had traveled, waited to catch his lines at the pier. The two newcomers needed breaking in despite their enthusiasm. They tried doggedly to keep up with Seth and Odds, but lacked the stamina. Meanwhile, Seth's splintered finger slowed him for jobs like coiling. Hank tensely controlled his need to push. Stupid injuries on board would affect insurance and rob them further of time on the grounds. They fished more slowly and delivered less crab.

Mo and Terry had returned from the hospital in time for the eight-inch season around Egg Island. The greenhorns were toughened by then, but they still ran continually weary under Hank's drive. Yet with experience gained they could now barter a berth on an easier boat, and they seemed relieved to go. Hank's team was intact again. They fished to their endurance limit. With half the king crab season lost or compromised, season's highliner was a gone dream, merely catching up the reality.

They had fished three days around Egg Island with no more than four hours' sleep a night, and Hank himself, ever plotting to outwit the crabs, had slept only one hour in the past thirty. Suddenly both the VHF and the sideband channels paged him urgently, Swede on one and John Gains on the other. Gains made contact first. "Come to port immediately, prepared for flight to Anchorage." And from Swede moments later: "Hank, your kid's in the Anchorage hospital. I'll have a car dockside. They'll hold the afternoon flight as long as they can."

"Which one? Which one? How serious?"

"Don't know any of this. Sorry. Sorry."

It was two-year-old Pete.

With enough rooms in the new house finished and Hank's income diminished, Jody had moved there a month before to save money rather than renew the lease on the rented place in town. It made mornings hectic. Three children needed to be readied for nursery school or daycare before starting the long drive to town over roads that were unpaved in places. An hour's commute in dry weather, it became twice that if rain slicked the potholes and flooded the creeks. Often she was late to work, eventually with more a scowl than an apology. Her co-worker Marge, divorced from a fisherman but hanging on in Kodiak rather than returning to Omaha, understood, stayed ready (eager!) to commiserate although Jody seldom complained openly, and privately wondered how long before Jody said to hell with it and left the boat-kissing jerk. By now Adele and Jones Henry had moved south for the winter, so that no eager Aunt Adele waited to take the children.

On Fridays Jody gathered the children with grim relief, bought them all hamburgers and ice cream for dinner—it had become a scheduled treat—then drove the potholed distance from town and shut herself in for the weekend. She now declined weekend commitments, whether parties or council affairs beyond official duty. The logistics of moving the entourage had become too great. On the other hand, the new place had a great peace about it, even beauty. The children were developing personalities she could enjoy, and they roamed without danger as long as they stayed away from the water. Five-year-old Henny's first challenge to her authority in that direction was announced by Dawn's shrill call. Jody found him waist-deep in the water looking for a special rock. The resultant walloping turned so severe that even Dawn, who had begun watching the punishment with complacent satisfaction, started crying in sympathy. Although a year younger than her brother, she grabbed any chance to take charge.

So when, at the end of a November Friday with the day rainy and already dark, Pete seemed listless and pushed away half of his hamburger, Jody paid less attention than she would have with her first child. The dark had glummed them all. During the long drive home through the rain, Dawn started a fight with Henny over whether a book cover was more red or orange, and then over who missed Auntie Adele most. Since Dawn had already learned to write simple words better than her brother she had the upper hand. By the back light in the wagon she crayoned in big letters "book to red" (she'd originally chosen that color for argument because she hadn't learned to spell orange), and regarding Adele: "I me do," then announced: "There, see, that proves I'm right." Henny responded defensively, annoyed that letters still refused to form words for him. Jody, who had a headache, snapped, "Each in your corner and *quiet*." Her tone settled the matter and they retreated to opposite sides.

Dawn maneuvered the last word. She tried to pull Pete over the center seat of the wagon to her corner in the back with, "Petey wants me to read to him, don't you Petey?" Instead of coming gladly as usual, Pete beat her off and drew back.

"Turn out the light and everybody sleep," snapped Jody. "It's getting harder to see the road."

The bridge over the Pasagshak was awash. The river usually flowed obediently under the boards. If rains continued, the run from the mountain might flood out the road, separating them from town. With Hank at home that would have meant a vacation, but now it deepened her isolation.

When the car lights finally picked out the mossy tree trunks by the dark house, Pete, curled in a sulking ball, refused to leave the car. Let him stay until he's ready, Jody decided as she and the others ran in bags of groceries before water sogged the paper. The rooms were damp and chilly. Jody started fires in the stoves with wood chopped the weekend before. Soon they had warmth of sorts. "All right Pete," she said at last, wearily, and went to the wagon to fetch him. He was feverish in her arms. She gave him a Tylenol, and, until the bedrooms warmed sufficiently, tucked him under a blanket by the picture window overlooking the bay and distant Kodiak that Hank so treasured in concept. (When was he ever home to enjoy it?) "Look, honey, see if you can find your school over there," she muttered, although little showed through the rain wall but vapor lights from the cannery piers. If she considered serious illness, she dismissed it in favor of fatigue and routine kids' ailments. Henny and Dawn had given a full share of false alarms.

She slept poorly. The wind-driven rain, which had kept planes grounded in and out of Kodiak for two days, hissed outside as it blew through bent treetops. Around midnight she went to Pete's bed with a flashlight. The child's forehead seemed hotter, but after all, he was tucked under blankets.

A while later Dawn shook her. "Shame on Petey, he makes too much noise and I can't sleep. Tell him to behave."

The child was thrashing, but limp when she picked him up. She could feel the heat of his little body. "Come on, honey," she said uneasily, "Give me your smile." He merely whimpered. A thermometer showed that he had a high fever. It frightened her for the first time. She wrapped him in the blanket and held him as she dialed the hospital in town from the living room phone. Dead, lines down. Dawn trailed, watching. "Wake your brother and get dressed both of you. Quick." She grabbed some of the children's clothes at random and stuffed them into a knapsack as she dressed herself.

The rain now blew horizontal. It splatted against the windshield with such force that the glass blurred at once behind the wiper blades. At the Pasagshak River bridge her headlights showed ripples where the planks should have been. Nothing but to speed through. She reached the other side after rushing water spun the car over slick wood, but with brakes now too wet for traction.

At the darkened hospital she entered the emergency room with Pete draped over her shoulder, shouting for attention.

"Now, now, mother," grumbled a sleepy intern, buttoning his white jacket. A minute later he frowned, and ordered an immediate spinal tap. The hospital room came alive with nurses and a doctor. Pete had bacterial meningitis. Neither Henny nor Dawn showed temperatures; it hadn't spread to them. Jody phoned Marge, who said of course she'd take the kids. "Just leave 'em at the hospital, give me time to get dressed."

Within an hour an ambulance raced the nearly comatose child to the Coast Guard base where a helicopter pilot waited to chance the weather into Anchorage, since no commercial pilot would risk it. In the bouncing helicopter she hugged the limp, burning Pete in her arms while a nurse tended an intravenous bottle attached to the child's arm. At the Anchorage airport an ambulance waited. Jody carried Pete while the nurse trailed with the bottle and tubes, but soon other hands took him over and the language turned surreal. "Kid's on amp and chloro," called the nurse. "D-5 quarter at two- thirds maintenance. Two saline boluses inflight to keep him going."

In the emergency room, doctors and nurses eased her aside. Her arms still felt Pete's impression as she struggled for glimpses of the little nose and forehead through moving backs. She wanted to scream but held it in, straining to hear what they said that might give some clue.

"Better we'd had him sooner," muttered someone.

She swayed, damning remote house, remote husband, her irresponsible self. I don't pray and haven't believed, she said without voice. But if you're there somewhere prove it, please, please.

The doctor summoned her into the circle. "Talk to him. Try to make him do things. Like squeeze your hand. Or open his eyes. Does the little tacker know any words?"

The small fingers gripped her thumb. But no response came further despite her urgency, and after a while the fingers slipped limp.

"Losing consciousness," muttered someone.

"Shush," said another. "Keep talking to him, mom."

Hank arrived in Anchorage next day around midnight on the afternoon plane from Dutch Harbor. The pilot had held the day's single remaining flight for two hours despite weather closing in, and this only because some influential cannery person (it turned out to be John Gains) exerted pressure. The resulting head winds made it necessary to refuel in Cold Bay.

Hank knew many of the passengers but kept to himself, not trusting speech as he agonized. They all drank bitter hours-old coffee in the Cold Bay flight shack. One suited businessman from the East Coast declared loudly and often to another that he'd missed his connecting flight to Chicago because a hick airline couldn't keep its schedule. One of Hank's boat friends happened to stumble and spill coffee on the man from neck to waist. It changed the subject.

Jody, so hair-strewn and haggard he didn't recognize her from the window of the intensive care unit, gripped him silently, beat against his chest, then returned to stroking the unconscious child.

Hank rented a motel room near the hospital, forced her to bed (she had kept the vigil alone for most of two days, dozing in a chair), and started his own vigil. When she woke, her first words to him were: "I hate that house." Hank chilled and said nothing. When he tried to hug her she eased away.

Two days later, it seemed that Jody's half-prayer had been answered. Although Pete still spoke nothing, his eyes stayed open and followed movement around him. For one precious moment he smiled when Hank tickled him. (Hank then had to turn away, sobbing. Jody moved in quickly to reassure the child.)

Although sun shone crisply on the snowy Chugach Mountains, Kodiak, a hundred fifty miles south, still swirled with storms and zero visibility. By now, Adele Henry shared watches while she waited for Kodiak flight weather to clear, and Hank's parents were on their way from Baltimore. Adele would open her Kodiak house to take in Henny and Dawn, and announced that the senior Crawfords were welcome also "if Jane doesn't mind Jones's bed and we'll give Harry the sofa." Jody did not inform her own parents of the emergency. "If they came," she said, "they'd just worry over their own comfort. And can you hear my mother if I told her not to smoke in Pete's room?"

Adele had arrived in Anchorage from San Pedro, leaving Jones at his welding business "to rustle his own meals for a change, and find out what it's like to wipe up the mess." Hank put his arm around her, able to joke in light of Pete's recovery. "Got a grinder to get green fuzz off the pans?"

"Rather I'll use the stubble he shaves only if I make him!"

Jody stayed quiet, almost grim. Yet she was the one who held them together. She assigned watches over Pete, and remained in control when Adele or Hank became emotional. She also guarded their money, collecting all that Hank had in pocket—as a successful fisherman he liked always to keep a wallet with fifties and hundreds—and she bargained with the motel manager for a lower rate.

By day five, Pete sat up propped by pillows, an IV bottle attached to his arm and a light restraint around his middle to keep him from squirming loose. He had begun to eat and to enjoy everyone's attention, although at times he turned listless. But no urging could get him to speak the simple words and phrases he had so enthusiastically spouted just days before. Nevertheless, the doctor said that in two weeks if all continued well they could take him home. At least that would stop the drain on their funds.

That afternoon the sky around Kodiak was reported cleared, and flights began leaving. Adele and Hank's mother, friendly rivals, would go down together to take over Henny and Dawn, but everyone debated Hank's dad's role. For the time before he returned east to his office, should he make himself useful in Kodiak, or stay to help the kids in Anchorage? Adele solved it with a wave of her arm. "Harry, my dear man, you'd get in our way. Don't you think Jane and I have things to do together? And girl talk? Good Lord, with Jones on his precious boat I do all the work myself anyhow." Then, quietly, to him alone: "I don't like it, the way Petey's not talking. I heard one of the doctors, when Jody wasn't around, say the child might be losing milestones whatever that means. He's not out of danger whatever they tell her. I lost one of mine to meningitis you know. No, don't speak. My only little girl. Two childless sons we barely see because Jones can't— Don't, don't, I can't talk about it, even now. You stick around up here. And pick up expenses when you can. Fishing's been terrible."

A few hours later a phone call from Kodiak confirmed safe arrival, while the stomp of feet in the background told that the children had been collected in good health. "Daddy," said Dawn when her turn came at the phone, "you kiss Petey and tell him to behave. But keep Mommy up there. Auntie Adele and Gam-gam can take care of us just fine."

"That means," said his mother, amused, "that we're being exploited for all it's worth. I must say you have good friends. That Marge who took them in on such short notice delivered them clean, and the few clothes they had were all washed. If that's the way people take care of each other around here it's a nice place. However primitive."

"Better lock the door against raiding savages, though." He never would have expected his parents to adapt to new circumstances, willing to pack and come help on the instant. In his mind they had remained part of an East Coast culture that lived by things spelled out and no surprises.

Hank and Jody continued alternate nights dozing in a cot in the room so that Pete would not wake to strangers, while his father assumed a full share of daytime watches.

Jody lightened as things continued well. She and Dad enjoyed each other, although at times they seemed from different planets. She alone could tease him with a tart remark and receive no curt reply. "My fish boat past confuses him, even though now I'm home and a proper mom," she told Hank during an afternoon off. They strolled the wide, empty Anchorage streets after eating tuna sandwiches made on the motel bathroom counter. (No costly lunches for the time.) "He's such a gentleman. It's almost cute, the look he tries to hide if I drop an unladylike word without thinking. I do try. Funny, your mom takes it better with a direct 'oh dear.'"

"He thought he knew a woman's place. It works with most of the ladies."

She ignored the bait. "Your folks are decent, I mean it. But it's like going into battle. Less with Dad. I can handle him. Did I tell you Mom hinted the other day that Dawn isn't quite the proper name when her granddaughter comes out at the cotillions? That thank goodness the printed programs can read Danielle? She talks as if it's decided, that the kids go back to those Baltimore finishing schools. You're not doing anything to encourage that bullshit, are you?"

"McDonogh's a good place. I went there. We wore scratchy uniforms. Drilled on the field. Crazy, looking back."

"Little soldiers, Jesus! Don't forget I'm an Army brat."

"It wasn't like that. It set good standards." He grinned. "They even let girls in now."

She turned serious. "So that's the part of you I can't reach. And a bucket of money for tuition, not even yet for college. I know they'd pay. But then we're indebted forever. Cotillion! Don't worry, I'll keep it friendly. But they're going to find a word called 'no' in my vocabulary."

Hank wondered of fights ahead. At least she'd said nothing more of hating their beautiful new home.

Harry Crawford made a point of taking his daughter-in-law and his son separately to dinner each night—early for the one to go on watch, later for the one who was relieved—and urged on each a stiff drink followed by wine. He favored the top-floor restaurant of the hotel where he stayed: felt it his discovery, and tipped well enough that the waiters soon knew his name. It assured a table where wide windows looked directly past the low city to mountains and water. He liked to start the first shift around four in November dusk, when the snowy Chugach peaks glowed pink. This evening—the last before he returned to Baltimore "before they realize they can do without me"—he had reached a mellowing second martini when Hank joined him late. By dark a full moon etched the white ridges so strongly that the sight held its own against the inside lights reflecting against glass.

Hank stretched and tried to relax. His Scotch deadened rather than soothed. Could Seth manage the guys tightly enough to catch their share?

Crabs for bills now, not glory. They'd do more if he could be there to drive and scout.

The elder Crawford read part of Hank's thoughts. "A full moon's impressive in rough water. Bering Sea on your mind?"

If I asked, thought Hank, he'd lend me money to continue boat and house payments on time.

"Incidentally, I hope it won't hurt Adele's feelings, but her house isn't that big. I've reserved a room at the inn on the hill where we stayed last time. That gives your mother freedom to come and go."

Hank shrugged. "She'll understand." Adele probably wouldn't and Jody would need to smooth it over in some way. "I really like it, that you and Mom came up so quickly."

"We wanted grandchildren. Now we know where to find them." His father's guarded smile stretched the short mustache that, Hank now noticed, had turned gray. He seldom laughed out loud although his humor remained steady, a self-containment suited perpetually to the office. "Not that we wouldn't rather have our family closer to home."

"Baltimore's gotten pretty distant. I'm sorry." Silence. There had always been silences between them when they reached a point of difference.

"How's the fishing business? I assume all's well?"

"First rate, thanks." Hank said it positively enough to forget payments and bills. His father's career with an international steel company, bootstrap-successful, had always been an unspoken shadow over his own work. Given other drives his own way might have been paved. But the crab would soon be back in their old abundance. To change the subject: "Hope you didn't chuck any great plans to come up here?"

"We'll see how important I am. A few meetings have to go on without me."

"Meetings. Oh. Mom wrote a while back, something about London later this year. Theater tickets and Christmas shopping at Harrod's. When's that?"

"It was yesterday." Hank started to exclaim, and it was his father's turn to avoid with an upheld hand and hasty "Don't worry." Dinner arrived. "My king crab looks good. Hell of a fisherman I'm with, ordering prime rib."

"You gave up London?"

"It's always there. Don't you eat the crabs you catch?"

"You've never had them fresh from the bottom boiled in seawater. By the time they reach your table they've been washed, rebrined . . . whatever. I can taste their cannery smell. You can't, I guess." The knowledge was pallid compared to international conferences, but he kept on. "It's still good food. I guess if I worked in a meat plant I'd taste whatever they do to the beef, so I'd order fish. Dad, we'd have understood if you'd—"

His father poured the wine. He had ordered a sturdy red. "Believe me. Any excuse suits your mom to see her grandchildren." A self-deprecating chuckle. "We're both about to turn sixty. You might think it doesn't matter. But we don't mind excuses to see our offspring. Of course, if your mom has her way we'll have our grandchildren enrolled back home at Bryn Mawr, and Gilman or McDonogh, in a few years. I have an education fund drawing interest."

Hank stared through the window at the frosty moonlight on the mountains. "Dad, my moving to Alaska . . . It wasn't trying to get away from you. I hope you know that. When I first came here I didn't . . . But it's our place."

"I know. You found your own way." A pause. "I like what you're doing even if it wasn't what I'd expected. We do worry about the danger, I won't pretend that we don't. Of course we did while you were in Vietnam too. Gotten used to it. In my own life any danger came of necessity, early, during the War, and then with a family I pursued nothing dangerous."

"I'm sorry."

His father's eyes flashed a sudden blue. "I haven't been sorry about anything in a long time. Don't be." He cut a piece of crab leg and chewed it. "Not bad. I'm glad I'm not such an expert. You know, when you were born in 1944, I was on that LST in the South Pacific wondering if I'd ever see your mom again, or you. It all turned out, of course. But you were nearly two by the time I first held you. I've never held an infant—a really little fellow—until up here." Silence. "Then your mom had some problem, so we had no more children. Of course, I've been lucky in business . . ."

"You've worked hard and you know it."

"Yes, yes. But that didn't bring three grandchildren. You did." His voice warmed suddenly. "That luck's special. It's great at any point in your life to be around your own. Here's to 'em. Drink up, and think about things that matter. Crab's good. Your steak looks tough. Too bad."

Hank grinned back in surprise at his father's grin. They clicked glasses. If I asked for a loan now, he thought, I'd admit failure and lose what I've gained in his sight.

He remembered his grandparents in Baltimore, Dad's sober church-going people and Mother's livelier widowed Gram Lacey. Both his grandmothers wore black, yielding early to their years. (Dad *sixty*?) As they aged they had relied on his father, who eventually took over all their affairs and saw them through old age to death. It had seemed the natural order. But now he in his turn would be too far away. His parents wouldn't need money. What of the rest? "Sixty! What's it like?" he ventured, and regretted it at once. He didn't want to hear.

"*That's* a question." His father leaned back and dabbed his mouth with a napkin. The lips below the gray mustache had a gray tint of their own.

"Sorry—I mean, never mind. I shouldn't have asked. Look out there, how the moon makes the mountains look like chalk."

"I hadn't thought about it, but . . . well, I have. And it's a damned shock. At sixty, you might find that you do pretend. I won't say that I still think like a teenager, or like a young lieutenant with everything focused on survival and duty. But I don't feel older than forty. Frankly I sometimes wonder how it all slipped by so fast."

"Still a lot of years ahead!"

"Oh yes. But I know the day's coming. I'll retire, say good-bye to some things, stop making decisions that affect more people than my family. We'll travel, your mom and I. Do interesting things together. Not so bad."

"Do you want to retire?"

"Hell no." He started to eat again, then put down his fork. "If you really wonder, it's a little like facing the end. Not like that death lottery when you're young and strong and off to war. Rather like . . . you plan for it, you watch it coming. But until you're sixty you don't believe it, really. Then all at once you do. Even when you know there's probably years and years ahead."

"Let's change the subject."

"Very well. To the point. If you're strapped for immediate money, let me help. It can be part donation, part loan. I'm sure you understand that my cash has limits—I've invested to make sure your Mother's taken care of no matter how long she lives. And of course maybe we'll both have a long old age. But, a few thousand."

Hank's stomach tightened at the suddenness. "No. I'm doing fine. But I appreciate it."

When he relieved Jody at Pete's bedside, she kept her voice low since the child slept, but her eyes and mouth showed humor for the first time since the illness. "He almost started to talk, then twinkled for a second. Maybe he's playing a game. I'd like that in a way. Nice dinner?" Hank nodded. She kissed him. "Okay. Settle in with your critter there."

The warm feeling from the dinner continued. His son slept peacefully, fever gone. He brushed a cheek against the peach-fuzz face. Never stopped to examine what constituted love. When it came he took it for granted, from parents to courtship to kids. What fortune to have six people whom he loved, who loved him in return! And friends besides whom he'd hug in a minute, like Adele and Jones, Seth, Tolly.

His arms needed to be full. He eased into the bed, unstrapped the restraint and, careful to maintain the IV needle, drew in the small body, chest to chest and warmth to warmth as in nursery days barely more than a year ago. The sweet-smelling, downy hair parted for his kiss, and his lips lingered on the yielding baby skull beneath. So vulnerable. My dad might have looked at me like this, he thought. And what does he see now, in me? Give it a few more fishing seasons and this peck of soft bones in my arms will be tall, maybe taller than me, all muscle, sprouting a beard. And I'll be older. And my dad . . . will be older.

Suddenly Pete stiffened and yelped. His body began to jerk. His head beat back. The IV needle pulled out. His mouth chattered. Feces squished from the diaper. "Help!" Hank called, "Help! Petey don't die, Petey I love you, honey, honey, don't die. Help!"

Nurses pulled the child from his arms and sent him from the bed. "Don't let him die, oh please don't let him die. Petey, Petey."

A doctor shook him by the shoulders. "Your child's having a seizure. Not good, but he's not going to die. It's under control. Here's a towel if you want to clean yourself."

Instead he called Jody from the nurse's station, then hurried back to the room. The child was being wheeled away, still thrashing, braced by pillows. "Stop! What are you doing?" Hank cried, running beside the gurney.

"CAT scan, new technology," muttered the doctor. "Stay alongside, talk to him if you like but I don't think he'll hear until the seizure's over." As they walked, the little body stopped jerking and Pete whimpered. He looked up blankly at Hank's voice, and pushed away with his free arm. "Keep talking," said the doctor.

Jody arrived, hair askew, sleepy eyes blue-bagged. He ducked into a lavatory to sponge the mess from his clothes, soon rejoined her. They were allowed to hover in the CAT-scan room, calling encouragement as the child, groggy but strapped tight, went into the sinister clanking machine like a corpse on a slab. Two other doctors had joined the examination. "Yep. Subdural empyema," said one. "Need to drain it. Set up surgery."

The entourage bustled the gurney to the operating room as a doctor came to explain. "It's what we call a pus pocket. Evidently some H-flu germ—that's a bacteria—escaped our treatment, and it's lodged in a pocket the antibiotics didn't reach." He paused. "In his head."

"Oh Christ," Hank choked.

"Doctor Smitt's our neurosurgeon. He's very good. We're going to drain it."

Jody's voice was level. "What long-term effect?"

"I'm sure we'll have it in time."

"The full story, please."

"Well. If there's scar tissue there might—*might* be danger of more seizures. We won't know. But seizures can be controlled with medication. They can also ride their course so the patient returns to normal."

Hank found his voice. "Won't know for how long?"

The doctor patted his arm. "We'll spell out possibilities after we see."

It meant that Pete's recovery from the meningitis would be protracted. It also meant a continued fiscal drain since their insurance covered only basics. Hank's father quietly switched the motel billing to his own account. When Jody, who paid the bills, found out, she at first refused, then kissed him and accepted it. But she and Hank agreed that their independence was too important to accept a deeper donation.

Harry Crawford delayed his return to Baltimore for two more days until the worst had passed, spending increased hours on the phone. He left an open account with his rooftop restaurant. Hank and Jody used it once, for lunch, but only to appear not ungrateful. Jane Crawford stayed on in Kodiak. Phone reports indicated no discontent among two foster mothers greedy for children and two children happily indulged.

When Jody wrote her own parents they phoned. "We want you to keep us posted," said her mother in a husky cigarette voice. "Good Lord, kids' diseases, don't ask how many I went through with you. Thank God it's not my responsibility anymore."

"Why don't you ever come see us?" growled Colonel Sedwick. "You know I'm not well."

Two mornings after the emergency Pete looked at his parents brightly and started to squirm, although he still did not speak. "Give it time," said a pediatric neurologist brought for consultation. "Normal child's development might be delayed a few months. But he'll catch up. Now, the seizure . . . others *might* follow. "

"You mean for a week, maybe a month, right?"

"At least, sir."

Jody folded her arms. "What *do* you mean?"

"Worst case, a lifetime." Hank groaned. "Each body holds its own mysteries. Some things we can't predict. It might never happen again. But, ah . . . best not to leave him unwatched for a time." To a question from Jody: "Very like epilepsy. Sudden, intense, then over. Put pillows, anything handy to cushion him, head especially, so he doesn't harm himself. Do *not* put anything between his teeth. That popular misconception might choke him."

"I see," said Jody. "And medication. That'll help?"

"Definitely."

Hank shook his head. "You're wrong. You've got to be. My kid's not going to be epileptic. We'll get another opinion."

"I suggest you do, if it helps."

Jody continued steadily. "The drug has side effects?"

"Not debilitating ones. Does need to be taken regularly, on time."

"For a few months, you mean," Hank persisted. Jody put a hand on his arm. He knew the answer.

Nurses on all the watches had made a pet of the vulnerable but outgoing Pete. It became their project to make him speak. The child's elfish refusal with a wiggle under the covers, combined with the shadow of more seizures, increased his charm. The attention meant that he was seldom alone during the day, and Jody could bunk in the bedside cot each night. It made sense that Hank return to the boat. Her income had stopped, and he paced the route from hospital to motel like a caged tiger, scared for Pete and uneasily diminished by a situation beyond his control that included an empty wallet. Jody recognized the latter and issued a hundred-dollar bill above expenses: "To carry. Don't expect more if you spend it."

Hank flew first to Kodiak. They justified the expense so that he could check on the house abandoned in haste. The front door was secure. Marge had driven out to pack the children's clothes after she took them over, and closed up correctly. The first wrong he sensed came with the acid stench that swept against him when he opened the door. Chaos in the damp and chilly living room. Stuffing from the armchair and sofa littered the floor. Knobs of feces lay everywhere, some of it matted in a fuzz of white mold. Somehow raccoons or other creatures had found an opening, come in for shelter, and made it their playpen.

Hank stormed and shouted, then cooled enough to manage a laugh when he found that neatly shut doors had kept the creatures from the bedrooms. He scooped, swept, and disinfected while scheming traps, poisons, even night ambush with a pistol. At last he merely patched an obvious opening (wiry hairs stuck to the edges of a popped knothole) and shored other possible break-in points. If he built close to nature, then the nature of animals had to be respected as part of the deal. Would Jody see it that way?

Back finally in Dutch Harbor, all but Seth greeted the Boss boisterously.

Seth, with a captain's gravity, informed him: "We've done good as most everybody. Not everybody, maybe, but good enough. And . . ." The relief skipper's eye had a gleam new to him. "I've found my own hole, call it Seth's Sloo, that nobody else knows where, not even Mo." The bushy face, usually as open as a map, remained tight. "Nobody."

Hank understood. "Then the Sloo's your secret. Money bag when you get your own boat. When we head there it'll be my stretch on deck and yours at the wheel."

The reserve lifted at once. "Come on, man, let's go catch them fuckers!"

For the remaining fraction of the king crab season they highlined again under Hank's sleepless prod. But half his season had still been lost to courtroom and hospital.

The Seattle bankers understood. (The son of the loan VP had summer-seined in Puget Sound and—to the VP's voiced concern and probable disappointment—talked of following the boats north rather than start banking at the bottom.) The bank extended the boat loan period and in the process let Hank skip three payments.

Less flexible were Kodiak loans for the new house. Hospital bills crept above Hank's insurance coverage, then suddenly soared, requiring another loan and mounting payments. It meant that he needed to winter-fish for anything saleable in the water—no Hawaii break with Jody and the kids—hanging tough until the next Bering king crab season bailed them out.

11

TROUGHS

SPRING–FALL 1981

By midwinter the tanner crabs had all but disappeared. Hank hired the use of a crane in Dutch Harbor and installed the big net reel and davits that converted the *Jody Dawn* for trawling. He hated doing it—his zest had become the chase for big crabs, not tutti-frutti little fish that Asians mushed into paste—but he was glad he'd followed Swede's advice. He signed into a Korean joint venture. At least the *Jody Dawn* had that added horsepower for dragging, unlike the now-glum Tolly's new engine that he had scorned to upgrade. The conversion also opened his option to go shrimping if he chose. Shrimp stocks had plummeted from their previous numbers in the Kodiak bays, but no one considered this permanent any more than the king and tanner crab drops.

Aboard *Jody Dawn*, Odds dubiously touched the chains, bobbins, and steel doors of the new trawling gear. His experience since childhood aboard uncles' boats included only floating gillnets, baited hooks, and seines that encircled on the surface, so that the trawl's complications to drag the bottom required fresh, difficult thinking. Terry summarized the general opinion after two test sets with a cheerful: "Man, this shit's no fun. You drag and wait, and then what you get's piddlefish like they'd slip through your toes."

"Yeah!" echoed Odds.

Seth took to trawling enthusiastically and Mo, his burly shadow, thus accepted also. For Seth it harked back to his early days with Hank on a slave-driving shrimper. "Remember that hard-assed squarehead Nels? Old bastard like to killed us he pushed so hard. Then didn't pay us proper.

Dead, ain't he? Pfoo. But funny thing, looking back makes me laugh now, how bad it was. Man we could take it!"

Hank nodded, remembering also Nels's dogged fishing even after cold sea had crippled him, until at last the sea claimed him altogether.

Seth discovered he liked the thump of bobbins as they scraped down deck to the water, and relished grabbing thick chains to lash steel doors against the hull at just the right instant. Heavy stuff in motion; perils to overcome, all of it with tricks that he knew. He lectured the others on the danger to make sure they understood.

They caught pollack enough: bulging bags of the soft halfpound fish. It was the easiest fishing any had experienced, since a tender simply detached the bag and floated it over to the Korean factory ship. "No fun a-*tall*," repeated Terry as they watched indifferently the fruit of a two-hour tow bob through the water without ever touching their deck. Nothing of the passive creatures in the net earned their respect like a heavy king crab's clawpower or a salmon's angry thrash. The huge mass floated like a carcass, submerging, then sluggishly breaking the surface. Waves licked around glassy fish heads sticking through the meshes. Seabirds swooped screaming to peck dismembered chunks of fish. Bladders popped like muffled firecrackers, from the seafloor creatures raced up through too many atmospheres of pressure.

"Well, if you gotta be born a junk fish," said Terry, "this gets it over quick. Then maybe you matter next time, be a sockeye or something."

"Everything has a soul," said Odds. "Every one of them junk fish has a soul."

"Yeah, maybe. But then a sockeye has a bigger soul."

"Come on," said Mo uneasily. "They're *fish*."

"Set the fucker again," snapped Seth. "Nets out of water catch air." They straightened the alternate net that had been delivered back to them from the tender, and attached it to the trawl's warps. The few minutes' hustle came closest to work in their day.

Seven American boats were delivering to the Korean mothership. It went smoothly at first. Even at nine cents a pound—unspeakable price compared to that for their usual targets—the money slowly mounted since they fished a total volume tons beyond that for crab or salmon. The Korean in charge of the factory ship's tender hailed them with raucous cheer each time he came to transport a bag of fish. Terry gaily tossed over a girlie magazine to acknowledge a gift of leathery dried fish that none on the *Jody Dawn* but Odds considered eating.

Then, three weeks into the season, Hank radioed for his haul to be collected, and heard back in barely intelligible English: "Tender-boat wait." Each hour he called again with greater impatience as his boat and crew stood idle, to be told the same. The bag of fish dragged astern like a gross sea anchor, undulating with the swells. Birds, having eaten all the breakoff, drove beaks directly into the encased bodies. The occasional tail flick through the meshes soon stopped. The bag, originally a mass firm as a sofa, flattened and softened. Its brassy smell soon lost freshness.

"Goin' to rot on us," said Seth, disgusted. "Better call those gooks and *make* 'em come."

Hank radioed fellow-skippers. Same delay. Only one delivery had been taken in the last five hours. Hank glared at the factory ship, stolid in the water while his boat's anchor of fish jerked them with each swell like a leash to a dog. He itched to confront them, but the ship lay a mile distant, too far to safely take the dinghy in rough water.

When at last the tender came, no one joked. Hank in float coveralls signaled the skipper alongside rather than tossing a towline for the fish. Only after repeated waves did the man bring in his boat. Once-boisterous almond eyes regarded him warily. Hank jumped rail to rail. "You take me to factory ship." He waved off objections. The engine stayed in neutral during prolonged radio talk in Korean. The tenderman's face, no longer creased with smiles, had a child's sheen but a weary age. Not only his deck was slimy, but also his cramped wheelhouse where dead fish odors had concentrated away from the wind. At last the Korean started his engine, and without facing Hank placed a ragged cushion over the exposed springs of the single captain's chair. Hank acknowledged but remained standing.

A Jacob's ladder clacked against the ship's high rusty hull. Thirty-foot climb, Hank estimated. The Korean gestured to show the difficulty, then pointed persuasively back to the *Jody Dawn*. Hank shook his head. He knew they had a basket they could have lowered. "You want it tough buddy? You got it." He grabbed slippery rungs on an upswell and climbed firmly hand over hand. Even though in good shape he was panting by the time anxious hands helped him over the rail.

Fish filled the wide deck bins. He could see no room for more, but a crane lifted the *Jody Dawn*'s bagful with its green and yellow chafing gear dripping slime, to be emptied on top of the rest. Hank had expected to see the deck bustling with Koreans but saw only two. One of them, buried to his thighs in fish, steadied the bag and hammered open the drawcord. The gush of dead creatures knocked him off balance. For a moment his head disappeared in the mass and his hardhat bounced off. The captain on the bridge above shouted harshly and the single other crewman on deck laughed as the man regained his feet, groped for the hardhat, and returned it to his head, and started distributing the slippery bodies with a paddle.

The man behind the paddle scowled up, then away. His face had a purple mark that Hank had seen somewhere before.

In the wheelhouse: "Down-go," explained the Korean captain after working the crane controls. He walked barefoot on a worn carpet that covered the enclosed deck. (Hank had considered removing his boots, but scraped them outside instead.) The captain thumbed the thin pages of a dictionary, pointed to "blade," added "*Chop-chop* down-go," and drew a finger across his throat.

A trip through the factory area belowdecks confirmed a breakdown in the cutting machinery. Two men in coveralls sweated over a battery of blades still dripping fish scraps. The rest of the crew, in thick rubber coats, lined shoulder to shoulder wherever they could fit, furiously scraping and cutting individual fish. Hank had seen enough surimi lines to know that skin and bones needed to be separated from meat in order to make fish paste, and that only machines could do the work in volume.

"How long take fix-fix?"

The captain shook his head. He led to the wardroom through smoky corridors where rust bubbled through yellowing paint. Away from the processing, everything smelled of sour food. A messboy served cups of rice wine and laid out bowls of the spiced fermented cabbage Hank had tasted reluctantly on the Korean longliner arrested two years before in the Gulf of Alaska. This brought it back, the purple mark on the man's face. Captain of the longliner caught fishing illegally, who had begged on his knees not to be reported for fear of prison and beating. Hank nibbled at the *kimchee* out of politeness, sipped the abrasive alcohol, tried to picture the man. Not his fault, even though he'd been gleeful along with Tolly and the rest at having nabbed a foreigner cheating on American fish. It was the Coast Guard officer who'd refused to alter the report, following duty. One-two-three, inevitably.

Back on deck, as Hank waited for the tender to return him to the *Jody Dawn* after it delivered a delayed bag of fish from another boat, he watched the man covered in gurry behind the paddle. The man kept his back turned. "Hey," Hank called softly at last. The man turned for a moment. Same purple birthmark from temple to chin. His lip was now pinched by a scar that induced a permanent scowl and showed missing teeth on half-stumps. Yes. The pleading captain.

The Korean factory ship never recovered full capacity. It accepted only a single haul a day from each of its contracted trawlers. After a few days, five of the seven boats in the joint venture quit and left. Only the *Jody Dawn* and another remained: skippers both who needed the money. At least each could then sell two additional daily hauls. One night in the brief dark Mo on watch called him. "That the lights of our gook ship, Boss? Ain't she movin' away?" Hank radioed to no answer. By morning the horizon was clear.

Three months later the *Jody Dawn* had still received no payment for the pollack caught and delivered, nor were any of Hank's inquiries answered. He reported the affair to the State Department. The same people who had tried to ruin him a year previous for Seth's bullets at the Japanese trawler now filed his complaint in some remote drawer.

"Write our senator," said Jody. "You know how."

"I damn should." But he didn't get to it before going to sea again, despite her reminders. It seemed futile.

Back in Kodiak, Jones Henry, in port briefly during a bountiful salmon season, declared: "You bought it." Age was making him acerbic, and third Scotches didn't help. His winter welding business for the San Diego tuna fleet had entered hard times along with the fleet itself, driven from American ports by activists' pressure against setting nets on dolphins. "Serves anybody who does business with the foreigners and their boys in our so-called State Department. You can add the porpoise huggers, don't get me started. And now you've got a boat too big to gear for salmon like the rest of us. You can drag, but none of the draggers around here can find shrimp anymore, so what have you got?"

"Daddy!" snapped Adele from the kitchen. "Hold your tongue. Hank always knows what he's doing."

Hank turned defensive with Jody in the room. "I'll make it up this fall with king crab. As for shrimp, come on." He raised his glass. "*I'd* find 'em. This town's gone crybaby. If Kiliuda Bay's empty as they say, it means the shrimp's gone to other bays, or a little offshore. Or down by the Shumigans or off the mainland by Mitrofania. Anybody can fill a boat when the water's plugged. Now it's time for the *real* fishermen. Prospector time. When you separate the cream."

"Cream—that's you, I take it."

"Anything out there, I'll find it." He turned to Jody for affirmation. But she watched him, detached.

"Not even the biologists can find shrimp anymore, Hank," called Adele.

"Those guys have no more idea than a schoolgirl how to set gear for their samples, Adele. So what do you expect? Do they ever ask fishermen to show 'em? I hear not."

"That's one time you got it straight," growled Jones.

Jody had turned strangely quiet, even in their home with the beautiful view. Whenever they talked of the house, conversation became stilted. Pete was their heartache and the subject they shared most freely. It had been nearly a year since the meningitis, but while he hopped in all directions like any three-year-old, he still did not speak. Bills now accumulated for therapy that produced no results. At least the precious child was healthy. Hank hugged him and played with him all the time, when he was home, until Jody needed to say: "You have two other kids, you know." Then Hank would gather all three against him and read, giving Henny and Dawn the chance to spell out some of the sentences themselves. The two older children had settled into a pattern. While they played together easily, Dawn continued to chatter and boss. Henny ducked his head as if to let the words flow past, and soberly followed his own course. Both, in their way, guarded their mute little brother.

At last, in mid-September, the Bering Sea king crab season opened. Hank and his men, like crews in the rest of the fleet, stationed themselves tensely for the set and haul. Up came the first pot, the second . . . the twentieth. Just last year they had frothed to the rail with a routine hundred big, sluggish male keepers in each. Now they contained no more than two dozen, plus more fish for hang-bait than could ever be used. Radio talk repeated over and over: "Just not feeding yet," and "Probably all still dug in the mud," and "You see all those foreign draggers? There's your fault." Hank shrugged off his unease. If old standbys were dry, it meant the crabs had found other holes to challenge his prospecting skill. Time to push.

Ten days later the hold contained no more than 60,000 pounds, compared last year to a routine 160,000 fished in half the time. With Hank's drive from ground to ground each crab had cost him double or triple the fuel of other years, while the men worked harder since they stacked pots after nearly each haul to run and test a new area. They returned to Dutch only when barely enough fuel remained for the 150-mile trip. No other boats waited at the plant pier to compete for space. Workers grabbed their lines, leapt aboard, and opened hatches even before the circulating water had time to drain. In little more than an hour their ten days' haul had entered the cookers, and seawater gushed again into their tanks.

At least the price rose. Last year Swede had paid eighty cents, finally ninety cents a pound. This year he'd posted $1.27 but Hank, making a noisy climb to the office, managed another seven cents without argument. "Only a dozen boats in so far," Swede admitted. "Some had only thirty, forty thousand pounds. Your scratch is the biggest delivery yet. My lines are hungry."

Hank refueled and returned to sea at once.

The king crabs did not appear. By October the average number of keepers in a pot had dwindled from the two dozen at season's start—poor enough compared with better days—to three or four. The big pots rattled instead with other creatures that ranged from flapping skates to spiny red-fish that could spike through gloves, and with cod that some who had fished only Alaska had never seen before. By now everyone could identify cod by the fleshy whisker on the lower jaw.

To save money on the *Jody Dawn* they ate fewer steaks and more from their catch. Mo reluctantly learned to batter thick cod fillets. Hank wondered anew at the savor of the flaky white fish fresh from the water, bemused by the way he'd avoided cod in the past through memories of cod liver oil. The taciturn Odds almost smiled since fish had always been his village food along with game. ("Cow meat's got no taste," he'd often declare, while stuffing down his share.) Seth put it glumly for Mo and himself, great eaters of beef. "Fish is nice, but it don't fill the corners."

Many boats of some 250 on the grounds gave up to cut losses. Increased fuel costs devoured most profit. Some of the homeward Seattle boats diverted to crabbing grounds around Kodiak. They competed with the local fleet for a supply that had dwindled there also, depleting it further.

Ashore in Dutch, snow lay untracked between buildings, where in other years paths would be trodden to ice by men headed for supplies or a drink. Loading cranes screeched only occasionally. Swede decided it was cheaper to pay return fare for half his plant crew than to feed them, heat the dormitories, and deal with fights that inevitably arose from idleness. John Gains had long since gone to Japan to confer with company officials on other sources in the world for crab, since shortage in one region did not mean the end of it for those who could pay.

At the airport, where planes once arrived full of people and left with only special boxes of iced crab for high-scale Tokyo and New York restaurants (most of the product went frozen by ship), outgoing flights were the crowded ones. Cannery hands flown in weeks before to work double shifts on overtime now sat glumly by their bags nursing pennies. Some had logged no more than fifty or sixty hours in a month. Puddles slicked the floor from their pacing in and out during long waits—sometimes days— for flight weather and space to take them home.

Hank drove harder. Finally his crew begged a break ashore—implied mutiny to get it. After delivering a thin load he agreed curtly to a three-day lay-in ashore (glad at least to take a few hours' rest himself). Vacation started with a listless dinner of fried bologna, no match for celebratory delivery-day roasts of other years.

Odds appeared before them in shore clothes with his seabag packed. "I'm going."

"You can't!" exclaimed Seth. "You're part of my deck."

Odds picked his words gravely. "I prayed over it lots. People here from church is going to put me up till I figure how to get home. Some day out there, the way we push, one of us'll get hurt bad, not just smashed fingers. And I got a family. Not worth it, the way we've been doin' this year."

Hank rose to take the initiative. Privately he was relieved since small shares would now stretch further despite extra work. He shook Odds's hand and wished him well. The others followed. Hank promised to send a check at the end of the season. A minute later, Odds had become part of history. It subdued even Terry.

A day's sleep later, Hank restlessly lingered over a single beer in the dim Elbow Room where once he had ordered $180 six-packs of Scotch for a joke. Cold wind straight from the sea weighted the vestibule door of the weathered frame building when anyone opened it. Hank glanced at old Nick, the bartender, half asleep on his stool. Start Nick talking with no customers to divert and he'd do the good old days nonstop. Although it was evening—in other years time for shouts to start spilling over the snow— the few tables were empty except for two men in hard hats. To increase his gloom the hard hats reminded him of the Korean with the purple birthmark and smashed teeth. Not his fault. Yes his fault.

"You guys from those new oil exploration rigs?" he ventured, to escape his thoughts. That's right, they said without interest in further conversation. Why didn't they stay at their usual bar of choice over the bridge at the Unisea, a place new like the bridge with nothing of fishermen about it? Different men, who hustled greasy ton-weight drills on a platform protected from all but the worst of the ocean. They lacked the foam and lilt that came from pulling live creatures from a clean sea.

Pat Saunders, one of the biologists from Fish and Game, pushed into the bar against the blown door. Ice beads flew from his parka. Hank waved him over more eagerly than in normal years. He'd always considered bureaucrats incompetent to set trial pots accurately enough to trust their data. Said so at meetings. Neither smiled as the newcomer pulled up a chair.

"Where you guys hiding the crabs, Patrick?"

"You tell *me*." The biologist's face, ridged as a leather scarecrow and now wind-reddened, always looked clenched, and the eyes seldom relaxed. "You know how to set pots."

"Nowhere, nowhere."

The admission brought a calming breath. "Well. We think warmer water might have pushed males north and west of traditional range."

"I've *prospected* further north and west."

"We predicted a shortfall."

"You talked about a short year-class, but come on, Pat, how could anybody . . ."

"You fishermen never listen. Never do. For two or three years we've warned you birds and the politicians both. Spare some of the matures for next time."

"What did you do, poison the water to prove your point?" When the biologist's mouth pursed he grinned to soften it.

The bartender interrupted with Pat's drink. In other years the tab would run, but now payment per round was understood. Hank slowly reached for his wallet, relaxed when Pat waved it aside and paid himself.

The man's glare continued. "You'd like to blame the biologists at the public trough, wouldn't you? Well, we have our opinion of you birds too. With you it's all for today. You and the politicians both. You pay us for our science but never listen. Then things collapse and it's our fault." He tasted his Scotch and, in a milder tone: "Nick, times are hard, but this stuff's water."

"Sorry. My eyesight." Nick came over heavily, holding the bottle by the neck. He topped Pat's glass, and started talking. "Ever see times like this? Ask me and I'll tell you. Plenty. Back in '47, that's thirty-four years ago exact, I keep count, when I paid off from the Navy here, honorable discharge and the War over. They shipped the Natives back home to Unalaska here from evacuation, but there was broken stuff everywhere—you know the Japs bombed the Navy base at Dutch Harbor other side of the creek but it was vandalism too—and I met my Aleut lady Stella and decided I could do worse than settle down here since I like it quiet . . . where was I?"

"Pouring the booze, Nick," said Hank mildly.

"Yeah, well, this bar, called it the Bluejay then, sometimes only open if a Coast Guard ship come in for bunker, didn't even have a vestibule door against the wind, door then opened direct facing the beach, and the one store, long white building and a boardwalk around it, company store for Native welfare, that's where I worked. Don't think I don't have stories to tell. You think there was all these crab factories and crab boats back then? No sir. People left us alone. Except for government Indian Affairs, in and out again fast as they could go. And Coast Guard now and then, come in for fuel. Did I say that before? Where was I now? Did I tell you yet about the famous Native lady with tits so long that for a quarter she'd—"

The two oil drillers saved them with "Hey Pop, over here, another round."

The biologist resumed his own train as if it had not been interrupted. "Ever consider your own stupidity?"

"Don't be such a firecracker, Patrick. I just wanted to tap your wisdom. You're the one who knows what's going on."

"Oh shit, Hank, any wisdom I have now, it's hindsight." But the slight flattery eased him. He took a long drink, stretched, and cracked his knuckles. Then, quietly: "What do you birds do out there? I'll tell you. You're in such a push to grab more than your share that you slam those seven- and eight-hundred-pound pots to the seafloor in seconds. Ever think how many crabs you splat under each pot?"

"But they were everywhere. They crawled in your dreams."

Pat sighed and drank again. "Not the whole answer to why they've gone, but look. Say what, you work three hundred pots roughly? And you smash 'em down fresh every day or two? Four, five crabs busted each slam. Some two hundred and thirty boats last year all did the same." He dipped a finger in his drink and traced wet figures on the table. "Round it to seventy thousand pots, fifteen times to the bottom for each in a month. No, make it ten, be real conservative. And stay conservative, say only three animals busted each time. That's two hundred thousand and some, no, shit, over two *million* crabs wasted. Wasted!"

"Food for the survivors," Hank said lamely.

"Then count the females and undersized that keep chasing your bait, brought to the surface, tossed back, over and over. That stress stunts some, kills some. With throwbacks, do your guys ever rip off a leg or claw when they're too tired to care how they toss? You know they do. Some animals don't survive, so that's more that never hatch eggs or grow to keeper size for your hold." Pat emptied his glass and went to the bar for another.

"None for me."

"You're not on the wagon. Forget the beer. Two Scotches, Nick, and adjust that ol' eyesight."

Hank shrugged. Now the rounds had started, end of a twenty he'd hidden, probably also his hundred. It had to go sometime. When the biologist returned, having gently sidestepped another barrage of the bartender's reminiscence: "Maybe we wasted and busted our share of crab, Pat, but we've done it one by one. The foreign trawlers do it wholesale. What about stopping *them*?"

"Is that whining I hear?"

"Never!"

"Well you're right, they kill their share. Blame that one on D.C. and write your congressman, it's nothing I can help. Everybody's screwing the crab for something. I'll tell you this out of office. For years Alaska's managed king crabs to let you birds take all the keeper-sized males of each year class, and always counted on the following year class for a new crop. Nothing saved for future even after we warned." Suddenly he pounded the table. "Don't tell *me*. Big crab money dictates in Juneau. Nobody who's making out lets it go."

Hank glanced at the men in hard hats. Their eyes returned to their drinks. "I'm not arguing, Pat."

"Yeah, well . . . money's approached me to change my data and stop warning, as if anybody ever listened. Realistically, I suppose a million bucks would buy me. I've had good offers but not that size. Lucky I'm a bachelor with simple tastes."

"You see us as the rapers of the universe, don't you?"

"I see you moving with no tomorrow in your heads. And ignorant of yesterday. Turn old Nick back on and he'll tell you. Think king crab was always this abundant? Never. Read statistics before the sixties. Back then crab was a cog in the ecosystem, not the engine. That was before the factory fleets started scooping those voracious feeder cods and groundfish that gobble baby crabs and shrimp and everything else, when nature kept a different balance. The crab population exploded, with their predators down as never before, and probably water conditions we don't yet understand. But now you're regulating the foreigners. Their catches are down, however you bitch, and that shifts the balance again. It means more fish to gobble baby crabs. And God knows how many trawlers out there besides the super-crabbers, all of you hungry as feeder-fish."

Hank gulped enough of his drink to burn then soothe. He wished he'd let Nick chatter on.

"And how about it? Ever talk to the old-timers? King crabbing started around Kodiak, not out here. Heavy fishing, so the animals got scarce. But fuel was cheap and the fleet was small and flexible, thus the world didn't end. Boats could target other creatures or could chase the crabs all the way along the peninsula and into the Bering Sea. Of course those salmon boats easily rolled over with too many pots. But they were the covered wagon into the Bering. These boats you've put your millions into are great crabbing machines. But inefficient for anything else. Maybe drag for groundfish with modification and compromise. Easy credit has put your ass in hock. Back twenty years ago guys had small boats they owned. You did yourself. I know. Now you've reached the Bering Sea, the far corner of your country. You've gone to the last frontier, you've got no new grounds, and you're stuck with luxury liners."

Hank shook his head. "Seattle banks are already calling in loans. Repossessing, even. Guys are scared. What's your valued advice now? To pray?"

"Stop crabbing. Before it gets worse. Do something else. Aren't the Koreans looking for boats to deliver groundfish?"

"Boy, you *aren't* on the grounds. Your salary's there whatever we do."

"Steady mortgage and retirement, but *you* get to wear the gold nuggets and have the Maui condos. That's if you listen to us and stay lucky."

"And you stay dry behind your desks. No risk, no glory."

The biologist looked at his watch and slipped a five under his glass. "Normally I'd welcome another few hours of insults on a lousy November night, but I'm expected."

"Those drinks to give you courage?"

The restless eyes actually lightened. "Life's not all crabs for a single male, even for an aging one." Pat paused in his parka, put three more dollars under the glass. "Old Nick's not getting rich tonight either." At the door, another pause. "Maybe you and the foreigners have raped the crab, maybe. But that's not the whole answer. They've moved away for their own reasons. We're still scratching our heads."

Hank nursed his drink. The fan that circulated the close, heated air made the only sound except for a whine of wind outside blowing straight from the water. Northeaster, sloppy sea. What kind of a life, away from Jody and scratch besides?

"It ain't my business, fellah," said one of the oil men. "But out drilling we see fish and crabs wasted floating everywhere. You ought to stop."

"Your goddamned oil kills more fish then we do!"

The man rose. He was big. "I can make something of that. It's our fish too, you know. Say the word."

Hank rose automatically, craving action. "Say the word."

"Outside, not in here," called Nick.

The second oil man grabbed his partner's shirt and eased him back into the chair. The challenger shrugged and obeyed. Hank resumed his seat quickly. Busted knuckles took long to heal. Jody would have been pissed.

"What's your poison, bud?" said the second man easily. "Join us. It's blowin' shit outside."

Hank would have done so at once. But he'd had drinks enough and saved both his twenty and the single hundred-dollar bill Jody allowed him. He made cheerful excuses and hurried out into the wind feeling diminished. His style was to peel bills he'd hard-earned, not nurse them.

A light shone from Swede's office. Hank entered after a quick knock. The desk drawer shut abruptly and a shot glass tumbled to the floor. Swede retrieved it unsteadily. Despite the whiskey that neutralized Hank's nose, no amount of ammonia from the plant below could mask the smell of real boozing. Swede's voice was thick. "Crabs not there, Crawford. Dozen boats quit today, dozen prob'ly tomorrow. Sit down. I'll tell you about it. I'm free to talk." Hank made excuses and left.

On the dark path to the boat, whirling snow shadowed the bare wooden houses and the onion domes of the little Russian church. It all looked like a Christmas card. A shaggy kid hunched in a jacket hurried from a door. "Mr. Crawford. Sir. Been waiting since I saw you go in the plant. Somebody said one of your men quit, that you needed crew."

"Not a thing." Hank hurried to avoid contact.

"Just make enough to fly out of this shithole, sir."

"Nobody's making money out there. Try the canneries."

"They're layin' off, not hiring."

Hank slowed. Take him to the boat for a meal? A sidewise glance showed other heads blocking dim light at a small dirty window. His guys had their own problems.

"Maybe I could come down and clean out your boat, sir."

Shouldn't have slowed. "I've got idle men with nothing to do but clean the boat."

"Got you. Thanks anyhow, sir. Good luck out there." The kid had a steady voice. He headed back toward the window with the heads.

Hank called, and gave him the twenty.

"I really do thank you!" The hand that came from the pocket to shake his was soft, but nicked and scarred. With the charity settled, Hank asked a few questions. The kid, Jeff by name, had come six weeks before from California to get rich, had worked a few shifts in a couple of the crab plants while looking unsuccessfully for a boat—didn't look strong enough for deck work even if they replaced Odds—but without a contract had always been the first laid off. He bunked in a rented shack with five others like him, pooling what money they had. One of the chow-hall cooks passed them leftovers.

Hank scribbled a note to Swede: "Do me a favor. Find this one a ride on some boat going south." The kid asked for his address to return the twenty. "Address it to the *Jody Dawn* in Kodiak," Hank called, confident he'd never hear.

Down at the pier by the boat, three other bundled figures stomped in the snow. Hank waved them aside with "Sorry, guys, we're not replacing our man."

The door to the boat was locked, and a hand-lettered sign taped to it read "NOT HIRING." His crew sat at the crescent table in the overheated galley. Seth, slumped with a book whose pages remained unturned, wore only skivvies and thong sandals. A fly walked unchallenged over his thick shoulder. Mo and Terry, slightly more dressed, flicked cards at each other. Most cards lay scattered where they landed. Hank started to pour a mug from the coffee on the stove, but it smelled old and bitter. He glanced at his watch. The holiday of their near-mutiny had lasted twenty-eight hours. More than another negotiated day and a half to go. "Guys having fun?"

"We always have fun," muttered Seth without looking up. "And you'd think we was the kings of Persia the way everybody's pestering us."

"You were once hungry on the dock yourself."

"Probably be again. We all got problems. You might not have noticed."

"Slept round the clock, Boss," said Mo more respectfully. "Slept so long it's in my mouth."

Terry managed a dispassionate wink as he aimed a card at Hank's face.

"A dozen boats quit today," said Hank.

"So we hear." Seth jerked his shoulder and the fly moved a few inches down his arm.

Hank dumped the old coffee and started making new. "Means less competition out there."

"Won't be the same without Odds," said Terry. "Now who we goin' to kid?"

"We could take on one of these apes still hanging around." They all looked up warily. "Or we could fish one less man on deck, and go find the fuckin' crabs wherever they are. After you've all had your sleep, that is."

"Boss," said Mo, "I sleep any more, I'll stick to the mattress."

"Have some fresh coffee."

Within an hour they had banged on a door to buy depleted basics and were calling good luck to the huddled figures on the pier who cast off their lines. Another hour at the fuel pier, again waking irritated people, and they pitched into the wind and black open sea.

12

JAPS

By late November, the men were looking up from deck with blank faces. The same cold sea still gurgled across their legs as the boat rolled, while lines still had to be coiled on the run and the same pots maneuvered perilously. But one or two keepers to the pot, if any? It was more than most of the remaining boats found, but scraps compared to the great old banquets. Swede's price, although raised steadily, did not fill the gap.

Seth stopped on a mat outside the wheelhouse to let his oilskins drain, then entered and peered at the electronic screen. He pressed a button to search other charts. Since relief-skippering and discovering his own Sloo (as bare this year as the lamented Hank's Hole) he'd become partners to the search, nearly as aware as Hank of the seafloor's slopes and trenches where crabs might school. "We tried that fathom curve off Misty Moon last trip, right?"

"Right."

"At least there was one or two there in most pots, sometimes three, four. Better than here."

"Try anything. We'll go back after this string soaking to the west."

"Want me to relieve you?"

Hank started to say yes gladly, but looked him over. Eyes wind-veined and dull. Had barely washed during a week at sea. Black tape covered rips in his orange oilskins, and a hole in his sweater showed red long johns beneath. Little shout left in him on deck where danger lay. Indifferent, nearly. Hank held out his mug. "Just have Mo brew some fresh. We won't pick for another three hours, so hit the rack, you and the rest."

Seth lingered with arms against the window bar. "Should have gone back and married that Marion. Wouldn't come to Alaska, she said. But she'd've come around."

"Too late now?"

"Oh yes, too late. Married some guy named John, writes my mom. Fuckin' asshole name. Got a little boy. I guess *John* goes home at night and plays with his kid."

Seth ambled below and Hank watched alone again, lonely and deep-tired. Steady swoosh against the hull. The ocean hadn't changed in the three years since the *Jody Dawn* sailed new-minted to the Bering Sea. Himself with thousands more hours of eyes watching seas. Unseen forces still drove the water from below like figures crawling under a blanket. Seabirds still scanned for food, rode the surface from sky to dark hollows, squawked staccato. And gray water gathered as always into swells that lift-ed the boat above the horizon, followed by troughs that buried the deck in spray while walls of water hid the sky, all in rhythm as steady as breathing. "Oh Jody. What am I doing so far away?" he muttered.

"What's that, Boss?" It was Mo with fresh coffee.

"Just singin' to the crabs."

"Maybe the crabs all swam back down to Kodiak. At least down there you'd see Jody and we'd sometimes see our girlfriends."

"We don't show up on Horse's Head with a 108-footer designed for the Bering, to compete with 58-foot-limit seiners rigged slambang. Any-way, it's scratch there too."

"Pride, eh, Boss? Guess that's life."

"Life it is, Mo. Get your sleep."

Christmas, back home at last by season's end, turned selectively fru-gal around town. The smaller-boat salmon fishermen who geared their economy to the summer season alone had fished bumper runs and done well. (A Christmas photo from Jones Henry, inserted in Adele's letter reporting their second trip to Europe, didn't help. Scribbled over an image knee-deep in sockeyes: "Too bad you didn't stick with the old seiner, Hank.") As for the crabbers, those gold-nugget men of other years, the agency that rented them Maui condos stayed dark, while formerly lavish hosts now penned hearty suggestions to bring-your-own. Hank fingered invitations with a weary thought for ice outside and the long drive. After the Bering Sea push he craved sleep. A mere day's crash no longer invigorated him for parties. Jody shrugged and agreed to stay in. She moved through the house with restless efficiency. The wood she chopped piled high outside.

Little Pete, now past his third birthday, more than a year after the meningitis, had had no seizures. Jody relaxed her surveillance, which earlier had kept the child in her sight or, at work, beside a phone even at lunch in case his preschool called. But, although he jaunted with a chuckle that proved his vocal cords functioned, Pete only squirmed and looked away when urged to try words. Dawn peppered him with words, teacherlike, Henny with quiet persistence. Hank cuddled him and read slowly, lingering over each word in hopes that one might entice an imitation. Pete plainly enjoyed the attention and began to expect it. He was being spoiled. Jody, aware of it, alternated between urging and aggravation.

Hank placed his table for the vista over water and faced bills she laid before him. Her salary covered daily expenses but not the obligations. "What the hell does therapy do for Pete? They charge like brain surgeons and he still can't talk. Maybe pull him out?" At her narrowed eyes: "Just joking."

"Expect first to sell this house and even your boat."

He caught his breath, hid panic, and pretended to study the next bill.

"You needn't have paid your crew their full shares before checking with me. They're all bachelors since Odds left, they'd have managed on partial till spring."

"Make excuses? They're my *men*. You used to understand."

Her explosion made no sense. At least, he thought, we'll make it up tonight. But when his arm went around her in bed, and he leaned over to begin kissing, she rolled away with "Good Night." It was final.

Want ads had virtually disappeared from the *Daily Mirror*, even for laborers and hash slingers. He inquired casually, then swallowed pride and asked direct even at the fish plants where they knew him as a highline skipper. No work.

A crab settlement from Swede in late December enabled them to make the September and October boat payments, September mortgage, and the summer portion of Pete's medical bills. And a check for four thousand dollars arrived from the Korean joint venture of the spring. It was only partial payment, but: "I wrote our senator and now I'll push him for the rest," said Jody. "Ted Stevens helped start this two-hundred-mile business, so I told him to see it through."

"You never told me."

"When are you around? You didn't do it yourself."

Nothing she said anymore gave him an inch. Nor did the nights improve. Yet she remained as brisk and efficient as ever.

Hank wrestled with his pride and considered calling his father for the offered loan, just to bring debts up to date. Then a check for $8,000 arrived unsolicited with a note: Dear Son. Gift. In case Pete's medical bills get out of hand." Hank debated accepting, and finally wrote a grateful thanks. But in so doing he vowed not to ask for more.

The mail also brought a money order for twenty dollars, from the kid named Jeff stranded in Dutch. Now home safe, he thanked Hank profusely and reported that because of his note Mr. Scorden found room on a Seattle-bound tender for himself and all five of his buddies. A thanks note also from the kid's mother added how welcome he'd be anytime in Sacramento. It made Hank sunny as he crawled along his roof to tar a leaky flashing.

At the Kodiak bank, Jody, her hair tied more neatly than usual of late, negotiated crisply. Hank's hands twisted under the table as they listed his *Jody Dawn* as security for the house and added years to the mortgage payments.

The Seattle bank also needed reassuring. He spent New Year's Eve aboard a friend's tender, southbound in a Gulf of Alaska storm, braced at night in a storeroom bunk hemmed by clacking tool boxes. It saved airfare. In Seattle, the bank executive who had extended the loan on *Jody Dawn* a year before gravely drew up new papers that cut monthly payments even further, to a quarter of the initial agreement for a dozen years' more indebtedness. "We'll float you all we can, Hank. God knows we don't need more repossessed million-buck crabbers on our hands. Guess you've heard the bank joke going the rounds, that we'll offer a free boat with each new account?" Hank bit his lip and pretended to be amused. "Do you know Terrance Smith?" continued the banker. "I'm afraid he crashed so deeply we couldn't keep floating him. Any bidder can buy his boat, *Star Wars,* cheap. We can't even *find* a bidder."

The news of Tolly jolted Hank, first with concern and sadness, then with fright for himself. After inquiries, he found his friend working in a machine shop down at Fishermen's Terminal, bent over a valve grinder. Goggles beneath a cloth mechanic's cap hid all of his face but a pursed mouth. Ponytail gone. Even his coveralls sagged—lightweight things compared to the padded ones worn on a cold deck that could stand by themselves. No gold earring. He looked so ordinary Hank's voice softened. "Tolly?"

"Minute." Tolly finished and glanced up. "Hey man!" Suddenly the old gleam for a moment. But, after a handshake, Tolly jerked his head toward a glassed-in office. "Time clockers. Gotta keep busy."

They met for dinner. Tolly's face was less lean and tuned, was turning fleshy in fact, or was it the close-cropped haircut? But "Well," he said, breezy enough that Hank's worry eased. "You stole the march on me this time, you fucker. Snuck in the horsepower, and now you've still got it all by the balls."

"Not exactly."

"Close enough. Henry Crawford and the *Jody Dawn* are still one and the same. How's my boy Henny? And little Dawn, that honey?" Hank vouched for their health, and added that they spoke often of Uncle Tolly although in fact they did not. "Sure they miss me. Jody's so organized she probably keeps 'em in line like a concentration camp. No offense, I just meant she's organized. Which is what I ain't. Know what? Jennifer from two years ago when I'd blow five hundred on a single night? She's stayed with me. We're getting married. The woman I'd call my squeeze, and now nobody better say that about her."

Hank congratulated him enthusiastically and started to call for another round, then realized he might have to pay for dinner. His thin wallet depressed him at once. Why wouldn't Jody let them get a credit card?

"And your little guy that was born just when we brought our new boats up from here—jeez, that's hardly more than three years ago—what's his name? He's gotten all better?"

"Pete. Still can't talk. Or won't. But he's bright enough. He'd be the one now to play with Uncle Tolly's—" Hank caught himself.

"It's okay. Still got my gold earring. Just it's in a drawer now. That was good times. Remember the boxing between my Ham and your Mo that Fourth of July? All the rest of the gold's sold and gone, along with my *Star Wars*. Had to keep something."

"You'll get it all back . . ."

"Like how? Banks run scared now of fishermen. Forget it, how they kissed all over us a few years ago. Start back on Swede's slime line or as somebody's deck ape? But you know what? Repossession meant no more payments. I don't worry so much anymore. I sleep nights." Tolly glanced toward a window across the room, then took a gulp of his drink. "Don't miss it so much. I stay dry unless I want to take a shower. There's worse."

Hank nodded while his unease deepened.

"I thought at first like, my life's over man, when the bank said they was going to auction my boat. I'd scratched in the Bering, even pushed down off Kodiak, until my eyes was so shut I couldn't see that my guys on deck's eyes was shut, that's how hard we tried to find them fuckin' crabs. Then all of a sudden, call from Seattle, seven payments behind and nothing to make 'em with, 'we got to talk to you sir'. I shut the door to my cabin and beat on the bedcovers for a while. When I come out I knew from the guys' long faces they'd figured without my saying."

A finger of diluted Scotch surrounded melting ice in Hank's glass. He wished for another.

Tolly pointed toward the window. "She's tied up here now at the Terminal, my *Star Wars*. Walk over and look out and you can see her. That's why I said let's sit over here. Mainly I take a route to work so I don't have to see. Maybe now and then I go by in the dark." He glanced away. "Sort of apologize to her if you know what I mean. I just wish whoever buys her won't still call her *Star Wars*. That's *my* name, not theirs."

Hank considered the horror of losing his boat. Work in a machine shop and find reasons to like it? Do anything, he told himself. Anything to keep his boat.

"One thing does bug me, Hank. My guys? We really all worked together, you know? Well, Walt, my deck boss, he's from Alaska anyhow and he's gone up to work on the Pipeline. And Rufus, he's gone on back home to Alabama and shrimp boats down there where he started, writes it's not as much fun but a lot warmer. It's Ham can't find himself another berth. The big guy's right for up here, knows the work, never complains, always good humor. A lot like your Mo that he boxed. Last I saw Ham he looked like a kid who'd lost his mom. Couldn't find a berth these times, no machinery skills like mine, not even canneries hiring. You wouldn't have a place on *Jody Dawn*?"

Hank told Tolly the truth. He was hurting, and without some break would soon be desperate with all his own crew in danger of finding themselves on the beach.

"Oh, man," Tolly sighed. He reached absently for the earring that wasn't there. "I guess I'm lucky I'm through it and out the other side with part of my ass left. Solvent even, each payday like today. Hey, I'm thirsty!" He ordered second drinks. At the end of dinner, when the waiter presented the combined bar-restaurant bill, he slapped his hand on it, allowed Hank to protest, and paid it himself.

"At least let me pay the tip," said Hank, hiding his relief.

"Sure, sure, buddy. If you insist."

After he and Tolly parted—Tolly bunked in a room near the Terminal—Hank walked by the boats to find the *Star Wars*. He passed four other Bering Sea crabbers the size of his own, all of them posted "For Sale" and ghostly dark. It was like being among tombstones. He slept badly. Stared at a basketball poster illuminated by a streetlight, in the bedroom of a friend's teenager where he stayed.

Since the king crab season was ended and the season for the smaller tanner crabs had not begun, Swede had returned from Dutch Harbor to Seattle headquarters. Instead of an office, Hank found him in an open cubicle enclosed by frosted glass. No bottle came from a drawer. A suit replaced his usual open shirt. A tie fell like loose string over the jacket bunched at the shoulders. Swede's gaze remained the appraisal Hank had known for twenty years, but the eyes—not red-veined like a month ago although turning a permanent yellow—now shifted after a moment. His proffered hand moved from a grip on the desk to a quick trembling return.

Hank glanced over the low glass wall at other cubicles in front of the executive doors behind which his friend belonged. "Fresh air for a change. Wise choice." Like joshing a hospital patient.

"The rugged privacy of Dutch will be my pleasure again in three weeks. You're down here to consolidate your wealth, I take it."

"How to squander. That's my great problem."

"Have a drink. Coke? Sarsaparilla? Root beer? The office ice box has it all."

"Root, eh?"

"Don't doubt it."

At least they've forced him off daytime booze, thought Hank dispassionately as he drew up a chair. "By the way, you've endangered your reputation. What if word got out that you staked six worn-out kids to a ride home on the strength of my note? People might begin to think you're okay." Swede shrugged, not picking up on it as he would have once. To business: "You planning to buy tanners for what they're worth, next month?"

"We'll pay the least we can." No smile to ease it.

"What's your word from the biologists?"

"No better than for kings. We see crabs nowhere." Swede automatically reached into his bottle drawer, banged it shut again with a grimace. "Last fall we scheduled double shifts in Dutch. Flew in the bodies, fed 'em while we waited, then had to ship 'em back home, all at our expense and no profit to cover it. Don't mention the supplies bought, rotting and rusting up there. Cost more to bring 'em back. The good corporate news is that our Japanese lords have other fish plants around the world to absorb losses. Bad news is who they blame for what happens here."

"I'd thought of bringing *Jody Dawn* down here to gear for browns, for rockfish. They were abundant last I heard."

"When? Two years ago? We're all in the wrong business."

Hank's mouth went dry. He focused on the nubbled glass wall. "I might have to give up the *Jody Dawn*." Saying it sickened him.

Swede's voice softened. "Good luck selling your elephant, Hank. I doubt we can help."

"Any work I could find here in Seattle? Might send Seth to scratch for the tanners, still get my boat share." A pause. "I mean *any* work."

"I can tell you nobody's hiring at the plants or boatyards, either office or line. A while back my sister in Spokane reported logging camps hiring for the winter. I told that to a kid last week stranded here when his boat went bust. He thumbed out there and they hired him setting chokers. Broke his leg the second day. You're too old to set chokers anyhow. Got a license for heavy equipment? Thought not."

"I'm not too old for anything! If it pays."

"Grow up. Drag heavy chain through brush all day? I did it out there when I was stupid seventeen. By twenty I'd have first robbed a bank."

"You always were delicate."

The door guarding the executive offices opened, and a brisk young man hurried to one of the desks. "My secretary's sick today. Would you confirm these Tokyo-Kushiro reservations? Thank you." A moment later the man stopped at Swede's cubicle. "Crawford. That's a coincidence. We just mentioned you in conference." It was John Gains. "Let's see you in, say, twenty minutes." He left without waiting for a reply.

Swede's grin was tired, even mean. "You're heading up."

"Fuck that. I don't jump. He'll wait all day."

"Crawford, my boy. Hank." Swede leaned forward with hands tight. His fingers fidgeted like folded wings. "If you're desperate enough to consider—even consider—winter forest camp at grunt level, synchronize the watch for twenty minutes. You ought to see now that *I* don't have clout to help you." "Wait here," said a pleasant secretary outside the wall that guarded the executive doors. She touched a phone signal and spoke his name. "He'll see you. Follow please."

Gains wore a dark suit that looked freshly pressed. His face had lost the leanness that helped him bloody Hank in the July Fourth ring so long ago. (Only three years. And a half.) Gold-patterned tie. Black hair trimmed close. "Yes Crawford . . . uh, Hank . . ." The hand was soft. (Could take him in the ring now.) "Coffee? Tea?" A smiling Japanese woman offered his choice of regular or decaf. "My usual *ocha*, Miho." Gains settled into a heavy swivel chair behind his desk, and brushed a flake of dust off the polished surface. Suddenly he seemed uncomfortable. "Well. Hank. I hope your little, uh—was it boy or girl?—is back running around after that scare?"

"Pete's doing fine, thanks."

"I . . . enjoyed your little girl, back during that Bristol Bay summer. I guess she wouldn't remember how she crawled on my lap. Some day I'll hope to have my own children, of course, once I'm established. Family all well?" All well, Hank assured him. "And your man, uh, *our* man, Seth?" Attempted smile that came out thin. "Stopped shooting at Japanese trawlers? No more grief from the State Department?"

Hank kept his voice agreeable. "You seem to have taken care of it, John. Seth was grateful." He checked the urge for feet on the shiny desk.

"My pleasure." The superior edge returned. "Folks here were very upset at first. You can't plan ahead too carefully for the Japanese. The unexpected throws them." He straightened a single sheet in a pile of straight papers. "We're in luck this morning. Mr. Moritaka Shintami can give us a few minutes, shortly. He's glad to meet you. I've made it clear that you're one of our best producers. So . . . how's life on the old boat?"

"New boat. Life's fine." The padded chair sank low, so that Gains looked down at him. Arrogant twit. "Had you wanted to see me about something particular, John?"

"Yes. I thought you might enjoy a trip to Japan. A reward for your good work—and an inspiration for the rest. Never been, have you?"

Hank hoped that his face didn't display a flush of interest. "Most who made it to Vietnam had a look at Japan."

"Oh. Vietnam. Oh. That's . . . interesting. It shouldn't make a difference, but I ought to tell Mr. Shintami. No surprises, as I've said." Another lame smile and heartiness. "I'm sure you behaved yourself in Japan, no arrests for raucous shore leave?" Hank kept his expression neutral. "So. We've discussed sending one or two top producers over to Japan. Your name came up. I brought it up myself."

"That's nice of you, John." But hell, won't work, need to make money somehow, he thought, and decided to kiss ass no further. He rose. "I'm so tied to the fishing grounds these days that I couldn't afford the time."

"Well you know—sit please, Hank, your coffee's coming—if Mr. Shintami approves, we'd be prepared to compensate for lost fishing. We don't always count pennies, you know. Because you'd give us full attention while you're there, wouldn't you? You might even want to meet one or two of our lawyers . . . if you're not happy with your lawyer here." He readjusted papers to make room for separate trays with tea and coffee. "Thanks so much, Miho. For instance, Hank. An easy loan to help cover that conversion to groundfish, say. With commitment, possible other things that might interest a highline captain. But here." He pushed over the tray with pot, cups, and biscuits. "No use talking until we see Mr. Shintami. It *is* lucky he has time today."

Hank settled back. Unreal. As he poured coffee into an uncomfortably delicate china cup he calculated the most he might essay for lost fishing. Not committing, of course.

Mr. Shintami looked to Hank like the quintessential balding Japanese. He bowed, offered his card, and waited to receive a card in return. Hank prepared for the usual Japanese dead fish handshake as he said affably, keeping his voice deep: "Sorry, I don't carry cards."

"We should order you some," said John Gains. "Don't you think so, sir?"

Suddenly the Japanese laughed, slapped Hank's arm, and offered his hand for a firm shake. "Thank you for drop in, Mr. Crawford. Please come, sir, sit here. John calls you good fisherman. Very bad season for king crab, but you produce more than other fishermen. Very very good!"

"I see you've been watching."

Another laugh. "Oh, we watch, we watch. Isn't it, John?"

"Yes we do, sir."

Shintami went to a display case and drew a bottle and glasses from a drawer beneath. "Japanese make Scotch whiskey, Mr. Crawford. Did you know?"

"Pretty impressive. Just a little one, please."

As if on cue the serving woman brought in a tray with ice bucket and tongs, glasses, napkins, and green cakes. The host carefully filled two shot glasses, and handed one to Hank. "To cheering the good health, Mr. Crawford. John . . . ?"

Hank noted that John barely covered the bottom of his shot glass, and cupped his hand to hide its emptiness. Shintami, on the other hand, clicked his glass against Hank's and drank half, then put the full bottle on the tray. Getting me drunk? thought Hank, amused. Am I really worth something to them? He sipped. Ersatz Scotch to a serious drinker, but not bad. "Nice." But watch out, he decided as he began to enjoy himself.

Shintami moved back to the display case. It held an assortment of elaborate cups, letter openers, and Japanese dolls. "My friends, Mr. Crawford, they give gifts that I please to place for all to enjoy. This carved tusk from walrus, to tell the truth, is gift of your very former Secretary of Commerce, Mr. Elliot L. Richardson. Such very friendly meetings! But your government changes, doesn't it. No longer President Ford, no longer President Carter. President Ronald Wilson Reagan, the famous actor, who is very good man but difficult to understand." Raised brows. "Possibly you know new Secretary of Commerce, Mr. Malcolm Baldridge? Or possibly new Secretary of State Mr. Alexander M. Haig Junior who is famously aggressive?"

The ersatz Scotch began to buzz pleasantly. Play games? Why not? He grinned. "Ronnie hasn't found time yet to introduce me."

"Oh?"

John Gains watched him, expressionless.

"Let me be frank, Mr. Crawford. We wish goodwill of some American top fishermen. Therefore it is our agreeable—how to say?—gamble, to invite you."

That night he phoned Jody. "You're *what*?" she exclaimed.

"That's right. Three weeks in Japan, all expenses, plus three thousand bucks a week, nine thousand no strings for my trouble. Donation, not income, not reportable as tax. I was thinking, honey, on the way back, if I broke the trip in Honolulu you could—"

"Am I hearing this?"

He'd anticipated her reaction. "Listen. What harm to see the enemy's eyeballs? One thing I made clear, that I spend time on their fishing boats. Meet fishermen. Of course I didn't spell it out, but let's see how these guys *think* on the grounds. As Seth would say, 'fuckin' strategy, Boss'". She didn't laugh. "Look, Seth can skipper *Jody Dawn* for the last weeks of the tanner season. There's no way around dealing with the Japs, uh, Japanese. They've got the markets."

"Sounds like you'll be having a good time." In the background a child began to cry.

"Didn't you hear me? Then you'll meet me in Honolulu."

"Be serious. Kids have to get to school every day, money as tight as we've ever seen it." A pause. "I wonder if Jones and Adele will ever speak to us again."

"It's time Jones caught up with the rest of the world."

John Gains briefed him with all the admonition that Hank would tolerate, from "Even in the most expensive hotel expect the room to be small. You're not being cheated; Mr. Shintami goes first class," to "Pass name cards to everyone, of course, even at a meeting with twenty people." A bow not deep upon greeting, but necessary. When drinking sake at a banquet wait for the host to refill your drink, although feel free to refill his as a reminder. "Whatever you do, don't confront. Japanese hate confrontation, they really work to avoid it."

Should cancel, thought Hank with sudden unease. No way this won't have strings. But in his mind he'd already allotted the nine thousand. And to see Japan *was* a way to learn, to make contacts maybe useful some time.

Not like he was signing anything.

As he warmed to the subject, Gains wagged his finger teacherlike, earnest and protective. "Never lose your temper, Hank, or raise that famous voice. Those are sure ways of scaring off these, uh, folks. And of losing face yourself, believe me. And keep this in mind: if you phrase questions for a yes or no answer you might as well not ask. A blunt 'no' makes folks cringe, so they'll say 'maybe' when they mean an absolute nix. As for 'yes,' sometimes folks are just embarrassed to admit ignorance, or they think that's what you'd like to hear."

"Folks? You make it sound like walking through booby traps."

"No, good manners, distilled by centuries of overcrowding. I should come with you but I've got to testify in Washington. I'll fly straight to Tokyo when it's over."

The idea of the trip suddenly lost some of its savor. "You don't have to trouble, John. You've briefed me."

"Well, you know, inviting you puts me on the line too."

At least for the first week he'd be left to handle things for himself.

Back in Kodiak as he packed, Jody turned snappish. Didn't she understand this was business? And she was used enough to his being away on fishing boats. "What's eating you?" he asked at last.

"Nothing!"

The kids were playing outside noisily. There was a thump. Pete came in whimpering with woebegone tears, followed by Dawn who declared: "It was all Henny's fault, not mine, Mommy."

"Yes yes yes," said Jody automatically. She let Pete hug her leg, but her look was somewhere else.

Hank watched uneasily. He wouldn't want to be stuck with kids either, he realized. But he continued packing.

PART III

APRIL–MAY 1982
JAPAN

13

THE JAPANESE

TOKYO, APRIL 1982

In late April a delegation of three greeted him at Narita airport. By now he had cards to exchange. His stiff bow in response to their deep ones brushed his beard against their heads. One of them chuckled as his hand rose to feel his own smooth chin.

He settled into the long chauffered car that drove them from the airport into Tokyo, and fielded politely his hosts' polite questions. "No, not my first visit to Japan. But the first in a long time." To an uneasy look as they probably thought of wartime soldiers: "Little vacation." The visits from Vietnam had been with others in frantic search of pleasure, memories that no longer counted, filtered through a buzz of alcohol. Fields outside the car's window had greened months ahead of green in Alaska, good for a comment that received nods and smiles. He confused the three name cards. His mistake in addressing Mr. Hayashi as Mr. Asakura broke ice for laughs all around. A festive banner in the yard of one neat house announced the birth of a son, they said when he asked, brightening at his interest. Definitely he needed no John Gains to Japan-break him.

It grew dark as they entered the city, deeper and deeper into traffic and bustle. Steam rose from food stalls and shops. He'd forgotten, living in muddy Kodiak and the Anchorage of empty streets, how a metropolis vibrated. Crowds moved chin to shoulder. How did they breathe? He watched, uneasy and excited. Too long away from New York, too seldom even in Seattle. Neon flashed big Japanese characters. Shop windows had smaller signs, some in English. He controlled a hoot at "Panty stocking.

177

Makes your legs striking sexy." Another read "Fashion hair. Permanent hair." Might enjoy this place after all.

His hosts left him with bows, limp handshakes, and smiles perpetual. He had a morning pickup at ten to call at the fisheries office. The hotel room was indeed small. His knees bumped between the bed and the furniture. At least the mattress was decently hard. He lay for a while, expecting sleep after ten hours' flight connecting from Kodiak and a reversal of days. Finally he dressed again and went outside.

A turn around the hotel corner brought him into lights and energy. People swept past in straight directions. A cart offered roasted squid on a stick. He fingered a five-hundred-yen note from the three thousand they'd handed him in the car as he calculated its value—something like two hundred to the buck, have to nail that better—and offered it to the vendor. Coins in exchange, and the squid: rubbery, not that good. Further along the street drifted smells of grilled meat. He followed into a wide alley with sidewalk tables. Spits on coals, twin signs in English: "Yakatori," and "Exciting Stadium." A group of Japanese men occupied several tables pushed together. They waved tall bottles toward him with politely hearty greetings, then returned to their own business. He pointed at objects, soon ate savory skewered chicken downed with beer in an oversized bottle.

A western woman paused at the yakatori sign, hesitated, then sat at the farthermost table. Hank watched her idly. Tailored clothes but not severe, softened by a scarf, nice. The men quieted and muttered to themselves. Hank waved to the waiter and pointed for more yakatori which came immediately, but the woman remained ignored for fifteen minutes even when she turned to signal. Oh yes, Gains-wisdom, no woman of virtue traveled the streets alone, especially at night.

She prepared to leave. The large beer had mellowed him. He passed a finger across the smooth gold of his wedding ring and kept it prominent, walked to her table, and said affably: "Excuse me, ma'am, this isn't a pickup. I just thought if you joined me you might get served."

"That's very kind." She looked him over, then crisply: "Mind greeting me like an old friend so that it doesn't *look* like a pickup?"

"Sure. Why, you *are* Daisy Mae Scraggs from back home, aren't you? Mother'll jump for joy to hear that we met!"

Up came her hand. "Cousin Herbert, I do declare."

Her beer and kabobs soon arrived at his table. "I was famished," she said between bites, "and didn't have time for a restaurant tonight. This country certainly belongs to the men. Can I buy you some more of this for your gallantry?"

"Kindest thing is to let me be. I'm stuffed and jet-lagged, asleep on my feet."

"Just from the States? Some wild part to judge from that bully bush on your chin. I haven't seen a proper beard like that in ages. Not afraid of scaring the Japanese?"

He leaned back, enjoying himself. Brightness appeared to be her habit. "Don't hurry. I can snooze till you're done."

"I won't keep you long. I really am in a hurry." It turned out that they were going in the same direction.

She stopped at a marquee roofed in a pagoda sweep. "Do you know Kabuki? I'm here on a Fulbright to study it. I suppose the name Ennosuke means nothing? Never mind, he's doing seven roles including the ghost of Iwafuji. The play's called 'Kagamiyama Gonichi No Iwafuji'—don't laugh, it's a classic. It runs through the month. I come now just for special parts after seeing it a dozen times. The whole play lasts five hours." Hand on his arm. "Come in! No, not when you're half asleep, it's too special. Take a breather some night and see it when you can stay awake." She held out her hand: "Thanks again, Cousin Herbert," and entered the theater smartly. Hadn't even exchanged names.

Photos outside showed pop-eyed actors in the poses of Japanese prints. He headed away, then returned, paid the fifteen hundred yen minimum, and entered a lobby as busy as the street. Shops sold candy and elaborate souvenirs. No sign of her. Just as well, probably. Some of the women wore kimonos. Unmistakably Japan. Damn, here I am!

His seven-buck ticket put him high in a gallery sharing a rail with Japanese. Below, on a dark stage, phosphorescent bones rose from the ground to assemble themselves into a completed moving skeleton that became a woman. Like nothing else he'd ever seen. In the next scene, full of flowering trees, a chalk-faced actor or actress—maybe the same one who played the skeleton but now in a bright kimono—rose on a trolley and floated around the ceiling, exclaiming in a singsong voice that was half rusty hinge and half cat yowl. The figure moved close to Hank's face, close enough to show sweat oozing through a man's white makeup. His red-veined eyes met Hank's for a moment, impersonally, but Hank jolted at the flesh-reality. This man was working hard, was no more part of lazy everyday than were crab fishermen on the grounds. Later, actors in fantastic costumes declaimed in sounds that could have come through a grinder. Some swaggered shouting from a side ramp. In a wild battle—wild as scud on the ocean!—one actor brandished a dagger from the top of a ladder held by stagehands. At the end Hank left his seat grinning, and glanced unsuccessfully for Daisy Mae to tell her what great stuff it was.

Back at the hotel a message from John Gains: "Be my guest for a massage to celebrate your first night in Japan." What the hell. He gave an okay to the desk clerk and went up to wait. To hear Jody's voice was what he wanted, but they had agreed to save phone expense since in an emergency she could reach him through Gains. He lay drifting. Pete, mister honey dear, keep healing. Dawn, push him to speak, keep at it. Henny, stay out of water. His arms ached to hold them. Seth, don't screw up the boat. Money would come from somewhere.

A knock woke him. At the door stood a solid middle-aged woman. Her smile showed two front teeth missing. Might have known, coming as a gift from Gains, nothing to behave about. She started to roll down his pajamas. "Uh uh, mama, just do the best you can otherwise," he laughed. As compromise she bunched up the pants legs. Her mattress-crackling rub and pull started on the left foot, slowly. A long fifteen minutes later she had worked up to the groin. An erection rose through his fly despite efforts to conceal it. "You hold baby," she chuckled, and patted it impersonally. He felt the blush as he cupped his penis and scrotum from her busy hands. She started on the right toes. It *was* relaxing: every part but the groin which had started teasing. Oh Jody. After a long while she rolled him on his stomach. He woke to find her walking barefoot on his back. Sonofabitch, here I am.

He started awake. Deck didn't roll. Boat might have hit a reef. An automatic bound for the wheelhouse tripped him over his hotel baggage. Oh. Tokyo. His watch said 9:30 and still dark outside. Meeting at ten! Oh. Hadn't set. Four thirty local. Back in bed his head pumped with energy and half-dreams. Sweating Kabuki whiteface-on-a-wire merged with a grope for gaskets in *Jody Dawn*'s engine room to morning sun backlighting

Jody's hair through the picture window. He stared sleepless around the little room. Twenty minutes later he strode the near-empty street, following a hotel map away from the darkened theater toward canals.

He knew Tsukiji Market was drawing closer when trucks rumbled, people pushed in his direction, and lanterns flickered over stallkeepers' stolid faces. A man in a rubber apron stood with a bowl close to his mouth, chopsticks shoveling noodles. Hank dodged men pulling long plank carts at frantic speed, but no one challenged his entry into the warehouse spaces. He followed the carts toward noise, through an acre of stalls empty except for some women scattering ice into trays. Clean fishy odors.

Suddenly he entered an action space: dark figures busy as Dante's Inferno, smells of cold sea, rasping shouts. Dozens of bulletlike tuna big as culverts cluttered the floor: bluefins up to five hundred pounds live, he judged—fighters in the water. They appeared to be fresh. That probably meant they'd been flown direct from boats around the world, given the price of fresh bluefin. Overhead lights glistened on their blue-black hides and on the wet floor. He walked gingerly to keep from slipping. Each carcass bore a tag and a painted number. Their chopped ends revealed ruby-colored meat. The largest still had powerful heads, tapered and noble. Fighters brought to earth and market.

Buyers in tagged caps squatted by the tuna. They examined discs of meat cut from the tails, thumped the skin, sniffed, scribbled notes on pads pulled from money pouches. In an area empty of buyers an attendant slapped lettered paper on carcasses, and laborers in sweatbands immediately locked hooks into big gills to grunt the tuna onto carts. Cart men gripped thick shafts, bent forward, and hurried off with their loads. The main noise centered around auctioneers on a platform surrounded by men in caps. Arms shot from the crowd. The lead auctioneer barked fierce monosyllables while his assistants documented. Transactions appeared to last only seconds.

He dodged and enjoyed, ignored, although his head ached from jet lag catching up. At length the wet floor gleamed increasingly empty. The auctioneer actually paused to sip from a bottle and chat with colleagues. Hank wandered the warehouse spaces toward other sounds. He found a loading dock carpeted with hundreds of smaller tuna—skipjacks probably —all frozen and steaming frost. A crane carried the rigid carcasses five or six to a cargo net from boat holds, and thumped them down on the dock like cordwood. Stevedores up to their boot tops in ice-fog dragged the fish into rows. The steady pace had not the frantic drive that dealt with fresh tuna worth many times more. One young stevedore sat on a crate smoking. He regarded Hank sullenly: envy, maybe. In a side room with bandsaws men cut the hard carcasses into irregular chunks that they stacked on end. The men actually stopped at Hank's appearance and waved fish slabs, enlivened by his interest. At their urging Hank lifted a piece the size of a fencepost and, surprised by its weight, pantomimed dropping it on his foot. His mock yowl started gleeful shouts.

Further wandering took him to an elevator accessed only with a key. What the hell. He waited for an officious pair and entered with them as if he owned the place. Their conversation stopped for a moment, but they didn't challenge. The elevator opened on a circular gallery with windows looking down over the warehouse roofs. He followed the men through a door into a vast, low hall. Open crates stood on tables throughout. Men passed down the aisles inspecting their contents. The crates held handful-sized stuff dried and fresh (some of it live): pale worms with pinpoint black eyes, snails, spidery crayfish waving dainty antennae, grubs like coughs of phlegm, silver minnows.

A man in a stiff gray shirt planted himself before Hank and challenged him in Japanese. Hank tried innocence with outstretched arms. It didn't work. The man ordered him to the elevator and watched frowning until the door closed.

Back down in the warehouse spaces the floor of the big tuna lay empty except for a man with a hose. Hank passed a quieter auction with no product in sight but long lists on a blackboard. Between bids some of the buyers actually smiled and visited. Heavy action had shifted to the area he'd first passed where women had been scattering ice. People and carts now jammed the aisles, frantic but as focused as the Kabuki actors. Women and men arranged the contents of crates, their sound a buzz punctuated by shouts. It could have been a flower show for the careful arrangements on ice beds surrounding each merchant. Variety he'd known, but this outdid anything previous. There were domino rows of small fish laid head-to-tail, purple tentacles peppered with white suction cups like firework bursts, spiky urchins laid so that their orange meat formed a uniform line, spotted crabs whose claws interlocked in drill precision. In contrast to the humans' nondescript kerchiefs and aprons there were red blocks of tuna, olive sea blobs that quivered, big individual fish still silver-gleaming (an elusive quality he could appreciate, gone within minutes on a careless deck under hot sun), fat maroon squid big as party crackers, stacks of little squid dried to a leathery brown-yellow, more.

It was the freshness that clung to his mind most as he stepped from cartways and squeezed against display rails. He could have been aboard *Jody Dawn* with wind across the deck for absence of the usual ripe fish market odors.

Back at the hotel he debated his dress for the day, decided to shed the jeans he'd worn since leaving Kodiak in favor of brown cords, a jacket-coat (compromise for all occasions, selected by Jody), and shined leather shoes (packed at Jody's insistence). Maybe wear the nice clothes back at Kabuki tonight, spring for a better seat. A car waited exactly at ten. Mr. Teruo Hayashi of the afternoon before greeted him with a limp handshake but eager warmth. He wore a suit but seemed less formal than he'd been in the presence of others.

Call Hayashi forty, Hank decided, although he could have been thirty with an old face or fifty with a young one. Short as a kid, brown, wiry. Earnest expression. Tense but likable.

"You have slept well, Mr. Crawford?"

"Restless, thanks. Hey, since I left you I've been to a Kabuki play and to Skeeji Market. Really impressive, both!" He had expected pleasure, but:

"By yourself?" The balding forehead contracted in anxious lines. "Oh, Mr. Crawford, I should to stay having guide you. It was thought you are sleepy." Chewed lip. "We have fish market on the schedule, there is no need for you to take yourself."

When Hank cheerfully reassured him, Hayashi attempted to lighten, but the effort was pale. To ease it: "I've never seen such a range of good-looking fish under one roof. Do I pronounce what's spelled Tsukiji right—'skeeji'?"

"Yes. Yes. I would gladly have to take you, Mr. Crawford."

"Call me Hank. What's your name?"

"Ohhh . . ." Uncertain smile. "Mr. Hayashi best."

The car entered a clot of traffic that moved in spurts. The road led to an avenue skirting walls of huge stones that Hayashi said surrounded the Emperor's palace (Hank craned but saw nothing more), then into crisscross streets between ubiquitous tall buildings. The car stopped by a dull chrome entrance. "Please beware the traffic, Mr. Crawford. Traffic does not move on the American side."

The fourteenth-floor fishery office was nearly as wide as a Tsukiji auction space. Desks formed precise double rows from wall to window. Each row ended at the window with a facing desk presided over by a man gravely neat in dark suit and tie. Those at subsidiary desks formed ranks of white shirtsleeves and dark ties.

Hayashi escorted him to a head desk to meet his supervisor. Hank exchanged cards and did the bow looking down on lips stretched over gold teeth. Mr. Matsunaga was a caricature of careful reserve as befitted his station. He became alert when Hayashi spoke in Japanese. "Tsukiji Market alone, Mr. Crawford? This is very dangerous! And unnecessary since it is on your schedule. Tsukiji is very busy. A vehicle might have injured you."

"Oh, I know how to step out of the way." Their concerned talk continued in Japanese as if he were not present.

After Mr. Matsunaga returned busily to his telephone, Hayashi led Hank to a conference room. A smiling woman brought in tea. Soon he faced six members of the shirtsleeve staff. With cards exchanged, Hayashi introduced them. Levels of English appeared to vary. Hank greeted two afresh before realizing they were the ones who had fetched him the night before. Except for an older man they all did look alike despite varying degrees of hair. It made an easy joke to arrange their cards by seating pattern to keep them straight.

One man—Yukihiro Kodama from his card—appeared better built and more self-contained than the others despite the same kind of white shirt and dark tie. A gym bag decorated with smiling cartoon animals lay at his feet. Hank pointed to the bag. Maybe exercise. "Judo? Basketball? Soccer?"

"Every morning run, Mr. Carford."

"Hey, I'll join you!"

"Starting half-four in morning." Hank slapped his forehead and declared he'd never make it. General polite chuckles.

Hayashi took charge, passing each a copy of the schedule. Tsukiji Market indeed figured prominently during three days allotted to Tokyo. Lunches and dinners all specific. (No Kabuki, too bad.) Train then north to a place called Shiogama to visit typical fish plants and officials. Then a flight farther north to the island of Hokkaido, for a long list of visits to more fish plants and officials. Then—unexpected but nice—a train for a cultural visit to Kyoto. Then a return to Tokyo for meetings with officials. No boats.

"I'd expected to meet some real fishermen."

"Oh, naturally, Mr. Crawford," said Hayashi brightly. "They will be invited to the offices."

"But I want to check out their boats." Hayashi assured him they'd go to the harbors and look at vessels. "I mean, I want to go fishing with fishermen. Go out for a few days on the water. I've packed my own boots and oilskins." Everyone scribbled notes. "That's understood then? I'll be going on some fishing boats? Right?"

Hayashi glanced around for help, said quickly "Perhaps, of course," then added: "No worry, Mr. Crawford, very interesting, all."

Hank turned to the others and addressed the older man—Mr. Suzuki from his card—whose gaze had never left his face. "I'm really hands-on, you see. Hands-on?" He flicked his hands, then made rope-pulling motions. "Meetings are nice, sure, for a while, but I like to see how things operate. You don't learn just by listening."

Suzuki nodded vigorously, then spoke to the others in Japanese. *He certainly understands*, thought Hank. Mr. Asakura, part of the airport greeting party, cleared his throat. "Mr. Crawford, Mr. Suzuki does not speak English. He wonders if this is American game you wish to show us, this you call hands. On-hands? Does this mean perhaps on-hands of friendship? We wish very much friendship with America. And thank you, all agree with you that meetings are . . . nice."

Work this out away from the conference tables, he decided. "Sure. Friendship. Good stuff." The others murmured and nodded. Mr. Suzuki leaned across the table with dignity and shook his hand.

At lunch, held in a restaurant's private room, Hank sat cross-legged at a low table with a new set of name cards. Except for Hayashi and Kodama the men represented agencies with long names. They treated him so graciously that he felt ashamed ever to have mocked Japanese manners. Hardly a sip lowered the level of his tea or his beer before one of them replenished it. As his ear became accustomed he found them easier to understand than those at the morning conference. Discreet women in kimonos knelt behind them to serve seafood, the first of it raw, arranged with flowers. Whole small fish in a subtle sauce followed, along with plates holding decorated single large prawns and other sea life. He had eaten Japanese in the States, even aboard Japanese ships, but this tasted better in every way.

"Do you have pleasure to be in Japan, Mr. Crawford?"

"Well, I've just arrived. But I'm glad to be here." He described his Kabuki visit enthusiastically, and his desire to see it again.

Discussion in Japanese, led by a confident man shiny and fat as a Buddha. Hayashi declared that Mr. Endo wished to invite him to Kabuki tomorrow night although a dinner meeting with officials had been scheduled. "I do not Kabuki for me. But Mr. Endo very important and insists to be hospitable. I must therefore alter the schedule."

"Why, thanks. That's really obliging!" (Should impress Daisy Mae if they happened to meet.)

"Since Mr. Endo informs that Kabuki ends at half-nine," said Hayashi, "we must ask officials to meet at ten."

"Maybe we could just skip that one."

"Oh no."

He waited, relaxed, for the inevitable pitch defending Japanese fishing in Alaska, ready to listen politely as he'd promised John Gains. The pitch never came. Rather they asked him about American fishermen: their level of prosperity and acceptance in the society, their expectations. It took him by surprise and forced quick introspection even while eating delicate food. "Ohhh. We want to make a living, I guess. Raise our families. Do work we like to do." He grinned and raised his glass. "Be prosperous, like everybody else."

They all laughed and toasted.

"And Mr. Carford," asked Mr. Kodama the a.m. runner, "do American fishermen feel dutiful to their employer?"

"We don't work for companies, we work for ourselves. That's our duty, to our boats." Another grin. "And to our wives of course. They handle the money." Murmured translations. After a silence to absorb it, uncertain laughs and further toasts.

The luncheon became a convivial blur. By the time of another session back at the fishery office Hank needed sleep. Hayashi was sensitive enough to shorten the meeting and return him to the hotel in a taxi. "You must rest, Mr. Crawford, after your long journey. Tonight I will wait for you in the lobby at half after seven, for the dinner banquet with high officials. Please rest quickly."

As the cab passed the Kabuki theater Hank noted customers entering even though it was only four in the afternoon. He needed a moment to stretch. After Hayashi left him at the hotel he strolled around the corner and studied the Kabuki posters, not sure what he wanted.

"Why, it's Cousin Herbert, I do declare."

"Hey! That's a coincidence, I was just—Daisy Mae, sight for sore eyes. Hey, you know, I went in for the performance last night after you left. It was *good*!"

Soon they were talking like old friends. He learned that her name was Helene Foster, and he was no longer tired. Nice, the way she flung scarves around her neck and shoulders. And a whiff of light perfume. Women in Kodiak had forgotten how to be feminine. And how to tease.

"So you've caught the last act of Iwafuji, and there's a soul behind that great beard. I never doubted!" Her face, not necessarily pretty, had all kinds of lights and expressions. "Well, the whole play starts again in a few minutes, and you've got to come in." She took his hand and pulled him along. "Don't worry, I get in free."

"I'm supposed to sleep, so I can stay awake for a meeting tonight."

"Do you think everybody stays awake except for the good stuff? Come on. The seats downstairs are comfortable."

"Just for a minute."

The long drama started indeed full of talk. But, now sitting close, he found the exotic makeup, gestures, and costumes too interesting to turn away. Each time she whispered translations he enjoyed a whiff of light perfume. Smelled fresh, like apples. Sudden tremor so far from Jody. Nothing he couldn't handle as long as he kept it in public places. Enjoy it. Vacation. During a break he bought them sweet drinks and cakes, and joked with her over the complications of Kabuki.

A glance at his watch. "Sonofa, almost seven. Hey, look for me tomorrow when I get escorted here. What's your phone in case I? . . . " He in turn noted his hotel room for messages. He sprinted to the hotel in time to dash water on his face and put on a tie.

"I see you have rested, Mr. Crawford," said Hayashi a few minutes later in the lobby. "You are looking now fresh and vigorous."

"Very vigorous, thanks."

At the banquet, held in a place that must have been killer-expensive to judge by the individual waitresses dressed as geishas behind each guest, beer soon gave way to sake for toasts. His geisha was unbelievably charming and attentive, even to feeding him morsels with chopsticks when he permitted. After the first hour he began to long for sleep: could have laid back in the woman's lap and drifted off as she stroked his head. If Jody could see him! (But she'd snap something and change the fun. Daisy Mae, now, would laugh and take notes.) Warm sake soothed like no other alcohol. Cups of it continued to be raised to friendship. The hosts talked no deeper of fisheries than to urge sea delicacies on him, including whale, while commenting on the importance of seafood to all Japanese.

On the way back to the hotel (the Kabuki marquee was now dark as they passed it), Hayashi reminded him: "Sleep well, Mr. Crawford, and suggest you sleep quickly. Better leave wake-up at the desk. I will come for you at half-after four in morning for Tsukiji Market."

"Couldn't we make it later?"

"Oh no, time for the tuna auction and then appointment with Tsukiji officials. Do not worry. We will eat breakfast there."

A note waited at the desk from Helene Foster. "Be fun to lead you by the beard through some of old Tokyo that your keepers might not show you. Could do it with lunch tomorrow, or day after. Even backstage at Kabuki-Za. Advise." He folded the note in his pocket, too groggy to think it through beyond: Nice. Vacation. Nothing couldn't handle. Tomorrow that damned schedule listed another lunch. In the room he heaped clothes on the single chair (no hooks anywhere), brushed teeth, started to pull off socks but lay back first, and woke only to the phone jangle for his four-fifteen wake-up call.

The tuna auction proceeded as before, although now he watched it without zest while an official chattered statistics. Next they rode the elevator to the room of boxed small seafood. A recognized man hurried over from the office space to greet them—the enforcer who had kicked him out the morning before. Hank winked. The man looked away, flustered, not amused. After being taken to the head desk for the usual formalities, the man toured them with statistics that Hayashi translated. The man continued stern as if Hank might after all be a spy or imposter.

Breakfast at last, among shouting people at a raucous counter just outside the market. Hank pointed to slices and dollops of seafood glistening on ice, which the seemingly slapdash waiters behind the counter presented in petal patterns. Hayashi urged him to mix a pablum of green horseradish with a brown sauce, but the original flavors were so fresh and subtle that he savored them plain. Only when he ate his own catch immediately from the water was the taste ever so sweet. No wonder the Japanese were such fanatics about handling. When Hayashi received the scribbled bill he glanced over and calculated the yen. Nearly a hundred dollars for just the two of them! No wonder Jones Henry's hated Japs could pay fishermen a higher price than any competitor when they chose and could dictate terms.

By the time they returned from breakfast the wholesale market had entered full swing. Two merchants knelt beside one stall hand-sawing a big tuna into pieces. They left the head intact, probably as proof of freshness. Hayashi pointed to blocks of a ruby meat on ice. The kerchiefed woman behind the trays smiled and bowed. "Whale meat, Mr. Crawford. Very now expensive because the U.S.A. leads the world to restrict Japan whaling."

"Out of my field, I'm afraid."

They drew aside for a long cart piled with baskets of small fish. The puller shouted for way, keeping momentum, his face tight beneath a yellow sweatband. He turned a corner sharply. The cart veered. The baskets slid off and overturned. The man stood with mouth open, expressionless, at a heap of fish nearly as high as his knees. A few of the merchants chuckled and paid little attention, but a man in uniform began to berate him with raised arm.

"Why doesn't that jerk who's yelling shut up and do something helpful?" said Hank. "Poor little guy."

"An official surely does not do helping, Mr. Crawford. You see this worker not careful. So. Consequently. Now he must pay, for the fish is unfit."

Hank strode over, scooped one of the tumbled baskets with fish, and started filling other baskets. The cart man jolted back, then followed suit.

"Oh Mr. Crawford, this is not necessary." Hank continued. "Mr. Crawford, your shoes and clothing will become filthy."

"Nobody else is helping."

"It is this person's problem." Hank shook his head and lifted a filled basket onto the cart. "Mr. Crawford, most unseemly that you do this. See how the official disapproves."

When the mess was down to the need for a shovel Hank straightened. The cart man bowed uncertainly. Hank's hands were slimy, but after consideration he pulled his wallet, wadded a yen note in his palm, and pointedly shook the man's hand. "Good luck, guy." The man started, looked at the note, frowned, and handed it back.

As they returned to the hotel so that Hank could change from the clothes he had messed, Hayashi observed politely, "Americans are very interesting, Mr. Crawford."

"So are Japanese, Mr. Hayashi."

14

AGGRESSION

KYOTO–TOKYO, MAY 1982

The elderly woman slid back the paper doors and entered on her knees, bearing dishes of food arranged like paintings. Serving them seemed her greatest pleasure. Whenever they entered the room her forehead touched the floor and she waited on them with the greatest smile.

Hank, cross-legged on straw mats he now knew as *tatami*, adjusted kimono flaps over his bare knees. Across the low table Hayashi stayed covered easily with an identical kimono provided by the *riyokan*. Of course, Hayashi was shorter by a head. His knees barely knobbed beneath the printed blue cotton.

Hank, now expert with chopsticks, detached a soft orange marble of sea urchin from its prickly shell. Clean flavor, tart. All the urchins he'd cursed for spiking through thick gloves, then smashed and kicked through the scuppers! And here they were food, a product to sell. "I liked the one on stilts best," he continued. "Those gongs and people. Then the view."

"Kiyomizu Temple. Yes, very old and beautiful. In Japan, when a man begins thing very difficult, like marriage, hehe, we say he jump off Kiyomizu. And the Ryoanji—your impression please?"

Hank stretched comfortably. "Which one's that, Yashi-san? We saw five or six temples today."

"Garden of stones and contemplation."

"Oh. The rocks in the sand. Well . . . interesting. The big productions are more my style. Ceremonies, priests waving things . . . like Kabuki, you know, action. What about those schoolgirls outside Kiyomizu who wanted my autograph? Fifty at least. What do they do with all their little books?"

"Souvenirs. Places and persons of distinction, Hank-san. You gave gracious time to sign books. Made very happy."

"Not hard to oblige over here." He smiled up at the woman who was discreetly removing the urchin shells and replacing them with thin silver fish nested between green sprigs and a yellow flower. Good food at a Japanese inn after Kyoto's great sights helped keep in perspective the frustrating previous days watching boats only through windows while officials droned statistics and shy women served cup after cup of green tea.

Hayashi poured him sake and he reciprocated. With raised cup: "*Gampai.*"

"Chin-chin." Hayashi smiled. "You see, I learning to say like you in America. Or is more correct to say 'Mud in the eyes'?"

Hank considered. Where to begin? "In Japan, what did they say instead of *gampai* say, ten years ago, twenty?"

"Always *gampai*, naturally. My grandfather."

"In America we change such words every few years. It's called slang. Nobody says 'mud in your eye' anymore, and I've never heard 'chin-chin' except in books with English butlers."

"But is books where I must learn. And why should word change when it . . . expresses the thought? Very confusing. Is not Japanese."

Later in the evening he phoned Jody, to catch her at wake-up time in Kodiak. Her cheerful voice relaxed him at once. The boat under Seth was managing, although the tanner crabs remained scarce. Kids were fine. Pete remained silent but progressed normally in other ways. Then Henny and Dawn told him how Auntie Adele was back so they didn't miss him so much anymore. He laughed and yearned to hold them.

"We're at a place called a *ryokan*, hotel without beds or chairs, just this straw mat they call a *tatami*. Bedrolls tucked in a corner. *Great* seafood, never had it so fresh. Japan R-and-R to Tokyo from Vietnam a dozen years ago was never like this."

"Jones Henry predicted right. You're brainwashed."

"Let 'em try." He glanced around the courtyard garden where an alcove sheltered the *ryokan*'s single phone, and lowered his voice. "If they've left out any statistic it's oversight. Everybody they drag me to meet is supposed to be important. Since they're so polite I've done my duty and listened. Even accepted that the closest I'll get to handling a net here is boat walk-on's with my keepers. They're so *anxious*. Now we're back to Tokyo with John Gains showing up, too bad. I'm doing fine by myself." He started to add that now he'd get another look at all the Tokyo attractions but skipped it. "Now. Just tell Jones to relax. I can separate their bellyaches from mine."

"I'll tell him. He and Adele arrived in town last week to gear for salmon. Dawn's already spent two nights there. We're going for dinner tomorrow."

"Say hi, say hi! And I don't need brainwashing to see that when these people pay premium for freshest fish they *know* the difference. I'll have new respect for fresh back on the boat. Guys might not like it, too bad. We'll get better price. And Yashi-san, my keeper here, he's okay. Little stiff. Worrier, pain in the ass at first. But after a few hot sake's we talk like buddies. He's putting this phone call on the *ryokan* bill, nice guy in ways like that. Wish you were here. The temples we've been seeing for the last two days are . . . *unusual*."

"Thought you went over there to work." Her tone had changed.

"I really miss you."

"Glad it's going right. I don't know what we'd do without that bribe they gave you to see sunny Japan. The bills are just stacking. And this phone call's racking up your obligation. Don't get in any deeper."

"I love you."

"I know, I know. Take care."

She didn't say "I love you" back. It left him tossing on the futon long after Hayashi's regular breaths proved him asleep.

When they left a day later for the Tokyo train the woman who had served them insisted on carrying his bag to the taxi and refused the yen notes he offered. With a low bow she handed him a wrapped box. Lacquered chopsticks. "What do I do, Yashi, I don't have any gifts."

"Not necessary. It is her great honor. But perhaps your pen?"

He started to grab it with his left hand, remembered an admonition from John Gains, and presented the pen with his right hand. The woman held it to her cheek, and bowed and bowed. Should have coughed up something better, too late.

The train sped them through hilly countryside, past tile-roofed towns. They ate smoked eel from neat boxes sold by a vendor passing through.

Hank pinched his chopsticks neatly around each last rice grain that had absorbed the rich oil. The Japanese were all right. Friendly and generous.

Back in Tokyo, the largest meeting of all that they had dragged him to took place in the boardroom of the Tsurifune Suisan Fishing Co. Ltd.

Director Kiyoshi Tsurifune officiated. His bald head glistened under the flourescent lights. Wrinkles extending from eyes to chin gave him the look of a sack drawn tight, but a cheerful sack and aristocratic. He beamed across the table and talked rapidly in Japanese, then tittered in that strange Japanese way without losing any of his natural dignity. His eyes were active, almost merry.

"'American art is my . . . excitement, Mr. Crawford,'" Fred Nishimori, the hired interpreter at his elbow, translated smoothly. "'Abstract, but also what you would call very of the flesh.' It is at this 'of the flesh' that Mr. Tsurifune was laughing, Mr. Crawford. Mr. Tsurifune continues: 'And you should know that I learned to play golf expertly, not at Saint Andrews in Scotland, but on famous American golf courses with American friends. Thus you see how deep I'm very in friendship with America.'"

The big room had a map of the world on its main wall directly behind Mr. Tsurifune, and beside it a poster with paint scratches from the Museum of Modern Art in New York City that announced an exhibit of American Abstract Expressionist paintings. The Tokyo pleasantries had already lasted more than two hours. A dozen Japanese businessmen faced Hank around a long polished table. All wore dark suits and subdued ties. Behind each sat assistants who scribbled notes and passed up papers at a nod from their boss, while behind Hank sat members of the fishery agency, including friendly Hayashi and grim Kodama. Discreet, smiling ladies replenished green tea around the table, though not for staff. Fred the interpreter flanked Hank on one side, and John Gains, newly arrived from the States, on the other.

"I'm really impressed with the way you handle your seafood," Hank had declared to approving nods and even grunts. "Very impressive, your passion for freshness. I'd like to thank Mr. Hayashi for first showing me this." He winked back at Hayashi whose face exploded into gratified nods. "I've always respected fish and crabs as food. Now that I've eaten 'em your way, so fresh they practically quiver, and served up like a picture besides, I'll respect my seafood even more. And I'll tell my friends that when Japanese insist on quality fresh, they are, uh . . . sincere."

"Good word. Translates well," murmured Gains. "But keep sentences simple."

A large, nervous man with slitted eyes spoke up, growling. "Mr. Sukisumi says he is very gratified to hear this information. But he fears that American wages are too high. Therefore the case, that Japanese attention to their own product will be too costly when demanded of American workers. Thus better that Japanese perform."

"Tell Mr. Sakasumo that high pay gives Americans plenty of incentive. We can catch and deliver Japan quality."

MR. SUKISUMI, wrote John Gains in large block letters, and underlined the vowels.

Hank grinned. "Mr. Sukisumi. Sorry." The gentleman nodded, pleased. The gesture appeared to satisfy him as much as an answer.

"Everyone would like to know more of your good impressions, Mr. Crawford."

Hank told them more of what he knew they wanted to hear.

On it went. At length the lean, bald Mr. Tsurifune cleared his throat loudly, and the others fell silent. All faces turned grave. *He's big cheese,* scribbled John Gains.

"Mr. Tsurifune wishes now to make a statement that he hopes you will listen with full attention, Mr. Crawford. He wishes to tell you this in all seriousness: 'I am up to my temper at the moment with the issue with the United States.'" Tsurifune threw up his hands, then slapped them on the table. "'I *love* America. I buy works of American artists. Why are you forcing us to make alliances with the Soviets instead? Don't Americans understand that alliances are permanent?'"

"Well, sir, I don't make the law, so please don't be angry with me."

"'You're right, so I won't be angry with you.'" General laughter. Hank liked him.

"'We are such friends with America, that it gives us only greatest pain that our friend now treats us like—'" Fred turned smoothly. "I will use an idiom you will understand, Mr. Crawford, rather than Mr. Tsurifune's expression which you will not understand. Like an old shoe, discarded when no longer useful."

"Thanks. But you can let me figure the idioms for myself." The Fred fellow could have been John Gains's Asian cousin. Same latest glasses encircled by large, dark frames, same black hair groomed to a shine, manner not quite slick nor condescending but close enough. Prissy little mustache, that difference. And at least Gains had earned his authority, give him that.

"Back now exactly as Mr. Tsurifune speaks it: 'Without more pollack quota from America for my company in the Bering Sea, it is *banzai*! Banzai.' Does this word need translation, Mr. Crawford?"

"Tell Mr. Tsurifune that it does not," Hank said coldly. "Americans have encountered the word."

"Easy now," muttered Gains.

A confident-looking man Hank's age by Tsurifune's side whispered in the older man's ear. Tsurifune waved him aside. A smile intensified despite his words. "'Americans have no use for this fish that Japanese need. Yet Americans *contend* that they must more and more capture this fish in vessels they do not possess, and merely sell it to Japanese producers. It is disaster for my company with two hundred and twelve employees who depend, founded in 1917, my father founded, my son here beside me soon to become director if the company is not destroyed. I wish to say that this you call Joint Ventures is unrealistic, Mr. Crawford. Not good friendship."

"Tell Mr. Tsurifune that I'm only a fisherman myself. I have one boat, not a ship. And I've got bills to pay and a family to support like everyone else. What does he hope that I can do for him?"

"Mr. Tsurifune says, Mr. Crawford: 'You are a famous fisherman and influential. We admire that you talk to United States senators. And, it is reliably said, you are friends to the Secretary of State Mr. Haig and even to President Reagan himself.'"

"What the hell," Hank muttered.

"You pulled that know-'em trick yourself," Gains muttered back. "So live with it. Don't worry. Not the main point here. Be sympathetic."

A thickset man with glasses that caught the light spoke bluntly. "Mr. Satoh says: 'Only Japanese know how to capture fish by Japanese standard.'"

"Well . . . Japanese may have lessons to teach us about care and handling. But Americans know how to catch fish by anybody's standard."

"Mr. Satoh says that much of fish captured by American vessels is wrong size and wrong species."

"Tell him I've visited Japanese factory ships that receive from Japanese boats. They take what they find in the water like anybody else."

"Ah!" declared Mr. Tsurifune when he heard the translation. "'But we do not waste. All product not used for surimi becomes fish meal.'"

Hank smiled. "Maybe."

The director tapped on the table and began to speak deliberately. "Mr. Tsurifune says: 'Americans are not aware of the . . . ah . . . complications of Japanese culture. It is directed toward efficiency, and at sea it is directed toward order in the fishery. Japanese fishermen must attend school. Yes, did you know, Mr. Crawford?. And Japanese fishing masters must attend very much school. On the other hand, any rich American, even a barber in America, can freely buy a vessel and capture all the fish he wishes.'"

"Come on now, that's not—"

The interpreter raised his voice to override. "Mr. Tsurifune continues: 'I wish to say, Americans are overdoing it. They do not know where' . . . excuse me . . . '*when* to stop. Fish belong to the world, not only to Americans. You do not understand to share.'" Fred's lips curled and his tone, unlike Tsurifune's, became insinuating. "'Frankly, Japanese feel they can trust Europeans more than Americans. They have a longer history, and because of that, people in Europe really value relations and friendship. Excuse me for saying it, but more American individuals are you might say cunning. And tactical. They don't hesitate to change friendships. For example, the U.S. has many divorcing couples.'"

Hank turned to Gains. "Where's this bullshit leading?" he said louder than he'd intended.

Fred leaned forward, absorbed it, and translated with the satisfaction of a child tattling. A silent instant, then Mr. Tsurifune snapped something so directly to the translator that it was clearly a rebuke. The fellow's tone suddenly changed. His voice nearly trembled until it regained composure. "Mr. Tsurifune wishes not to argue with such a distinguished guest, Mr. Crawford. He only wishes to inform his American friends—"

Gains's interruption sounded more casual than his grip on Hank's arm. "Mr. Crawford has enjoyed sharing opinions with Mr. Tsurifune. As he told you, he is learning to appreciate Japanese culture. And has been grateful for the opportunity to observe, uh, Japanese culture." He scribbled to Hank: *Ride with it!*

Hank guarded irritation as Tsurifune droned on. The old man's voice peppered the air with such conviction that the translator regained confidence. The heavy, bitter green tea had begun to thicken in Hank's mouth. Why didn't they serve their usual flavorless little cakes to help the stuff go down? He covered the notepad in front of him with squares and triangles, then connected them, shaded some, enclosed some with circles.

"'It is aggravation to us, Mr. Crawford, how Americans do not honor friendship and commitment. Perhaps you're not aware that historically, Japanese have fished in the entire Bering Sea and also in the Gulf of Alaska. In these fisheries we have made great, yes, tremendous investment. We have put so much money into the market for black cod. Then it was deprived and we're driven away. After all that Japanese people been through, it's like they've been stretching their lifetime for a gold mine, and after they struck it, it's taken away. And then this American guy says—'" Fred assumed a sly, sarcastic voice. "'Out you go, go away.'"

A brisk woman dressed more severely than the tea girls hurried in with a phone on a long cord. As Tsurifune listened, his face tightened and he held up a hand for silence. "*Hai, hai,*" he snapped at intervals over the phone.

Hank took the opportunity to beckon the tea girl. "Some water, please, miss?" Fred translated curtly, his manner different toward a servant. She bowed and hurried away. "*Mizu,* that's the word for water," said Hank, remembering.

"Buy!" Tsurifune declared, in English, his face as fierce as a sword thrust. A moment with pursed mouth, then another "*hai,*" and his lips parted in a slit that revealed gold teeth. A further moment and he had handed back the phone, waved the woman away, and returned businesslike to his notes.

"Mr. Tsurifune says: 'Let us continue, Mr. Crawford. Japanese captured king crabs long before Americans thought to do it. My company has records crab fishing there in Bering Sea 1920, at that time managed by my own father. Then when Americans saw how profitable, you took equipment into areas of Japanese fishermen who unfortunately work to feed their families. Took equipment far from the American shore in waters once understood by all to be international by entire world.'"

"You mean, sir, by those in the entire world strong enough to kick out the others?"

"*Nix,*" wrote Gaines. But Tsurifune nodded, understanding.

"'Then, therefore, even before you demanded possession of two hundred miles of water, you made control of king crabs, which consequently forced Japanese fishermen into very great loss. However, Japanese graciously changed to the capture of only snow crabs—tanner crabs, I think you call them—which were smaller and of no interest to Americans. Now, seeing this, Americans have captured the king crabs to extinction and have therefore decided to capture all the snow crabs for themselves.'"

"King crabs have disappeared from places we never fished. Nature changes its—"

"Please allow me to finish translation, Mr. Crawford. Mr. Tsurifune continues: 'It is even more ironic that Americans possessed no economical way to extract meat from the very thin snow crab legs until their Japanese friends demonstrated. Yes, we gave away to you our method. Therefore, now, you're telling Japanese friends go home, do not capture *our* snow crabs.'"

Hank's scribbles had blackened one note page. He started another.

"'The next case in point. It is that of pollack—bottomfish you call it—in the Bering sea. And decidedly sablefish—black cod you call it—in the Gulf of Alaska. When did Americans ever bother to capture these creatures before seeing that their Japanese friends needed to capture them for survival? Now it is, we see clearly that'—now, Mr. Crawford, I will report Mr Tsurifune's own American idiom that he uses especially for you— 'Americans become a dog in the manger, demanding what you cannot need or use, in order to deprive Japanese friends.'"

"Please tell Mr. T that this might sound unfair to him. But Japan has its own water out to two hundred miles. It's not our fault if you've fished it out. In our water the foreign ships—not just Japanese, also Soviet, Taiwanese, Korean, whatever, but mostly Japanese—were taking so much fish there was nothing left for Americans. Your ships were a city out there. I saw it many times. I was just a crab fisherman in a small boat, and Japanese ships sometimes destroyed my gear. *You* were the ones who overdid it. You forced us to take back our own."

Tsurifune absorbed the message looking directly at Hank, nodding with a "*hai!*" at each point, then leaned back frowning. His son, who had made notes throughout the meeting while saying nothing, passed him a slip of paper. Tsurifune read it, and pushed it back abruptly. But his tone became chatty. Fred's voice in translating reflected the change. "'Let us have a friendly discussion on this. Even in Japanese regions, Koreans with fishing boats are coming in within two hundred miles. Sometimes they fish illegally, and that's when we also start criticizing. Those things happen. We also get angry. We have a saying, "we really expand the hole of a needle." We ignore Japanese fishing, get angry at Korean overfishing. Americans also fish illegally. Do you know this? All do it. So let's not make that too much of an issue. What America is doing now, they send search planes looking for Japanese illegal fishing. And I think the cost of this airplane comes from money made by American fishermen, and do you know where the fishermen's money came from? From Japanese buyers.'" The old man raised his eyebrows to make it a joke. The prompt produced appreciative laughs from his colleagues.

"'Seriously, Mr. Crawford. Do you know Japanese eat up to ten million tons of fish annually, one-seventh of the worldwide amount? You've got to realize we have such a big market, and you have to take good care of it. So what I want to emphasize strongly is that if American people catch all the fish, and ninety percent is sold to Japan, it's only fair that you let Japanese capture equal amount.'"

Hank was becoming increasingly restless. "That's not in my hands, sir."

Tsurifune returned to his notes and continued in his earlier tone. "'Let me tell you frankly, Mr. Crawford, we are in anger and upset that our supposed American friends now deprive us of more and more quota that we have harvested historically. And, even with unfair quotas allowed, which you call Domestic Allowable Harvest I believe, you are trying to deprive even this unless we agree to buy also from American vessels in program called Joint Ventures, which therefore puts Japanese fishermen off boat thus to starve their families. Even now, too many vessels driven away from our historic fisheries off the U.S. must try to fish off Japan which crowds away Japanese home-stay fishermen and upsets the order.'" Tsurifune held out his hands. "'Excuse me, but is this what Americans call friendship?'"

Thick Satoh leaned forward. His tone was harsh and the interpreter quickly reflected it adding a snide tone of his own. "'Japanese have shared you our maritime research. We have shared you snow crab and black cod processing methods. In Japanese culture which Americans evidently do not understand, friends do not betray friends. But this way you have betrayed your good friend. Isn't it customary for people who accept favors to give back favors?'"

"Hold on here." Hank laid down his pen and pushed away the pad. "You're who? Mr. . . . Satoh. I don't think you know your damned history. Sir." He turned to Mr. Tsurifune. "What were you doing forty years ago, sir? You yourself? Excuse me, but I think you were playing some part in trying to destroy America and the rest of the world. Japanese started one of the dirtiest wars in the history of man." He threw aside Gains's urgent hand on his arm. "But we defeated you. If we hadn't, the world would now be hell for everybody but Japanese. But we did not destroy you, sir. We helped you to recover and become strong again. *Helped* you! So that now, it's possible for you to sit here today, the important head of a powerful company. You rattle on to me about favors and friendship—"

"Please, Mr. Crawford, let me catch up," interjected the interpreter with breathless awe.

"What Mr. Crawford means to say—"

"Shut up, John."

Hank calmly sipped his water, again brushed off Gains's anxious hand, and scanned their startled faces. Tsurifune's son studied Hank with narrowed eyes and a stretch of the mouth that was possibly a smile. Only the old man himself waited without expression. "Caught up, Fred? Okay. Sir, don't tell me about favors this year or last year. Remember the many, many years of American friendship that has made you strong instead of wiping you out. Remember why it is that all of you are sitting here today rather than . . . well, excuse me, but . . . instead of in some prison."

After the translation, silence. Get up and leave calmly, Hank told himself. Catch the first plane home. Around the table, wary eyes had focused on Mr. Tsurifune. The aristocratic face remained a mask.

Suddenly the old man chuckled, then laughed. Everyone else did the same, cautiously. Gains joined with nervous excess. The son, unsmiling, raised one eyebrow and scribbled notes. Tsurifune resumed in a calm, pleasant voice, his eyes again merry. Fred cleared his throat. "Mr. Tsurifune says: 'We will now leave this controversial subject to discuss other interesting matters. American painting of the . . . for example . . .'" The interpreter asked a puzzled question, and Mr. Tsurifune's reply in Japanese contained the English words. "Ah. Abstract expressions, for example. 'This is achievement of great consequence for America. I myself possess paintings by the great Americans Jackson Pollock, Mark Rothko, Sam Francis. And now, today also Jasper Johns. Does this amaze you?'"

Hank forced himself to settle back. "Very amazing, sir." Not just paintings that amazed! He fingered his beard, feeling light as his battle tension eased. *Painters*? The guy named after a fish was the only one he'd heard of: man who sold scribbles for the price of a crabber. To play the strange new game he said: "*One* I like, I guess. Bellows? John or George Bellows? Those prizefighter paintings?"

Tsurifune wagged a finger and his eyes sparkled. "'Your tastes are literal, Mr. Crawford. And *aggressive*.'"

"Just like Japanese Kabuki, sir. Which I like very much."

"Ah!" Several of the dignitaries nodded eagerly. But further talk revealed that none of them had attended Kabuki in years.

The meeting lasted another hour and covered the full range of Tsurifune's interest in pleasures American from golf to bourbon. Hank listened politely with wandering attention while his buzz settled. Jones Henry, you should have heard your old buddy tell 'em off, seen 'em back down! Now he knew how to handle Japs . . . Japanese.

Yet he continued to like Mr. T. The word gentleman applied. Grace under fire. At last the director concluded, voicing flowery praise for Japanese-American friendship at that. "'Photos now, Mr. Crawford.'" As translator Fred folded notes into his briefcase, he regarded Hank with subdued respect. Now that he wasn't parroting other people's bold words, he seemed to have no presence of his own—little face behind a smudge of mustache. Mr. Tsurifune in passing dismissed him with such an absent wave of the hand that Hank said something kind to compliment Fred's English. The guy lapped it up like a puppy. Hank turned to the fishery people. The dependably friendly Hayashi—who had greeted him that morning enthusiastically—bustled with papers and averted his eyes.

A photographer snapped the whole party (minus staff and fisheries), in front of a vast abstract frieze outside the company boardroom. Frame after frame followed of Hank and Tsurifune together, with Hank's arm lightly on the shoulder below him and the old man's arm reaching high. As soon as the photos ended, the dignitaries and their staffs vanished.

A banquet would follow in four hours. "'Since I am an old man and must rest,'" declared Tsurifune with a twinkle, (in English!) "you must please accept hospitality from my son."

To Hank's dismay the meeting would resume next morning at ten. "What the hell's left to say?" he muttered to Gains.

"Now it's your turn to shut up."

"Well . . . ," Hank ventured in the cab back to the hotel. Beside him, Gains said nothing. Afternoon traffic was already thick. Get moving, Hank silently urged the cab, begrudging every car that blocked their way. John's obvious disapproval penned him in, while the meeting had left him pumped up, needing to let it out. Call Jody. Then, maybe, catch the first acts of Kabuki before the banquet grabbed him. Admit it. A little harmless joking with Helene would be nice, if she was there. Tell her about the meeting, hear her laugh... He returned to the grave game-play with John. "Well . . . Old Tsurifune took his medicine like a gentleman."

"You *don't* know Japanese, do you? How he acts now is the surface. He'll never forget. Maybe never forgive."

"Want me to ship home tomorrow?"

"Wish I had the option. No, you stay. See if you can hold your tongue tonight and tomorrow. At least see it through on the surface. God knows what they'll make of you now." When they reached the hotel: "Freshen up. We can meet for a drink in, say, an hour, and I'll try to—"

"Uh-uh. See you when they pick us up for the banquet."

"See here, Hank—"

"No thanks." In the cramped room he placed a call to Jody, showered quickly listening for the phone, dressed slowly, checked the hotel operator who assured him he'd not been forgotten, then waited restlessly. At last the operator confirmed: no answer. He'd wanted her voice. And wanted to relate how he'd told off the Japanese. Have her give the message to Jones Henry: Pearl Harbor remembered.

Time for Kabuki to start around the corner. When the elevator opened onto the lobby, damn, there was Gains, seated with a group of Japanese talking seriously. Gains rose and beckoned him over. "Sorry," Hank called. "See you back here seven-forty for pickup."

Gains started toward him. The smooth face framed by neat black hair and horned glasses turned anxious. Hank hurried to the street and quickened his pace without looking back.

Soon he stood by the box office of Kabuki-Za to buy the cheapest balcony seat.

"My stars it's Cousin Herbert, I do declare!"

"Hey Daisy Mae!" Without thinking he held out his arms. "My dear ol' cousin!" Her agreeable scent surrounded him. Apples again. Her arms closed, more than the casual greeting he'd intended. It triggered an unexpected surge. He released the hug quickly and stepped back. There she stood, scarf over shoulder, interesting as ever. He realized she was part of Kabuki's attraction.

"And dressed fit to kill!" she exclaimed. "I'd suspected those were *some* muscles I finally felt beneath the padding." Her eyes drifted to his chest, then back to his face directly.

He stepped back, wary, and uneasy for being so. "Dressed for banquet tonight. Got to leave by seven-thirty."

"A shame." But did she look relieved? As they walked into the lobby a knot of Japanese matrons in traditional dress tittered. "You know, don't you, Cousin Herbert, that your splendid barbaric beard is part of the show here?"

"Plenty I don't know."

He followed to the good orchestra seats she commanded. The program was no longer that of the actor playing seven roles in a long drama, but a series of shorter ones. "They change every month," she noted, and began to explain the plot of the first play. The curtain parted on a chalk-faced woman. ("That a man?" "Of course. Shush.") Backdrop of moon-rippling water. The character swayed as she/he whimpered and agonized in a high singsong voice.

He'd hoped for warriors with growls and gnashing. Helene's perfume kept pulling his attention from the static drama.

When she escorted him out to catch the banquet transport: "You do have my address and phone number, Cousin Herbert?"

"Somewhere." Best to have lost it.

"Here. I wrote it down again. In case you'd say that."

He tucked it in a pocket of his suit jacket.

"Enjoy the air up in that male tree."

He started to ask what she meant, decided better not. Her half-saucy look made him uneasy. But lighthearted. Now that he was safely leaving.

15

THE MALE TREE

The restaurant admitted only members. Its proprietor bowed deeply to each. The place smelled of teak and money. They entered a private room raised from the floor. Waiting beside each cushion knelt a smiling girl dressed like a Japanese doll. The men settled cross-legged around a low table. They started with beer. This washed down courses of sea tidbits tucked on individual plates among fronds and blossoms. None were less than delicious. Sake followed, accompanied by raw, bright red slices of tuna and whale. The toasts began. On Hank's left, Tsurifune's son headed the party. A subdued John Gains sat at the turn of the table facing Hank. The other six guests were dignitaries from the earlier meeting. Hank studied their faces. Some were pompous, all overly convivial even to the blunt Mr. Satoh.

"Call me Mike," Shoji Tsurifune had said at once, in easy English. He had the direct look of his dad, though without the knowing twinkle of age. His dark suit and tie were as impeccable as Gains's, but the way black hair flopped casually over his forehead showed an ease foreign to the straight-slicked Gains.

"Whoever taught you English did a good job," said Hank.

"Thanks. At Harvard, I guess." In warm-up conversation Hank learned that he played sax in a jazz ensemble (not for pay of course), had never seen Kabuki, seriously honed his golf and tennis skills, and had assumed from birth that he'd take over the family business. "Do I like my family business? Sure. Why not? What difference would it make?"

Under Mike's easy translation the talk flowed from one light subject to another, with fish business barely mentioned except to identify some exotic species when it came to table. It forced Hank back to his own college and Vietnam days when fishing hadn't dominated his thoughts. Not as difficult as he might have expected, especially since new toasts interrupted often. Time passed quickly.

"We've toasted friendship," Mike declared. "Then once America, and once Japan, and Hank-san, and John-san who brought him here, and—" He counted with his fingers while some of the others who seemed to understand English nodded to each: "Baltimore Orioles, Boston Red Sox, U.S. Open, Boston Celtics. Any others? Oh, dog races, Iditarod. What next?" The kneeling girls behind each guest filled their cups from individual blue-striped carafes.

"Been here only what? No more'n two hours, man," said Hank, fingering the warm cup. "Want to get us drunk?"

"Why not? Ah." A door slid open. Smiling, bowing older women handed in platters of fish that still twitched and glistened silver against nests of small yellow chrysanthemums. The young hostesses received each dish ceremoniously, and with further bows arranged them around the table. The girl behind Hank leaned past him to cut out a piece of bright red meat and offer it to him between chopsticks. Her soft silk sleeve brushed his cheek.

He looked comfortably into her eyes—after a toast or two he'd accepted being fed—and opened his mouth. Delicate flavor. (Poor critter now surely dead, forget it.)

"You like?" she asked gently.

"Ummm."

There followed conchs, uncooked, their guts hidden way up in the shell to be picked with little forks, then spiky urchins served likewise. Then some reddish sea vegetable with a taste so suddenly disgusting he coughed it out as everyone laughed and laughed.

He looked around at the grinning faces of men who had been all tight business in the afternoon. Fat old Sukisumi whose eyes had slitted like a snake's with each pointed question now rolled on his side when Hank told how fishermen sneaked around the corner to a cash buyer in Bristol Bay if the price was high enough and fuck the cannery. They all had roared. If Mike had been translating for the meeting it would have gone sweet. No snide bullshit. Nobody remembered anymore what he'd said about Japs in the war. Not from the way they acted now. Poor asshole Gains sitting there tried to laugh out and toast like the rest. He'd never get it. Hank told more anecdotes. He made each funnier than the last. They loved it. Who said all Japs were frozen little pricks?

Cooked food began to arrive, first single big clams, then baked salmon and other fish, then soup with whole king crab legs. With each bite that the girl fed him, he declared he'd never eaten better. "You are *nice*! You know?" She giggled in the cutest way with a hand over her mouth, so pleased, and her whole little body bowed. Glad he'd said it. "You're what they call a geisha?" Giggle again. "What's your name?"

"Machiko."

Mike Tsurifune leaned toward his ear. "Like her?"

"Uh-*huh*."

"She's yours for the asking, you know. Easy to arrange. Very private. My guest, of course. She'll sing for you. Then, naturally, whatever you like."

Hank kept his look blank. He'd been daydreaming of this, but . . . He turned to find her watching, anxious and coaxing. "Ohh, Mike-san my man!" He leaned back laughing, and found his head in her lap. "I've got a wife. Don't you know?" But he refrained from mentioning his wife by name. The silk of Machiko's lap smelled of . . . what? Whatever.

"Oh Hank-san. Who doesn't have a wife at home? Home where they belong, eh?"

"Straight ol' Johnny Gains over there watching my every move," Hank pretended to whisper. "You don't want to shock Johnny Gains, do you?"

"Part of the hospitality, Hank," said Gains quietly.

Hank shook himself and sat up. "Let's eat a while. I'm good at eating." Machiko started to select a large prawn from a platter that had just arrived. On impulse he brushed away her arm and used his own chopsticks.

"Mr. Hank-san angry?" she asked in a small, hurt voice.

"No, no, just . . . Americans like to wait on themselves."

"Then you angry with Machiko?" Her hand crept to his chest.

"Get her off my back for a while, okay?" he muttered to Mike. "Don't hurt her feelings, she's nice, but she's all over me."

An amused word from Mike, and she drew back. "Want her gone altogether? Plenty more. Look them over. Any here, any." Hearty hand on his shoulder. "You're guest of honor. Or we'll send for more."

"Let's eat a while." Hank watched sober Gains, poor guy trying to be jolly and drunk. Probably drunk enough. Uh-uh, this wasn't all friendship. Not with feeding him geishas. But they'd swallowed his hard talk that afternoon. What's the most they expected? That he not bitch if their ships ran over his gear? No way. But he knew now that Japs were nice. Be glad enough to speak up for the way they needed their stuff fresh. What the hell, good word for their keeping some quota, maybe. He chuckled to himself. If ever he did actually meet Mister President, or Haig, that is.

No question, he could handle the Japanese. "Reminds me," he began. They all quieted and leaned forward, looking pleased, as he told another funny yarn.

He stayed on top of the blurred evening, although food kept coming until it lost its taste, and the sake turned crummy in his mouth with succeeding toasts until he demanded water in between. He wandered off to the restaurant's head—Jap toilet a hole in the floor, watch your feet—and puked out some of it.

John Gains appeared at his side as he washed his hands. "Save something for tomorrow, Crawford."

"That's what I'm doin', man. Don't plan to carry all this in my gut all night, Mr. Johnny-san."

"I can't just cart you off the way I'd like. Impolite. But I suggest you stay with the water and fake any more toasts. Empty your cup into a plate, discreetly. That's what Shoji Tsurifune's been doing, if you haven't noticed. And if the girl attracts you, take her tomorrow night. She'll keep. Old man Tsurifune's going to be fresh tomorrow. He's in bed asleep right now."

"Sure. He's old. And you've got numb nuts, John. That girl's got me roused. Easy for you to postpone. Well. No. Kidding. I'm too . . . wifed up. Even though it's ten time zones away. Or what, nine? Eleven? Fuck." Cold water on his face and deep breaths cleared his head briefly. "Whatever you say, John, it's a great fuckin' party. Hey?"

"It's a typical fucking party, Hank. For certain occasions. The old man has things to say to you tomorrow."

"Oh shit. More friendship gabble? Got to tell off old Tsuri . . . fuckie . . . fookie . . . again?"

"That mouth's going to screw you some day. Splash more water on your face, then let's get back in there."

Back on the cushion, Machiko's hand touched his thigh discreetly and her sleeve brushed his face whenever she served. They now took turns singing Japanese songs. Stuff sugary as lollipops. "Okay," he announced at their urging. "Here's mine." Good way to forget that little hand. He wouldn't have guessed how good "Love Me Tender" sounded in a full, rolling voice, but from the way they applauded and called for more he knew it was good.

The banquet broke up with bows all around. Little Machiko did more than bow. She touched her head to the floor by his feet. He swayed, not sure how to take it. Like to hold that package, he thought, pulling against Gains's firm arm to look back. Her eyes followed him. Hold her. Smell her. Feel smooth flesh. Some dancers he'd seen once—Spanish?—tightened their butts and led with their cocks, shook it when they walked, knew how things could boil down there. He knew.

"Still not too late," said Mike Tsurifune easily. "Or tomorrow."

"Shit, Mike, ol' lady faithful back home, all that."

"You Americans. I love you. Thrash it out for yourself. See you tomorrow. I'd invite you to breakfast, but tennis comes first when you're going to play tournament end of the month."

"Oh you Jap . . . Japanese. Love you too . . . your fuckin' tennis."

At the hotel Gains parted with: "Eight-thirty for breakfast. We'll talk. Don't be late, leave a call. They pick us up nine-thirty for ten o'clock meeting. Get sleep."

In his room Hank tried to pace but could only bump between bed and washstand. No answer from calls to Jody. Should be just the time she was getting up. Or having lunch? Time wouldn't stay straight. As he thought of it, though, if he told about the jolly banquet, she'd say something to spoil it.

Now Helene, she'd listen. She'd have a laugh. Her address had sweated in his jacket pocket, but the blurred number remained readable. When she answered sleepily it was barely hi before he declared: "These people can grab you in more ways than Kabuki, you know?"

"I wondered if you'd call."

"Let me tell you. Food like no tomorrow, and sake out your ass . . . ears, but that wasn't . . . Know what they did? They had a *geisha* there behind each guy, and mine—get this—they said she was *mine*. My own geisha. They said take her home and do whatever!" Silence on the other end. "That shock you?"

"Oh, shocked. Especially if it really was a geisha. So what did you do?"

He laughed to cover the fact that he suddenly regretted doing nothing. When ever a chance like that again? Let the laugh be his answer.

"Did the beard make her tickle?"

"Oh. Sure."

"You seem to have dismissed her early, for all that."

"Not my type. After all."

"What *is* your type, Hank?"

He lay back on the bed and scratched his thigh. Silence waited. "American type, I guess." Silence again.

"Ready to climb down out of that male tree?"

"Hey?"

"Want to come talk about it?"

"Talk about it. Good idea." Silence. "Where?"

"I live near Kabuki-Za but you'd never find me. I'll walk over. Seven-oh-five's your room number?"

He closed his eyes. Turn back now or not. "Streets this late, pretty empty . . ."

"Streets are safe in Tokyo." Silence.

Wasn't he on vacation from everything? "Well then, come on!"

"Expect me in twenty minutes."

He hung up, reached for the phone to dial again and cancel, laid back waiting.

By the time she knocked he was eager. Her perfume, just like he'd remembered. Soon they pressed naked against each other. He went in with a grunt of relief, enjoying even the teeth in his chest.

Too fast. Booze had made him too fast before she was ready. They stayed skin to skin and she assured him it was all right, just keep trying. It embarrassed him. Finally, after a fashion, slowly. But now he was sleepy.

She began to coax. Suddenly he woke and felt his nerve endings come alive. Now he wanted to please her, to show what he could do. When she responded, he responded further. It became all new, all different than with other women.

"Ohh, you're good!" she exclaimed. It roused him to perform further. A cry from her, then a new surge of pleasure.

At last they lay satisfied. He rolled in her warmth. I still have it, he thought. They chuckled at how it had all happened.

"Yes," she repeated. "You *are* good."

He woke to find her dressed again, ready to leave. She kissed him lightly. "Call me tomorrow?"

"Or today."

She left. Her perfume remained. He started to doze back comfortably. Suddenly her spell vanished and the perfume smelled bitter. What had he done? Jody! Try to call her. He picked up the phone, then replaced it. Not with that damned apple odor everywhere. He opened the door and swung it back and forth to air the room, finally gave up. Odor lodged on his hands and in his nostrils. He scrubbed, then sat on the bed holding his head. It was Jody he wanted, more than ever.

Come on. Jody had slept around before they were married, just as he had. Just dumb biology. (Kidding whom? came back the answer.) He rose and swung the door again, then crawled into bed and wrapped a clean towel around his nose. The thing was done. Sort it later. After all, I'm way off in Japan where such things happen.

The desk call jangled him awake. Something wrong, he knew. It took moments for the malaise to focus. He lay breathing into the towel. Way off in Japan, he reminded himself. Just as he dozed into a fantasy of all's right, a knock on the door. John Gains, making sure he got up. Gains camped on his bed, already dressed in his suit.

He made himself stretch. "Feelin' shitty, John."

"That's news."

He forced a grin despite hangover head and rubber-sided mouth. "Don't worry. Fishermen can booze all night, then be at the pots first light. Don't think I haven't done it."

"I'm sure you have." Gains picked up a green patterned scarf that was crushed against the pillow.

Hank reached to grab it. But too late. He shrugged, at once self-conscious.

"Not my business, Crawford. But I hope you're not playing Madama Butterfly here."

"Who's that?"

"Oh, never mind."

His legs took him to the shower. Hangovers used to be easier. Couldn't be *that* much older. He felt like retching and his head thumped. Jody. No, not the same, oh not the same damn it. Just Japan stuff, not real. What would he tell her? *Would* he tell? Whether he told or not, he knew himself. And now Gains knew. Sort it later. Forget it now. The decision made him easier.

Coffee downstairs helped. Thank God not green tea to gag on. Gains knew enough to steer to the American dining room rather than the Japanese one that before this Hank chose as part of the game. Hank tightened the tie against his neck to force himself alert. Clink of china helped dim the warm night memory. "So. What's the drill today?"

"I'd like to say be yourself, but that's clearly a snake pit. Just please remember that you're a damn good American fishing captain, one of the best."

"From you, John, that's very nice."

"Never doubted. I hated crewing under you. But that's because I'm not the deckhand type."

"You can say that!" But this was the guy who'd knocked him around in the Kodiak ring. Too soft for it now, if they went again. "At least under me you kept down that flab."

Thin smile as Gains rearranged the flowers and silver condiment bottles on the table. "I know you're hurting back home. Like all the other cowboys who staked the whole bank on king crab. Don't think that Mr. Tsurifune and his heir don't know it too. Remember this for yourself. Your trump card is, you're American."

"Damn right I am. So?"

Gains reopened the napkin that he'd folded twice and laid it on his lap. "Don't ask me, Crawford. I'm a company man for the Japanese. You'll have to figure it out for yourself."

The waiter brought scrambled eggs with toast and jam. "I didn't even know we'd ordered. Damn that looks good. I've been doing Japanese for the hell of it, but—"

"Commendable. But this morning I figured you needed Stateside."

"Maybe you're sometimes okay, John."

"Don't get carried away."

The comforting eggs settled his queasy stomach, partly, and the sweet of the jam soothed. It diminished the swim in his head and refocused the rest. Jody and trust waited back home whether Gains knew or not. What *did* Gains know, or figure? Hank leaned back. "Well, if you're through talking business, your geisha last night, could you have laid her?"

Gains closed his eyes and sighed. "Hank. Your private life's your own business. And I'll keep mine to myself. Those were waitresses. Yours was something special, but no geisha. Geisha's a trained professional. Sex, maybe, but certainly not assumed. Only way, way down the line after rapport, maybe. Remotely. You wouldn't have appreciated a geisha."

"Hm." He felt foolish. Then remembered Helene, started to grin. But Jody. Sick feeling. Think about it later. Coming up in the office elevator, a sweating, cheerful Mike in white tennis shorts joined them. "Terrific night, Hank. Your stories were a riot. Sleep well? I'll be there by the time Dad finishes showing his trophies."

Mr. Tsurifune rose from his polished desk and strode around to greet Hank with lively eyes, a firm handshake, and (reaching up) a pat on the shoulder. Gains received a lesser nod. "Happy to see you, Mr. Crawford. Good banquet last night?"

"Hey, sir. You speak better English than I do!"

"Ha ha. Only little. Please to look around?" The old man's hand remained on his back, guiding the way.

A niche in the walls of polished wood held a Shinto altar of the kind Hank had seen in less private Japanese offices, but the blue and yellow vase in this one could have come from a museum. Hank commented. "Ah!" Tsurifune's smile revealed gold teeth. "Your eyes very good, Mr. Crawford. Imari, seventeenth century." One wall held a big painting of nothing but one fuzzy red square and a smaller green one. "And this do you recognize, American master Rothko? Very expressive you see. And, ha ha, very expensive must say, but soon I think worth more." Could have done the same with Christmas paper and glue, thought Hank, but he nodded politely.

"Come, Mr. Crawford." With a flourish, Tsurifune threw open a door in the paneling. It opened to a long room with art work hung and stacked. Workmen in smocks were moving some pictures from a white wall that others were repainting white. Tsurifune's hand led him from one picture to another. There were two big ones by the dribbles guy with the fish name, one of nothing but an empty bathrobe, another of thick, black streaks of the sort done to test a brush. A smooth statue of almost nothing "by Noguchi of course. And here you see also early work Kunyoshi, America and Japan together—friends from many years ago. Now making room for Jasper Johns, purchased through my agent in America yesterday. Yes! Did you know that I have approved this sale by trans-Pacific telephone just while you and I talked of fishing matters in great earnestness?" He looked up at Hank triumphantly. "You are amazed, Mr. Crawford, to find such important and valuable American collection in Tokyo?"

"Really amazed, sir."

Tsurifune gestured to framed canvases and drawings stacked beneath the emptied wall. "All these, American Sam Francis. You know? All Tokyo period, value increasing."

"You met Francis during his five years painting in Japan, didn't you, sir?"

"Ah, hundred percent, Mr. Gains, you have listened and remembered." The hand led Hank back to the office. They moved to a wall where spotlights from the ceiling shone on the contents of a floor-length glass case. "And here, Mr. Crawford. Trophies from experience around the world." It almost duplicated that in the office of the big Seattle Jap . . . Japanese. "You recognize the hat—you call it cap? U.S. Coast Guard Cutter *Sweetbrier* which I make visit in Alaska. See there scrimshaw on walrus bone, and paperweight with U.S. state seal, and cup with girl painted inside most cunning, gifts of—" He named three powerful U.S. senators. He pointed out other celebrity gifts one by one and finally pointed offhand to a silver ashtray far in the corner of the lowest shelf. "Present of Mr. Sweden Scor'en, I think he is friend?"

Swede too!

Mike Tsurifune joined them, as cool and dark-suited as during yesterday's meeting. His father led the way to thick leather armchairs. A smiling girl immediately brought green tea. Mike's spicy lotion wafted strong. No hangover that Hank could discern. His own stomach felt sour, his head stuffed.

Tsurifune leaned back, tapped fingers together, and spoke in Japanese. His lean, aristocratic face assumed a grave but still friendly expression.

"My father first wishes to apologize for speaking again only Japanese. But he thinks it's better in order to make all clear, since he's paid a lot of money to make sure I understand English." Appropriate polite laughs all around. "Now Hank—it's okay if I call you Hank?"

"Sure. Is that your dad talking?"

"Oh no, of course not. Me. I haven't begun translating again. Don't be offended. Older generation in Japan is very formal." Mike spoke curtly to the girl with the teapot. She bowed (not as deeply as last night's waitress) and hurried off. His voice eased again. "Now Hank, I'll just speak for both Tsurifunes. We know king crab times are hard in America. It's the way things go. And yesterday we told you of Japanese hardship since the U.S. claims more and more fish quota for itself and eases out foreigners."

"Well, as I said yesterday—"

"Needn't defend. Please let's not go through all that again." The chuckles included Mr. Tsurifune, who had not received translation. "We know the reality whatever yesterday's rhetoric. You're claiming your own. We would too, if we had it. Now. We've made inquiries. No offense, but it's no secret that you're having trouble with payments. We know your little boy was sick, and we're glad to hear that all's now okay except the bills. And, with your 108-foot crabber *Jody Dawn*, you've rigged expensively for bottomfish also, but the Korean joint venture turned out to be a mess. We're not surprised, I'd like to point out, since this is typical of doing business with Koreans, and also of such joint ventures your State Department proposes. Also, we note that you are building a new house twenty miles from town not completed or fully paid for."

Hank flashed Gains his sudden resentment. Gains's gaze remained steady.

"We didn't need John to tell us, Hank. Don't be offended, but we have plenty of access. We also know your catch record, not just what you deliver to our plants. You produce, because you seek product even when others give up and go home."

"*Your* plants?" Glance again at the stoic Gains. "I thought you were a small private company that owned five or six trawlers and longliners."

"That too, of course. It's complicated. Don't let it worry you. Except as reassurance that there are resources." Mike spoke in Japanese to his father, businesslike, then leaned toward Hank. "What would you say to immediate clearing payments on your *Jody Dawn* and all other bills? Then, perhaps, some time later . . . who can say?"

The girl laid down a tray of Scotch and shot glasses. The day continued with little time for pause. After a long luncheon and the usual toasts,
Hank spent the afternoon with Tsurifune Company lawyers. They
explained the terms of an agreement by which the company paid off the
Jody Dawn and assumed co-ownership. Hank would amortize the debt
with future earnings and regain full possession. The terms were more flexible than any with his Seattle bank. He refused, however, a further loan for
his house and medical debts. Gone deep enough.

No question but that the Tsurifunes had an agenda for him. But as
everyone talked he began to see it as mutual interest. If Japanese controlled
the world's fish money and markets, why not be inside with them rather
than nose-against-the-window looking in?

He tried to call Jody to tell her about it. No answer. She was busy in
town probably, the kids in school or at Adele's, whatever. He'd tried.
Admit it: was afraid she'd answer and break the spell. Let Japan continue a
while longer and sort it out later.

By the end of the day he craved sleep. Sleep first, then—this was
Japan, other side of the world. But energetic Mike Tsurifune had planned
another dinner with waitresses as attentive as little Machiko the night
before. His new girl brushed against him often. It left him warmly restless,
anticipating. Wasn't this his time and place? His earned vacation from the
cares?

Back at the hotel he lay back, still restless rather than sleepy, wishing
he were not alone. Faintest stimulating perfume smell lingered. Phone her?
The phone rang.

"Cousin Herbert."

Sudden guilt. Should hang up. "Hey. I've had a pretty long day."

"Sounds like you're up that male tree again."

"Huh?"

"Men. They climb a tree and pull up the ladder."

A relief to laugh in spite of himself. "That what you think?" Her
creamy voice, pert and funny. Soft skin, thigh to thigh. Just her voice started the itch. The itch grew. He could almost smell fresh perfume. Knew he
was waiting for it.

"Look. I'm so embarrassed. I left something there last night."

"Found it, yes." There it lay in a closed drawer covered by a towel, where he'd tucked it that morning. He leaned over and opened the drawer. That's what he smelled, not imagination. Better hang up. But he didn't. "Pretty careless."

"Oh my, yes."

Think about it later. "Maybe you want to come claim it."

"Twenty minutes?"

"Waiting." He lay back and stared at the ceiling. Once, twice, had to be the same. On vacation and sort it out later.

16

SKIPPER DREAMS

H e needed to hear Jody's voice, and nobody responded all day and night. Her voice would keep him from slipping further. Adele answered the Henrys' phone only after he'd spent hours trying. Didn't fishermen's wives ever stay home?

"Jody's father had a stroke, Hank. They weren't close from what Jody says, but she felt she had to go. Now shut up, Daddy, wait your turn. I can't believe I'm talking to Japan."

He felt a new surge of guilt. "Is Jody all right? Is she upset? Are the kids with her?"

"I have Dawn and Henny so they don't miss school, no trouble at all. Jody took little Pete. It all happened suddenly, the way those things do. Daddy! It's very, very long distance. *Japan.*"

"Give me that thing, woman," growled Jones Henry. "Hank!" He shouted into the phone as if he were calling boat to boat. "They brainwashed you yet?"

"Not a bit."

"Listen, Hank. Give me your opinion. Got an offer to buy a Bristol Bay gillnetter and permit. Bay reds bring ten, twenty times Kodiak pinks. I figure with crab and shrimp gone, the one good investment these days is salmon. Biologist fellows predict a thirty-four million run in Bristol Bay this year. Five, six pounders they say brought over a buck a pound last year. One year like that pays the second mortgage I'd take to buy in, most of it. What's your opinion?"

Hank remembered the tides, and his grounding with the *Orion*. "Bristol Bay's a different game, Jones."

"I know the game. I fished a Bay double-ender thirty years ago while you still sucked lollipops."

"Daddy!" came Adele's voice. "It's Japan. Hank's paying money!"

"Japs are paying, Mother, trust Hank to make 'em. Now listen, Hank, quick other question. This fellow Ham Davis. Crewed for your buddy Tolly. What about him?"

"Well, what about him?"

"He's on the beach. Mebbe I'll take him. Can he work? Is he reliable?"

"Yes to both, Jones. Good man. To the other—a Bristol Bay permit costs a lot."

"That's for me to figure."

"Then go for it, I guess. Jones, this *is* long distance. And Adele hasn't given me Jody's number yet."

"She's here. The woman's fingers are in my face grabbing for the phone."

Adele gave him the numbers of the Sedwicks' home and the hospital. "I have all kinds of questions I won't ask till you're home. But I'm sure those people aren't as civilized as the French. Just tell me this, because I can't believe I'm talking actually to Japan. What on earth time's it there?"

"Eight. Nine. Thereabouts. And the day's yesterday, or maybe it's tomorrow, I can't keep it straight."

"They *are* strange people. Daddy's got that right." Her voice dropped. "Hank! He's just left the room. Listen. This idea of Daddy's is crazy. We don't need another boat with second mortgage and new debts at our age. The boat welding business in San Pedro's gone bad since the porpoise huggers started driving out the tuna fleet. That's why Daddy thinks he's got to do something new."

"Change keeps it all interesting, Adele. Bristol Bay's hopping they say."

"But it's our savings he's fooling with. Oh, here he's coming back. For heaven's sake don't encourage him. You take care!"

Jones again. "Hank! Something I ought to read you about the Japs taking over in Alaska."

Hank turned restless. "Show me when I get back. Now, Jones, on this Bristol Bay thing. Maybe talk to Adele, think twice—"

"I'll worry about that. Hank! Remember Pearl Harbor!"

Hank crushed a matchbook from the bedside table. "I'm . . . remembering."

Hank placed a call to Jody's Colorado number. He waited in the small bedroom with elbows on knees. Had Jones ever cheated on Adele, maybe to get a breather from her pecking and her France-foolishness? And Adele? Long weeks alone while Jones fished?

The home phone in Colorado didn't answer, and the hospital passed him from person to person until the line clicked dead. When he called again the Tokyo operator couldn't make a connection but told Hank he'd keep trying.

He lay back, too depressed to think of sleeping. She wouldn't cheat on him. Jody wouldn't. The bedside phone rang. He picked it up eagerly, prepared to hear her voice.

"Cousin Herbert. You are some scarce."

"Look, Helene. I . . ." Silence.

"Oh my."

"I'll . . . We'll talk later, right?"

Now he waited by the phone feeling even worse. Helene was a nice person, too nice to be hurt.

The little room was oppressive. For some reason neither Mike Tsurifune nor John Gains had usurped his evening, just when he wanted their diversion. He cancelled the Colorado call and left quickly. On the street he took a back route that avoided both Kabuki-Za and the yakatori stalls. As he stood looking at the wide Ginza and its overblown neon signs, wondering what to do next, he heard noise and followed it to a side street packed with people. In the center surged a teak and gold palanquin shouldered by raucous young men. He didn't know the meaning, but he gladly lost himself laughing and shouting with the Japanese. He rose nearly a head taller than most. Several around him looked up and started joking. He became a willing part of the entertainment. It cleared his head.

Next morning he reached Jody at last. He did it from a hotel lobby phone rather than the bedroom with its trophies. Her dad had died. Funeral tomorrow. "Mother's on a sedative. I didn't think she cared about anything but herself, but maybe I was wrong. My God I never knew the work to bury somebody. And his papers! I thought they were organized. And Pete's just a pest! Thank God for Adele keeping the others, but without his brother and sister he's suddenly all over me. Clings! He's never done that before. When are you coming home?"

"I'm sorry Honey, about your dad. But listen. Stuff you won't believe. Are you sitting?"

"*Sitting*? You don't know what it's like here. Pete! Stop that! Okay buster, you asked for it!" Sound of wailing.

He waited while money-seconds ticked. Wanted to hold her. Felt sick with shame. John Gains walked into the lobby from the street. He wore jeans and an open shirt, and carried an overnight bag. Gains? Didn't know he owned such clothes since deckhand days. Still an hour before they'd meet for breakfast.

Finally she returned. "This is terrible. I forgot you were on the phone. What is it?"

"Honey, they've offered to pay off *Jody Dawn*, maybe promise of more later. Convert me to longline for black cod in the Gulf of Alaska."

"What's the catch?"

"They know I can deliver."

"There's got to be more to it than that."

Didn't she ever concede anymore how good he was? "We fought for our two hundred miles. Now we own the fish, and *they've* got to kiss *us*. I'm American don't forget. I can get quotas in my name that they can't. It's a deal. A trade. They'll set me up with fifty-one percent ownership, and I'm their fish supply. The way it works, gradually I'll buy back full control from my profits. And listen. They'll give me an open line of credit with their Seattle bank. Honey, you wouldn't believe the money these people have to throw around."

"What happens if you don't catch fish?"

"Are you kidding? Gulf of Alaska's got more black cod than . . . ants in a hill."

"When did you ever longline for black cod?"

"It's fishing gear, honey, I can handle it. Just a bigger version of the halibut hooks I baited years ago with the Norway squareheads, remember? Take me a day, no, four hours to figure it."

"Oh Hank. There's a hitch somewhere."

"No hitch I can't handle. Listen. They didn't tell me more than that, but I get their thinking. These guys see the writing on the wall. All their markets and plants back here? Committed for black cod—they call it sablefish—and in a year or two they'll be down to zero quota. Enter an American who they know can catch whatever fish or crab's out there. They need me, honey. We've got 'em by the balls. Every day over here I'm learning more how to handle this."

"Pete! Get out of there! Damn it, Mommy said stop! Hank. There's *got* to be a hitch. Who can advise us? Swede?"

"He's in their pocket. I didn't know how much until I got over here."

"Pete! You sit in that chair and don't move. Do it!" Sound of wailing. "If he'd only talk he wouldn't be such a—Hank, what do you have to sign for all this? Oh God, wait. Mother! Stop that! Stop it. Hank, she's having hysterics again in her bedroom and throwing things. Hank, what about your father? Ask his advice."

"I've thought of that, honey, even though he doesn't know anything about Japanese. But they're on that damn world cruise they said for years they'd take."

"There's the doorbell. *Mother*! Pete, if you don't leave that—Hank, I've got to go."

"But you agree. Right?"

"To what? To what? *Pete!*"

"It's our opportunity."

"Sit on it for a while." Prolonged loud buzz of a doorbell. "*Coming!*" Sound of a crash. "*Pete!*"

"They want an answer."

"Then do what you think's best. *Mother*, for Christ's sake!" She hung up.

At breakfast Gains was as efficiently dark-suited as ever, smelling of his usual lotion strong enough to waft across the table. When Hank asked if he'd been out for a morning jog: "What makes you think that? Now Hank, it's gone beyond my advising you. Frankly I thought they might offer you more. Your bluntness probably screwed that now until you're proven. Hopefully that's all. They've already talked to your Seattle bank, I've learned that much. But last night they said my job here's done, go back to Seattle and make us some money. Flying late this afternoon. Bags upstairs packed. I'd planned at least a week over here."

"*Leaving*?" Suddenly he wanted Gains around. "Will they stick to what they promise?"

"Japanese always honor their contracts. That needn't worry you."

"I've had a sinkhole of crabs hit the pots and change things a little. But there's no little about this. Too fast."

"They'll honor whatever contract you sign, don't let that worry you. It's in the negotiation that you've got to hold your own." Gains frowned, and for once the careful black hair and studious gravity didn't seem superficial. Younger than Hank by a decade, he seemed older. "I think you know that I was the one who focused them on you. And I was kind of responsible for your conduct over here."

"Well, then. Sorry. Hope I didn't screw you. But nobody jerks me around like that. You're important enough to them to stay on top, aren't you?"

"I can only hope. It's probably . . . Not many Kansas plumber's sons make it to where this one is today at twenty-seven. Scholarships, night work. Made sure I got educated with the best I could. Step by step including your hell boat."

"You weren't worth shit in an emergency, but you didn't shirk any work I gave you."

"I do what's needed." The thin smile. "Incidentally, not that it matters anymore, but when you hired me I said I'd finished only two years of college. You wouldn't have hired me if you'd known I'd just gotten my degree in business administration. You see, the fish business was what I'd planned to target, and I'd decided to start at the bottom."

Hank leaned back and enjoyed his laugh.

The waiter came and respectfully leaned over Gains to point toward the lobby. A Japanese girl in street clothes, holding a small package, bowed directly to him. She appeared to have been crying. "Ah, God." His voice softened. "I *told* her not—. Excuse me."

Gains put his arm around her gently. Nearly a head taller, he bent to talk as he led her out of sight.

It seemed too serious for banter when Gains returned with a small box. His veneer dropped. "Well, I guess it's no secret since you saw." He gestured for more coffee, looked at Hank, then away. "I lecture you about Madama Butterfly because I've slipped into it myself. Started two years ago when they first invited me over. I made it clear from the start, just happy time. Now, whenever I show up in Tokyo, it's all so nice. But then so sad when I go. Neither of us expected I'd leave as soon this time." The thin smile, but this time wistful. "If you were going to make trouble, I kept hoping you'd make enough to keep me here."

"John, John, John. You're human after all."

"I'd appreciate your not joking."

"I'm not. And it's your business all the way. Your secret."

"Thanks." Gains played with his filled cup rather than drinking it. "You're a lucky devil. You know it?"

"I guess we both work like hell for what we get."

"Hank, you've yet to see the measure of work-like-hell."

They provided a lawyer comfortable in English to explain the proposed contract and didn't rush his signature, but they wanted his commitment before leaving Japan. Another banquet waited that evening, at a different club. Mike raised a playful eyebrow. "Girls, new choice." Either father or son remembered his taste for Kabuki. "Tickets for the best seats await you at the box office, any day, just tell me."

Hank no longer wanted Kabuki. Wanted not to be near it.

That evening at six, with conference over and John Gains now in the air (and missed, that was the strange part), he lay in his room while the hotel operator dialed Colorado. Seconds later, too soon for a connection, the phone rang. He left it unanswered, then called the desk at once for its message. Helene, indeed.

In Colorado, Jody's mother answered. He expressed his sympathy. "That's nice, Hank. But at two in the morning?" Her voice was even more husky and cracked than he'd remembered, and with a whine to replace the old frank disinterest. "The funeral today *drained* me. Then an hour ago my pills finally kicked in to let me sleep. You might have considered— Never mind. Jody'll be glad you've finally called. I'll wake her."

"At least it's quiet here now," said Jody, awake at once. "It's been a day. Not much of a funeral, I guess they didn't have many friends. But plenty of hysterics and self-pity. And Pete. He's been a brat."

"Guess he's not talking yet?"

"You'll be glad to know he's decided to say one word. Only one. It's 'daddy'. I suppose it's the one thing he can't get these days by pointing. Three and a half now, and if he has one word he can damn well say others. He's not sick any more and I've had it. Let me settle this mess, and I'm going to stop buying his permanent terrible two's."

"'Daddy'? He says '*daddy*'?"

"'Daddy daddy daddy.'" Her voice softened. "All right dear. It was going to be a surprise but it just slipped out. I was thrilled too when he said it. But now I'm just so—"

"Put him on. Let me hear it!"

Jody complied and waited through his excitement. Then: "This is costing, Hank. Do you have news?"

Hank pulled himself together. "Well. I've been pretty positive about what I want. But amazing, they come up with things before I ask. Gear breakdown? I just call my bank and these folks'll guarantee what's needed. Bad times and I miss a payment or two, which won't happen? Up to three in fact, they'll cover it, just put it on the bill. Insurance? They pay."

"Hank, there's got to be strings."

"I'll tell you, less strings than my original bank loan. The strings are: they expect a highliner who can catch what's out there. That's me. And access to the quota I'm entitled to claim as an American—that I own. Which translates to an automatic market for whatever I catch."

"What about Seth and the boys?"

"They'll go along if they want to stay with me. Probably have to get another couple of apes to do the baiting when we finally convert."

"Sounds like you've planned it for everybody."

"It's my time, honey. It's my place."

"Used to be ours together."

"Ours. Sure. Still is."

Jody lowered her voice. "Mother? Are you still on the line? Hank, it's all I can do to get her hands off me. Literally hands. All that damn smoking, fingers yellow, they tremble all the time, and they clutch. The woman won't let go. Little Pete? She hugged him so hard he wriggled like a fish to get free. Now he runs when those arms come at him. Then *she* whimpers that I've alienated her grandchild. Hell, he didn't exist before this. Now that the Colonel's dead—that's what even his daughter was expected to call him—she's scared. We might be stuck with her. Not if I can help it, but . . ."

Hank chilled. Whining mother-in-law in their home? "She's never given you anything."

"Not that simple. I'm old enough now to realize it. I *feel* old."

"Not you, Honey, dear, Jody. Not you." He wanted to hold her. How could he have even played with someone else? He asked to hear Pete say the magic word again, and praised the child until Jody, in good humor but firmly, ended the call.

He lay in the bed and cast his glance around the small room, cleared now of Helene-trophies. Damned suit worn all day draped out to wear again in an hour. The phone rang. He let it, then checked the desk. Helene, indeed. An hour later the same, as he gingerly sniffed to separate used socks from clean and dressed for the banquet.

When he returned late—banquet in a more subdued place with fewer people, different girl but as available as little what's-her-name, Michico-Machiko—a saucy note waited at the desk. Midnight phone call, again ignored restlessly. Next day a more dignified note. Face her eventually and break it off, but for now there was enough to figure out without that. Didn't even want to think her name.

With a tentative agreement reached, Mike took him over. They went out one night with Mike's friends (all men) to a place where they drank to a state of guffaw and staggered up to sing into a microphone. Everyone demanded encores of Hank's "Love Me Tender," until he was tired of singing it and stumbled over the words. Next night they visited a section of Tokyo called Rappongi. The place was an excess of lights, crowds, and glitz. At another time Hank might have liked it. They entered a place of chrome and purple neon guarded at the door, and sat drinking and playing roulette while Japanese girls in tight silk dresses visited. Mike knew them all. Hank had liked the Machikos better, thought of Helene despite himself, wished he were leaning unencumbered over a top rail of Kabuki-Za watching the chalk-painted actor float past.

The toasts were many, as usual, and delicious seafood tucked in fronds came in volleys. Stuff of dreams in hamburger days to come, but now he longed for a hamburger and milkshake.

Next morning, calmly: "As the lawyers explained, Hank, we co-sign with you, assign you fifty-one percent ownership. We'll need your house signed over for security, of course, you understand that. Just formality."

"My *home*?"

"Formality, Hank. Business. In two years you'll be buying your own Rothkos or whatever your taste."

The man's confidence relaxed him. "It won't be squares and dribbles, count on that. Maybe a Hawaii condo."

"Don't knock the squares and dribbles. My dad loves them, I think. He loves anything American. For me they're money. Everybody else over here's paying too much for Dutch sunflowers. Our agent in the States insists that in five years the jump will be to the abstract expressionists we're collecting. And American all the way. Give it a thought whether you like the stuff or not."

"Likely. Jody'd kill me."

"There you go again, letting the ladies lead. Our Kabuki seems to be your taste. Your Jasper Johns had a whole period based on Kabuki play *Usuyuki*. If it's not too late when your money starts rolling in, you might consider at least a print from those before the price hits the sky."

"Does the thing look like a person?"

"Don't make me laugh."

Step by step it happened. Hank alternated between wonder, fright, exhilaration, and disbelief as the process unfolded. During the remaining days in Japan he managed to elude further banquets except for a planned farewell evening.

There was a wistful, unsatisfactory ending with Helene, safely mid-day over lunch. He was ashamed not to have faced it earlier, and he regretted it even more because she took it so gracefully. "All the woolly bears seem to be firmly locked in their trees," she sighed in good humor, and took his face in her hands to turn it to her. He closed his eyes. Perfume working and the itch started. Three times no worse than two? He made himself picture Jody, kissed Helene lightly, and walked away.

At the fishery agency he now moved as a creature of great importance, greeted with a rush to the door by the once-too-busy Mr. Matsunaga, only cautiously greeted by old companions Hayashi and some of the others who now evidently perceived themselves his inferiors. He gave Hayashi politeness but no more. The little guy's snub at the Tsurifune meeting might have been intended to save his ass if Hank's war-frankness had gone wrong, but it had been real.

That evening, old Mr. Tsurifune himself attended the farewell banquet. He and Hank sat in double seats of honor and filled each other's sake cups. No interpreter was needed. The company photographer took the two together arm to shoulder while Mike, less easy in his father's presence, stayed discreetly aside. With a flourish Mr. Tsurifune presented a velvet box. Inside was a pearl necklace.

"I can't take this."

"For your wife, Mr. Crawford."

"I can't. It's too much."

"Bad manners to give it back, Hank-san," said Mike. "Don't worry. It's nothing. Done all the time, for special guests."

During the long flight home across the Pacific his head ached from the toasts. The hangover was reality in what otherwise seemed a dream.

17

ANGERS

"Hank. Dear. It's all right, dear." She said it gently, but she was firm. "You can't hold me all day. Get our bags. And you'd better hug Pete again before he falls apart."

"Daddy Daddy Daddy."

Hank released her with one more brush of his mouth against her hair, then swooped Pete into the air and hugged him close.

"Don't you have at least one little kiss for your mother?"

"Mrs. Sedwick. Hi." He kissed her as quickly as he could, avoiding the wrinkled lipstick mouth that sought his own. Stale tobacco. (Why wasn't smoke in a barroom as intrusive as in open air?) Tell Jody first thing that he'd not call the woman his mother, that she'd earned nothing from either of them. It didn't help that, halfway during the drive to the house, after commenting "My God, kids, don't you know you left all civilization thirty minutes ago?" she said: "I hope to God this trip doesn't take much longer. I'm dying for a cig. Jody darling, surely one little ciggie while we're driving won't hurt anything. I could even roll down the window."

"You know my terms," said Jody coolly.

So much he had to tell Jody, and the wagon held a stranger. The woman sat behind them blocking him even from Pete who had quickly crawled into the rear. A drizzle kept the wipers clacking slowly.

He had arrived back in Kodiak five days before to a town suddenly less his own. Jones Henry and his seiner crew were off fishing the reds at Igvak before Jones left for his new venture in Bristol Bay. It postponed reaction to Hank's Japan agreement, but emptied the piers of seiners and

233

bustle. He wandered apart, wondering when he'd net another jag of salmon and feel them thumping around his legs. The house was bleak without Jody. (Did she find it bleak when he was off fishing? Not with three kids to keep her busy.) Even the precious view over miles of water to town lights had become lonely. Stains on the counter previously unnoticed (Jody probably kept it cleaner, he decided) appeared whenever he laid down a cup or dish.

Since Dawn and Henny attended school in town they remained with Adele, and he dined there nightly. He met his children outside school and walked them slowly to Adele's, buying treats and wine for dinner on the way. Henny, sturdy at seven, had no intention of holding his father's hand, but Dawn did it possessively. Henny, now in second grade, proudly displayed his homework while Dawn in mere first watched with envy. After homework, Hank lay with them on the floor with *The Wizard of Oz*. They took turns reading and spelling the words. Adele left them alone while she busied in the kitchen, but by dinner she had taken over with questions of Japan and her own opinions of how it compared (unfavorably) with France.

The shadow of Helene hovered over him like a malaise. Why had he done it? Did restoring faith mean confession, or keeping guilt to himself? After all was it that bad, when everybody shacked around? He knew the answer. Jody was the love of his life. The decision of whether to tell came down to what it would mean between them if she learned, and that he feared.

At last they drove from the potholed road into the leveled space before their house. "Home. Thank goodness," said Jody. She left the car and stood for a moment in the mossy quiet beneath the tall trees. "Never thought I'd get tired of endless sun. I'll say this for Kodiak rain. It brings out the pine smell."

Hank listened gladly. She'd grown to accept the place. He grabbed Pete out in his arms and snuggled him, answering "Daddy Daddy Daddy" with "Petey Petey Petey."

"My God, it's Hansel and Gretel, witch's house in the dark, how do you stand it?" exclaimed Mrs. Sedwick. "I need my cig, but is it safe? What about bats and things?"

"Stand close to a tree," said Jody drily. "Maybe the bats won't see you. And make sure you stamp out any ash when you're through."

"In this wet? What would burn?"

He had washed all dishes, hung up his clothes, pulled kinks from the rugs, bought flowers, and raised the heat to welcome Jody back, but: "I can see *you've* been baching it," she observed cheerfully.

He resisted an injured retort, gently disengaged Pete, and held her in a long kiss. "Boy, how I've missed you." The strength of her returned embrace reassured him.

Wouldn't she forgive?

"Ohh. Lovebirds. I'll just shiver outside a while longer and give you your privacy."

Jody drew apart and sighed. "Come in, Mother. I'll get your room ready."

"I don't want to be any trouble. My God, out there in that wilderness at night, what do you do when you . . . need a cig?"

"Where's she sleeping?" Hank muttered.

"Pete's room. He'll take Henny and Dawn's room while they're at Adele's. When school finishes . . . he'll have to come in with us." She put a hand over his mouth and shook her head. "By then you'll probably be on your big boat."

He had bummed a sockeye from one of the cannery hoppers. Outside he filleted it angrily. When Pete followed to watch he calmed. "Hey Petey, what's this?" He pointed to the fish.

"Daddy."

"No. Fish."

"Daddy."

"*Fish.*"

Pete giggled. "Daddy."

Hank tried also with tree, knife, and house. Same answer. Like a game, but with the child calling the shots. One more try. "Mommy, Pete. *Mommy.*"

"Daddy."

Hank gripped the child face to face. "*Mah*-me. *Mah*-me." Pete began to cry. Hank released him, looked away upset and uncertain, then hugged him.

Suddenly: "Mommy."

They danced with the word, said it over and over, then rushed inside to show it off.

Jody was cutting potatoes. Pete declared his word triumphantly. She slowly put aside the knife and pot, kneeled down, and held the child's shoulders.

"Mommy."

Her eyes filled with tears. Hank had seen it seldom.

By the weekend Jones had returned from fishing Igvak sockeyes. "And he's simply impossible around here now," Adele told Jody over the phone. "There's this time every year when he's caught the fishing fever, of course. But he *would* buy that gillnetter, and now he's got to fly up to Bristol Bay and get it ready. So naturally all of a sudden he's not so sure he should leave his seiner and crew down here with somebody else. Exactly what'll happen, I told him last spring. I know the man better than he does himself. We were doing fine until those porpoise huggers, as Jones calls them, drove the tuna fleet out of San Pedro and Daddy's welding business fell apart."

"Hank's going to Bristol Bay too, you know. Of course the *Jody Dawn*'s too big to fish, so he's tendering whether he likes it or not."

"I hope he'll be able to look after Daddy, then." Lowered voice. "I wouldn't say this if you-know-who was listening, Jody, but Daddy looks worried to me. God knows we hadn't expected the salmon price to drop this year. Of course he's going to do well in Bristol Bay, and we won't have this second mortgage for long. But you know the boys out at Igvak didn't get nearly the price they'd expected for their reds, and what if it happens up there too? People say the price dropped because of the botulism scare. But that was way last winter for one little can of salmon and these fish go for frozen. They say pink salmon around Kodiak won't bring more than five cents a pound this year, and that's a scandal. I'm awake nights worrying, like in the old days. And I thought we were free of that."

"Jones is uptight already, so don't start anything," Jody told Hank as they drove to the Henrys for dinner.

"He's got to hear it eventually."

"I know."

"It's nice that you have friends who bring you into civilization once in a while," observed Mrs. Sedwick sitting between the front seat and the children crowded away from her in the back of the wagon. By now no one listened or bothered to reply. Pete in particular, from longer acquaintance with his grandmother, avoided her.

Jones opened the door. His expression, while often half a scowl, was indeed more tense than usual. "Well, you come back brainwashed?"

Hank chose to answer with a hearty: "Not likely."

Jones's crew, near-strangers to Hank except for big Ham Davis, late of Tolly's crew, kept Adele's Sunday dinner tradition by her summons as in years before. Hank's crew had also been invited, although only Mo was there. Seth and Terry, also just back from a discouraging tanner crab season in the Bering Sea, had flown home for a break. Adele's hostessing recalled the way poor Steve and Ivan had squirmed under her benevolence, funny at the time. (Still not real after all the years, those deaths, thought Hank.) And even more like old times when Adele stood over the crewmen, kids with fingernails scrubbed for the occasion, to announce ominously: "We're informal here, boys, so I want you to make yourselves at home."

"In other words," Jones muttered when she had returned to the kitchen, "no cussing and don't pick your noses."

"We got it, Jones," said Ham Davis respectfully. Tolly's former crewman winked secretly at Mo, his one-time boxing opponent. Hank had seen the two hanging out together with their girlfriends when their boats were in port. He asked Ham for news of Tolly. "Only, Captain, that he and Jennie's got married, and he's still at that machine shop in Seattle."

As the men discussed the plight of Tolly, losing his boat, their voices dropped. Jody put her hand on Hank's. She understood what it meant. Ever since she'd returned from burying her dad she'd been more accepting. Hank squeezed her hand gratefully. But then he thought of Helene and it poisoned the moment.

"How do you stand this weather?" declared Mrs. Sedwick, returning from outside, trailing the odor of smoke. "Now, how can I help?"

"You can set the table," said Adele agreeably.

Jody's mother did her chore, then remained in the kitchen. Her cigarette-husky voice, lowered to a stage whisper, drifted out in snatches. "My late husband, the Colonel, of course, always insisted on . . . Who do you think you're talking to? I said . . . like I don't exist, so lonely I could scream . . . absolute end of the earth . . ."

Jody rolled her eyes. "I should go rescue Adele."

But Adele's voice, raised with no pretense of hush: "I went simply berserk until I dragged Jones out of here winters, and to France of course. After the children grow you've got no life here unless you work, run for office, or . . . Florence, why don't you volunteer for something? What can you do?"

"*Do*? Once you've earned retirement, the Colonel always said—I suppose I could teach bridge. Or lecture wives on military etiquette, since there's supposed to be a military base around here. I *would* like to be useful."

"Well . . . I suppose that's a start. But you've lived so many interesting places, close to France even. Germany, you said? Jones and I don't approve of Germans, of course, after what they did, but . . ."

"Let the hens go at each other," said Jones drily. He waved toward the bottle. "Help yourself as long as she's in the kitchen. Just keep it looking like it's your first." He winked at Jody, who responded with a grin from early days.

Hank realized how much of the old Jody he missed, and ached with the memory. He gulped part of his drink. In those days, hadn't they all slept around, selectively? Different now and he knew it.

Jones gulped also, and faced Hank. "I reckon it's no secret what your Jap friends paid us at Igvak this year. Prime red sockeye salmon firm as this glass, and they give seventy cents, fish that went last year for buck sixty-eighty. You think they're not bandits? Because one foreigner dies from what's-that-they-call-it? In one eight-ounce tall?"

"That one can had botulism, Skipper," said Ham. "It's bad stuff."

"Scary," echoed Mo.

"The way foreigners kill each other all the time, and one dies from a can of salmon that has botulism, in Europe at that, Belgium or someplace—if you ask me, a few Frenchmen could go and except for my wife everybody'd be happier."

"Don't think I didn't hear that crack," called Adele from the kitchen. "I'm sure a Frenchman would have known a can of bad salmon before he ate it. They're civilized beyond our understanding."

"So civilized they eat worms."

"Snails, Daddy. Phoo." Adele bustled in staunchly with a platterful of halibut steaks. Florence Sedwick trailed carrying the baked potatoes, her wrinkled lipstick-mouth stretched in an uncertain smile. "You *know* once you're in France you enjoy yourself. And what about those French fishermen you met down on the Seine below the bookstalls, who showed you their nets?"

"The ones who couldn't talk English?"

"You had a lovely time with their wine and cheese and you know it. You went back often enough."

"That or museums and perfume stores." Jones turned back to Hank. "Like I was saying. One can of fish gone bad in Europe, and over in Japan the Japs cut the price."

"Not good, Jones." Hank became cautious, although he too suspected the Japanese of taking advantage. He was glad when Ham and Mo changed the subject by quietly jibing each other on points scored in a basketball game they had just played together in the high school gym.

"Captain Hank?" asked Ham politely. "They got a gym up there in Bristol Bay?"

"Nothing you'll have time for," snapped Jones.

"So," said Hank. "New adventure for us all. The famous Jones Henry back in Bristol Bay after thirty years. Guess you remember those killer tides?"

"That I do. And I ain't forgot the screwing that cannery management used to give us."

"Daddy's mailed off his dues to the union the fishermen have up there now. He's doing it all the way."

Hank thought he was steering Jones safely. "Guess you'll deliver to Swede then, and keep the old tyrant in line?" Jones nodded. "Well, you'll be on the fish and into the action. I envy you. I'm stuck again tendering. This time at least with my own *Jody Dawn* instead of Swede's *Orion* boxcar. At any rate, Jones, since you're fishing for Swede you can deliver to me. I'll see you get the best price I can manage."

"I assume that means you've got a direct line now to the Japs." Everyone fell silent. Jones eyed Hank directly. "You sell out to the Japs?"

"Noo . . ." Adele flashed a warning, but Jody shrugged and nodded him on. The two men drank, not shifting gaze. At length Hank: "I came back with expectations, maybe."

"*Mebbe*? Then it figures like I expected."

Get it over. Hank kept his voice light. "They've paid off the *Jody Dawn*. As part of the deal I'll tender this summer. Then gear for longline and go for black cod in the Gulf." Jones studied him without speaking. "Look, it's a hell of a break. Black cod's a guaranteed market for one thing. And Japan's the market. You ought to see how they take care of their seafood over there." Jones continued to stare. Hank leaned forward urgently. "You're either in the world or you're left behind. Why else are you starting something new with that gillnetter in Bristol Bay?"

"In other words, you've sold out to the Japs." Jones rose and walked out of the room.

"Would anybody care to tell me what's happening?" asked Mrs. Sedwick.

"I'd better go talk to him," volunteered Hank.

Adele pursed her mouth in the way that made pug-dog leather of her face. "Stay there. He'll just have to absorb it. New ideas were never Daddy's strong point." They concentrated on Pete who, now that he'd begun talking, eagerly crowed each proffered word. Mrs. Sedwick went into the kitchen and washed all the pots and dishes. The others were too busy covering the tension to notice.

Jones did not return, even with Adele's anxious coaxing or then her irritated command. With the strained dinner ended, the crewmen had no trouble escaping.

Florence Sedwick took Adele's hand in parting and thanked her. Then she said quietly: "I know how it is. When you're tied to a man with opinions you might as well reason with the wall. Certainly the story of *my* life."

Adele turned cool. "Daddy has his reasons, I assure you."

Hank phoned the Henrys next day. "No, Hank dear. Daddy can't talk. He's still sulking."

"Sulking *shit*, woman!" shouted Jones in the background. "Hang up that phone."

"Don't you dare use boat talk to me!"

Next day Adele confided to Jody, when they happened to meet while shopping groceries: "I've never seen Daddy this bad, even with the porpoise huggers. It's eating him." She looked tired. Wisps of hair poked untypically from under her bandanna. "I think it's because he cares so much for Hank." Jody's mother alongside her knew enough to keep quiet.

Hank worked on the house and on his boat in the days before he needed to leave, but nothing he found to do could lift the weight. Jones would surely cool down. Their friendship was too long and deep. But he knew the grain of Jones's intransigence and part of him recognized, uneasily, that it might go on.

Of the other weight: He started twice to tell Jody he'd cheated, but both times backed off before speaking. Things were going so smoothly. The strains before he'd gone to Japan seemed lifted. Jody now moved in harmony with everyone. She treated her mother kindly and dealt with the children as friends (but always with each, in charge). In bed with him she was warm and relaxed—so giving in fact that his guilt interfered with his performance.

On the final day before leaving, he checked the *Jody Dawn*'s electronics once more while Seth lubricated the windlass and Mo and Terry noisily carried aboard cartons of supplies. Later he stood by Fishermen's Hall looking out over masts at his boat and all the others. There was Jones's crew aboard the *Adele H* running the seine through the power block. Jones was undoubtedly somewhere, readying his boat to function for six weeks without him. While Hank debated whether to risk a visit, he looked up to see Oddmund Anderson. "Odds! Look at you, man." His former crewman, always self-contained even when doing the messiest work on deck, now wore a dark suit and a serious expression to match.

"Captain." They shook hands cordially although Odds's reserve remained. His grave, smooth Aleut face and his bearing had a new assurance.

"Family all good?" Hank appraised him as they talked. Reliable crewman, even though he'd deserted them in Dutch less than a year ago. At least Odds had a known capability, and extra crew would be needed when he converted to longline.

"Fishing with anybody?"

"No."

"Miss it?"

"*No*. I work for the Native Corporation. It's nice, because I go home every night. And church Wednesdays and Sundays. And AA. It's nice. I done right."

Odds meant it. When Hank brought up the new venture, his former crewman could barely summon the courtesy to listen, eyed the sidewalk

and people passing, finally glanced at his watch while legs moved restlessly. "You see, Captain, I've got a meeting soon. With our advisor, he's an
important lawyer from the United States."

"We're the States right here, Odds."

"I guess. Anyways, I got to go."

Hank watched again the activity aboard Jones's boat. The sun was
shining. Shouts drifted up from among the masts, everything alive. It was
the sort of day to settle differences. He strode down the ramp.

The *Adele H*'s crewmen were running the seine through the block
inspecting for holes. "Captain? . . ." said Ham warily.

Hank kept it casual. "Boss in?" He started to climb the rail as he'd
done routinely over the years.

Ham stuck his needle into web and hurried over. The others stopped
to watch. "Skipper don't want to see you, sir. I'm sorry. Said if you ever
came, not to let you aboard. I guess you know why. Sorry."

Hank studied him. Ham meant it. "I'm sorry too. Not your fault." He
slowly climbed back to the floating boardwalk and left, avoiding the hands
in pockets and the slump he felt. He headed back toward the road, passing
the bows of other boats—boats smaller than any he'd ever own or run
again, seiners of the size that hugged water and talked to the fish. One crew
stacking web called out a collective Hey, man. He was known. This was
his country. Even the tarry diesel smells and damp of the pilings were his.

He stopped, considered, strode back to the *Adele H*.

"Captain . . ."

"I'll take the blame." Hank threw open the cabin door.

Jones Henry glowered up from the galley table. His stubbled face
looked aged. "I reckon messages don't come through clear. Ham! You
want to stay with me, you get this man off my boat!"

"Captain Hank. Like I told you—" The big crewman's hands curled
uncertainly into fists.

"Ham's not to blame, you thickheaded old pisser," Hank said heartily. "I pushed past him." He slammed the door. "We'll have this out."

"Anybody sucks up to Japs—" Jones banged down his mug and rose.
"If they don't get off my boat I throw 'em off."

Hank turned his back, pulled a mug from the overhead cabinet, and
started to pour from the coffeepot while he hoped for the best. Jones's

strong hand clapped onto his shoulder. It caught Hank by surprise. With a sick feeling: Let it happen, he told himself. Just take it.

Jones spun him around and pushed him toward the door. "Fuckin' Jap-kisser, think I'm kidding?"

"I know you're not. But still, you hear me out." He turned too suddenly. Jones hit him in the mouth. The cup fell and broke.

They stared at each other, both shocked. Maybe this'll bring him around, thought Hank.

Instead: "Well, ain't you hitting me back?" Jones muttered. "You afraid?"

Hank licked blood from his lip. He controlled his sorrow. "I don't hit friends."

"Get out of here, Hank."

"The world's bigger than you want it to be, Jones."

Jones opened the door. "Your fancy talk's nothing but shit." His voice shook. "Mebbe I could take it from anybody else. But you and me— Get off my boat." Ham and the other crewmen shifted feet on deck. "See this man leaves my boat if you want to stay crew for me."

Hank walked a straight line numbly from rail to pier, along the floats, and up the ramp. His breath came as labored as if he'd run a mile. By the Fishermen's Hall he paused. Shaggy young crewmen were stretching a net along the pier to inspect for holes. Down among the masts, nets aboard the seiners rose through power blocks like sails while crewmen mended them. Once it had been all joy. He felt his life burning away.

Black hole everywhere. Then let it be complete. Face Jody. He bought roses, and drove the long road home. "You could have expected that from Jones I suppose," said Jody sympathetically. "I'm sorry." She handed him ice cubes wrapped in plastic for the lip, then continued stuffing clothes into a hamper.

Never had he wanted her touch more. He put aside the laundry bag and wrapped his arms around her. Just to stand and sway together, then go gently to the bedroom. Her returned hug was like balm. Don't tell tonight and spoil it. He started to caress.

She rested her head on his chest for a moment, then sighed and eased away. "You pick strange times. Can't you see I'm hurrying to town?"

"Just for the laundromat?" She was dressed for more than house, he noticed now. "Dear, don't you ever hear anything but the fishing news?" She said it almost fondly. "A zoning bill tonight that half the town hates. Everybody's going to need a say. Don't worry, I'm taking Mother with me, she won't be in your hair. Suddenly she's showing interest in things and it's time she saw something to keep her busy. Meat loaf on the stove."

"Let them do without you."

Her flare took him by surprise. "You don't understand anything but boats, do you? Nothing anybody else does is important. I'm on the city council. I ran and got elected, remember?"

Face it! "Wait." He brought the roses from the mudroom where he'd left them. "I'm sorry." His face must have shown he meant it, even though she took the flowers with barely a glance.

"Hank, dear . . ." She faced him seriously and forced a smile. "Wives in Kodiak have to make a life of their own while their big men are out on the boats." She touched his cheek and her look was both amused and wistful. "Sometimes the pieces don't fit that neatly."

"Jody. Darling. I'm sorry for something else."

"I could have guessed that. This isn't roses country. What did you do, lose bucks at poker?"

He sat with elbows on knees, looking down. "In Japan."

After a silence: "Well, Hank?"

"I met this woman. American, on a study grant of some kind. I missed you and she was good company. One night I got drunk. And we slept together."

"You son of a bitch!"

All the way, get it over. "Slept together again the next night. Then I ended it. You're the one that matters, Jody. I was lonely."

Silence. He looked up. She had not changed position but she looked away.

"It's tormented me ever since, Jody. I'll never do it again. Otherwise why would I have told you?"

Pete ran in from somewhere. "Go play in the bedroom, honey." By her tone the child obeyed.

Mrs. Sedwick followed from outside. "I've had my cig, I suppose for the night although I can't imagine people not smoking at a meeting. Oh, hello son. Don't you have a kiss for your old mother-in-law?"

Jody told her calmly to leave them. Again her tone brooked no questioning.

Hank rose and held out his arms. "Please understand. Never again."

Jody walked to the window and looked out. "Don't be so sure. I suppose she was fun to be with?"

He hesitated. "Yes."

"Well, Hank." Her voice had become detached. "Japan seems to have made you break faith all around. You and I've been playing by different rules."

He started toward her. "I love only you."

She took his arm and guided him to the mudroom. Along with the roses she handed him his boots and oilskins. "Your boat's now your address."

"Darling. Jody. Please. I love you."

"Take the truck, leave me the wagon. You can come in the back way and pack your things." She returned to the kitchen and closed the door.

PART IV

JUNE–JULY 1982
BRISTOL BAY,
ALASKA

18

GO DRY

". . . bill of lading's in my *hand*, I fucking know what I ordered, checked piece by piece in Seattle and then the hatch sealed. Count again, don't make me come down. Should be sixty boxes raingear, not fifty-seven. Seventy gloves not sixty-three. Forty of welding rods not thirty. Hundred-fifty cases of those Filipino noodles, got that right." Swede glanced up from his radio-phone and waved Hank to a seat. "Any stealing, I'll find it. Your memory's not so gone you know I'll see it through from charges to jail, you can say that around."

Speakers crackled with boat talk. "*Orion*, yeah, I don' know." Hank recognized the father on the Italian gillnetter, what was his name? It returned the whole scene four years ago when he'd skippered the *Orion*, that barge. Was the old fart engineer—Dork or Doke was it?—still trying to take charge? A good summer, turned happy when Jody and the kids came aboard. Pete not even born. But happy.

"And nobody loses three hundred feet of four-inch pipe, check corners of the damn barge." Swede's voice continued, grating and efficient. No bottle and shot glass from a drawer, but otherwise he was more like his old self than for years. Jaw as squared as the tractor cap, shoulders taut. Maybe it happened like this every year at salmon shakedown time, Hank decided, and he'd been seeing only the autumn Swede with more time for brooding and bottle. At least some of all that had seemed eroded had come back right again.

The old Italian's voice assumed the drone Hank remembered: "Go on strike when the run's maybe two days away? Meeting today, maybe we go, I don' know. I don' feel like no fistfights, too old for that, maybe Chris here, maybe he's lookin' for a fight, huh Chris? He's restless, I don' know . . ."

A telephone rang. "Then get to it!" barked Swede to end the radio conversation, then gave a curt "Yes" into the receiver. "No, Rhonda, *four* more carpenters, it's three more electricians. That's right, and five machinists. Get 'em on the plane today, tomorrow latest. They can expect to stay through August shutdown, don't send me whiners who want to run home to momma. I'm not finished, hold on." Swede leafed with one hand through an ordered stack of papers as he growled to Hank: "Japs entertain well, don't they?"

"That they do."

Back to the phone with a paper: "Copy these names and don't ever send 'em to me again or they go back same plane your expense. Roger Foley. Joseph Todd called Junior. Sam Michaels, I think his nickname's Shithead it's apt. Lazy. Bitched I worked 'em too hard. I thought you sent me people who wanted overtime. Collective sitdown—of course I fired 'em, this morning, and please replace with bodies that plan to last. Soon as you can, my dock gang's now short." Pause to listen. "If your Local 37 calls that a legitimate strike I'll start hiring off the street in Anchorage, you know that's in the contract. We're clearing decks for a real strike up here." Pause again, then dry laugh. "D'you talk like that to your husband, Rhonda? I pity him. Thanks, girl." Swede put down the phone and, to Hank virtually in the same breath: "John Gains in there's anxious to see you. I suppose it was only a matter of time before you joined the Rising Sun along with the rest of us."

"They've made me a hell of a deal."

"They can be generous when they want."

"You make it sound sinister."

From one of the speakers: "Bugeye calling Switchblade, go to channel green, over."

"Switch green." Swede reached to dials on a shelf above his desk, and motioned Hank to leave.

"Switchblade, you listening?"

"Listening." To Hank: "On second thought, stay. You're part of it now."

"Hey, Switch. Condition Gatsby."

"Interesting. Is Mrs. Gatsby still pregnant?"

"Swelled up thirty-three, thirty-four inches something like. Doctor wishes she'd delivered yesterday, maybe operate today."

"Poor Mrs. G." Swede scribbled numbers. "She's an interesting lady, so better luck to her next time. Any more news? Good. Good. Out." He turned to Hank. "Escapement almost reached, so Fish and Game could declare the first opening any time. The big mass of the first run started through False Pass yesterday and should be storming the Nushagak late tomorrow. They weigh six to seven pounds each, a whole pound bigger than two years ago. Fishermen had better decide to fish."

Hank shook his head. "I thought with these new radio scramblers you didn't need code games anymore."

"I don't trust gadgets." Swede smiled.

"You pisser, you're enjoying this."

"It's my work." Another phone rang. Swede listened, then: "Forty cents, Sam, sorry, that's all we're prepared to offer. Call it shit but that's how it is. Yes, Sam, I'll wait." To Hank: "You didn't sign anything not in English?"

"Hope not."

"Welcome to the company. You'll end up rich. Or if you don't watch out, back in a hold pitching somebody else's fish. What's Jody think of it?"

"She's . . . all right with it." Nobody yet knew.

"Don't leave her out of it. Am I the only one who knows what a catch you have in Jody?"

"I know," Hank said casually. Keep his distress private.

John Gains, in rare open shirt without a tie, came from a closed office and put a sheet of paper in front of Swede. He shook Hank's hand. "I want to see you. Five minutes?" And back into his office.

Swede glanced at Gains's paper and, into the phone: "Correction, Sam. We'll break our asses and give fifty cents. The best we can do." He listened, then said drily, "If you guys haven't read the market reports you don't know how many cans of salmon from last year's pack still lay in the warehouse. England's stopped buying all Alaska canned salmon since the botulism death. That's our prime market for canned reds, closed by their government itself. I know, I know, one guy dead in Belgium five months ago, from a pack out of Ketchikan in another part of Alaska a thousand miles from here." Pause to listen. "You won't get a better price this year, Sam." Phone down.

"You paid over a buck a pound last year. No wonder boats might strike."

"This isn't fun. I'm on a tight leash. I can offer an extra spring settlement if the price rises retail, but don't count on that. Nobody's buying canned salmon."

"Japan buys frozen, not canned. You can't tell me that market's crashed."

"Japan grabs opportunity. Your friend old Tsurifune might sweat, but he won't go broke. If we can get it cheap that's how we'll get it. "

"*We*? That's your line now? Fifty won't pay for gas."

"It will with volume. And *Jody Dawn* still gets its standard tendering fee."

"You mean I'm supposed to cheat the fishermen who deliver to me? I didn't bring my boat up here for that."

"Read your contract. You bring your boat when they tell you. I'd suggest you give breaks on supplies where you can. For the rest, suck it up like the rest of us."

From one of the speakers: "This is Alaska Department of Fish and Game. Anticipate an opening within the next twelve hours. Boats: Do not stay dry."

The lines around Swede's mouth drew down wisely. "Switchblade gets the facts."

"You do enjoy this. You know how tough it'll be for the guys, now the fish are coming. When I just left my *Jody Dawn* the tide was still headed down. Four, five hours before we float again, that's the time they have to decide."

"When she floats, you be out there. By the way, I assume you know your friend Jones Henry has the gillnetter *Robin J*. Has a big kid for his net picker. Told me he'd deliver to any tender but *Jody Dawn*. What's between you?"

"He thinks I've sold out. He hates Japanese. It's out of hand and I'm worried."

"Cry on somebody else. I told Jones to suit himself unless Crawford's the only buyer of ours around, then get his ass over to you."

"He took that?"

"Jones and I go back to before you ever came to Alaska, Sonny."

Hank shook his head, suddenly depressed. "You wouldn't have one of those old Swede Scorden bottles in that drawer?"

"Shut the door." Swede produced a flask from under a folded coverall. "Just drink it from the mouth, and keep the smell away from me."

"You're on the wagon?"

"Trying."

Hank returned the flask unopened. "Hide it deeper. Hey—" He tried to sound casual. "D'you have a phone line open, so I could call Jody? Maybe an office nobody's using?"

Swede pressed a button on the phone console. "Honey, give this man a priority line to Kodiak. I'll be down on the wharf." He rose and indicated his chair. "I've been glued here six hours. Time to count missing cartons." The door closed behind him.

Hank took the chair, gave the number, and waited, tension growing. He'd tried to think of other things all day, often succeeded during the business of preparing the *Jody Dawn* to collect fish and sell supplies. On the desk, Swede's scribbled numbers showed he'd subtracted 27 from 33 and 34 to reach fish poundage. And added 3 to "yesterday" for the time fish would storm the Kvichak. Cracked their code.

Connections beeped and clicked. He wiped his sweat from the receiver. On one of the speakers above the desk the Italians, his old friends among them, were wondering as usual what they'd do, and on another one Fish and Game instructed boats again not to stay dry.

"Hello?" Her precious voice, with the edge that sometimes bit but had its own music, voice that he loved.

Keep it light. "Hi."

"Well. Fish jumping?"

The cool tone hadn't changed, but at least she'd offered a question to keep talking. On other tries during the nine days since he'd left the house she merely put the children on the line, and told the last one to say goodbye. "The run's started, but things are pretty tense. Low price offered. Guys say they won't fish until it's raised, and I don't blame 'em. I'm caught in the middle. Since Fish and Game predicts a thirty-four million run it'll probably turn out all right for boats to stay tied up a few days, but

I hate to see all that fish go home." He didn't want to ask about the children for fear she'd put them on and not return. "Things . . . running all right?"

"Running as usual."

Risk it. "I really miss you."

"That's too bad."

"You're really . . . the most important thing to me."

"You'll hurt your boat's feelings."

"Jody. Darling. Please. Believe me, I'm so sorry. It sets me crazy I'm so sorry."

"We'll talk about that someday. Have you seen Jones up there?"

"Not yet. They say he's in with the strikers." At least they were speaking. She volunteered that Adele now worried both for the state of Jones's health because of his tension, and for their new debts.

John Gains opened the door without knocking, frowned at Hank, and pointed to his watch.

Hank waved him off so strongly that the door closed. He drew a breath and interrupted her talk of Adele. "I . . . listen, Jody, you're the most important thing to me, not the boat. And the kids. Don't leave me. I want so much to hold you." The silence lasted so long that he wondered if she'd walked away.

"Look, Hank. We're busy here. Let me fill you in. This morning I took Mother to the airport and sent her back to Colorado. She knows now there's worse than living alone with bridge games around the corner and having a smoke whenever you like."

"That's good!"

"Now I'm packing."

"Jody!"

"I need time to decide things. There just has to be time. You might actually see me and the kids before long. We're going fishing."

It turned out some people he barely knew, friends of hers from earlier days, had a setnet camp on the Kvichak, and she was flying up to join them.

"Without *me*?"

"How otherwise?"

"Look, look, it's great you're coming up. I'll rearrange bunks on the *Jody Dawn*. We'll make plenty of room for you and the kids. Just like four years ago up here on that *Orion* boxcar. Remember what a great—"

"Toot your whistle when you pass our beach, Hank."

"But you'll be with—my kids'll be with strangers."

"With old friends you don't happen to know. Drop ashore for coffee and I'll introduce you."

"Pete's too young. He might walk into the water."

"I know how to watch Pete."

"I've got to take out the boat in three hours. I can't even meet you at the airport."

"You're not expected. I'm back on my own, Hank."

He was in no mood for John Gains and hurried past the door. Hands in pockets, he watched only concrete paving downhill to the piers. Doing this without him! A backing forklift beeped and he jumped aside ready to shout at the driver. Machine shop oils, ammonia smells, people themselves bumping him in their hurry, it grated on him, all of it. The hulk of a container barge rose above the boards of the pier, along with the top of the *Jody Dawn*'s mast. Swede stood on the gangway of the barge facing two subdued, respectful men, his face as wiry and mean as the first time Hank had ever seen him in the role of tough cannery boss. Everybody else had a place while his own eroded.

It had begun to drizzle. Below the pier, boats lay half-tilted in muddy sand, their hulls exposed. Rivulets drained seaward from puddles around the pilings. Out in the river, shrieking gulls attacked salmon stranded to their fate on humps of land exposed by low tide. He remembered how the hateful birds pecked eyes. At the far end of the long pier a colony of the thirty-two-foot gillnet boats were braced together. Men aboard them buzzed hivelike, rail to rail, spots of orange and yellow raingear, their shouts like pepper above the grinds of machinery. Some of the men were climbing the twenty-plus feet of ladder to the pier. Everybody in place but himself.

A familiar face passed. Lean, about his own age, always tense, gray now around the eyes. The man's raw wrists protruded from torn sleeves of red long johns covered by a plaid shirt cut at the elbows. Oh yes. When tendering the old *Orion*. The fisherman who argued with John Gains over payment when Gains kept the brailer suspended long enough to drip out gurry and lower the weight.

"Oh. Sure. You were crewing on the *Esther N*, right?"

"No more. Now I own her. Bought last September. Jack Simmons."

"Congratulations, Jack."

"Bought on the strength of at least the same buck a pound we got last year." Eyes red and restless searched Hank's face. "You're with the office up there, right? Have they settled?"

"Not yet, I hear. But I'm not office."

"Fish and Game's going to open soon. Don't stay dry they've said."

"I heard that too."

"You think they're going to settle in time?"

"I . . . guess it's up to the Association."

"That Association, Christ! I paid dues since all the skippers in our bunch belong and look out for each other, and now I'm one of them. Why don't you give us a fucking price and let us fish? I hocked my house for this boat and license. Even the building in Tacoma where I have my diner."

"Jack, I'm not management."

"Now we're going up for another vote. I can't afford to stay dry."

"I understand."

Jack glanced toward the *Jody Dawn*. "Understand? With a boat like that? Guys like you can't be both one of us and one of them." He hurried off to join others headed through the buildings toward the road.

Hank descended a long, slippery ladder to the *Jody Dawn*'s deck. Seth waited, hands on the hips of thick, greasy coveralls. Water beaded his beard and eyebrows beneath a wool cap pulled low. "Supposed to be five cartons you ordered of toilet paper come aboard I haven't seen. You going to let every deck ape who delivers fish use our crapper?"

"Part of the tendering, remember? You'd be glad for it if your boat had just a bucket on board. But we'll open only the deck head, not our head inside."

"I ought to go ashore. Terry needs a belt for his water pump. He didn't stock an extra. And Mo wants hooks to catch dinner out there, and we forgot Terry's strawberry ice cream he eats all the time. Does this shithole have stores?"

"I don't remember. But we'll be delivering to a big floater-factory, they'll be stocked." He thought of Japanese tastes. "Maybe not the ice cream."

"It's American, that factory, ain't it?" Hank kept his expression neutral. Seth sighed. "Oh man, the way you're fuckin' around with the Japs and all."

From the pier twenty feet above someone shouted, and a ropeful of cartons bumped down against the pilings. "Well, that's your toilet paper." Seth looked around restlessly. "So we're going to be stuck out there? Tide's still on the way down. We got hours. I'm going ashore."

As it ended, Hank used his influence to commandeer a truck. They all crowded into the cab, with Terry on Mo's lap both joking about it and Seth gravely riding middle. The wiper blades cleared the window with a slow *shlock-shlock* that Terry began to imitate. Suddenly they all fell into good spirits, even sang snatches of "Home on the Range." The bumpy road led from the cannery complex through scrub, to the single paved strip connecting Naknek to the airport. Sparse weathered structures started dotting the barrens after a mile, and their numbers increased the closer they came to Naknek. Pickup trucks sped in both directions, crowding the lot in front of a big store built of new boards.

Inside the store, between aisles of hardware, gloves, and boots, Hank and a younger man with curly hair stopped face to face, remembered each other, and shook hands. "My dad still talks about that fishing ride you took with us four years ago," said Chris Speccio. "He knows now you're a bigshot crabber, read some interview in *National Fisherman*, but he says, 'Maybe the man knows how to crab, but I'm the one taught him all he knows about picking Bristol reds.'"

"Sure. Tell him that's how it happened. Nick's your dad's name, right?"

Chris laughed. "That's a good Wop name too, but no, it's Vito." Hank asked about the others in the Monterey fleet, and whether their code was still based on opera. "All the same, every bit, uncles and cousins just like always. Maybe Tony's new on my uncle's boat 'cause he's just turned fifteen; time to be a man. You think we'd change? Don't even switch code operas no more, might get us confused ourselves. Anybody who wanted, they've figured us out long ago."

Hank, cautiously: "You guys ready to fish?"

Chris rubbed his fingers along a packet of innersoles in his hand and studied Hank, suddenly quiet. "You know our Monterey guys. Should we do this, maybe do that instead. Here the fish are comin' in. Should we strike with the union where we've paid dues for twenty years? Should we go fish like we want for the cannery that's bought our fish for twenty years? It hurts, man. You see those reds swimming in on the flood, and what was it you came to this wet dump to do except catch reds? I want to lay out nets and see 'em smoke. Get my hands around those big sockeyes. Not buy chewing gum in some fuckin' store."

Hank understood so well it hurt to consider it.

Chris was headed to a strike meeting at a nearby hall he pointed out through the brush. "You oughta hear it. But you're sort of management, I don' know. But you oughta hear it."

Hank and his men made their purchases, then followed where Chris had pointed toward a wide frame building half hidden by brush. They picked through a rough path hemmed by growth. Men moved in and out of the building, guys like themselves in shaggy wool with greasy cuffs. Many younger men had beards, older ones tight, grizzled jaws. Their boots had trampled the ground into a gumbo of mud and cigarette butts. The place had the same undercurrent of hive-buzz as the beached boats—edgy, voices suddenly staccato. Occasional shouts came from inside.

"I've listened around," said Seth. "How the Japs are jerking everybody."

"The Japanese have their problems too."

"That's your company line now, ain't it!"

"Come on, man," said Mo. "Boss sees things we don't."

"And you see nothing at all."

"It's like a movie here run backwards," said Terry, in stride with short arms swinging. "I see guys here delivered to us four years ago. But they all look different, and nobody says hi back anymore. Know what I mean, Boss?"

"I know."

They followed others inside. Men sat on folding chairs and clustered standing. Damp wool made it steamy, and smoke formed a haze. A middle-aged man peered over glasses from a raised lectern, his voice raised but difficult to hear.

From the chairs: "You think those independents are staying dry? They're out in the *water*. So if we stay dry we're stuck through another tide even if you get us a price, and the scabs get it all."

"If you go wet," said the man on the platform, "you signal you'll fish whatever their price. Just an hour ago they raised it ten cents. We've got to keep up the pressure."

"Pressure, yeah. Look at the two years ago we struck, and what it got us was days lost on the first run, same price for boats that struck who delivered to floaters, and a hike for only cannery boats that didn't strike. The Japs played us and won, Sam."

"That's the point! The fish started running, and when our blockade didn't work we panicked. Fish and Game has predicted plenty of fish this year. We'll make up a few days lost. But if we give in again, they know they can tough it a little more each year and we'll cave in. This is the year to draw the line, or we'll be doing it again and again."

Lean Jack Simmons popped from his chair. "Some of us can't afford to wait." Grumbles and assents from others.

"It's for the long run—long run, Jack. This is your future. Hang tough and you'll make up any loss. You think I don't need to pay bills?"

"Yeah tell us, tell us, Sammy," somebody shouted. "You've fished the Bay twenty, thirty years, boat's paid for and your license came free. What about the rest of us?"

A man with long sideburns and a smudged cap raised his hand from among the standees. "Get it straight for me, Sam. We started out asking ninety?"

"Ninety-one."

"Whatever. Now we're down to eighty-five, right? And they've just gone from forty to fifty. We ought at least expect halfway from them before we settle."

Voice from the chairs: "My Dillingham buddy's just told me on radio they're close to settling up there for seventy."

"Still too low!"

A red-graveled face in camouflage hunter's cap: "We'll lose the fish while we fuck around here."

Sideburns: "You didn't hear Fish and Game? They've promised thirty-four million fish this year, and man just told us they're running late. The run hasn't barely started. Clean your ears."

"You trust fuckin' biologists?"

"Sit down, sit down, that's asshole talk."

"You want to make me?" The two lunged for each other across chairs and knees. Others intervened.

"Wow, Boss," whispered Mo. "These guys are pissed. I didn't know about any of this."

Seth pushed his shoulder. "Wake up. You never pay attention to the important shit. Japs kicking everybody around." He glanced significantly at Hank. "You got to stand up to the Japs or they'll eat you."

Hank listened, troubled. Back in Swede's office they were indeed playing games with these people, and it *was* the dictatorship of Jap money. Japanese money.

A large, heavy man rose. It was Chris Speccio's dad. "All these years, Sam, you've just called on the cannery bosses and we made deals. I don' know how, shook hands, right? But they *listened*. Before we had our union nobody listened. So we need the Association. So just do what you done before."

"Everything's changed, Vito. Since the Japanese started buying to freeze in '79. That's what I'm trying to drive home. Canning used to be the only show and I talked to four or five bosses. Now freezing's a different monkey with a different market. Dozens of bosses, some far away. It's changed the rules."

Jack Simmons had remained standing. He started out against close-packed knees.

"Where you going, Jack?"

"They say cash buyers already pay up to sixty-five. Stay dry if you want."

The big man blocked his way. "We don't break up like this. We stay and vote."

"You standing in my way?"

"I'm telling you!"

Others intervened. Voices called for the vote on fifty cents. Sam at the lectern tried to state his case further, but finally acceded. Someone called the men milling outside. Shoulders of damp wool and slicker rubbed closer as others crowded in.

A familiar grating voice cut through the noise. "Throw those men out. They're spies!" It was Jones Henry, just entered, his arm pointing at Hank like a shot. The noise quieted. Eyes turned toward Hank. Jones's face worked. "Don't you check members at the door? Those men are spies for the Jap-controlled management!"

Jones's crewman Ham towered behind him, scowling to match. His broad young face, usually open and friendly, had become as mask-frozen as a cop's or soldier's on duty.

Hank caught his breath, but kept his face expressionless. The awful scene continued dreamlike.

"Hold on, this man's invited by me," declared Chris Speccio, stepping forward from a wall. "He's maybe no member but he's fished with us and he's okay. A fisherman. I don't remember seeing *you* here before, though, mister."

"Fished here under sail before you were born, so I don't need your shit when I say these men are spies. The Japs own the boat he's tendering, they bought him out. So shut up."

Chris clenched fists and tried to move toward Jones, but the press was too great. "I fished here twenny years, mister, and you're a stranger whatever you once did, so don't give *me* no shit either."

"Hold it," called the man at the lectern. "I was about to clear the hall of anybody not a voting member, and that's what I'm doing now." To Hank: "Ask you to leave."

"Of course," said Hank. "Just let us through." Keep neutral face, he told himself. His whole being felt hollow.

Men around him, some whom he knew, made way against each other. "Tell your bosses," said one, "that nobody here's going wet until we get eighty cents minimum."

Hank stopped to face him. "You won't get that this year," he said quietly. "That's the truth, not management crap."

"You *are* on their side!"

"You hear that?" cried Jones. "He's sold out worse than any scab. That man in here's a rotten apple!"

Hank controlled outrage as he walked toward the only exit, where Jones stood. Beside him Mo rumbled: "Boss, he hadn't ought to talked to you like that. Don't worry. Nobody's goin' to hurt you while I'm here."

Hank half-turned. "Cool down."

"We're all behind you," said Seth calmly. "Let any fucker try anything."

At the front a discussion began over whether the vote should be by open or secret ballot or by show of hands, and the focus shifted from Hank's departure.

Hank tried to brush past Jones at the entrance, but Jones faced him. "Canal to Iwo taught me things."

"You've taken this too far. Calm down."

"Yeah," said Ham with a twist to his voice. "Guam and Iwo. Some people who don't listen are ignorant. You got to tell them over and over."

Suddenly Mo's face pressed against Ham's. "You shut up." The two stood at equal height.

"Make me."

Mo punched hard enough to stagger Ham against Jones and others. Ham recovered with a flying jab that Mo, prepared, dodged and deflected with his elbow. The two scuffled, bumped against others, soon rolled against boots and brogans exchanging blows.

Hank tried to pull Mo back, while Seth and Terry leapt to control Ham, but neither fighter separated. A kick in the stomach landed Terry doubled up against legs. Jones watched with a tight smile, making no attempt to intervene. Others finally separated the two, glaring and spitting blood. Mud and cigarette butts covered their clothes.

"Get it fuckin' straight," panted Mo in his deep voice. "No shittin' on my skipper."

"Don't give me *fuck* about your skipper."

Terry slowly straightened and sat up. "You're some kicker."

Ham turned. "That was you, Terry? Sorry. You okay?" His cheek bled enough to drip on his jacket and redden one of the butts that clung to it.

The fight had blocked part of the entrance, but the meeting was too noisy to be interrupted. "I reckon," said Jones calmly, "that we'll go in now and vote. Against the Japs and Jap-kisser. You in shape, Ham?"

"In plenty shape, Skipper."

Hank gripped Jones's shoulders while tightening his stomach against the opening he'd left. "Jones. Stop this craziness. We've been friends too long for this. I . . . care for you, man."

"Let go." Jones turned into the crowd. Ham looked back at Mo, hesitated, then followed.

Hank and his men walked slowly back to the road and uphill to a dark bar in the village center. It had been emptied by the meeting. He bought them shots (except for Mo who asked for beer, Coke, and water at once and gulped them indiscriminately), and secured ice for Mo's jaw and knuckles. They drank without savor. Terry attempted to describe the fight as a joke to their advantage, but the effort died. After another beer wolfed with jerky and peanuts Mo declared he felt good, and they walked glumly outside.

Hank remained numb. Just accept it, he thought. Decision's been made. It wasn't dishonorable.

High weeds surrounded a cluster of houses with rusty corrugated roofs, but a painted fence enclosed a clipped graveyard and church. The church had a plywood onion dome, painted not long before, and a bell on girders mounted by the door. Most of the double-hatched Russian crosses stood straight although some sagged in the wet ground. Artificial flowers draped on the crosses ranged from newly garish colors to weathered chemical reds and blues. *

"Looks like people up here do more with theirselves than just fish in July," observed Terry. "Remember ol' Odds? Odds, he liked to fix them little Russian churches, so this would make him happy except nothing to fix." Nobody answered.

Gray clouds reflected on the river below and on the multiple roofs of cannery complexes flanking either shore. Each cannery looked larger and better kept than the village itself. Rising tide had begun to swallow exposed humps of mud, and the predatory gulls had dispersed. Hank finally felt he could end the walk and escape to his boat. "We'll float soon. Time to go back."

They followed Hank back downhill to the truck. Raised voices punctuated by shouts came from the direction of the meeting hall. Jack Simmons and a few others hurried into view from the path.

"How did the vote go?" called Hank.

The men stopped and eyed him cautiously. "You going back to Swede's cannery?"

"Come aboard if you want."

As they climbed into the open back of the truck: "Don't do it!" shouted someone who had followed them. Hank jerked the engine into gear and started off.

Stones and mud clots thumped on the cab. "Fuckin' scabs!" Hank looked back. His riders had hunched down. Their expressions were tight and far away. Jack buried his face in his hands.

19

STRIKEBROKE

ockeyes now frothed into the Naknek/Kvichak river system, and reports confirmed the same volume farther north in the Nushagak system off Dillingham. Union boats remained dry. The men ashore smoked and paced their cramped decks, or, between meetings and votes, they gathered in front of stores to discuss and rationalize or, if they could afford it, drank too much.

Out on the water a spooky quiet prevailed. The usual easy chatter on open radio bands had become cautious quick messages, sometimes so elaborately coded that the speakers themselves acknowledged without humor that they'd lost track. The lights of tenders and processor ships glowed day and night so no strike-breaking fisherman who chose to deliver could miss them. Hank was committed to paying fifty cents although cash buyers with "60" or more scrawled on banners cruised the edges. The latter boats maneuvered to provide a side concealed from binoculars (including Hank's) to shield skippers, committed to companies, who risked delivering for the higher price in bills paid them hand-to-hand on the spot.

"Who's that delivering for cash, Boss?" asked Mo.

"Can't make it out," although he had seen indeed.

On the beach was Jody with his children, working for some set-holder named Joe Penn. Fish and Game marked the location for him—had given him a UHF band to call. Nobody ever answered. It was miles from his anchored position.

Mo, aching still from his fight with Ham, walked both in a kind of peace for duty done and in gloom for the buddy he might have lost. Terry had inked little skulls on the tape that patched his cracked knuckle. But boredom ruled life aboard the anchored *Jody Dawn*. Seth turned snappish. Even Terry's attempts at humor irritated him. When a boat came to deliver —usually in the time of most reliable dark between 11 and 1 A.M., or at least during fog or heavy rain—they all leapt to deck grateful for the action.

Aboard the boxcarlike tender *Orion*, when Hank pulled alongside for food he'd forgotten to stock: "Where's that pretty lady your wife?" It was Doke the old engineer. It might have been the identical greasy coveralls that hung by a strap, but in four years fat had sagged his face further to the sad-eye of a sleepy hound. "Wish I could say the crew Swede sent me this year's more respectful than yours. Course yours had Johnny Gains, that's a man made something of himself."

The factory freezer ship they served, *Dora*, radioed often to see if they had fish. "I've got a whole classroom of college kids signed up to get rich," mourned Dave the captain. "Playing cards and worse while they eat my food. And little Jap egg men—uh, Japanese egg men, hello Mr. Fukuhara—mooning to themselves in a corner."

Without question those gillnetters who broke ranks had tapped a thick run of fish. Hank and his men watched wistfully while sockeyes grand as footballs—still silver although crosshatched with bloody net-marks—sluiced from brailers and thumped into their hold. But no one showed the spirit that usually accompanied big catches. Few even bought supplies. Especially ignored were the comfort foods that men in other years bought massively as soon as they made money.

When Jack Simmons delivered he raised his eyes from deck only to check the scales, even handed Hank the signed receipt without a word or look. He and his crewman forewent the *Jody Dawn*'s toilet, even though the *Esther N* had no facility except a bucket. Hank put the carbon copy on a box with Fig Newtons, apples, and ice cream when he handed it back. Jack took the paper only.

"Don't punish yourself."

Jack shrugged and returned to his boat. His crewman cast off and the boat disappeared in the rain.

By daybreak no one else had delivered. Hank took his single load to the *Dora*. Japanese faces appeared at the rail above and watched silently while Americans brailed up the fish. "Come aboard for steak," called Captain Dave.

Seth, Mo, and Terry had already shucked their oilskins preparing to climb the ladder but: "Thanks, not this time. Got to get back on station."

"Boss!"

Hank steered in the expected direction until the factory ship dimmed, then altered course and sped full engine toward the chart mark of Jody's beach site. "Oh," said Seth grudgingly when he saw why they'd lost their steaks. He and the others loosened the life raft and readied it on deck.

Along shore, smoke drifted from half a dozen buildings no grander than sheds and A-frames, scattered in the middle of sand and brush. He eased in, watching the fathometer. Draft barely a foot, but the tide would still rise for another half hour. Men and women on the beach were pulling into waders or had entered the water alongside a net. He scanned with binoculars. They wore padded clothes, while caps covered the bulk of their faces. He couldn't identify Jody.

But there was Dawn by the shacks! Running somewhere with another girl her own age. He pressed the boat's whistle. It made her stop, look, wave, and divert toward a shack painted green at the door and weathered white at back. In a moment out came Henny with Pete jumping beside him. Hank blasted and blasted, but dared not leave the wheel to go out and wave. The people on the beach looked up momentarily, but were too busy to pay further attention. Jody. Which among them?

They anchored, and with Terry (the lightest) he paddled the raft ashore. Dawn and Henny splashed in boots to meet him. Pete, leashed like a puppy to a post driven far from the water, crowed "Daddy! Daddy!" and strained against a halter. Hank jumped out, tucked a child under each arm and ran with them up to Pete, then hugged and hugged. They rolled on the damp ground together. How to hug them all enough!

"Daddy. I have a new girlfriend, her name's Melissa, and she's my very best friend in all the world. And Petey can say lots of words because I taught him but he can't go near the water, and—"

"I taught him words too," said Henny.

"Don't interrupt, it's not polite. And Daddy, the bugs are just . . . ferocious sometimes but we spray from a can and it smells bad, and Mommy sings a lot it's very noisy—"

"I like her singing. It's nice and—"

"*Henny*! And Daddy? When all the nets are pulled we make a camp-fire if it's not raining, and Melissa and I whisper ghost stories to each other, and Melissa and I help put the fish in the skiff if the water's not rough—"

"I do too."

"Not as careful as Melissa and me—and I—no, me. So don't inter-rupt. And Daddy, listen to this, we've got fireworks! The men have a whole box full and Mommy's bought firecrackers and I just can't wait. For some-thing tomorrow."

"It's for Fourth of July, stupid."

Hank forced a laugh as he studied them, suddenly devastated. Ruddy cheeks, smudged faces washed maybe once a day, clothes so unwashed he smelled them as if it mattered, Henny seemingly grown an inch since last he saw them—all healthy. They were flourishing without him. He'd become incidental. He pulled himself together. "Which one's Mommy?"

Henny kept the initiative long enough to point out a figure with a red pom-pom on her wool cap before Dawn declared: "See it? That's how we can tell, even if it's raining very hard and we're supposed to stay inside. Melissa comes to visit sometimes when it's raining. Her mommy lets her. Everybody's nice. Except a man who's very bossy."

"She means Mr. Penn. Of course he's bossy sometimes. He's in charge. I'll bet you're bossy enough on your boat, Dad." He said it with admiration.

The figure with the red pom-pom stood waist deep in water, pulling the net alongside men a head taller. He wanted to rush to her, thought better of it.

Instead he followed them to their house, first trying to carry Pete after unsnapping him. The child had always asked to be carried. Now he struggled free and trotted behind. The single room was warm and soot-blackened. It smelled of bacon and old socks. but it was orderly. Pieces of carpet covered planks of the swept floor. Wooden crates augmented two folding chairs. Air mattresses against one wall had sleeping bags folded on top. Each child's clothes were stacked in a separate box tiered into shelves. Utensils lay in a basin of warm soapy water atop a plywood counter where Henny had been cutting onions for a stew. A pot of water puffed lazy steam atop of a propane stove as it would in a boat galley. Hank removed his boots, which had shipped water when he jumped from the raft, and started barefoot toward the door to wring out his socks.

"Give me, Dad." Henny said it deep-voiced for a seven-year-old. The boy took the socks outside, and returned, flicking them expertly. He was sturdy and calm. Hank watched with a shock of emotion. His son was no longer a young child.

Time was moving. Tide now should have peaked. Hank checked his watch minute by minute, walked to the door to peer down the beach. The adults were still hauling and picking their net. "Hen, maybe you'd go tell your mom I'm here just for a few minutes?"

"Sure, Dad." Dawn continued to inform him of camp details. She stopped long enough for Pete to speak two sentences, mainly to prove her teaching skill. Hank contrived to hug each as he praised them. Pete cuddled for a moment, then laughed and ran behind a crate for peekaboo. Dawn needed to be coaxed and caught, and then she snuggled with: "Daddy, I love you." Little package! Maybe the image of young Jody. They were all positive.

Henny returned, breathless from running both ways. "Mom says she's glad you came but she can't leave work and come again when you can."

He left the house and stood watching the netters from a discreet distance. Jody was picking fish from the net and pitching them into a skiff. Now he'd have recognized her without the red-pommed cap. Her movements were Jody's alone beneath the bulky clothing. They had the perk and assurance of a decade before when the two of them rode together on the same boat and he fretted that she didn't want to marry. What had he done to her? He held his children closer, hugged each as long as they tolerated it (they've all become independent and don't need me, he groaned to himself. What have I done?), and left step by step.

"I was wondering!" said Terry by the raft. "Look how far the tide's gone down. The raft's just where I tied it when you jumped and got wet." It now lay beached and they needed to drag it to water. The children waved a noisy good-bye with demands that he come back soon. As he paddled back to the boat, the figure of Jody stopped work and waved. And she called. Was it to come again? Too much child-noise to hear. But yes, that. Back soon. At least that.

The *Jody Dawn*'s keel was just brushing bottom. Another few minutes and they'd have been beached for at least eight hours, perhaps more than embarassed had a high wind blown.

On station again, despite daylight, a boat delivered with the now-expected haste and reticence, while another boat hovered to discharge its fish after the first had safely disappeared among choppy waves.

Dave called from the factory ship. "Been trying to get you. Radio dead? Look, if even one boat's delivered bring it over so we can work."

"But then I might miss others."

"Full speed and take the damn chance."

Hank's mood had lifted. Full-gun across the water, he felt the push of the sea. Seth, in oilskins, stayed on deck. The invigoration of wind and spray brought him to life also. He stomped and danced. "Look at that bear," said Terry from the dry wheelhouse. "Man who says all he wants is a kootchy-koo wife and hot blankets, and he don't know himself he's all boat. He'd blow like a teapot if they trapped him ashore."

Hank swiveled in his captain's chair. "Funny thing to say."

"That's if anybody even knew what you was talking about," rumbled Mo. "If you didn't always say things people don't understand, I'd say when Ham kicked you that day it loosed a screw. But it was loose already, eh Boss?"

Terry tick-tocked his head and rolled his eyes. "Doodle-doodle-doo."

"For a little guy you're sure nuts." Mo said it like a fond pat on the head. "Seth's just havin' a good time, and I think I'll go out there too. Yeah." He swung down the wheelhouse stairs holding the rail, to land below with a thud and "Ow!"

"Now we got to patch a fuckin' hole to the engine room," called down Terry. To Hank: "He still hurts from that fight but he don't want to admit it. Phony in the movies, you know? How guys bonk each other and don't hardly bleed."

Hank watched the choppy water. They now rode a strengthening flood. Occasionally he circled against it to create a spray plume that doused Seth. Soon Mo had lumbered out in his oilskins. Seth found an object in the scuppers and threw it. Mo caught and returned it with a full slam into Seth's chest. Hank enjoyed their play, wished he was there. "Suit up, Terry. Join 'em."

"Naa. I get wet enough times. They're the kids."

"And you, what? Twenty-five? Younger than either."

"Depending on how you count. I'm short, so I might look like a kid. And I like to kid about things."

"What made you say that about Seth? We've all got boat in us."

Terry stretched. "I could leave it tomorrow. Just put me ashore and push me towards town. Someday I will. No rush. And Mo, he's nothin' but passing through. Although he'll prob'ly stay unless somebody pushes him. Your friend Tolly who lost his boat? Doesn't sound like he's so bad over it. Hear he got hitched."

"When you go, where to?"

"Ohhh. Back home to Oregon. Work in the forest a while, maybe. Or the boatyard in town. Get me a hamburger franchise. There's plenty of things."

"And have a family?"

"That too. My first old lady's left town, my mom writes. She married somebody else last year so I'm done with alimony which is good. This time I'll marry only when I'm done fishing, I guess." Pause. "Find some tall girl so our kids ain't short like me. Tell 'em stories about how I went to Alaska and worked for some shithead skipper."

"I didn't think it bothered you to be short."

"Try it some time. You don't mind that I called you a shithead?"

"Try it some time yourself." Hank veered the bow to spray white water across deck, and was rewarded by Seth's fists and yells. Mo held up his arms and yodeled. To be out there! He slowed to clear a gillnetter's corks. "Mind my asking what broke up your marriage?"

Terry stared at the water a while. "Maybe it ain't you and Seth's the only ones has too much boat in him."

Hank understood, but: "Oh?"

"Well. Seth, he don't even know all the things he wants, though he sure wants 'em. He's like you that way but you control yourself. Seth don't. He cooks over too fast. It's bang, so angry so fast he forgets what's important, even how things go. But what's the same in both of you's this: you're more boat than house. Lucky you, got a wife understands. And, well . . . don't take it wrong, Boss, it's your life, but . . . any old lady of mine, I'd be pissed if she worked on the beach alone like that when I'm workin' hard to pay the bills and her job is home. You and she sure have something special."

Hank shifted and swiveled the chair, trapped in its padded arms. Oh Jody.

"Ol' Seth with his temper, he might keep losing. Like he did that girl he was engaged to. He says she just went with some other guy. But it was because he blew up at her one night then ran off to catch a boat, and when he come back she wouldn't open the door."

"I thought I knew everything about Seth."

"Maybe you like to think it, but you're not a deck ape no more. You're Boss. It's a lot nobody tells you." Terry's glance was mild but monkey-playful. "Don't worry. You're no shithead. Guys ask us all the time how did we get so lucky, and is there maybe a site aboard for them."

The water that should have been clustered with gillnet boats was only dotted. Unlike the little Mafias that fished together and cared for each other like those from Monterey, Anacortes, and Native villages, the few boats now strikebreaking kept whole horizons between them. Hank saw the *Esther N* through binoculars and approached slowly. Her net was coming aboard. About two-thirds of its nine hundred feet remained in the water to judge by the ride of white corks. The end of the corks bowed with the tide as Jack Simmons steered crosstide to intercept fish. Hank maneuvered to the net's lee, kicking his engine against the increasing current.

Jack and his crewman stood on opposite sides of the roller, pulling in web over the stern. Their backs were into it. Fish and net entangled them to the knees. Web continued over the roller. Lumps of entangled fish squeaked from the strain against the moving cylinder. The part of the net that stretched between water and stern was clustered with fish. Seth and Mo on deck clutched the rail and leaned toward the sight.

"Ah. Ah," breathed Terry. "Ah, Boss. Why ain't we out there like that?"

Hank's mouth had gone dry with the desire to be pulling fish. He collected himself. "*Jody Dawn*'s three times legal length for this fishery, for starters."

As they watched, Jack and his man stopped the roller to grip both sides of the net-fish mass on deck and drag it forward. The weight was such that they struggled.

"Go rail to rail," cried Seth. "We'll help!"

Hank could feel the twist of Seth's body, the craving to grip such web, because he felt it himself. "Give you a hand?" he called from the wing.

Jack, without looking up: "Stay off." He and his man grimaced, and with a grunt together slid the mass of net over the battened aft hatches. "Go. Go 'way. Mind your own business." They returned to the roller, walking so stiffly their backs must have hurt. Jack throttled controls by his rail to adjust the boat's heading, and the two began again to pull lumped fish and web over the roller.

Hank left slowly, feasting on the sight as long as possible while space cleared between the vessels. Down in the water pale bullets of fish swam in ranks. Fish seemed even to brush and thump against his hull. Seth and Mo had run for a hand brailer. With Seth gripping his pants Mo leaned far enough over the side to lower the rim. The press of fish into the small net strained the long aluminum handle. Mo gripped tight and his body inched further over the rail. Terry rushed down to hold Mo also. Hank slipped into neutral so the boat floated with the current, and this eased the brailer. Mo brought it up packed with half a dozen fish.

Seth waved a thrashing sockeye. Mo and Terry grabbed others. It was like a tribal dance, complete with whoops and yells. Hank watched enviously. When they started to ready the brailer for another dip he sighed and called down: "Can't do it, guys, sorry. Breaking the law. We don't have licenses or gear for here. You've even got to throw those fellows overboard." To groans: "Keep one for dinner. The rest over the side before they die. Do it." The flicking fish went back one by one like toys relinquished.

Instead of enlivening the day, the incident left them gloomier than before.

At the processor ship, Captain Dave, full-bearded even for Alaska, his eyes sleepy from too much sleep, asked for news of the strike as if Hank knew more than he did. Young men and women, clean college types in sloppy clothes, pulled slowly into oilskins and headed for the gutting table on deck. "No use building a fire under them for so few fish," said Dave. "I'll kick ass when I need to." A faintly sweet odor of marijuana drifted through the corridors. On the now-emptied mess deck, where a kid in an apron aimlessly cleared cards, crusts, and full ashtrays from the long tables, Hank and his men picked at steaks larger than they wanted. A

Japanese in neat brown coveralls marked with Japanese characters came in crisply, received a pot of tea from the galley, looked around with a frown, and left.

"Message for you, Skipper." It was Swede on the scrambled radio band. Amid electronic squeaks and whirs he instructed Hank to return to the cannery before the tide lowered.

Entering the river close to midnight they passed colonies of gillnet boats moored together, still on strike. Light beams flashed and dark figures swarmed. The anger in voices carried across the water.

As soon as lines were secured a dock foreman hurried Hank by electric cart to the office. "Strike breaking up?" Hank asked en route. "We wish." John Gains and Swede waited. A bottle stood on the table along with water, a can of cola, and glasses. Gains's signature neat hair was rumpled and he wore coveralls, but the starch in the cloth along with a tie maintained his image. Swede's rumpled coveralls and red tractor cap had seen their usual service.

Gains smiled: a suspicious act for him. "Hank. We haven't talked since Japan since you didn't drop by the other day." Hank offered no excuse. "Pour you a drink?"

Hank looked at Swede. "You having?"

"One. Yes."

"I don't need it if you don't."

For answer Swede filled three shot glasses. John mixed his in another glass with the cola. Hank would have preferred diluting with water, but to show disdain for the cola he clinked shot glasses with Swede. The two old friends gulped neat.

Gains only sipped his drink, but held out the bottle. Hank shoved away his glass, and contrived to shove Swede's along with it. "You didn't call me in to booze. I see activity on the boats. Strike about to settle?"

Swede looked up with the old weariness. "Some are going to break it on this tide, say my people. Impasse otherwise. The processors can't find the market to offer more." He cleared his throat. "The union doesn't understand. All that TV and newspaper crap about botulism, and the British embargo. People are still afraid to buy salmon." It sounded rehearsed. At least spoken before.

"Even frozen? Even the Japanese?"

"We'll get to that," said John Gains calmly. He leaned back in his swivel chair and locked arms overhead with studied casualness."You see, Hank, it's the canning market that needs to recover. But we've got to keep some parity with prices paid for the frozen sockeye market."

"Then just freeze it all for a while."

"Look around you. Thousands of tin cans waiting to be filled, a few hundred workers waiting to do it. And freezer warehouses have limits. So does their shelf life."

"So? You called in my boat when it could be collecting and delivering fish for whatever."

"My *Orion*'s still there." Swede shuffled papers without looking up. "You see, on record we have to pay the price we've offered the union."

"We have an assignment for you, Hank."

Panels had been painted to cover "Jody Dawn" on the bow and stern with "Arctic Lion", and canvas mounts painted with "60" along with other numbers to affix if needed. They had a locked metal box for him with bundles of fifty- and one-hundred-dollar bills. The *Jody Dawn* was to move to a different location, take a different radio call signal, and serve as a cash buyer advertising more than the price offered the strikers ashore. The code for his prices was locked in the box.

"Not me! Let *Orion* play sneak."

"*Orion*'s too recognizable."

"You can go to fucking hell!"

Hank's hand was already on the doorknob when John Gains said: "Kiyoshi Tsurifune paid cash for your boat. He owns it until you pay him back. This is how you pay."

"Sorry, Hank," Swede muttered. "You signed."

Hank continued out and slammed the door. He started toward the dock breathing heavily. Take *Jody Dawn* back down the river before the tide changed, straight south through False Pass and home. No words. No discussion. Never return. Safe in Kodiak let them try to grab his boat! How could he pick up Jody and the kids on the way? Would she come? He stopped with hands in pockets to stare at his beloved *Jody Dawn*. Her bow was high enough above the pier to show her name. Obscene, obscene to change it. Fucking, fucking Japs. Done it to himself. He wanted to pound something, stepped in the shadow of a building to control his rage.

There was still tide left for the getaway. He walked the pier to calm himself and think, toward the clustered gillnet boats. They could have been found by sound alone since the rest of the cannery was quiet except for generator hums. Some boats were maneuvering free. Sounds as angry as those he felt himself came from down among bows caught by flashlight beams: "Comin' the fuck through, release the fuckin' line or I'll chop the fucker, I mean it!" "Fuckin' try it you'll fuckin' see!" "Don't let him through." "Let him through, let the fucker through, fuck him!"

Hank crouched by a wall behind an idled forklift truck. The dock foreman walked past calling his name. Silently he remained in limbo out of sight. Time to think. But his thoughts merely rounded to the same wrong conclusions.

Familiar rasping voice: "You're going wet! I knew you for a scab since you defended that Jap-kisser."

"Out of my way buddy." The shadow of Chris Speccio with a load in his arms, outlined by a single dock light, moved around the crouching shadow of Jones Henry. When Jones moved forward and planted himself again: "I'm telling you, fellah, mind your own business."

"We all fish," said Jones, "or nobody."

"Lot of nobodies out there grabbing the fish I came for. Strike two years ago didn't get us nothing. What the fuck, you're here just this season think you run it? And you smell like booze besides. So I'm telling you, fellah, out of my way."

"Hear me. We all fish or nobody. Put down that box."

"You're nuts and drunk."

"Ham!" Jones shouted. "Come here help me." The big crewman appeared from somewhere. "At least one Jap-kisser ain't going to make this tide. Ham, take that box from this man."

"Skipper . . ." Ham didn't move.

"Don't you hear me?"

A heavy older figure joined them. "Chris, that you? Got the bananas? Let's go."

"*Minuto*, Papa." Chris spoke something in Italian.

"Why don't you talk like an American? Ham. You going to take that box?"

"Skipper . . ."

Vito Speccio's voice lowered to a growl. "I don' know who the hell you are, mister. But leave my kid and me to our boat and mind your own fuckin' business."

"Ham, you going to take that box?"

Something clicked in the older Speccio's hand. It sounded like a switchblade.

Hank rushed to face Jones. "Chris and your dad, go." They left. Jones swung. Hank sidestepped, then caught Jones from falling. "Come on, let's find you some coffee."

"Do Jap-kissers just drop out of the sky? Get away from me. No. Wait." Jones threw another punch that missed. "Ham! You going to take care of this Jap-lover for me or not?"

"Skipper . . ."

Hank gripped one of Jones's arms and told Ham to take the other. The crewman obeyed without question. "Where's your boat? Let's go."

"Middle of that mess of boats, Captain."

Hank considered. The trip over rails could exacerbate the nightmare. "My boat's at the far pier. Help me."

Hank called for his crew and Mo appeared. They brought Jones aboard alternately struggling and passive. In the galley Jones smashed a mug and plate from the table before they cleared things and hemmed him in. Mo brought him coffee, and handed a mug to Ham also. Jones would not be pacified. He demanded to be taken anywhere else.

"I'll talk to him."

It was Swede. "Sure your money's safe in the office without you?" Hank snapped.

"Nice job of stalling. You went dry about fifteen minutes ago." Swede squeezed around the table to Jones and his voice softened. "You're a good man. Take your coffee, then come up to the bunkhouse and sleep it off. I'll make sure you're afloat when the strike's settled."

Jones quieted, turned slowly like a hunched turtle, and studied Swede. "You working for the Japs or not?"

"Whatever, I'm your friend. Listen. The old days are all yesterday. Change or go under."

"Nothing's changed of Iwo or the Canal."

"Even there, except in your memory."

Jones groped for some way to express himself, slammed his own cap against the wall, then grabbed Swede's and did the same. Hank had never seen Swede without his cap, Jones seldom. The exposure revealed them both to be gray, balding, older—old under their strain.

"I have D-Day tales, Jones. We all fought. It was the thing we did. We had to. The thing of our time. But forty years ago. Make your peace. You can't do it all alone, that's why you've got that fellow there. Expect these men around you to understand?"

"I do," said Hank. "I *do*." Swede ignored him.

Ham hesitated, then turned to Mo and pointed to Mo's skull-decorated knuckle. "That from me?" Mo nodded. Ham touched a tape on his chin. "Nice hit."

"You okay?"

"Good as you."

Seth appeared from deck, trailed by Terry. "They're doing something screwy to our bow. D'you know about it?"

Hank leapt up. "Son of a bitch!"

Swede had retrieved his cap and become Swede again. "Accept it, Hank. You've got no choice. It happens when you sign papers. My apes are making the change as discreetly as possible. If you hadn't disappeared we'd have had you out in the dark." To Ham: "Help me get your boss to my quarters."

Hank knew he was trapped and taking it like a brat, pout and all, yet he kept his angry expression. Terry and Mo wouldn't care, but how to explain to Seth?

Swede in passing put his hand on Hank's shoulder. "Tell you what. It's about eight hours before you float again. Come settle business after we tuck in this very fine mutual friend. Then I'll have my chopper fly you to Jody's camp for a couple of hours."

Hank hesitated. Being bought. But he nodded.

Jones had a final word. He pointed at Hank who was about to help him up. "Keep that man away from me."

When they had left, Hank looked for something to do: took crackers from the closet, poured himself orange juice, brought a spoon for jam, left it all idle on the table. His men watched and waited. "New assignment, guys. Consider it orders, like the military." But what if they talked on the dock? He attempted a smile. "Sealed orders until we get to sea, like the military." They still waited. "That's it. Hit the rack."

"Skipper Jones has sure gone off his rocker." said Terry. "It's too bad. Time for him in the old folks' home."

Mo became solemn. "I sure don't like the way he talks to you, Boss. You hadn't ought to take that." He considered. "Poor Ham. Not his fault Skipper Henry's gone kook."

Seth reached over to take the crackers and jam. "Jones Henry used to be a great skipper. Now let him stay down in California with the other crackpots."

Hank decided to make a speech. "I want you to understand. We'd be worrying about how to speak German or Japanese except for men like Jones. And others who didn't make it back. Nothing we've done matches what they did at our age. I might have been pulled into lousy Vietnam, but I did my year's hitch and came home. Jones and Swede had to stay for the years until their fight was over. Their own skin was on the line every day. The stakes were homes and families. And along the way they saved our future who hadn't been born yet to piss them off." His voice was turning husky in spite of himself. "I'm not being corny. If Jones Henry hates and won't forget, let him, he's earned it. Don't ever badmouth Jones in front of me. And don't let me hear you've done it somewhere else."

Seth and Terry nodded, each impressed in his way. "Didn't know any of that," said Mo in wonder.

Hank left. He walked heavily along the pier and up toward the office. With low tide and boats beached the issue of strike-breaking was moot again for a few hours. Boat noise had quieted. The steady hum of generators had taken over. In soggy ground away from the boardwalk he found a few stems of yellow survivor flowers to pick. A drizzly pale light etched masts and gleamed over emerging humps of mud in the river. Gulls began to gather for their next low tide's fill. He hated and loved it all.

20

JODYLAND

A thick buckle snapped into a thick belt. Hank had not ridden a helicopter since Vietnam days. The pilot turned the engine key, and the cockpit filled with odors of oils finer than those on boats. He hoped the metal floor wouldn't heat and melt the chocolate bars in the box his feet straddled. He laid the yellow flowers safely on top. The chopper rose straight, engulfed in noise, as the brush beneath blew flat and panorama unfolded.

Except for the straight road, the land stretched nondescript. Life lay along the wide Naknek River where lights still twinkled in pale morning. From above, the cannery roofs became a pattern of clustered gables and long metal strips hugging the shore. Masts of gillnet boats beached together formed a leafless forest. His own *Jody Dawn* at the other end of the pier looked small and vulnerable. A handful of the small gillnetters carefully plied the channel toward the mouth, but two larger boats had grounded on the mud. Four other cannery complexes squatted like bright towns along the shore. The village itself was scattered wider. Its buildings blended with the ground. Beyond the river mouth the sealike Bristol Bay swept into misty horizon.

The pilot shouted above the noise without having thought to give Hank earphones. Hank tried to listen and asked for repeats, at last nodded and pretended to understand. He needed space to think. First face-to-face with Jody since they'd parted. Near the largest cannery on the south shore the pilot circled a weed-filled graveyard and yelled "Old Chinamen." Hank remembered reading somewhere about the first canneries on the Naknek River built in the 1880s. Those were the days of the imported coolies,

before the advent of the heading-gutting machines called Iron Chinks. Ol'
man river, seen it all. Would Jody let him hold her?

Beyond the river they began to traverse swampy land pocked like
Swiss cheese with water holes. Gray sky reflected back at them from each
puddle. The pilot tapped his shoulder, then swooped low to startle two caribou drinking. The creatures ran and he chased them with glee audible over
the engine noise. Get on with it, thought Hank. He pointed ahead and tapped
his watch while trying to remain pleasant. The pilot nodded. He headed
across the water, passing the anchored factory ships and scattered gillnet
boats. On the opposite shore they passed small encampments of tents and
shacks. Smoke drifted from most even though it was four in the morning.

Finally they reached the camp that Hank recognized by Jody's green
door. Beach empty. She'd be inside. He yawned and stretched to cover his
trepidation. They eased down on flat sand away from the buildings. The
pilot shouted "Two hours," then pointed to six on his watch and held up
two fingers to make sure Hank understood. As soon as Hank descended
with his package and crouched to safety the helicopter lifted and throbbed
away. It left silence nearly as intense as the engine noise. Then dogs began
to bark. A trio of them came to meet and challenge, but when he held out
his fist to be sniffed their tails started to wag. A swarm of gnats found him
at once, insects so fine he breathed some in and started to cough. The route
to Jody's led over ground too boggy for running. It held some of the same
now-limp yellow flowers he clutched.

The green door was hooked loosely from within but a stick raised it.
The hot, stuffy air inside at least discouraged the gnats. With only a small
glassed square for a window he needed to wait. Slowly the outlines of
objects emerged: pot vaporing on the stove, boots lined in a corner. There
lay his beloveds rolled in sleeping bags alongside each other. The dim light
caught their cheeks and nosetips. Jody's long hair spilled around her face.
He eased behind her head, knelt, and kissed her.

"Mmmmm . . ." she murmured, then started up, freeing an arm and
striking.

"It's me, just me."

She woke all the way, recognized him, and freed her arms for a spon-
taneous deep kiss. He held her, breathing hard and blessing her response as
he tried to maneuver around and alongside. She laid a hand on his arm and

stopped him. Calm whisper: "The kids'll be pleased. How long this time?" He tried to hold her again in the same way, but she eased from the bag impersonally, slipped on shoes, and walked to the stove. She was fully dressed.

He followed. "Less than two hours."

She turned up the propane and drew over the two chairs. "Well. Nice to see you. I'll make coffee."

"Isn't there any place private around here?"

She pulled back her hair. "I'll wake the kids for you in a minute."

"I want to be with *you*."

Jody shrugged and shook her head.

He reached for her hand. "Look, in two hours we can pack you out of this mess. The chopper takes us back to Naknek, and by the time *Jody Dawn* floats we're all together aboard. Like a new honeymoon." She squeezed his hand but drew it away and busied herself at the stove. He continued, encouraged: "The kids'll love it. We'll keep Petey in halter and life jacket the way we did the others four years ago. My guys won't mind sharing a cabin so the kids can have their own. They all like my—our kids. And my cabin: you know it's good for two."

She poured hot water over instant coffee. "You still don't understand, do you?"

Her tone frightened him. "Understand that I screwed up, but for God's sake Jody I love you. What happened isn't enough to lose what's between us."

"No, no, I agree." He leapt to embrace her, but she held out his mug to block it. "Just sit and control yourself."

"But I love you."

"Well, Hank, I love you too. Sit and drink your coffee."

He gulped the hot beverage and burned his mouth. If she'd only let him hold her it would do what words failed. On impulse he went to the doorway and brought over the box and flowers he'd left there—an excuse to stand facing her. "Chocolate bars. I made Swede open the canteen."

"I'll pass them around next campfire."

"How about leave them here as a good-bye gift to everybody?" She looked at him so steadily that the answer was clear. "You're not coming with me today. Are you?"

"Not remotely."

"In a few days, maybe?"

"Sometimes you begin to understand, and then you just slip back. Flowers for me? Thank you."

"Sort of wilted from a couple hours ago. I didn't think they'd be growing here too." She put them in a plastic cup with water: didn't discard them. He was grateful. "You know, the chocolate bars—I thought you'd hide them somewhere for the kids one by one, not the whole crowd."

"Hiding? Do you know your daughter? And just where around here, incidentally? Hiding would challenge her to find them. Although then she'd probably try to ration them herself with lectures to Henny and Pete about rotting teeth."

"We're raising a little Jody." He laughed, hoping she'd take it right. She did.

"And a little Hank I believe, assuming you were sober and thoughtful as a child. Pete's the wild card. His speech may be coming late, but he's got bubbles I don't see in you or me."

"We have a beautiful family. When are we coming back together?"

She remained standing. After a few sips of coffee: "I've come to accept your adventure in Tokyo," she began quietly. "It untied my apron strings. I found the energy to shoo Mother back to Colorado where she belongs and to quit my job in town. And now I'm here being Jody again, not Mrs. Hank. Life's become less complicated."

Where was this leading? he wondered uneasily. "That's good, I guess. But what about us?"

"The children are fine," she continued as if he had not interrupted. "They're having a big experience. They miss their daddy now and then, but they're used to his being off on his boat and there's no reason you can't come see them when you want. We're doing all right without you, Hank. For myself, I don't need that house so far from town, or any other part of future aggravation—"

"Jody!" Now he was frightened.

"—if it comes with the wrong price."

"What would have happened if I'd never told you?" he blurted. "Wouldn't things be just as always? The reason I told was so it wouldn't—"

"You simply don't listen, do you? Well, to answer it, you're not that good a liar, Hank. We'd have gone on for a while. But in your mind it would have come between us. And someday again you'd have felt oh so lonely and sorry for yourself away from home, and eventually . . ."

"No, Jody. I love *you*. Never again. Look, we're rid of that mother of yours and it can all go back to where it was."

"I never paid that much attention to my mother, but she did used to say that men are all excuses and good intentions but deaf. That was her experience. I didn't expect it to be mine. I've never admitted that fishermen's wives fall into the same danger as Army wives. Their men away and lives to keep filled. The Army was like a club that absorbed its wives into little excuses to keep out of trouble. There were coffee klatches after the kids were safely dumped into school, and committees, and bridge parties, and four o'clock martinis, stuff to fill the day. I vowed it would never happen to me."

"It hasn't. Leave your mother out of this. It's about *us*. About getting back to *our* life."

"When I brought Mother up here," she continued, "I'm not sure what I'd expected to happen, but she was falling apart and I was all she had. We'd never really got along. Well, she did pull herself together, whether you saw it or not. Even though the kids couldn't stand her and she didn't make a place for herself here, she pitched in with the chores and stopped feeling sorry for herself. She even phoned one of her club friends back in Colorado and found they missed her. I sent her back in shape to resume the life she'd made. And, important for me, watching her reminded me again of what I won't let happen here."

"I'm not some army colonel. It won't happen." Hank glanced at his children soundly asleep, but refrained from looking at his watch. Precious time running out before the chopper returned. "Jody, tell me what you want. Move back to town? We could do that, I guess."

"Too bad you don't see for yourself." She poured more coffee. At least they were talking.

"I never had a place to call home until Kodiak, since the Army sent my father all over the place. Dad's death and Mother up here started me looking back. We were on post in Germany, I think. Somebody on the club grounds had a big shepherd or Doberman on a chain. The dog was crazy to get free. Snapped and barked all the time. I was about Dawn's age, about five, ready to do anything I wasn't supposed to. That dog didn't scare me. I couldn't get enough of watching how he'd leap, and the chain would catch him midair and jerk him back. He'd choke, whine a little, then leap again. Maybe I liked the way he didn't give up, or maybe I was just contrary enough to think it would be fun to set him loose. Whatever, I walked into his circle. All of a sudden teeth were in my arm and I was on the ground with more teeth coming and all I could do was scream. You can guess the noise. Mother came from her bridge game or something, all dressed in high heels. She might have just stood there screaming for help since there were gardeners around. Instead she ran straight into the circle and pulled me out while the dog tore up her leg."

He glanced secretly at his watch and hoped her tale was over. "Wow. Good for her. Bad for both of you."

"Blood and stitches, you can imagine. Poor dog shot of course. Father rushed home from his maneuvers somewhere. After he made sure I was all right, he whacked me where there were no stitches to make sure I understood that dogs on chains stayed that way." She laughed deep in her throat, and he joined. "But what I really remember: no praise or sympathy for my mother. He gave her hell for not watching me better. We went by rules. I felt sorry for her, just for a while. I don't know whether my father had a girlfriend in every foxhole but I never saw him affectionate. In this case it was the rules that mattered, not Mother's feelings. I suppose playing bridge was what Mother settled for. It's not what I'm going to settle for with you, Hank."

He rose and held her shoulders, hoping she'd put down the cup and come to him. "Never, never again, Jody. If you'd only believe how sorry . . . how sick I was after . . ."

"Another dog story," she said less seriously. "I had a mutt that would tear up the garbage even though he was smart enough to know the rules. Then he'd whine on his belly to show how sorry he was. But a week later, garbage over the kitchen floor again and the dog on his belly. Mother finally gave him away. It was my pet but I didn't hold it against her. Mother did have a standard."

"I'm no dog. Never again. I swear it, Jody."

"Being married to a fisherman is one thing if that's his reason to be away from home. But, swear all you like, if you then give yourself excuses when you're far from home or long time away, you might as well be sneaking around corners in Kodiak. We know that's the way some do here, men and women. I'm not giving myself up for that. It's trust, Hank. I've given you mine. I don't want you regretting things you can't do. If your mind's not clear about it, take back your freedom and give me back mine."

He pulled the wilted flowers from the jar for want of something better, and took them to her. "I pledge you my trust. It weakened once. It won't again."

She accepted the flowers, and kissed them lightly. "Then expect us back in time for school in September. Meanwhile come visit as often as you can. Even if I'm busy you know you'll find your children, and they miss their dad. So do I."

Relief, and suddenly he began to weep. Just as suddenly she was holding him.

"Come outside," she said, and offered her hand.

A few houses away she motioned him to wait, slipped the hook, and entered. Soon a woman he'd met before, fully dressed but rumpled and sleepy, left buttoning a parka and carrying floppy waders. She nodded to him pleasantly and continued to Jody's cabin.

"Come," said Jody. Instead of hooking the door she bolted it. Then she held out her arms.

They tore at each other, strewing clothes. Still half-dressed, skin electric against skin, they eased together into lumpy quilted folds on the floor. Their mouths sought everywhere like parched drunkards. At climax he capped her cry with a groaning roar. Then panting, together, his face between her breasts. Her smell was dark, soapless, salty, like earth and sea.

After minutes he roused and felt with one hand for a blanket alongside the futon. He picked a splinter from his knee where it had slipped from the padding, and she kissed it. Then they helped each other undress all the way, and lay covered making love again serenely.

He caressed and caressed. She accepted, did the same. "Oh Jody, my God I've missed you."

"I've missed you too."

Bangs, clicks, and voices outside. Suddenly firecrackers rattled. Jody stretched, kissed his chest, then rose businesslike and began to dress. "Barbecue and Roman candles tonight. Can you make it?"

"How I wish!" He reached up. "But I still have forty minutes now."

"That's you. Work time for me."

"They'd understand."

With hands on hips but in good humor: "Apparently *you* still don't."

"Sorry, sorry." He watched with head propped on arms, admiring, his spirit full. It was the bright, sure Jody of their courtship.

They could now chat again as friends. He told her the humiliating corner into which Swede and John Gains had driven him, and of Jones Henry's obsession. Her advice was practical: Avoid Jones. Make the best of cash buying and remember the lesson in future. But: "Do you think Jones can still take care of himself?"

"When he's sober, sure. And he's never been a drunk. This is just an aberration. I've never seen Swede as solicitous."

"Adele's worried."

"Then so am I. To this point just for our friendship."

"You may have lost it, you know."

"Not for good!"

"You've heard about old dogs."

They calculated Jones's age from anecdotes since Jones never spoke of it. Something beyond sixty. "But not far beyond," said Hank anxiously. (Sixty? Old!) "Damn that Japan trip for all its loss! Everything went right before that!"

"Except for no crab, Pete's doctor bills, and the fact you'd overextended us for the house and the big boat."

"But I was managing." At her expression he held up both hands. "*We* were."

Dressed now, she peered down as she tied back her hair. "Try to remember that 'we.'" She said it in good humor but he heard the edge.

"We. Always."

She left with "Go see your kids. And thank Jeannie if she hasn't already gone to the net."

Outside she bantered and laughed with the old tough freedom. By the time he'd made it back to his children and had jiggled them awake in their sleeping bags she was down with the others, about to wade out into the cold water.

21

FIRES OF JULY

The chopper returned him over the river to the cannery. Below, a handful of gillnet boats had flaked from the pack and were heading to open water. A firework trace arched toward one of them from a boat still tied.

"Be sure to tell Swede I gave you a smooth ride," said Marvin the pilot, lightly. "Swede's got a chopper pilot's license, you know. Means he's always watching how I do. At least when he flies with me I can relax, since he takes the controls himself to stay in practice."

Hank's *Jody Dawn* waited with engines humming and Seth on deck irritated and restless. "What the fuck are we up to?" Seth exploded. "Boards with some crazy name painted on and ropes to flap 'em over the sides across our own name. And asshole John himself's waiting in the wheelhouse with tin boxes, says nobody else should come up except you. You'd think he'd never been a deck ape under me the way he acts. And I stood up for him once when you wanted to fire him, remember?"

Hank patted Seth's shoulder. "Are we afloat yet?"

"Just. Better give it more time to be safe."

A sputter of explosions made Hank jump. "Somebody shooting?"

"Chrissake it's Fourth of July. Mo and Terry made some bottle rockets we're going to shoot as we leave."

"No. Don't. No attention to us. Sorry, but I mean it."

"Awww," came from Terry as Seth told him the news and Hank climbed to the wheelhouse. Out by the strikebound boats other rockets arched toward the departing boats, accompanied by hoarse shouts. They were aimed by the men still on strike, who were not playing.

John Gains turned from the chart table. He wore freshly creased coveralls but hadn't shaved since the night before. "Nice visit? That's a wonderful family, yours. I should get started myself and no more Japanese girls, however attentive."

"Don't mix 'em. What's up?"

"Count the money and sign for it. I'll trust the bank with just a pack-count on fives, tens, and twenties in this box, but we should do the fifties and hundreds together. Swede's on his way."

They each counted packs, then exchanged them to verify. It became tedious. Between packs: "Mike Tsurifune says hello. We talked an hour ago."

"Early evening in Tokyo? He's still sober then, I guess."

"At home and sober, sends warmest. He parties only with visitors he wants to impress. Do well here and I think the old man'll forgive. They did have bigger plans for you."

"When I buy back my boat they'll never see me again."

"Don't be hasty. They're your future."

Retort was saved by Swede's appearance. He, too, looked sleepless. "I left your friend Jones snoring. That's a hard nut to crack. I've always respected him. This burn against you isn't funny. It *is* strange. He doesn't care that the Japanese pull my strings, but your connection sends him wild."

"It's no compliment to you. Jones and I had a different kind of pact."

Swede unfolded a chart he'd brought and showed Hank where he wanted the newly christened *Arctic Lion* to anchor. "A few miles on the opposite side of the processor than before. I'd planned to send you further toward the Nushagak, but Dillingham just said they're close to settling for seventy. You were to pay sixty-five, but now seventy-five's got to be your price."

"And you're still offering these guys fucking fifty? I curse being part of this." Swede looked away.

John Gains studied him coolly. "You *are* naive."

Swede handed him the chart. "Don't change identity until you've collected from the boats committed to us and delivered."

"And I'll pay them seventy-five?"

"Don't be difficult, Hank," said Gains. "You know they're on the books for fifty. Eventually they'll get whatever we bargain, but not seventy-five, I hope."

"*Pricks.*"

Swede continued in a drone: "Suggest you change identity on an empty horizon, preferably in the dark or fog, just after delivering to the *Dora*. Then put up your banners and advertise. After that, deliver back in the dark, best if nobody else is delivering. But on your way out now, pass close to whatever boats you see to give us an idea how they're doing. Codes are in this book."

"I feel dirty."

"Sorry to hear it." By the time *Jody Dawn* passed the clustered boats on strike the defectors had cruised far enough ahead to reach open water and disperse. Hank's men usually gathered in the wheelhouse underway, but none of them appeared. He called down for coffee and Terry brought it. "Where's everybody?"

"We're pissed, Boss. Try working on bottle rockets all night, all ready to shoot, then like some prison warden says you can't."

He called them up and explained what was happening. Seth fumed and called it betrayal, Terry declared it kind of interesting, and Mo silently studied the deck.

Boats were still scattered distances apart. Hank told Seth to cruise among them and check their nets discreetly with binoculars, and to wake him if anyone wanted to deliver. "I can write their tickets," said Seth. "Get your sleep."

"No. Wake me."

Sleep had closed deeply when Mo shook him awake with: "Sorry, but you said to, Boss." It was lean Jack Simmons. He and his man were working the end of their last shackle. Little more than a day had passed since the plugged gear that set the *Jody Dawn* men wild, and again it was on a flood when new fish poured in, but now the net came over the roller with only an occasional lump. They picked as they reeled, scattering individual fish around their boots where netfuls had piled before.

"Where've you been?" asked Jack without looking beyond Hank's chest. "We picked all night on that good set, then tried to find you. Nothing like that now. You ask me, I think the first run's passed."

Hank took the tallied fish ticket from Seth. He beckoned Jack to his cabin and closed the door. "If you're smart you won't talk about this." He entered the delivery in the book for fifty cents a pound, then paid another twenty-five in cash.

Before they changed identity Swede radioed instructions to offload an extra net to the *Orion* that they carried as service to their fishermen. ("You're not going to be offering service now.") The old engineer Doke stood at the boom controls outside the wheelhouse. He acknowledged sententiously when Hank nodded.

As soon as the two vessels exchanged lines the *Orion*'s skipper climbed across the rails and introduced himself as Jeff. He indicated Doke. "That lardpot prick, I hear you put up with him once."

"That I did."

"He'd better watch I'll throw him overboard—he'd fuckin' float—if he don't stop bitching about everything we do. You know he has a lock on his special teabags and counts them each day like we'd steal them? Fact is we figured his combination and now and then we do slip one out when he's down with his engine. We ought to sell tickets for that circus when he counts and counts, then looks all around, then counts again. Of course now he takes his teabag can, lock and all, down to the engine room with him and we've got to figure some new way to get even."

Hank laughed. "We'd all have paid to watch that." He considered. "Don't injure him. He's more vulnerable than you think. And—you're passing through. That boat's his life."

"I didn't think you and him got along. Whenever he brings up your name it's to say you don't deserve such a wife."

Hank laughed again. The exchange at least put him in a lighter mood. When they left the *Orion* he waved merrily to Doke, who was still guarding his post by the boom controls, and received back a suspicious nod.

The days became nondescript, governed by tides more than the sun, which seldom shone. After collecting from Jack Simmons they found two other boats ready to deliver. None had recent catches to match their earlier ones.

At the factory ship: "Get me fish for Chrissake," said Dave the skipper. "My classroom's sitting on its ass eating my steaks and smoking pot. Let 'em smoke since it keeps them quiet. My boom lowers when it affects their work. But these restless little Japs, they creep in and out of their holes, little mouths like prunes, act like it's my fault we don't have fish. Get me *fish*, Hank!"

Hank watched uneasily the conversion of his *Jody Dawn* to the *Arctic Lion*. Like a thief taking his boat. The mechanics of the change were simple enough. Planks with the new name were flapped neatly over the old name, although it would be easy with a boat hook to peer under them. Wouldn't fool somebody like Jones. Swede had furnished sets of canvas banners with numbers by tens from sixty to a hundred along with attachable fives, allpainted in big red letters outlined in black: two of each so that they could face both port and starboard. Old-time Norwegians called it bad luck to change a boat's name. He himself might be free of superstition, but this was one more reason to hate it.

Once his men accepted the idea they took Terry's lead to enjoy making the trick work. After they had mounted "75" and entered an area of boats: "You can shoot your bottle rockets now to draw attention" Hank called down. When Terry and Mo pranced on deck they wore red bandannas pirate-style, and Terry had blackened curly mustaches and long sideburns on their faces. Seth followed soberly with a smaller token mustache.

Hank wished he could stay out of sight, but he needed to be paymaster. He chose a corner of the galley table which he darkened by unscrewing the ceiling light, and hoped it made him less identifiable. After debating Terry's and Mo's pirate fantasy he let them keep it. But to Seth: "Think you're fooling anybody?"

Wry smile. "Just ourselves."

The first boat to deliver came alongside quickly in dark rain, choosing starboard since other boats nearby were fishing to port. Watching from the wheelhouse Hank recognized them from the strike meeting. In the galley he offered no coffee as he had on the legitimate *Jody Dawn*. The skipper kept his eyes down. They finished the transaction as quickly as possible. With no further commitment after cash passed hands no one needed to sign off. Hank started to enter the name of the boat in his log. "That necessary?" asked the man. Hank wrote instead "Gillnetter One."

But later that night: "Heyyy man, you!" It was Chris Speccio. "Who are you and me working for? D'you quit Swede? You some spy?"

Hank banged the table in sudden good humor. "Arrest this cashmonkey and throw him in the hold with the fish!"

Chris leapt up, fists clenched, then looked around and realized it was a joke. "Oh man, this tension, I don' know."

"Get some coffee."

"The old man, he's so upset he talks about going back and joining the strikers again. Half our guys are still ashore. We'll never live it down with the older ones, but two of my cousins? My own age, their papa died last year left them the boat? They're fishing. It's old against young, and I'm pulled in the middle. First time we're all divided. For me and my cousins, we remember two years ago we struck got shit, wives, kids back home want money. The old guys remember how the canneries jerked them around before they got the union. I don' know. If they'd just the fuck settle! Seventy-five you're paying they'd settle for that."

"Take the money, Chris. I can't advise you. Suggest you deliver to the *Orion* now and then to keep face with Swede."

"Then this ain't Swede here?"

Hank considered. "Not the Swede you know."

As word spread, more and more boats slipped to the *Jody Dawn/Arctic Lion*'s visual lee and delivered. While none of the catches were vast, they accumulated enough that Hank's boat, in tandem with the *Orion*, enabled Dave on the factory ship to activate his butcher-freezer lines for a full ten-hour shift. By the seventh of July a freighter bearing Japanese flag and characters had tied alongside to transfer icy cartons from the *Dora*'s full hold. Hank arrived with a delivery in time to see the hatches sealed and the ship head for Japan.

The cannery helicopter stood on the factory ship's helo deck. Marvin the pilot had brought some engine parts, and a carton of American candy bars from John Gains to the captain of the Japanese freighter. A return gift rested beside Marvin on the galley bench as he ate a steak and joked that this was the best chow place on the bay.

"Well," said Captain Dave after signaling the cook, "I like a happy crew." Soon a smiling older woman brought steaks for himself and Hank.

"Your old lady still pumping setnets?" asked Dave.

Hank nodded, annoyed at the choice of words. His mind wandered the site every night between sleep. To change the subject: "Marijuana smell's gone from your corridors."

Dave stretched comfortably. "Fish are here now, and I'm the law.

Said it's finished, class—finito. Caught two kids smoking anyhow, sent 'em ashore for Swede to ship home or whatever. At least the little prune-mouths approved." He glanced around, then imitated with jerky bows. "*Hai hai hai.* Prune-mouths in their little white boots everywhere, trying to chisel grade Number One fish down to Number Two's. Couple of hours ago with that freighter you'd have thought it was the Ginza here."

"I thought you had only three of them stationed aboard."

"So, like I said. Everywhere, everywhere." As if on cue one of the Japanese entered, filled a teapot with hot water, glanced around, frowned, and left. "Oh, they're okay. Just shy I guess. All out of shape if they see people not working, like it's their ass back home. They just never let go, like a dog with his teeth in the meat."

Hank remembered John Gains's prediction that this was his future. He sliced his steak so hard it scraped the plate.

"*Hai hai* all over the place maybe," said Marvin. "But when I ride those people back and forth you've never seen anything so polite."

Hank was summoned to the wheelhouse. "Tide's rising and strike's done," said Swede on secure radio. "Settled for seventy cents."

"Great! We'll pull our planks and return as we were."

"Negative. Negative. Continue as before. But now fly cherry vanilla."

Hank checked his code. It was eighty-five cents. "That must be a mistake."

"Cherry vanilla's never a mistake. First run's already started up the rivers, nobody's sighted the second. Get me every fish you can. My pilot there? Send him up for instructions." Hank returned to the table disturbed.

The strike news had already reached others by radio to judge from shouts and laughs. Two high-pitched voices chattered excitedly in Japanese, and from somewhere a string of firecrackers sputtered. The pilot returned from the phone and nudged Hank. "Come for a ride."

"I should get back on the water."

"Swede's instructions."

They rose from the ship's helo deck. Quickly the factory and Hank's boat alongside diminished and fuzzed in the mist. The horizon held only two or three gillnet boats in one vista. They headed toward land. Suddenly the pilot whooped and pointed. Boats were streaming out of the river like ants from a hill or cars on a rush-hour freeway. They moved rail to rail in the river confines, then at the mouth fanned out in all directions. "Cage door's open and the grounds are *hot*!" Marvin called.

Jones Henry's among them, thought Hank. Good luck to you. The pilot grinned and next swept across the water to Jody's setnet site. "Hour and a half, Skipper, gift of Swede."

Hank accepted the bribe buoyantly. He dashed across sand and marsh to Jody's cabin and flung open the door with a loud "Hey!" Jody sat by the table with Pete on her lap and a picture book in her hand.

"Daddy Daddy Daddy!" Pete ran to hug his leg. Hank fondled and roughhoused him. Jody stood smiling. When Pete had subsided: "Go find Henny and Dawn, honey. Tell them who's here."

They stood alone. Smoky odors of mildew, bacon, and boots had become dear to him. Arms out and they advanced together. She pressed against his chest and he breathed hard at once. Through layers of wool he felt her heartbeat. "Let's lock the door."

She rubbed against him like a purring cat. "You know we can't. Relax until the kids get here." Their kiss held until noise and chatter tumbled in. Pete jumped up and down while Dawn talked nonstop about the fireworks they'd had for two nights, and Henny stood looking up. Hank eased off Henny's cap and tousled his hair.

Dawn grabbed his hand. "Daddy! Come meet my best friend Melissa and everybody."

He turned to Jody hoping she could intervene. But she shrugged. "Come on. Meet the crew."

It ended as a sociable hour with handshakes and sips of home brew, first from door to door and then in a larger cabin with an iron coal-burning stove. Someone popped a few leftover firecrackers for the occasion. Marvin the pilot joined them. Hank knew most of the faces, but casually from the town world beyond the boats: teachers and storekeepers with the men normally shaved and the women in dresses. Everyone asked for news like long-isolated castaways, as if he knew of more than the end of the strike. (One of the women even wanted to know how Congress was voting on the Equal Rights Amendment.) The fish run had tapered—on that everyone could agree. The next run should start any day.

All too soon his family waved him good-bye with more firecrackers thrown, and the chopper rose to head into the expanse of water. Boats now streamed everywhere on the bay, leaving white trails.

22

JONES

A few sockeyes from the initial run lingered in eddies before their programmed journey up rivers to spawn and die. Lucky boats caught them—or those skippered by men able to figure the habits of fish. When the shortage became an acknowledged reality more and more boats delivered for cash to cut losses. By mid-July Swede had raised his cash price to one dollar. It kept Hank and his crew busy. Everyone waited for the second run.

A rare sun had shone all day. It reduced night to an hour of twilight between reddened final glow on one horizon and pastel wash ninety degrees to the east. When Hank furled his price banners and slipped his disguised boat to the factory ship to deliver, he found Swede's legitimate *Orion* tied alongside despite their agreement to come at separate times. The factory's boom raised a glistening brailerload from *Orion*'s hold. Lights of sunset and dawn etched it on opposite sides. Hank tied to the tender's outboard rail to wait his turn.

"Come over, man," said Jeff, the *Orion*'s skipper. "So little fish out there it was no point coming our regular delivery in the morning. Sorry. Stake you to coffee and a little something else? I guess you know the way."

In the galley Hank saw Doke the fat old engineer. He occupied the same corner of table that he had defended from Hank four years before. "Ehhh," muttered Jeff. "Hoped that shithead would be down in his hole. Come on to my cabin."

Instead: "Doke, good sir," said Hank, and walked over to offer his hand. He remembered the lonely old man at close of season, faced with

299

winter in a Seattle rooming house and the wait, until another spring, for renewed life aboard the Orion that he'd helped build. But the man who looked up slowly was the sour Doke of summer authority.

"You." The puffy hand came up grudgingly, for a limp shake that left a smudge and odor of oil on Hank's hand.

"Hear you're as much an old pisser as ever."

"You'd be too, putting up the way I do." Bags under accusing eyes, cheeks weighted into jowls. Mess of a man, thought Hank, but not his problem. "You and your boys was bad enough—except Johnny Gains, he didn't belong and proved it soon enough. But that lady of yours. She made it a good year and I wish she was back. Left you by now, I'd imagine. Gone to somebody who deserves her."

"Sorry to disappoint you."

"Well then, you give her my regards. She's one lady." Pause and seeming struggle, then: "Have a cup of my special tea?" Hank refused gracefully.

Seth came in, trailed by Mo and Terry. He took Hank's arm and drew him aside. "Maybe you'll want to go out that other door. You wouldn't believe. One of the little gillnetters come to deliver since it couldn't find *Orion* on the water, ties to our rail. Guy walks across our deck to *Orion*, stops, looks me over, walks our deck, leans over the bow and flaps up the board with our phony name. Says: 'I might have fuckin' known.' It's Jones Henry."

Instead of leaving, Hank poured himself coffee from the urn and moved into the bank of seats around the table. Face it out.

Jones strode in, hands at the ready like a gunslinger. His man Ham followed. They both looked around, Jones sharply, Ham guarded. Ham and Mo locked eyes and nodded warily. Jones turned his back to Hank and addressed Jeff. "Chased you over the ocean, Skipper. Not that we've got a holdful worth the trip, but you're supposed to be there so it don't rot. Now, you want me to deliver to you or direct to this ship?"

"Sorry, Jones. I broke schedule. When I'm done why don't you just brail it over direct?"

"I would if a scab boat wasn't blocking my way."

Mo rose and Ham stiffened. The two buddies of other times studied each other reluctantly.

Jeff looked puzzled. "Tide's slack and no wind, Jones. The other side's safe. Just move around to their starboard. I'll get Dave to take you right away."

"It beats me why I'd have to move my ass one inch to accommodate a scab boat."

Jeff glanced from Jones to Hank, uncertain. "Fish still running thin, Jones?"

"You could say that. If I'd stayed with my seiner in Kodiak, the pinks mebbe no price to 'em but I'd be catching fish. And keeping better company than Jap-kissers."

Mo stepped forward. "Captain Henry, sir. Like I told you a few days ago, we don't like shit dumped on our skipper." Ham sighed and advanced on Mo.

"Back down," said Hank calmly. "Jones, sound off in this direction if that's what you need. Leave others out of it."

Jones turned slowly. "Now here's a great sight I must have missed. A man playing tap dance on top his buddies."

Hank kept his expression neutral but didn't trust his hand to take a drink from the mug. He felt withered. "You've got an audience. State your case."

"'State your case?' What kind of college-boy shit is that?" Jones pointed. "This man, if you want to call him that, one time he learned to fish from me and once we were partners and once we nearly died together. But now what's he done? Ask him! Sold out is what. Not to foreigners from China or Korea that don't matter, even Russia, but to the very Japs! The same Japs that called him over for patty-cake and he played so well his lips stuck to their ass." Jones's scowl swept the room like a beacon. "Anything I've missed that this man hasn't sold?"

"Jones," said Hank, forcing his voice to remain steady. "Japanese are people. They shit and they bleed. They work hard, love to eat fish, know how they want it, and pay. We're in the business of catching fish for sale."

"There's a politician talking." Jones pointed at Hank. "I don't care what you do, all you strangers. It's this man breaks my heart, that I took for my own. Taught him. Brought him to my very house. He's the one I'd expected to know better."

Jeff cleared his throat. " But Hank's right. Not one of us here but he's working for the Japs." Jones gestured angrily. Jeff continued: "Whose money, Jones, do you think it is runs the cannery, and the factory ship, and my *Orion* that collects your fish?"

"And what do you know of the rest, any one of you babies? Know what you kiss for that?" Jones' eyes slitted. "One time there was a war the Japs started, and I'll tell you about the Japs. Starts with me and buddies I trained with, First Marines, landed from boot camp to a shithole Guadalcanal you've never heard of."

"You done the Canal?" exclaimed Doke, coming to life. "I was Seabees out there later, buddy. Don't say *I've* forgotten."

Jones was too involved to acknowledge. He continued to scowl the room, unshaved chin jutting from wiry neck. "Here's my paddy-cake with the Japs. Patrol with buddies one night. Ambush. All of us hit." Each word dropped precisely. "I saw their shadows coming, shot to the last, then knew to play dead. Chewed a strap not to yell from the pain, never mind that. Gripped mud and let the spiders and lizards do what they liked. Japs laughed when they stuck a bayonet into each of my buddies that groaned. Not to kill outright. To make 'em scream as long as they could." Glare from face to face. "Now which of you says they've turned different?"

Seth and the *Orion* skipper looked away. The locked gaze of Mo and Ham guarding their sides loosened uncertainly. Only Terry held Jones' look, interested and sympathetic. "You tell it for us, buddy," muttered Doke.

When Hank rose to start toward him Jones signaled Ham to follow and left. Hank called his name although uncertain what to say if Jones stopped. But Jones went straight across decks to his boat, barked at Ham to throw off the lines, and disappeared into the little cabin. Spurt of engine and the boat left.

The encounter drained Hank's spirits. Surrounded by his men's voiced awe at Jones's tale and sturdy conclusions in their boss's favor, all he craved was Jody and the dark of covers over his head. He stayed in his bunk when he could.

Another grabbed visit to Jody's setnet site helped little since she was busy with the nets. Now that his appearance had become routine, Dawn barely stopped her playhouse with Melissa for more than hello. Pete held his hand for a moment, then skittered away with Henny in chase. Hank stood watching Jody boisterously at work with the others. She looked so happy! They all were free of him and happy. He began to face it: Probably in future Julys, wherever he was, she'd be here. And his children, needing him less and less.

His thoughts didn't help the heartsickness over Jones Henry, or his uncertainty over the right and wrong of his course. He needed Jody's touch and her presence to talk and explore. But, like himself away on his boat, she was busy being herself. Soon after the middle of the month it became clear that the second sockeye run had failed to materialize. A few fish wandered in but the grand predicted run, if it existed, remained at sea. (In the end thirteen million anticipated salmon failed to appear.) Fish and Game wondered and searched for reasons. Their embarrassment could not match the emptiness of strikers' nets.

Tides ran a course that man could predict exactly, moving from high to low to high again in approximate thirteen-hour cycles. The *Tidal Current Tables* told it for the year, to the minute. Weather was another matter. Fog settled for hours or days, so thick that deck and running lights ghosted without the shapes of their vessels. Then in minutes a wind might blow the horizon clean. Calm water could churn into whitecaps during the course of a haul-in. The same calm sometimes produced mirages: spooky shimmers of nonexistent shapes. Winds often blew independent of flood or ebb, hitting the current head-on so that the two forces caught boats in the middle. Anchor chains needed wide scope so that, as the forces changed, a boat could pivot with enough distance from other boats for a full swing of the compass. It was a place to stay alert.

"We are scratch," said Dave on the factory ship. "*Orion*'s bringing us practically nothing." His eyes were red. He had just come from a belowdecks argument with the Japanese inspector over grading fish and his beard was flecked with gurry. It turned out that some of his own money was invested in the factory ship although the Japanese owned controlling share.

Swede from shore was specific. "Get those people fish. Add a nickel to your price for anybody who delivers regular and make it clear that's why. Under the table after you've settled, no tax reporting." Hank had fallen far enough into the game that he did it with a shrug.

Just finish the commitment, Hank told himself, and make it out of here. Inaction left him with hours for thought. Too much of it became brooding. Without the cloud of Jones Henry's judgment he might simply

have rejoiced in his marriage and family restored, and have spent the days
maneuvering his schedule to visit the setnet camp.

Here he stood aboard the boat he'd yearned to own and had sold himself for—no, bargained for—and instead of racing the seas in pursuit of
crabs (or anything!) he waited for the catch of others. Waited under the
humiliation of subterfuge that had even robbed his boat of its name.
Robbed him of his deepest rooted friend.

During one afternoon of calm water he glumly watched a mirage that
could have been hills or buildings—watched it collect, shimmer, dissipate.
With a drink or two under his belt he'd have begun to compare it to life itself.

The trip to Japan had cracked the shell. Broken the coconut. He
played with nonsense similes, substitute for thought. Busted the piñata.
Before Japan, his way had been logical progression, boat to bigger boat,
taking on that which befell. Now the way had exploded open. Money
scarce and money promised brought out the bedfellows. A lowering sun
sneaked briefly into view between layers of gray cloud and gray sea. Its
blazing orange swept the mirage clean and showered light on the world.
Reason enough to blank the mind and relax in the sight. If a world could be
so transformed, wouldn't all things turn right?

Soberly, where was he headed? Not Jones's way fenced by the past,
that was baggage not his own no matter how he empathized. Even with
friendship at stake, his future needed to be tied to the realities of his own
time and place. Be wary, that's for certain. Wish otherwise, but know it as
business, the geisha parties past and future.

Then there was Kabuki and Helene, wistfully. Now that he was safely removed, and Jody restored, he could indulge it a little. Scarf and apple
scent. He breathed a memory-whiff since it no longer threatened. A woman
with style. But Jody fear not. Helene had brushed a part of Henry Crawford
now tucked back like a scrapbook photo, safely bygone. He wished her
well. For him, the precious things were Jody's wide smile and tart sense,
her firm touch, clean smell . . . Pete's hop-skitch . . . Dawn's spiky alert-
ness . . . Henny's grave admiration. Precious realities, all of it gifted with
promise.

The blazing orange etched rigging and cloud stumps. It burned over
the caps of sudden little waves kicked by a fresh wind. He'd gear for longline and take on the new. The thought made him weary, all the work ahead,

but he felt a bubble of excitement waiting to explode and knew the energy was there. Drive. Make money. Buy back his boat's possession. Play into the great game where combat waited and reward glimmered. Become chess piece to nobody.

23

SAND

Lean Jack Simmons and some of the other strikebreakers pulled their boats for the season and flew home. They thus avoided witness to their shame and left what fish remained for others. They also escaped with the money.

Hank followed the fortunes of Jones aboard the *Robin J* as best he could, through information relayed by sympathetic Jeff of the *Orion* to Dave on the factory ship. Jones's fishing luck was as poor as the rest. But he had his teeth into the quest for fish, enough so that his man Ham confided to an *Orion* crewman that they hardly ever slept. Easygoing Ham had turned jumpy by report, and almost as irritable as Jones. Since Jones traveled without buddy boats or community, Hank had little chance to eavesdrop on his radio conversations, but one night the unmistakable voice started talking curtly to another man from Kodiak. "You're scratch too, eh? There's only one place they're left and that's the pockets close in to shore."

"Don't let the wrong wind and tide catch you."

"Who said you didn't keep alert? Ham! You turned moron? In that shackle double-speed, it's empty, use your eyes! We got other places to set. Signing off. Work to do."

Most deliveries to Hank's shadowy *Arctic Lion* came from the remaining original strikebreakers, who had distanced themselves from the union agreement with the canneries. "Here's how *we* worked it out, my cousins and uncles," said Chris Speccio lightly as he and his dad sneaked a cash delivery. "Fish tickets, they're all going into one big envelope. Then back home everybody who's family divides it, strike and strikebreak equal."

"Including this cash payment?"

Chris laughed. "We ain't saints, Hank."

Chris had tied alongside under the anonymity of fog, but while he delivered, the visibility cleared to reveal a vista of masts. "Whoa, get out of here," he declared only half in jest. Hank freed his stern line, then at Chris's "yo" the painter, and nodded to Vito through the wheelhouse window. The father had chosen to remain inside after strapping the brails. Since breaking strike he had said little.

On open radio the voice of Jones Henry told his Kodiak friend, "Go Channel Blue." Hank guessed the frequency Jones had used for years, and switched in time to hear Jones's rapid-fire: "Saying this fast and once. Head toward Banana Tree. I'll code you my loran coordinates another channel when you're close. Found a hole close-in to sands. Pocket of reds trapped on ebb. I figure enough for both of us since the strike shitted you too. Any scab boats hears this, stay away."

"Read you buddy. I'm down south line off Johnston waiting to set on flood. Looks like most other boats too. Miles from you so we'll stay here see what happens. Then I'll come hope not too late. You off by Deadman Sands? Don't have to answer. Just be careful if you're close in. Tide tables predict this one's a real strong flood coming in."

"In control, in control. Repeat. Any scab boats hears this, not welcome. Out."

Oh Jones, thought Hank. Pull it back together.

Seth yawned. "That pisser won't let go."

"Belay that talk!"

"He might be your friend, and he sure had it bad with the Japs, but I've been enough with Jones Henry to call him what I like. Admit it. The guy's turned the corner."

"And I tell you politely to belay it." Seth looked away, resentful, but said no more. Hank's gloom deepened. He'd begun to fear for Jones.

"The way he's talked to you is no good, Boss," said Mo. "But I hope Captain Henry's found some fish'll make him happy. I hope so too for my buddy Ham."

"The hell he's still your buddy!" Seth snapped it to cover his backing off. "Go fix dinner."

"Ham's just done his job last month, our fight."

Hank turned spontaneously. "You're a good man, Mo."

"I now pronounce the combatters deck ape and deck ape," said Terry. Mo, aglow from his skipper's compliment, reached around and pulled Terry's cap over his eyes.

They spent hours together in the wheelhouse while Hank cruised the radio bands. Identifying languages passed the time. Of a pinched singsong: "Anybody knows that's Jap," said Seth.

Hank grinned. "Chinese." He'd ascertained the Taiwan ship's call sign the day before.

Of another band: "Don't tell me that ain't Russian."

"Plenty of Russian around," said Hank easily, secure again in previous knowledge. "But that's Yugoslav, Croatian. The Anacortes gang."

"You sure know a lot, Boss," said Mo with admiration.

All radio talk halted at six P.M. for the weather roundup from Kodiak by fisherman's wife Peggy Dyson. She had committed to the service after years of nightly communications with her husband, Oscar, aboard his *Peggy Jo* in the Bering Sea and elsewhere, and now fishermen throughout Alaska relied on her broadcast. While less than two hundred miles separated Kodiak from Naknek, the mountains of the Peninsula blocked radio waves so that her familiar voice came in squeaks. Storms from the Aleutians that had brought the fog, she said, would be replaced by a norther bearing easterly. "Precipitation expected, with gusts possibly exceeding forty knots."

Jones had better leave his little sand pocket, Hank thought. Warn him? No, Jones was always careful, and it would only invite some insult. He tuned back to the foreign conversations. Two clearly Native voices spoke English softly, deliberating each word. "So what's that one, Professor?" asked Seth. "Mongo-Lapudian?"

"For all I know. Aleut or Eskimo, both are around."

Seth picked his teeth. "I've been thinking. Maybe I should shave my beard. Give a try without it. Maybe women don't like beards anymore."

"Make no difference," said Terry. "You'd be as ugly as ever."

"Sometimes you mouth too much!"

"You'd look *good*," soothed Mo.

Hank had watched Seth grow increasingly scratchy. He switched to a band that he knew the Italians used. "That's Wop, don't tell me differ-

ent," said Seth, still on the edge of anger. Hank nodded and switched to
an established Norwegians' channel. "Anybody knows that's Squarehead."

Seth was mollified.

The predicted rain arrived with splatting drops. On a clear day the
sun would still have hovered low on the horizon for another two hours, but
now the gray light darkened. Wind began to kick the water into chop and
whitecaps. "Terry or Mo, check the anchor." Each man for form's sake
declared the other should go, then traded recreational insults while they
slipped into oilskins and went out together.

"Oh man, we're fuckin' bored," said Seth. "I was almost going out
there myself. Mo hasn't even bothered to start chow and who cares. All we
got to do is eat."

Hank watched through sweeping wipers while his men felt and
kicked the anchor chain and then gave thumbs up. "Shitty night," they
declared appreciatively in unison, returning with a slam of the wheelhouse
door. "Ol' Jonesy's and Ham's gettin' wetter asses than us tonight," added
Terry. "But I wouldn't mind being with them, all that fish."

"Anybody who hears me." It was Jones Henry's voice on the open
monitoring channel. He spoke deliberately. "I've run into a little trouble.
Nothing we can't handle, Ham and me. But if anybody's close by we could
use a tow."

Mo and Terry made for the bow even as Hank ordered anchor-up. As
soon as Jones gave his location, Hank set course, then grabbed the chart
and told Seth to go full speed.

"To anybody hears this," Jones continued. "Propeller's gone near as I
can tell." His voice was calm. "Swells coming at us all of a sudden like a
roller coaster. A big swell slammed us, we hit ground, scraped over something buried mebbe part of some other boat wrecked. Too rough to see until
morning but, like I say, probably broke propeller since we're dead in the
water. We're safe enough on anchor of course. Tide still going down,
means sometimes we beach in a trough, then a wave slams us. My hold's
got mebbe fifty fish, not enough for ballast. Not yet at least. Water's kicking like a stewpot. Ham! Stand back!" After a static-filled silence, Jones
resumed: "Wouldn't mind having chain on that anchor line instead of
nylon, but she'll hold."

Hank bent over a detailed chart. At least only sand was marked at Jones's location, no rock. But Jones appeared to be trapped in the shallowest water, two feet low tide worst case, three at most, safe only in calm. The inlet was at least a dozen feet too shallow for the *Jody Dawn*, although depth lines on the chart indicated safe draft only a hundred feet beyond. The northeasterly wind and swells would be driving Jones straight toward the charted sandbars. And who knew what smaller bars lay shifting beneath? When flood tide commenced the current would be directly opposed to the wind. The forces would fight him broadside.

Jones resumed in a voice that stayed calmly deliberate: "Wind's rising. She'd blow us onto that hump of land but for the anchor. Getting dark, but I see white breakers along that hump. See it close enough to hear it. And smell it if you know what I mean. Ham! Just rest a minute, make coffee. If the boat ain't pitching it's bumping, but no reason not to have our coffee. Yup, we're being jiggered like some gull tied to a string. Well, work to do. If nobody's nearby we'll close off this frequency and give somebody else a chance."

Hank grabbed the mike. "Keep talking, Jones. Everybody else alert. Possible Mayday. Keep this channel open." Several voices agreed. "Jones! We're full speed toward you. Hang on."

"Sounds like Hank. Stay clear, Hank, your draft's too deep, you'd ground certain." Pause. "Go back to buying fish for the Japs." Pause. "Got no Mayday here, we're in control."

A voice: "Advise you put your gillnet back in the water, leave it full of fish as possible. Ride that instead of your nylon anchor line. The nylon could part in shallows with too much stretch and no bounce to relieve it. So when net-over gives any slack, pull back your anchor. Flood current about thirty minutes away and it's predicted strong. When it comes it'll pick up that net and drag you with it to deeper water. Not far away. Net'll ride you out like a tugboat. But secure that net on cleats, everything. Careful. When the pull starts it could bend a cleat, pull it out by the bolts. I've been there."

"Well," said Jones. "That advice noted. But here's only this one fifty-fathom shackle of empty net on board, two fish in the web. Test-dropped it half an hour ago, no fish left for it to catch. Can't say I'm proud of what happened. But I ain't ready to leave what we've got, that I'm looking at just a few feet out of reach. It's the rest of my net, detached and out of reach, and it's plugged with all the fish of the ocean. Ham's trying to grapple her in, and he'll do it. Hold on." Jones's voice turned distant. "Ham! Rest a minute till I get there." Voice clear again: "I've worked that boy too hard and wish I hadn't. He's numbed his shoulder just when we need his best muscle. Happened this way. My first shackle came in a near water haul. Then all at once, start of the next shackle, she was plugged. We'd found our mess of fish backed in here on the ebb. So I detached the empty net on board, buoyed the full one in the water, and figured I'd run in back of the full net and attach the empty one to keep all nets working. Back then I still had mebbe four foot of water, and I draw under three feet. Swells didn't seem so bad. Trouble is, a swell caught us like the *Titanic* high as our heads, and we banged in the trough, broke the propeller like I said."

"Suggest you stop talking and put out web, even if it's empty web."

"Not come to that, I'm saying. In control."

Come on, Jones, thought Hank. No time to get pissed. He'd seldom heard Jones so talkative. It either meant Jones felt safe, or had done all he could.

"Here we are," Jones continued, "looking at a net so plugged with big sockeye salmon it's dipping corks, and with a little luck we'll still reach it when the tide starts moving. But float that empty net? She'd drag us clear of those fish for sure. Mebbe we're dead in the water but repeat, anchor holding. Now I got to sign off. My man Ham's gone back with his grapple and I want to hold his belt. No way to fish him out if he falls over. Boy's gone crazy to get us back our nets full of fish and I don't blame him. Just one lucky throw mebbe five feet further, one lucky gust to carry it, and we've got our catch and our ride to deep water both. If we put out our empty net just yet, it'll drag us further from the full net sure, and good-bye the only money-haul of the year. Out."

"Forget the fish, man," said someone. But no further answer from Jones.

"Stubborn?" said Seth. "Well, he's so stubborn he's got style." He looked at Hank directly. "My kind of stubborn pisser. Got his fish, won't give 'em up."

"Okay, he's a stubborn pisser." To himself Hank added: and it's made Jones lose his trusted judgement.

"Ham's strong," said Mo. "He'll get that hook right if it kills him."

"Don't say it that way," said Terry.

"No no, didn't mean it that way."

From the cannery, Swede's voice: "All vessels keep this frequency open. Jones. Read me? Jones! You're in more danger than you think. A storm's bearing on us not adequately predicted. Why doesn't that man answer? Company chopper's coming to fetch me. Will then head to the scene. Hank. Give me your position and ETA-Jones. Any vessels heading to help, relay your position." Other boats called, but none were close.

Hank pumped the throttle and cursed his speed, although water was parting like a wall from both sides of the bow and fans of spray pelted the windows. At least the wind and swells that pushed Jones toward shore pushed him toward Jones. Mo brought him a sandwich. He set it aside. "Break out all our lines, you and Terry. Tell me how much we've got. Be careful on deck, we're hitting the water hard." They left.

"You got a plan?" asked Seth.

"Just as it goes. Any ideas?"

"No more than you but you're right, we'll need lines whatever."

"And . . . not sure how we'll use them, but break out survival suits."

"You ain't swimming in?"

"Every option. Do it."

"Right. But—" Panic in Seth's eyes and voice. "Don't consider that. I'll stop you."

A heavy gust independent of the prevailing blow hit the *Jody Dawn* broadside and rolled it with a shudder. The plate with the sandwich smashed to deck. The gust from unexpected direction would have been routine in the middle of a winter Bering Sea, but not for summer in Kvichak Bay. The overhead thump of rope and clank of metal fittings reassured Hank that Mo and Terry were coping topside on the open storage deck.

"Jones, damn it. Get back on your channel. *Hey!*"

At last Jones's voice, calm as ever. "Well, Hank. If you're going to stick your nose into it, we're jiggering here, out of the rain for a minute while Ham catches his breath. That hook almost made it. Three more feet and we've got her. Meanwhile, seems to me the wind has slacked. Soon we'll get out our bathing suits if this keeps up. Nobody need worry about us."

"Jones! Bad forecast whatever the wind's doing there. Just for the hell of it, you guys put on your survival suits."

"Now, you wouldn't believe this, but we've got only one of them things for the two of us. Ham forgot his. But I'm captain and responsible—should have checked any crewman of mine—so it's Ham's suit. But Ham, he won't take it. So the big orange thing just sets here between us like a pot of flowers. However, we ain't come to that by a long shot. Hank? You back now buying fish?"

"No, you turkey, I'm heading toward you."

"Well . . . Ham and me appreciate that." Pause. "Hank. You're a good man."

Hank caught his breath.

"Do not come close, Hank," Jones continued. "If I'm bumping ground you'd plow dirt. We're holding. Good little boat. Don't worry. Less breakers now on that sand hump. Tide's started in. Sometimes spray hides it, but that hump's going down while I watch, seems. That's how fast the tide's rising. Question for anybody hears me. Wind and swells keep pushing me at that hump. Wonder at high tide if the wind could blow us over it clean. My chart's spilled coffee on the numbers right there and light's not good, we're saving what power we have. But looks like mebbe a patch of nine-foot depth other side that should give my anchor line more play. Does anybody out there know? "

A voice: "Shifting bars all along that north side. Do not go over. Repeat. Do *not*."

"Then we'll stick it out since that's what we've got. Hank, you there? Mebbe you can float us a line with your rubber life raft attached. Then Ham can get in and grapple his extra three feet. Then we can pull out together with my fish."

"Forget the fish, you idiot!" exclaimed a voice.

"Sounds," said Jones drily, "like somebody who ain't into the fish. Hank, you hear what I said about your dinghy?"

"We'll anchor as close as possible—the chart shows safely deep water just outside the inlets—then try to float you a line attached to buoys and life rings. Then raft, whatever, we'll see."

"Current's making harder now by the minute, Hank, so you'll have to start pretty far down-current or she'll sweep past us. You figure."

Mo came in dripping to the eyebrows to report lines ready. "We'll get five hundred feet easy, Boss." He asked if he could use the mike. "Hey, Ham, you there man? This is Mo."

After a pause and Ham's voice muttering "Press this giz and talk, that's all?" Ham said cautiously: "Yeah. Hi, man. You hear me?" Mo affirmed. "Uh, well, that's good. Never used this thing before since Skipper Jones always—you, uh . . . Mo? Gettin' wet out there I guess?"

"No, man, I asked how about you first."

"Oh. Good. Good. Pretty dry in here." Long pause. "I just checked the lazarette. No leak there."

"Hey. Next time we're in Kodiak Fourth of July? Want to put on the gloves again? Let Lola and Judy hold our shirts. Beat your ass, man."

"Yeah. Sure. Sounds good. Oh Jeez!" It was a cry. "Skipper Jones! That water up through the deck?"

Static. Hank called and called to no answer. He told the others to break out the life raft and inflate it. Have whatever means ready.

Ten minutes later: "Okay, hear this," said Jones. "We're shipping water, just a little. My pump's new last year, doing fine, engine room's mostly dry. Wet no more than to our shins. Lazarette's dry, leak ain't there. We are bailing, just for recreation, taking turns. Hank, you there?" Hank affirmed. "Well, now, this is a mountain in a molehill since nothing's going to happen except me and Ham getting our pants wet. But Adele. She talks a lot but she's one fine woman. I'd hate to see anything go wrong for her. You hear me, Hank?"

"I hear you, Jones." Hank steadied his voice. "Don't worry about that."

"You can kiss her for me if you've got the nerve. Now Ham has something he wants to say. Here, son, I'll take the bucket now."

Ham's voice. "Mo? You there Mo?"

"Yeah, man? I'm here." Mo's voice was husky.

"Just a dumb thing. My mom? She's at the address I left at the harbormaster's in Kodiak. Someday if you get the chance? You see, the water's up now near to our knees."

"Sure, sure, man, but don't you worry, we're coming and Boss here knows what to do. Hang on! You hear?"

"My mom bakes good pies. Going to try that hook once more now."

Mo turned to Hank like a child. "Oh Boss, you gotta do something."

Hank grabbed the mike. "Damn it, Jones, put out your net."

"Captain Henry says tell you, just one more try with the hook. He's already out on deck waiting for me, sir, so I'm putting this thing down."

The throb of a helicopter passed overhead in the clouds. Swede's voice. "I'm approaching the scene. Dangerous downcurrents with this wind. Better to reach them by sea if you can do it, Hank. Safest we can do is swing them one by one to closest shore since I've got to drive and John by himself can't pull a man aboard."

"Marvin's not piloting?"

"Marvin became my former employee half hour ago when he said it was too dangerous to come here. My volunteer crew is John Gains."

"Gains!"

"Stand by. Calling any setnet sites vicinity south of Halfmoon Bay. Anybody read me?"

Voice: "Joe Penn setnet camp here. We're located due southwest the emergency position given, about two and a half miles southwest. Have no wood for bonfire, but will keep generator going and shine flashlight beams when we hear you coming. Lights will be in an area safe to lower, with everybody standing by to assist."

"Boss, ain't that the beach with Jody and your kids?" asked Terry. Hank nodded.

Jones's voice: "Wind and swells getting stronger than ever. My mistake to think it slacked. We've just now give up with the hook. Anchor line's stretched like a banjo string."

A voice. "Then that nylon anchor line's close to snapping. Urge urge urge put net in water even if it's empty."

"You're right. Ham! Throw down the bucket come help me." Sudden hoarse cries. Transmission stopped. Despite calls Hank could not rouse Jones again. He beat on the wheelhouse rail.

At last *Jody Dawn*'s radar showed the sketches of land in the middle of water that betrayed the long, irregular bars among which Jones lay. Closer in, when Hank slowed, the rain hit them harder because they no longer rode with it. He guarded the fathometer but sent Terry to the bow to take hand soundings. Seth and Mo on the open deck above him tied lines and readied the raft. All peered into the dark for signs of the *Robin J*.

Jones, Jones, you've got to be there. Please.

He turned on his sodium vapor crabbing lights, and scanned with binoculars. Water rolled under the boat like horses' manes, leading to empty horizons. The lights diffused against rain but penetrated enough to make out what might be a ridge of land. Swells rolled over it, sinister and glistening, while flurries of whitecaps kicked all around. But Jones, Jones, where? He allowed the wind to creep him in while backing the engine. "Sixteen feet," from Terry on the bow, confirmed on the fathometer. Risk three more feet, very limit. No. Risk four heading in since tide was rising and his bow rode lighter than his stern.

"Yooww!" called Seth. "Ten o'clock to port!"

Mo's voice bellowed "Yeah she's there! There she is!"

First sight was a faint light that jiggled. Suddenly it swooped, jiggled again, then swooped in a different direction. Hank directed his beams, and the *Robin J*'s small dark outline took shape. A trough buried it, while crests tossed it nearly out of the water. As they watched, the boat pivoted, a wave hit its hull, and the light spun, flickered, disappeared. The boat was out of control. Its anchor line must have snapped. Without the ballast of fish it was being tossed like a trash ball by the wind and swells, caught apparently in an eddy.

The figures of Jones and Ham staggered over the washed deck hugging a net. Both wore yellow oilskins, but Ham had his legs in the orange survival suit and the rest apparently belted around his middle. It appeared they were attempting to put over the net. But whenever they advanced a few feet the deck slanted so far that all they could do was cling. Then with a swoop the boat careened, and the deck became nearly vertical in the opposite direction. Hank's crabbing lights hit the *Robin*'s windows without reflection except on jags. It meant the glass was smashed. Pieces of white board surged around the hull. As he watched, a wave snapped off another piece of the cabin.

"Thirteen foot!" called Terry at the lead line.

Big swell. In its trough the *Jody Dawn*'s bow touched sand. Instant shudder and halt. It jerked Hank forward and his head hit the window. Terry on the bow, caught off guard leaning over with his sounding line, nearly tumbled overboard before clutching the rail. "Terry inside!" Hank cried over the speaker as he throttled reverse. His fear made him gasp.

Keep hold. A few feet back and the fathometer showed safe water. What if
his engine had failed? In old sail days without engines, that's how the
names piled for bell tolls. Terry looked up, waved his arms with a grin,
turned to take another sounding. "Terry! Inside! Go!" Terry scampered aft
to the housing, grip by grip on stationary handholds.

Hank called for anchor. When the anchor held, the boat spun half circle on the chain so that they faced Jones from the stern. It made the for-
ward-beaming sodium lights useless. Hank turned them off and activated
his searchlight. About three hundred feet of water roiled between the two
boats. Too far for any kind of throw to reach. To Hank's barked instructions over the speaker they tied a heaving line's monkey fist to a drift line
attached to floats. Mo, the strongest, threw it over and over. The wind blew
the weighted ball toward the *Robin*, but as soon as the fist dropped short
the current moved it far from target.

The helicopter arrived, to noise so great Hank needed to turn up the
speaker. A basket dangled beneath it from a line being blown nearly horizontal. Swede's voice: "Looks too rough for your boat to get in. Can't get
them on radio. What I'm going to do they'll see. Basket for only one at a
time. Can't risk the weight of both in this weather. One of them'll strap
into it. John here's on his belly tied in, looking out the bay to guide the tow
as best he can. But John alone can no way hoist the man up. Have to drag
him through the air to the closest beach camp. I'll come back then, for the
other. But I didn't start with a full tank, just grabbed the machine. These
fucking things gobble fuel, I've got to go refuel. Pray to hold tight."

Hank and his men gathered dripping in the wheelhouse to watch as
Swede's chopper hovered down over the thrashing *Robin J*. The helicopter's
blade wash flattened water slightly around the *Robin* and steadied the deck
on a starboard roll. But the basket blew beyond their reach. The helicopter
circled unsteadily to face into the wind. It removed the boat's downdraft
stability and the deck bucked. Jones and Ham each gripped stanchions with
one hand while they grabbed for the swooping basket with the other. On the
fourth try, Ham made a flying jump and fell to deck with arms wrapped
around the line. He disappeared in foaming water as the deck careened to a
different angle. Jones released his grip and leapt into the foam.

"Oh shit don't wash Ham over," cried Mo. He fell to his knees. "Oh
shit God, don't let 'em die." Hank prayed silently, belief or not.

The water washed clear. The yellow figures remained, thrashing. Struggle for balance? Hank knew as he watched through binoculars. Jones was forcing Ham into the basket.

With the chopper directly overhead the *Robin*, its downwash eased the boat's violent random thrash. But it held the starboard list in place. Glassy swells rolled over Jones and Ham and splashed against the hatches. Jones, Jones, thought Hank. You're seaman enough to have battened everything, aren't you, man? In answer, a wave rolled high enough to spill through one of the smashed windows.

Jones braced himself and waved up one arm toward the helicopter. The aircraft rose with Ham in the basket clutching the rim. The orange survival suit still encased his legs and the top was now pulled over one shoulder. For an instant the *Jody Dawn*'s searchlight illuminated Ham's anguished face with mouth open crying out, and Jones's calm gaze as he continued to signal with his arm. Sudden gust. The chopper dipped. A wave broke over the basket and pulled it underwater with Ham. Then with a roar the chopper rose and melded into the dark with the orange and yellow of Ham's figure flailing.

"I take back all the way that I called him a pisser," said Seth hoarsely. "He gave up their only survival suit."

Hank forced his voice steady before speaking. "Jones has his values."

With the downwash gone, the *Robin* should have rolled back to port, and begun spinning anchorless again, but she remained on a starboard list. Meanwhile flood current had increased enough to hold the boat broadside to the relentless wind and swells that blew in near opposition. Hank watched through binoculars as Jones crawled along the higher side of deck port-side with the net draped over his shoulder, gripping hatch covers for support.

"Do it, Jones," muttered Hank. "Get that net in the water." In malevolent answer a wave surged up the deck and covered Jones. When it receded, Jones lay flattened between hatches and the net had washed from him. Instead of trailing from the stern as intended, it stretched directly over the submerged starboard rail. As the current took hold, the net began to pull the *Robin J* further onto its side.

"Get the raft astern." Hank freed an orange survival bag.

"No, Hank."

"*Do it!*" Even Seth hurried to deck.

Alone in the wheelhouse Hank shook his survival suit from its bag, quickly wrapped plastic around his boots to slide rubber against rubber, and slipped into the thick legs. Focus, forget fear. Quick to Jody? No, bad luck, focus instead to be all right. Just the same, hand trembling, he scribbled on separate sheets:

"Dawn I love you. Dad."

"Henny I love you. Da."

"Pete I love you. Daddy Da—."

Then, breathing heavily: "Jody I love you. Flower of my life. Stay free."

Folded into envelope, "Jody" on the outside, tucked into the logbook.

The survival suit, neoprene rubber coverall seamless from foot to chin when zipped, might float a man dry and warm, but worn out of water it was flapping and clumsy. Even the gloves were only thumb-palm. He stomped awkwardly in it to deck, clutching the bag of a second survival suit for Jones.

"No!" cried Seth.

Hank was calm. "Those oars in place?" He peeled one arm free and bent over the tubular side of the raft to check for himself. Flimsy oars, but locked so they wouldn't detach.

Seth grabbed him. "This is one shit I ain't taking off you. If he's gotta die it's his own business."

Hank shook him off. He checked the bowline attached to the raft, retied it himself, jerked it to test. "Keep this tow bent on the winch all times, two or three turns no more so you can slack or pull in fast. Pay attention. Oh, portable radio."

"I'll get it," said Terry and ran inside. Seth also disappeared, even though Hank called after him to come back for more instructions.

"You can't do that alone, Boss," said Mo. "What it looks like you're doing needs four hands at least in the raft."

"Alone, Mo."

Terry returned with the portable radio, and: "Boss, Mr. Scorden just on radio, says Ham's safe delivered but he's got to go refuel. Says everybody hold tight till he gets back for Captain Henry."

Seth came from the cabin with his legs in a survival suit as he struggled to pull his arms through the top. "Coming with you."

"No you're not. Your job's here, to stay and handle this boat. You're skipper now." Hank squirmed his arm back into the rubber. Rain had already chilled through his exposed sweater and thermals. He threw the stiff orange bag of the other survival suit into the raft. Below roiled black water. Sky black. Wait another minute. If only Swede's chopper . . .

Terry pointed. "Oh Jeez lookit, Jones's boat. She's flooding straight through the windows!" What remained of the *Robin* above water merely dipped as swells moved over it. Jones clung to the housing with an arm wrapped into one of the empty window openings. Swells rolled above his waist.

"Raft over, quick." The flexible rubber craft bounced and skittered wildly.

Seth grabbed his arm again. "Jones is fuckin' old! He brought it on himself! *His* fuckin' stupid, not yours. Don't make it another."

"Let go!" Seth would not. Hank struck him. Seth fell on deck. Hank slipped into the raft. It bounced with his weight, then adjusted unsteadily. "Cast me off. Guard the line."

"You're all I got!" cried Seth.

As Hank settled to the oars and peered over his shoulder toward Jones's boat, a bounce in the raft and there was Mo's sheepish grin as he squatted beside him. "Get out," said Hank.

Mo looked up calmly. Rain dripped from his eyebrows. "Needs four hands, Boss. Let me row."

"Thanks. But get out. Risk one's enough. I mean it."

"Boss, Ham's my buddy and that's his skipper."

"*Get out!*"

Seth and Terry helped Mo back aboard. Hank looked up at their grave and frightened faces. "Tend that line, guys. I'm in your hands."

"In God's hands," blurted Terry.

Hank started to joke the joker, instead quickly dipped with the oars and rode a swell to make distance before he changed his mind. Mo in the raft would have been comfort. He yearned to be back with them. Soon the blinding circle of *Jody Dawn*'s searchlight washed out their faces. Sudden panic. Alone in black seas. "The Lord my shepherd . . ." It eased nothing. "Jody be with me." He kissed his wedding ring as the oar hand reached his lips, held her face and tried to row harder. The aluminum oars were mere sticks with small paddles, meant to hold way rather than make speed. His work with them was to buck the current that pushed abeam, since the wind by itself blew him steadily toward the *Robin*.

Faint call beyond the wind. It sounded like: "Sinking!"

He rowed wildly. The flimsy oars strained against grommets, but the rubberized material of the raft stretched to absorb the extra pressure. He was panting. The survival suit encased him like a steam oven and sweat gushed from his wool cap. Searchlight in his eyes gave flashed vision when he twisted to scan for the *Robin* in dark. Too blurred to see anything but the boat's dim shape, no details. At least it hadn't sunk. The rowing was work beyond his anticipation. Should have kept Mo. "Jody . . ."

Sudden gust. The raft bumped a hard object and bounced off. He tried to grab slick surface as the oar jerked from his grasp to sharp wrist pain.

Hands locked around his arm but began to slide. He looked up into Jones's slitted eyes, with glistening hull behind. The *Robin* had overturned. He dropped oars and gripped Jones's hand just as it began to slip away. Before he could counterbalance, Jones had tumbled across his knees, the raft upended, and they floundered in the water.

He clutched Jones's shoulder while groping at the raft with the arm in pain. His feet touched ground. A second of relief, then current pulled at his legs and a wave covered his head. With footing lost, the buoyant neoprene of the survival suit tried to float his legs. In the trough, feet on ground again, he sputtered salt water, gasping. Helpless buffet with arms locked around burdens, but to give in to pain meant all lost.

"Let go. Save yourself."

Without answering, Hank thrust Jones against the bottom of the raft. Jones instinctively clawed at its surface. During a moment with feet on ground Hank pushed him up enough to clutch the edge. It freed Hank's hurt arm but he still needed to thrash it for balance. Quick assess. No way in rough water, lacking firm foothold, to right the overturned raft without dumping Jones. But no chance, with it overturned, for a safe pullback to *Jody Dawn*. Exposed land lay a hundred feet ahead in the opposite direction. Would it stay bare long enough for Swede's chopper to return? There at least lay the only way to right the raft. He plowed step by step against the current, the hump in dizzy swing before his eyes, falling water-swept and regaining hold. Cold salt pushed sickening into nostrils and head. Each breath risked new slam of gagging brine. He gained inch by inch until the current lessened against shore and swells rolled far enough below his mouth to breathe without sucking water. When Jones's feet felt the bottom he bore his own weight and slowly helped to walk the raft.

The sand sloped upward to the hump. When the swells rolled only below his thighs Hank dropped to knees and crawled. He stopped to vomit, dragged the raft farther with Jones now clinging to it at a slow crawl also. On firm sand, Hank vomited again while Jones disentangled himself from the raft an arm and a leg at a time and fell alongside.

The hump, while submerging, still rose three feet above the water's grasp. Rain poured. Hank clumsily righted the raft, then draped his arms over the inflated rim and retched seawater. Why I'm not stronger than this? he wondered, annoyed, and drowsed into warm stupor. Arm pain restored focus. He forced himself awake. There lay Jones shivering in a ball. Hank groped for the bag with the extra survival suit. Gone. Floated off. And the radio. He peeled down the top of his own suit and with freed hands rubbed Jones's chest. Wet clothing squished under the oilskin jacket. Cold wind twitched a tuft of Jones's hair, gray in the glare from *Jody Dawn*'s lights.

"Jones! You hear me?"

Jones raised his head as sluggishly as a crab brought from cold depths and muttered urgently. Hank put his ear close. "My net. Tell Ham get it. Plugged. Prime reds."

Startle warning of hypothermia, first slip into death. Hank shook him. "Make sense, Jones. It's Hank!"

"Good. Good. Throw that grapple, son."

Hank rose and peeled down the rest of his survival suit. As each sweated part of him became exposed the wind chilled it. The water had lapped closer to their feet, making it harder to keep Jones dry as he pushed him leg by leg into the floppy coverall. Rubber boot against rubbery material required pull and stretch. A wave leapt the mound and filled one leg of the suit. He lifted Jones's leg to let the water gush out, then hurried to encase arms and zip the front. His own arm was turning numb with weakened fingers, but at least the pain had thus eased.

He stood, and his own shivering began. There lay his *Jody Dawn* only a few hundred feet away, the dash of half a minute on land. A thin rope from the raft still attached him to its deck. Line too thin now to risk against the longer distance from the bobbing, upturned *Robin* than in his initial calculation, not with wind unslacked and current still making. Their shouts came from aboard in a formless volley. All he could do was shout back and wave at their blessed light (*his* light, light of his ship!) as he listened for helicopter churn.

The water advanced further. "Jones. Can you stand?" He tried to help him up. Jones slowly cooperated but his weight fell limp in Hank's arms.

Hank looked up at the sky. *Jody Dawn*'s lights reflected ochre against solid clouds. Not a sight or throb of blades. Somewhere to the southwest stood Jody and his children, probably helping Ham, even holding the big, slow crewman. Damn you, Ham! Safe and warm.

Jones sagged further. "Jump up and down, Jones. Increase your circulation, man!" Hank tried to jiggle him as he forced motion for himself. The rising tide now licked around the soles of his boots.

"Doing thin, Hank," Jones whispered. "But warmer, seems."

Jones knew him! Coming back! "But you've got to keep moving."

"Hank. Stayed . . . you . . . should stayed in boat. No friend when . . . I say . . . said . . . Hank's no friend, said. Didn't mean. Sorry . . . Hank. Cold. Mebbe . . . most stupid . . . whole life." With a sudden jolt Jones raised his head and looked around. He clutched the sleeve of Hank's jacket, felt it, then touched his own. "No. No Hank. Get this thing off me. Back on you." Just as suddenly he collapsed. Hank laid him in the raft. Rain had already puddled inches on the bottom and there was nothing to bail with. He leaned over and tried to splash out water with his hand. The chill seeped further into his hands. Into bone.

Dark empty all horizon except for light of endless distant *Jody Dawn* and its gleam on the *Robin*'s rolling overturned hull. "Now what are you going to do?" Saying it aloud kept him company. Random shouts continued to wind-blow from his boat, his vessel, his ship, his own *Jody Dawn* separated by raging shallows. "Aiii," he called. "Aii-ooo" for the sound of his voice alive.

Water now chilled the calves of his legs through socks and thin boot rubber. Old sweat iced against his chest. "Aii-ooo." Their shouts came back. Image of their dear faces: "Seth. Ivan. Steve. No . . . Seth. Mo . . ." He struggled with it, frightened. "Oh, shit, Terry. Terry of course, no problem."

The frigid water that sucked life trickled over the edge of his boot tops. It slowly invaded his thick socks, and started on his skin.

"I have Jody. And Henny, Hank Junior my namesake and shadow. I have Dawn to see into a woman. I have Pete who needs to grow against my leg." He looked down at the shadowed figure of Jones Henry. "I have Jody." The *Jody Dawn*'s lights flashed madly, riding glassy swells toward him like signals.

"God help me!" Without thinking further he bent over Jones, unzipped the watertight garment, and began to yank out the limp arms.

Jones roused sluggishly. "Hank?"

"Forgive me." Hank continued peeling down the survival suit. "Forgive me."

"Ha. Kiss the girls."

"Oh Jones forgive me."

"Stop blubber. Forgiven."

Hank stopped. With a sigh for life itself he pushed Jones's arm back into the suit and zipped it up.

The raft now floated and water lapped at his knees. Chill burned his legs. Tide had risen enough that current began to tug. Hank wriggled boots into the firm sand and steadied the raft. As soon as he got in himself, he knew, current would careen the flat-bottomed craft out of control into water bottomless and drowning-deep. "Chopper, chopper, come Swede fuck you."

Like a click the lights of the *Jody Dawn* went off. Hank gasped. Had engine room flooded, generator gone? Anchor would still hold them. To sink in place, his ship? End of his own! Nothing left. The vanished light took sound with it except for water's suck and thrash. Black world on all sides. Panic. Wild. Alone. Further cries stuck in his throat. Had she sunk? The water, now to his thighs, pulled in earnest. The raft had begun to buck in the swells. Harder to hold on. Raft would soon tilt. Decide something. He groped with his lips for Jody's ring and kissed it. His legs no longer burned. They had turned numb. And heavy. Sleepy thoughts began to warm him like a mother-hand.

Flashlight beams waved from the *Jody Dawn*, and blessed shouts. They floated! Listen, he told himself now voiceless, pulling together all his effort. Listen. Jody on the beach, Dawn Henny Pete all waiting. Think! No chopper. No Swede and can't wait longer. Into raft. Grab the line hand over hand. Maybe Seth'll feel it, start pulling other end. If line breaks, raft floats even if current carries it. On to edge of earth. Life's journey so be it. Slack tide to come on schedule. So also daylight. Wind stop eventually. Strand on flats in daylight. Chopper search. Ai—stay awake! Vision of gulls picking stranded salmon's eyes.

As soon as the anchor of his feet left sand, current swung the raft into depth cutting his option to stand again. At the mercy . . . He clutched the rim and crawled over it, forward on belly over Jones's limp legs. The umbilical line was strained taut as rock—danger it might tear grommet from rubber. Line seemed even to groan, or was that Jones? Hands turning numb. At first grip he cried in pain. But cry and hurt woke him to grip harder and blank against all but focus. Think! In trough of each wave came a second's slack. Play line like there's a fish on the end. Pull, give way, pull. Soon the only way he could grip the line was to clutch it into his body with arms and elbows.

Slowly the sea gave up line by inches until he'd gathered aboard a few loops, keeping them clear of Jones and himself. With the work he began again to shiver, back to life.

"Jones! You hear me?" No answer from the blackness. Toward the flashlights of the dark *Jody Dawn* he shouted "Coming in! Pull me!" and gripped back the line harder with each slack. Rain blurred his eyes and salt burned them too much to see more than waving spots. At least that bit of light.

Helicopter throb. Overhead, Swede's machine passed, low enough for an instant of flattening downwash. It circled into the wind. Too late for steady legs on ground to catch the basket, so what did it matter? How could Swede find the raft from nothing but thin flashlight beams? Circled again. Mere luck if basket slapped raft, and no hands to grab it since nothing on the raft could belay the line he'd gathered. Let go the gathered loops, and the raft's zip back over gained space would surely snap them wild and gone. "*Jones.* Help me!" No stir. A swell smacked him and entered the raft. What if Jones's face had slipped beneath? "*Jones.* Least raise your head, man!" Nothing. "*Jones.* Your life! Wake it!"

"No more," muttered a shell of Jones's voice.

"*Yohh, yohh,*" Hank cried mindlessly. And suddenly, knowing Jones: "Fuck *your* life, you asshole. Get up and save *my* life, *Hank's* life! *I need you.*"

Groan. Foot kicked out slowly against Hank's leg.

"Up, Jones, *up*. Just sit up. For Jody's sake! Save *me*."

Lights exploded from the *Jody Dawn*. They blinded like a knife in his head, and no hand free to shield eyes. His ship again in blaze whatever the breakdown! Suddenly the umbilical had slack. Snapped? He pulled wildly. It jerked back taut. Then slack. His ship's whistle blew and he shouted with it. Gleam on the swells, on the vibrating lifeline itself and knuckles clutching, life again throughout the water!

Blurred sight, but the lights seemed larger. Then he realized. Seth was driving the *Jody Dawn* head-on toward the raft. Figures of Mo and Terry moved on the bow, shadows in the glare. They too pulled slack. "No," he called. "Too shallow. Need at least sixteen feet aft these swells. *No*." His ship came closer. "*No!*"

The overturned hull of the *Robin* reared glistening a moment before the *Jody Dawn* hit it. Thud and crunch. The shadows of Mo and Terry disappeared. Hank watched helpless. No sound remained in his throat for the cry he felt.

So be it.

The line his men had gathered on *Jody Dawn*'s bow flopped back into the water. Sudden slack and the raft raced backward. Hank clutched, tried to buffer with his arms. The jolt pulled his shoulder in its socket, agony beyond pain.

With knees pressed into the side of the raft, he held with all his body. Flashes, sick. Don't faint. Hold. He wanted life. Jody. He pressed his head against the thrumming rock-hard line and held.

Chopper downwash. An object glanced his head. Jones's voice behind him: "Got it."

The line he held eased. Arrested motion jolted him forward, face into sea before he pulled himself back. Automatically he pulled in slack, pain like screams through his shoulders.

Knees pressed into his back. "Got 'im. Won't let go."

Hank managed to turn his head. Jones, face frosty-old against whisker growth, eyes like beads, teeth bared, had arms wrapped around a line leading to the sky. The rescue basket bobbed beside him in waist-deep water.

Swede's chopper was towing them the final distance. So be it.

Dark minutes or hours later, hands pulled them up the stern of the

Jody Dawn. Hands tried to pry open his elbows locked like gates against his chest. He cried in agony, then felt warmth and buzz and blackness.

When he regained consciousness he lay beside Jones on the galley floor, face to face. Jones was asleep, whitened hair slapped like seaweed, mouth open fishlike. Hank's own mouth gasped into a puddle. Engine throb beneath deck plates. He looked to see Terry rubbing his legs, but felt nothing. "Boat smashed?" he managed to voice.

"Starboard bow's a mess, Boss, but we're still running. Seth's on our way to the factory ship, factory ship's steamin' toward us got a doctor on board from Dillingham for you and Captain Henry."

"Jones? Okay?"

"He sure looks tired, Boss."

Hank tried to rise, fell back in pain.

Jones stirred. "Kiss the girl for me, Hank. Adele. If you got the nerve."

"Kiss her yourself."

"I will. I will."

A moment later: "Guess he's fainted," said Mo.

But Jones had died.

24

OCEAN'S CHOICE

When Adele met them at the Kodiak airport Hank walked to her in a straight line. With his shoulder in a cast he could use only one arm, and stiffly, but he drew her close, gently kissed her cheek, and held it. Explain later. A black scarf around her neck still had the store-shelf smell.

Jody embraced Adele next. Serious Henny held back with Pete in tow. For once Dawn said nothing, but took Auntie Adele's hand and stroked it.

"I knew it could happen someday," said Adele calmly. "Always hoped it wouldn't." She wore the darkest brown of her wardrobe including slacks.

They walked to the dusty green pickup truck that for a decade had framed the face of Jones Henry at the driver's window. "Pastor Hall for the service of course," said Adele. The Anchorage hospital had only this morning released Hank, but Jones's body had arrived three days before. "I said good-bye to Daddy and had my grief. Then I gave him up to be cremated."

"I suppose you'll take him back to San Pedro where you live most of the year?" asked Jody.

"Daddy doesn't like to be cramped. It was never his place the way it is here. And I'd miss him as much wherever he went. This way's best."

Under a warm July sun the children climbed willingly into the back of the truck and settled on dusty tires. They still wore their half-washed setnetting clothes.

Adele handed Hank the keys automatically. With a light excuse Jody took them from him, climbed to the driver's seat herself and motioned him onto the passenger side. "Take the middle, Adele, so we can talk." Hank started to object, then acquiesced. For a while he watched on the way to town. Jody's easy shift of gears and then mountains turning green from snowmelt, but soon dozed. He woke to hear Jody explain: "He's slept most of the time since. The doctor said expect it. You remember how they were eight years ago, after all those days on that life raft."

Hank turned from the window, seeking shadow. Raft again. Death again. Steve and Ivan dead that time but Jones, hadn't he himself saved Jones by goading him back to life? But Ocean, you never give up trying, do you? This time you won. He heard Jones's dry laugh while the warmth of detachment reembraced him.

"After that experience I'd begun to think my Jones was indestructible."

"They were cold then, but they weren't immersed. That's the difference. Sixty-something's not old for most things, but the coroner said Jones's heart just gave out."

"It was a big heart, Jody. Didn't seem so sometimes but it was. Many's the hungry kid looking for a boat he fed. And Lord knows the poor man didn't like France any more than having a root canal, but he went because he knew I loved it." Her voice wavered. "Paris won't be the same without him, if ever I go back. I'll associate every place with him, even if it's to hear his opinion about eating snails." Jody's sympathetic laugh joined hers. "And Daddy thought the world of Hank. He'd never gotten on with our two adopted sons, you know. Those boys had hated the water from the start, and after Daddy tried to force it, they all gave up on each other. So he'd really come to think of Hank as his—. This last, about the Japanese, it about broke his heart."

Silence, then: "It broke Hank's."

"Oh Jody."

Hank roused enough to wonder what had been broken, then remembered. The sadness of it clouded his vision even with closed eyes. Facts drifted, then reordered in bearable form. There sat Jones across from him instead of Adele, telling how it was all in a day's work. *Jody Dawn*'s bow rose as pristine as the day she came from the shipyard. King crabs stormed back to fill the pots. Jones raised his whiskey and they had a laugh over bad 'ol good ol' Japs . . .

He woke to hear Jody again. "Dislocated shoulder, and left arm so sprained it swelled triple. Seth said they had to cut him out of his wet clothes. All the guys looked older when I saw them."

"I can imagine. But they're so young they'll bounce back."

"Seth's aged in a way that makes him seem more confident. Hank credits him using his head. If he hadn't pumped out the *Jody Dawn*'s tanks and dumped their fish to raise the draft before running in, the boat could have been damaged worse. Seth did do something unnecessary. He turned out all the boat's lights while he put the pumps on max, to keep from over-loading the generator. It certainly gave Hank and poor Jones some bad minutes. But he was thinking."

"And Daddy's crewman? Is he all right?"

"Ham. Yes." Jody measured her words. "You know that Swede's chopper dumped him at our setnet site? Rode him over in an open basket through the storm. By the time we grabbed his legs and eased him down I think he'd forgotten even his name. He shook so much he rattled the bas-ket, although we had to pry his fists from the ropes."

"Poor boy. But he's recovered?"

"Ham's . . . having a different kind of trouble. I don't know how much anybody's told you. But there was only one survival suit."

"Then it was certainly Daddy's. He never sailed without that big orange bag."

"Well. It was Ham who'd come aboard without. But Jones made Ham wear the one suit. Hank confirms it from their radio talk."

"Oh, Jody. Daddy'd be alive today. He's left me alone because of a big stupid kid!" She broke down. After a while she wiped her eyes. "Didn't I tell you Daddy had a big heart? If I know the man, he probably reasoned it was his job to make sure his man came equipped. So he took the blame. Oh, the fool. Why do men have to be heroes? I already miss him so, Jody."

"Ham's afraid now to see you."

"Well he should be!" After a silence: "You saw the wrecked boat, didn't you?"

"I went for Hank's sake, to see what he'd been through. After Swede had me flown to the hospital and I'd talked to Hank and knew he'd recover, and went back to camp to pack and get the kids. Joe Penn, the camp boss, took his motor skiff."

"Was it bad?"

"Well . . ." Jody hesitated. "Waves did their worst. Somebody might have taken an ax to the housing the way it looked. And the hull, split. And a net half buried in sand, plugged with rotting fish. Gulls everywhere. You can guess the stink and screech. It was weird to see it on such a sunny calm day with water lapping against a little hill, after such a storm. Ham started sobbing. He scratched and dug till he found the seabags and some boots. Then he couldn't stop, he went kind of crazy, started throwing anything into the skiff. Rope scraps, empty soup can from what he said was their last meal, bent spoon, the cracked green shield from the starboard light. Joe and I finally just each took an arm and eased him away."

"He deserved to feel guilty. But men shouldn't cry like that."

"At least not be caught doing it. Well, I left Ham at the camp. The kid runs to do any dirty work he can find. Pushes out in water over his waist without waders, comes back shivering, then just sits with his hands to his head until somebody makes him eat. He wants to come to the funeral but he's afraid."

Another long silence. "How do we get him here?"

"I can phone Swede from your house. Swede'll see to it."

"Daddy would want it. Think he has money for the plane? Maybe I should pay from down here."

"Swede's taken charge. Let him handle it. He and John Gains between them, I'm impressed. That helicopter rescue put them in danger. No one would have blamed them if they hadn't done it. I'm . . . sorry . . . well, Hank's devastated . . . that it didn't help Jones."

"I know. I know. It should have saved Daddy too. It just didn't. Hank did all he could."

Back at the house it was Jody who marshaled the forces. While Hank dozed in a stuffed chair by his picture window, she arranged for repairs to the boat and saw to plans for the day of the service.

Hank watched idly as winds ruffled miles of water all the way to the Kodiak piers. Somewhere among the distant masts was Jones's nice little seiner *Adele H*, its door padlocked because the temporary crew had decided five cents a pound for pink salmon wasn't enough to warrant the work of fishing. No fishermen, they. Adele would need to sell the boat. Pity. Insurance should reimburse for the wrecked *Robin J*. This wouldn't be the the year to sell the Bristol Bay license if Adele could avoid it, with salmon prices down all over. Too much to think about. His legs ached and burned. Whenever he considered going to the kitchen for water, or beer, or a snack, he progressed as far as a preparatory breath, then decided to wait until Jody or Henny or Dawn came along. He desired nothing enough to seek it. The world was basically warm and cozy. His purpose was to observe its passage, nothing more.

Russ and Mark, the Henrys' two adopted sons, remained as shadowy as they had always seemed. Russ, the drifter, was so out of touch that a letter to his only address, GPO Denver, received no reply. Mark had flown in from Omaha, where he worked as a computer salesman, for what he assumed was to be the funeral. But since Jones had been cremated, Adele felt no pressure during the height of the local salmon fishing to schedule the service other than late on a Saturday, so that fishermen could attend after the weekend closure. "I certainly wouldn't have expected your *father* to give up a day's fishing," she explained.

Mark shrugged. "No, I suppose you wouldn't." He treated Adele sympathetically and even wrote a check (unsolicited) for a thousand dollars to handle small emergency expenses, but he remained detached. Bulging at the waist, he never removed his suit and tie. When she waved him off on the plane the next day she too was detached, almost relieved to see him go. A part of life that hadn't turned out as she'd hoped.

Adele had then remained at the airport, sipping coffee from a vending machine, while she waited to meet the plane an hour later bringing in Hank and Jody. Sitting still opened time for memory whether she wanted it or not. Jones, inevitably, the rugged man fresh from the Marines whom she'd married and adored. Happy years, even seeing him off on other mens' boats, since they were saving together for his own. Darling little Amy born. Busy mother as it was meant to be even with the shadow of birth complications that left her unable to bear more children. Horrible midnight spasms. Dead little body from meningitis so laughing only hours before. Oh Lord, if you were watching as they say: Why? Adele hurried from the seat and paced the room, benches to counter blurred by tears.

Jones might have shared her grief for a week or two—give him that—but then the man had returned to his fishing. Sure, if adopting a child would help, he agreed. Too hasty, with her heart still buried in the little grave. Orphaned brothers five and six, minister urged. Boys already hostile to the world and nobody bothered to say. Passive, sullen, hating work. Love and firmness would change that. She did try. But her heart stayed with the lost baby while time slipped away. And Jones, convinced by the relation with his own fisherman-dad that all any boy needed to be toughened no-nonsense to boats, demanded while they shirked and glared.

When at last the Anchorage plane arrived bearing Hank, Jody, and the children, Adele greeted her family. Her spirits lightened and she became efficient again though a widow still in grief.

.She postponed the funeral service on the first Friday when a predicted three-day storm moved in to ground all flights. Peggy Dyson relayed the message to the seiner fleet in the bays around Kodiak Island during her scheduled weather broadcast.

Hank's crew arrived midweek by sea aboard the damaged *Jody Dawn*. Jody drove Hank to the cannery pier. He watched without leaving the truck, despite her urging. It could have been someone else's boat. Life, after all, flowed along whatever he did. Things that needed to be done got done. Daylight, night, tides, they came in predicted sequence, whatever. Even storms. He dreamed back with curiosity on the things he'd cared about. Like watching a movie. When the lights came up you just went home.

Seth, in the wheelhouse, did appear more confident. He'd shaved his beard to reveal a stubborn chin, and he stood at the controls clear-eyed and solemn. Mo and Terry jumped smartly to his commands. After they secured mooring lines, they hurried to the truck. Seth sauntered over more slowly. They all were solicitous.

The repairs could be handled at a local boatyard. Hank's detachment continued as he surveyed the damaged bow. The boat, his possession, seemed now less his pride and soul. He'd allowed her name to be changed and desecrated her in the process, just as he'd desecrated by signing over control to the Japanese. He was so tired! Legs ached without pause—not like the shoulder pain accepted as part of fishing now and then—but rather like a snake in his system. When Jody drove him home he limped straight to bed.

By the second weekend the weather had run full cycle from storm to sun to squalls, but planes were flying. Swede Scorden and John Gains chartered a flight direct from Naknek and brought along Ham. Adele and Jody waited as the three descended to the rain-slick runway.

In the small airport waiting/baggage room, Adele clutched Swede and cried while he patted her shoulder, then hugged John and thanked him for coming. She broke down briefly at the sight of Jones's old seabag. Ham had not entered. Despite the rain he remained close against the plane with his gaze on the ground. When Adele had composed herself: "Oh for pity's sake," she exclaimed, and strode out in the rain to bring him in with an arm around his waist.

Ham, like Hank, had lost his spirit. His slumped shoulders seemed particularly forlorn for a man so large. Adele studied his sand-scuffed duffle bag with torn hip boots strapped to the side, sighed, and declared with her old officiousness: "You'll stay at the house until you decide what to do, of course. Daddy would have wanted it." Jody saw Ham's alarm, and cheerfully said that Hank needed him to help on the *Jody Dawn* so he'd better just bunk there too. Ham's humble look thanked her.

On the day of Jones's service the men of the salmon fleet—most from boats come to port for the weekend but some who flew in from as far away on the island as Uganik Bay and even Alitak —filled the pews at St. James the Fisherman. The service was thoughtful, delivered under the shadow shared by the congregation that Jones Henry's fate could be their own. Ham listened from a dark alcove. Neither Mo nor Ham's recent girlfriend could persuade him to sit.

Many strong voices turned husky while singing:

Eternal Father strong to save
Whose arm has bound the restless wave
Who bids the mighty ocean deep
Its own appointed limits keep.
Oh hear us when we cry to Thee,
For those in peril on the sea.

At the end of the service Adele rose to announce what she had already told those who had spoken to her. A wake would follow, down on the docks aboard the *Adele H*. "It won't be at the house. That wasn't really where Daddy lived, much as I loved the man. You give Daddy a proper send-off, and I don't mean a tea party." She herself chose to embrace people at the church, then stay at the house where some of the women joined her. Henny, Dawn, and Pete went with her to stay overnight. "They're even more precious to me now, the children I didn't have," said Adele as a matter of fact.

Jody had arranged a bar in the *Adele H*'s galley out of the rain—bottles, cans, ice, jerky, and other snacks, and plastic cups—and Hank's crew under Seth had prepared a salmon grill on the dock under a flapping lean-to. Ham stayed in the shadows filleting fish, and refused to drink.

Swede and John Gains both paid their respects. They'd planned to return at once to Naknek, but fog closed the airstrip. People learned of their role in the helicopter, and hand after hand slapped their backs. After a token drink at the pier, however, they chose to take a quiet dinner at the inn where they stayed overlooking the harbor.

"All those people for just a guy who fishes," mused Gains. "A man who always seemed to me ill-tempered."

"He did the work."

"For once I wouldn't mind being part of all that."

"You've earned a place. Go on back down."

Gains considered as he read the menu. "You more than me, and I don't see you moving. Is the steak good here?"

The section of floating boardwalk that berthed the *Adele H* and other seiners throbbed with voices and milled with glistening yellow and orange oilskins under blowing rain. Jones's virtues were discussed along with the pittance paid for pink salmon by the thieving canneries. Hank walked among them out of duty, but watched and listened outside himself, answering questions only with reticence. Everyone knew the generalities of the disaster since it had been reported at length in the Anchorage papers and the *Kodiak Mirror*. Hank had submitted to interviews, but some details remained his alone. Let reporters conjecture. Fellow-fishermen sensed most of it without asking: understood keeping the fish your net had caught; needed no reminder of the lonely doubt and fear in the face of the sea.

Jody stayed at his side most of the time. Occasionally her sharp or hearty laugh alerted him that she'd moved off on her own. None of the other wives had come to the boat, but she fitted in without apology. How precious she is, he thought. His luck in having Jody comforted him. He thought of it in a wave of gratitude, but then it drifted into the stuff of dreams.

"I'll tell you what probably happened," said a skipper who had taken instruction in treating hypothermia. "Anybody's got only a few minutes in that cold water if he's immersed. The blood in your arms and legs chills down. Your big danger is your heart can't take blood that's too cold. So you've got to warm a patient gradually. So you start with the torso, not what they call the extremities. Now if Jones started to freeze, and his body shut down—I don't understand all that but it's what's supposed to happen—but then if, say, he started doing something vigorous instead of resting to keep his circulation slow, then it could have pumped sudden cold blood from his arms and legs to his heart, and maybe his heart couldn't take it. It might have looked like Jones was okay. But then bang. Jones being older, that probably didn't help." Others with experience nodded.

Hank listened, and wondered dully whether Jones would still be alive if he hadn't been goaded into grabbing the helicopter basket. Could there have been some other way? The thought became too heavy. He wandered inside to sit at the galley table.

The urn with Jones's ashes—a blue Greek imitation with handles—had been placed discreetly by the porthole. "Hey, shit," somebody declared. "Ol' Jones needs a snort same as the rest of us!" He banged down the urn among the bottles. Someone else carried it further: lifted the stopper and dribbled in Scotch while others cheered. Hank started to object, then relaxed with the rightness of it and poured in a few drops himself.

He remained detached, skirting questions with "Oh, yeah, pretty bad." At length he slipped down the ladder and crawled into a bunk. The party droned and became louder with successive drinks, but now stayed for him at an easeful distance. Close to his ear against the skin of the bow, water lapped an inch away. So it had been on his first excited night aboard a fishing boat, hired indeed by Jones Henry aboard the dear old *Rondelay*. Green cannery kid exploding with desire to be a fisherman. Oh Jones. And it was the *Rondelay* that had delivered him from cannery drudgery under

who but Swede Scorden. So young, and so full of it. Full of joy. His sadness of memory came in waves, interspersed with sleep. Shoulder ached,
sign of healing. Feet and legs had a burn that throbbed and expanded. The
survival suit would have protected him from frozen legs. Jones died anyhow. But thank God he hadn't weakened to grab back the suit.

He woke shivering to continued noise and pulled a musty sleeping
bag around him for warmth. He next woke to Jody's voice: "There you are!
For a while we thought you'd wandered off. Are you okay, honey?"

"Just kiss me." She did. Abovedeck the noise came and went in
waves. Someone started the "Jolly Good Fellow" song. Nice, thought
Hank. "Toasting Jones, better not knock over his ashes."

"As a matter of fact they're toasting your friend John Gains. Some of
the boys started talking about the rescue, missed Swede and John, and
went up to the inn to fetch them. Swede wouldn't come. John did. Want to
go home?"

He left the bunk stiffly. Putting weight on the legs felt like jabbing
them with boards. Up the ladder slowly. There at the galley table encircled
by fishermen stood John Gains, holding a cup and smiling uncertainly. No
question but that he was enjoying himself. Top it off, thought Hank. He
walked through to John and held out his hand. "Thanks, John."

The handshake back had a tight grip. "Wasn't that much, Hank."

Six hours after the church service, the last well-wisher had patted
Jones's ashes for the final time. The salmon grill had long since been extin-
guished by accumulated water gushing from the canopy, but people agreed
that Jones had been given a good send-off. By midnight Seth and his men,
with Ham, had carried all the cans and empty bottles up the ramp to the
trash bins and had scrubbed the galley of the *Adele H*. One more job was
left them, by Adele's wishes conveyed through Jody. "Somebody else can
do it," said Seth. Ham shrank away, and "Spooky," said Mo backing off.
Terry shrugged, gingerly took the urn with Jones's ashes, and propped it
with pillows in the wheelhouse captain's chair. "Hope you're comfortable," he said, and hurried to rejoin the others.

Seth padlocked the door, and they trudged through puddles along
cannery row toward the *Jody Dawn*. A wind had begun to blow wildly. It
made the night sinister. Ham trailed. Mo stayed alongside him, cajoling. At
last Seth marched back although Terry kept moving. "Look," Seth shouted

above the wind. "You ain't the only one who walks around feeling guilty about something. What good's all that sorry-shit going to do you?"

"If only I'd remembered my survival suit," Ham moaned. "If only he hadn't given me his."

"He made you take it. We heard it."

"I was scared. I let him. He'd be alive now."

"And you dead!"

"Wish I was!"

"Bullshit!"

"Man, man, it's over," shouted Mo. "Ain't nothing you can do."

Seth clapped Ham's back and pushed. "Move! We're gettin' wet and we don't need to." Ham hung his head and obeyed.

Aboard the *Jody Dawn* Terry had fired the stove, so that the pot was puffing steam when they arrived dripping. They sat around the table with mugs of instant cocoa. In the warmth of the galley Ham became calmer. "Could maybe give all my money to Mrs. Henry."

"What money? What money?"

"Anything I ever make. Like what I'd ever spend again on boozing." He breathed heavily. "Or on having a family someday."

"Wow," breathed Mo at the enormity of it.

They all pondered until Terry declared: "She's a brave lady. She wouldn't take nothing like that." It seemed to settle the matter.

Ham sighed, relieved. He gulped his cocoa and nursed the cup. "Sure wish I could crew with you guys. It's no way though, I guess. Even if there was a site. No way after how I talked tough to Captain Hank and all, because of Skipper Jones . . . Even once almost had to throw him off the boat . . . No way."

"That would sure be great," declared Mo. "I wonder?"

Seth shrugged and glanced at Terry, who nodded. "Maybe we have influence. Beats having Mo got to risk his knuckles all the time because you answer to somebody else."

Next morning Jody drove Hank to town with his seabag. The rain had stopped, but fog drifted among houses on the hills and around masts in the harbor. They called on Adele at the house to report that the party had been one Jones would have enjoyed.

Hank roused enough from lethargy to wrap his free arm around
Adele and kiss her, and to explain that the kiss fulfilled Jones's last words.
She gripped his arms. "Are you making that up?" He assured her he was
not. She rested on his chest and hugged him. Then, shaking her head, she
walked away.

Adele and the children drove with them to the *Adele H*. On the way
she mentioned that Jody's mother and Hank's parents had both sent their
sympathies and invited her to come visit. "I was so touched, because I
think both meant it. Of course when will I ever get to do anything like that?
I have so many decisions. Thank God for insurance on the wrecked boat.
That leaves the licence. Would you believe that somebody offered to buy it
for one fifth what poor Jones paid? Yesterday Mr. Scorden and John Gains
advised me not to sell it until the botulism scare's over and prices go up,
and their company's found a way to lend me something against it. Means
I'll probably come out even on the debt Jones made to buy the cursed boat
and licence. Oh Jody, why do the kind of men we love have to prove themselves over and over like that? But now, the boat of his heart, the boat that
bears my very name. I'll have to sell it and that breaks *my* heart. A whole
life that was built around the two of us, without my ever thinking. Sometimes I gave the poor dear man such a hard time, and now . . ."

"When he deserved it," declared Jody from the driver's seat. "And
not often enough at that." Hank, beside her, woke enough to frown disapproval. Her frosty glance warned him not to challenge.

"I can't explain, but—" continued Adele. "In a way he's still with me.
It's a comfort. But Daddy was always in charge, and now I'll have to . . ."
She reached to grip Jody's shoulder. "Treasure your man while you have
him." Jody patted her hand.

Seiners all along the docks were leaving. One by one, boats weighted astern with net, corks, and skiff backed from their slips and slowly
headed down the corridor of moored sterns toward the breakwater. Their
circular wakes reflected masts. Crews of other boats hustled last-minute
supplies aboard for the week ahead. Hank's crew, with Ham, were waiting
aboard the *Adele H*, and Seth had started the engine.

Swede and John Gains arrived from the hill, their manner suitably
grave. Hank surveyed John. The man's hair was uncombed. "Feeling
good?"

"Hangover. Lousy."

"Glad to hear you've joined the human race."

"Maybe so."

Hank shook Swede's hand. His old cannery boss's face had accumulated massed wrinkles from forehead to mouth, but the eyes that for a while had turned bleary now glared clear and direct. "Give it all my regards," Swede growled. The two studied each other, then embraced.

Hank climbed over the rail and Jody started to follow. He stopped her with a friendly hand. "Jones's boat, remember? At sea or any time just before sailing?"

Adele followed to touch her arm. "Just this one last time, dear. Daddy hated a woman on his boat. He never let me aboard if he could help it. Let's leave the man his peace."

Jody shrugged and returned to the pier, then paused and frowned. "When did our Jones Henry ever want his peace?" Her smile widened for the first time in days, wickedly. "I was only going aboard to make sure the boys had cleaned up last night's mess, but I've changed my mind. I think I'll go with them. If you claim Jones is still alive with you, isn't it time to help the man grow up?"

"Oh, Jody . . ."

"Not without your permission." Her eyes narrowed. "You own the boat."

Adele's hand went to her mouth and the fleshy lines drew down. "I do, don't I?" Sudden resolution: "The children are fine at my house. Yes. You go. For both of us!"

Aboard the *Adele H*, Hank stood on deck directing Terry above him on the flying bridge. The blue urn with Jones's ashes needed to be secured and displayed prominently. Jody paused at the boat rail to watch before crossing the great line. Hank usually made decisions without backtrack, but with the urn he vascillated like a housewife arranging furniture. Just the fatigue. Gladly she'd have hugged him. For two days, ever since finding his farewell note while straightening the *Jody Dawn*'s wheelhouse, she'd turned unexpectedly tearful. Not her way. But the note had not left her pocket, and now and then her hand reached to feel it. He's my love, she thought. Strong, with the bullheaded part open to change. Thank goodness he worked to win me back, because I won't be his dishrag.

She swung her legs over the rail and stood on deck. Ham was the first to notice. He dropped the line he was coiling. "Miz Crawford, hi m'am." When she greeted him and started forward he followed, disturbed and uncertain. "If you stay right there, m'am, I'll really like to get you whatever—" Jody continued to deck center, then looked up at him pleasantly, a small creature about half his size. Ham's face grew red. "Captain Crawford, here's your wife," he stammered.

Hank turned. "Party's cleaned up, Honey. You don't need to come aboard." She remained. Hank hurried across deck, and gave Ham an assignment to send him away. "Hey . . . You know poor ol' Jones never had a woman aboard underway or even on the day he sailed. It nearly killed him when Adele wandered aboard in port, you know that. We're just trying to honor Jones."

"Something else managed to kill him."

"You don't understand."

"No, *you* don't." She surveyed him dispassionately. "At least the shock's brought you to life. First time I've seen you off your ass in a week. I've decided to come along."

"Don't kid. The guys are all watching."

"Do you boys always get so upset with things you can't handle? Set an example for poor confused Ham there."

"Dear, it just won't . . . This is a guy thing coming up."

"I'd call it a thing for those who've risked their lives on the water. How's your memory today?"

"When you fished with me? That was years ago."

"When we fished together. In *this* lifetime, Hank." When she sharpened her voice she enjoyed the way he stepped back warily. Never admit except to herself how much she loved him at any time, for both his assurance and his doubt. "Better not embarrass yourself in front of your men." Indeed they all watched while pretending to work. "I'm aboard and staying."

Hank turned for help to Adele watching from the pier. She stood calmly with arms folded, a dumpy figure in brown slacks, hair tidy under a flowered bandana that had replaced the black one of days before. "It's my boat now, Hank dear."

"I know. But Jones . . . Not *my* rule."

"I've been thinking, Hank dear. What if I could settle Daddy's debts without losing the boat? I'd need a captain. Maybe I'll just hire Jody to run my boat for me. Jody! What do you say?"

"Sounds good to me."

Hank glanced at his crew. They had stopped altogether to listen. "Come on, ladies. We're off on serious business today."

"Oh God!" Jody exclaimed. "They take a little step forward the size of a spider's, then at first threat to their guyness they scamper for a hole. And when they bring it on themselves they wonder why. Adele! You know I *have* run a boat. Let's talk when I get back!"

Adele's laugh was incongrously hearty for the occasion. "We'll damn well talk! Hank, you know I love you, but watch out. One day Captain Jody's going to make you ask permission to set foot on her *Adele H.*" She stared at each man in turn. "Boys. How'd you like a woman for your skipper?" Seth, Mo, and Ham collectively gaped and backed away. Only Terry held his ground, grinning.

Hank attempted the same heartiness. "I guess since the atom bomb's exploded anything can happen. Poor Jones would turn in his—" He checked himself.

Adele touched her breast. "I carry the man right here, so I daresay I'll be the first to feel it if those ashes start to roll. Now, Hank. Where do you plan to go? You know best where Daddy liked to fish."

"Uganik."

"Good. Good. He'd approve."

Hank turned respectful. "Want them to bring you the urn for a minute?"

She quieted. "No, my dear. That kiss you delivered will do."

Boats all around them backed from their slips puffing exhaust. Hank put his arm around Jody, and waved to his children. At least make it appear to be his own initiative. "We want to make Whale Pass at high slack so let's go. Lines off," Swede and John on the pier started toward the mooring posts.

"No, boys, that's mine," announced Adele. With the ease of a fisherman's wife who had done it before, she unflicked the stern line and tossed it to Mo. Then she strode to the bow where Ham waited. The big youth's eyes widened. She freed the line but held it, and, as the boat left the slip, walked it back. Ham gave her slack, but glanced warily toward the flying bridge. Hank at the open wheel above him shrugged, uncertain of Adele's intention himself. At last she threw over the line with: "It's all right, Ham. You take care, and come call sometime."

For all her push, Jody now chose to leave the others alone—they'd had enough shock for a while. If Hank on his own invited her up to the flying bridge, however . . . While the others assembled around Hank to enjoy the scenery leaving port, she busied herself in the galley. Cleanup remained whatever the men thought they'd done. Odors of whiskey, beer, and mustard still hung in the cramped space. She wiped the tables, noting racks and cupboards at first unconsciously, then with method.

　　　Captain this boat? Crazy idea. Just Adele's joke to make them squirm. She'd steered and worked on deck for Mike Stimson and others long before Hank entered the picture, albeit as cook. Idea for another day. The kids needed her, even though Adele was wonderful. But the thought made her look into space. Back at the setnet camp the children had looked out for each other and thrived on the freedom. She could fish day trips, like a job. No, a boat this size needed to fish around the island all seasons to pay for itself. She felt for Hank's farewell note in her pocket, fingered the paper. Would he be secure enough to accept a fisher-wife, and one not under his command at that? Suddenly she missed her children. Why had she insisted on coming today like some brat? She'd brought no clothes except the jeans, blouse, and thick old jacket she'd thrown on three hours ago.

　　　She glanced outside. The crew remained with Hank: huddled around him in fact. They wouldn't see her. She went back through the galley and slipped down the ladder. The area with bunks along the curved bow had musty damp odors of unaired sleeping bags and blankets. Any crew she ran would air bedding on sunny days. Cautiously she opened the adjacent door to the engine room, the only boat space strange to her. Steeling against the blast and airless oil stench, she entered, closed the door to face it, and forced herself to stay. Learn. But not while the thing pumped and threatened. She studied the tubes and wires and greasy metal without moving her back from the bulkhead. Retain the picture at least. It was a relief to return to the galley.

She stretched her arms on deck, gladly breathed the droplets of foggy air, watched the passing spruce hills of Near Island. The boys on the flying bridge still clustered and all looked ahead. Hank stood by the wheel graceful and straight, looking himself again. Breeze dented his beard. The urn of Jones's ashes, firmly lashed to a stay, made a spot of blue against the gray sky. Water gurgled against the hull. The boat had begun a gentle sea-rock. She'd forgotten how the motion soothed, how even harsh pitch and roll suited her.

Back inside the galley she tied open the door, started coffee brewing, and settled at the table where she could look out at the deck with its stacked seine and slips of sky, trees, and water.

A knock against the metal door. The short figure of Terry stood in the doorway. "Hey. Boss says tell you the view's nice topside."

The invitation pleased her, but it had taken too long in coming to accept at once. "Thanks. I'm fine down here for a while."

"When we start to roll you'd do better in fresh air."

"I won't be seasick."

"Boss said you wouldn't be." He hesitated. "Mo, he's cook? Can he come down and make coffee? Is that okay?"

"It's already making. Shall I call when it's ready?"

Terry hesitated further. "You know, none of us is sorry you're aboard, even Boss. Even Ham. It's just that everybody has to go through, like, some weird motions. We hope you don't feel bad."

"Thanks for saying it."

"Later, if you need warmer clothes . . . I'm the smallest here, mine'll fit you closest. Although my stuffs kind of stinky since I'm engineer. Kind of oily some of it."

"That's really sweet, Terry. Don't worry about smell. I've been around boats."

"I know. Boss is so lucky. My ol' lady? She left me from too much boat on my mind, and the smell was part of it."

"That's right, you're our machinist. Say. What do you know about the engine on this boat?" He started giving details enthusiastically. Although he continued to avoid calling her by name, he relaxed enough to sit at the table and sketch a basic marine engine.

After a while he regarded her directly. "Was that all just kidding? Could you really skipper this boat?"

"What do you think your Boss would say?"

Slow grin. "Atomic bomb, maybe. Something like that."

"What would you say?"

"Me?" He blushed. "I guess, maybe, like: 'Give 'em hell, Jody.' Yeah. That's what."

"Don't worry, it was just talk. But thanks." She sent him off with mugs of fresh coffee for everyone.

Hank had expected Jody to join them on the flying bridge as soon as they left the pier, but was relieved when she chose to limit her invasion of his domain. Her presence, added to their mission, kept his men from their usual high spirits of departure.

Beyond the breakwater, with farewell waves to shore behind them, he felt, gladly, the release from land and the water's fresh push. Jones's seiner had a different pitch than the larger *Jody Dawn*, quicker, more like the old days. With his shoulder in a cast he'd planned to give Ham the wheel through Marmot Bay, then turn Whale Passage over to Seth. But he felt the surge of command and retained the helm himself.

Fog descended in a rolling presence just as they entered the narrow gap of Whale Passage. The others fell silent instinctively. He had traversed Whale often enough, but he never ignored its potential danger. Whirlpool water bore them past glimpses of brown rock and hills of spiked spruce tops. Ghosts haunted the Passage for him, at one with the fog. There had been the end of Spitz the Prophet and redhaired Pete, drowned friends of his first fishing summer with Jones. He breathed more easily when they entered wide Kupreanof Strait, less for danger than from memory.

By the time they reached Uganik Bay it had long ago turned dark. Jody had found cans to open and had served a meal despite Mo's embarrassed protest that he should be cooking. They anchored. Jody joined Hank at last, quietly, saying little. But soon she yawned, and retired to the lower bunk of the small skipper's cabin. Hank duly followed to make sure she had bedding and to tuck her in, but was glad that she asked for nothing more. The ghosts of Whale Passage had remained with him, and solitude was his need.

Snores issued from belowdecks as he passed through the galley. He wandered to deck and settled on the high stack of web with his back against the skiff lashed on top. The fog around him thinned to show hazy lights of other boats around them, thickened again to muffle even the hum of their engines. Smells of briny water mingled with the fog to evoke memory with heartaching sharpness.

A full moon began to burn through. Its glow surrounded him and slowly intensified. At length the boat's housing stood black against silver light. The light etched ripples all the way to the dark hilly shores and throbbed on the beaded white corks stacked behind him. These were the waters where he'd first learned to fish. His ghosts paraded in the ripples. There bounced Jones's old saucy paint-chipped *Rondelay*, and aboard strode salty Jones Henry himself who'd hired him in near-charity for his eagerness and had drawled him the mysteries of fish from lookout on the flying bridge; gruff, amused Steve who taught him the gear and dipped him overboard when he whistled; sententious, protective Ivan of the skiff-next-to-God and fragrant socks. They'd all cuffed him into shape. He dozed, and they visited.

He woke in the dark with a start. Dew had seeped into his shoulder cast. He was shivering although someone had tucked a blanket around him. Jody? He thought of her with guilt and tenderness. A month ago his only dream was to have her back, and hours ago he'd been annoyed to have her aboard. He hurried to the cabin. There she lay, hair tumbled softly, the most precious part of his life. He knelt and kissed her, breathed in her cheek's scent. Kissed again, tenderly, ready to caress and make love when she woke. Her arms reached around his neck to draw him down, but she diverted his face. He tried to raise to her lips. "No," she murmured. "Come back tomorrow. Take a blanket with you this time."

A pause so long he thought she'd fallen asleep again. Then she caressed his hair. "I found your note. You're the flower of my life too. *Shh*. Don't speak." He remained in warmth until her breath steadied back into sleep, then took bedding from the top bunk and returned to deck.

He thought he was returning to his ghosts, but under sharp moonlight they had dispelled and he realized he no longer sought nor wanted them. The lights of other boats anchored around the lagoon sparkled like a Christmas garden, no longer hazed. *Splash!* announced a salmon, and widening silvered circles in the water showed where it waited to be caught. Above black-hilled treetops throbbed a distant patch of mountain snow.

Clean breeze entered his lungs in wafts sharp with spruce. He lay back against the pile of net and locked fingers into the roped web. Tangible. His life lay ahead, blessed by fortune. All of it mattered. He felt his energies. What life took he'd give back. This was his time and this was his place.

Sun in his eyes woke him next. Ham stood staring, hesitant. The others still slept, Ham said. "Can I do anything for you, Captain Hank?"

He needed nothing, felt strangely comfortable, but: "Sure. Make coffee and bring it out." Sturdy okay kid, he thought. The new adventure longlining for black cod awaited, with the need for additional crew. Needed guys he could trust to push under his drive: to catch enough quickly, pay off the Japanese, be free again. He'd offer Ham a berth. Sunlight sparkled on the water, and through a gap in the forested hills it sharpened the snowy peaks of the mainland forty miles away across Shelikof Strait. Up from the water arched a salmon and returned with a splash. Hank sat alert. Farther off another jumper arched. The water was alive. Other boats cruised, staking space. Fish and Game would soon declare the opening on radio and with a rocket fired from their patrol boat. By the time Ham brought coffee Hank strode the deck, newly charged for action.

Jody came on deck, stretched, and smiled. Her own jeans and shirt outlined her trim body beneath a vastly oversized wool shirt of his that she had comandeered. "Mo demanded back his stove. Suits me." He rose and they hugged. Then she eased away. "Now go do your guy stuff. I'm not going to interfere."

"Thanks for the blanket last night."

"Better than nursing you through pneumonia."

He started to make a joke of Adele's notion to hire her as skipper, thought better of it. Instead, sincerely: "I'm glad you came."

"Oh ho, don't get carried away." But she rested her head against his chest, and, when Terry called out "Chow, folks," took his hand as they strolled to the galley. Mo had laid out platters of stacked sausage, eggs, and pancakes. Everyone waited until Jody had filled her plate before they ate, and their forks clicked with only subdued conversation, but each in turn invented some friendly comment to involve her.

"Okay," said Hank finally. "You know why we're here. I'd normally take the helm but that'll be Seth's job."

Seth's chin jutted and his back straightened. "Right."

"And without this cast I'd operate the skiff alone, but today I'll need a second skiff man." He glanced from face to face at the others. It was Ham who needed to come. "You good with a plunger, Ham?"

"Yessir!"

They unlashed the skiff from the stack of web and launched it astern. Hank started the engine and checked its fuel, then settled in. The time approached for Fish and Game to signal the opening. Seth, at the controls, cruised while they all peered for signs of fish. Hank watched critically, restless to be in control himself. "Jumper ten o'clock starboard," muttered Terry.

Seth glanced at Hank, uncertain. Hank nodded to approve the spot, and there they waited. A rocket *swoosh*, and the opening began.

"Yo!" cried Seth. Mo's mallet hit the pelican hook. With a snap and clatter Hank's skiff floated free, pulling the end of the seine attached to its stern. It had been a long time since Captain Hank had handled the skiff-end of a seine. He forced himself to watch and obey Seth's gestures as he guided the skiff with the net to encircle water where the fish had jumped. At last they reached a holding pattern. Boat and skiff moved parallel through the water pulling the seine in a semicircle between them. Ham, without coaching, grabbed the shaft of the plunger and hit the metal cup at the end into the water with a loud pop and bubbles. No need to explain to him how to scare fish into the net.

It was time. Hank called Ham from the plunger and turned over the controls. He stood with the urn of Jones's ashes and held it up for the others to see. In the sky eagles flew. Down in the water salmon jumped. "Okay Jones," Hank cried. "God keep you!" He pulled off the stopper and upended the urn over the water as Seth sounded the *Adele H*'s horn. Word had spread and other boats blew also. Ham joined with a low cry in his throat that became a howl.

Nothing fell from the urn. Hank, startled, peered inside. Smell of whiskey and ashes. The mess had coagulated. Hank held the urn high and waved it. "Oh Jones, you pisser to the end," he bellowed. "Jones Henry has the last word on us all!" He flung the urn high with his good arm. Sun glinted on its handles as it turned in the air and splashed down. Whistles and horns echoed across the water.

Hank didn't bother to wipe his eyes as he watched the ripple where the urn had plunged. He envisioned its contents dissolving, becoming one with the sea. He threw after it a wreath given him by Adele, and a flower of his own.

Ham's howl subsided. At length Hank told him to take up the plunger again. "Yessir!" said Ham. His voice had cleared.

Seth signaled, and Hank brought the skiff with its end of the net back to the boat, closing the seine in a circle. At Hank's command Ham leapt aboard, a vigorous man again. Hank alone worked the skiff to hold the boat off the circle of net. He watched as his crew winched in the purse lines and then raised the net like a sail over the power block to stack it again on deck, his breath and body bending to each step.

That figure stacking rings! She wore yellow oilskins oversized as a tent with legs and arms rolled back. Admit it. She belonged.

When the time came to bring aboard the pursed bag, it surfaced smoking with the frenzied flap of salmon. His men, with Jody alongside, grunted up the heavy bag and fish poured to deck. Hank could feel the throb around their legs.

Back aboard at the end of the set, Hank faced them all. Scales and gurry clung to their oilskins. Jody stood as charged as the others. Their hands and legs, like his own, moved restlessly in the wake of action.

He made himself speak dispassionately. "Well, guys—uh, crew— Our job today was to scatter Jones's ashes and make a set in his honor. I guess we're all still worn out from Bristol Bay. Ready to go back to town?"

"You fuckin' kidding?" exploded Seth for them all, and Jody hooted with the others.

"Then let's fuckin' fish!" Hank shouted, and strode to take back his helm.